THE NEWEST NOVEL BY THE AUTHOR OF "AT PLAY IN THE FIELDS OF THE LORD"

FAR TORTUGA

By Peter Matthiessen

The publication of this novel has been received with extraordinary acclaim, the kind reserved for beautiful, moving, exciting fiction that creates a new vision and is full of the pleasures that delight the soul.

"An adventure story of great purity and intensity, worth comparing to the best of Conrad or Stevenson."
The New York Review of Books

"This is not merely a good novel. It is an exhilarating moment in the history of literature."
Chicago Sun Times

WHEREVER PAPERBACKS ARE SOLD

Bantam Books by Peter Matthiessen

AT PLAY IN THE FIELDS OF THE LORD
FAR TORTUGA

At
Play
in
the
Fields
of the
Lord

Peter Matthiessen

AT PLAY IN THE FIELDS OF THE LORD
*A Bantam Book / published by arrangement with
Random House, Inc.*

PRINTING HISTORY
*Random edition published October 1965
2nd printing. . .November 1965 3rd printing. . .February 1966
4th printing. . June 1970
Literary Guild edition published December 1965
Bantam edition / April 1976
2nd printing*

*Photo of Peter
Matthiessen on back cover
by Nancy Crampton.*

Published simultaneously in the United States and Canada

for
Luke and Carey
Rue and Alex

At
Play
in
the
Fields
of the
Lord

The way to innocence, to the uncreated and to God leads on, not back, not back to the wolf or to the child, but ever further into sin, ever deeper into human life.

—HERMANN HESSE

In the jungle, during one night in each month, the moths did not come to lanterns; through the black reaches of the outer night, so it was said, they flew toward the full moon.

So it was said. He could not recall where he had heard it, or from whom; it had been somewhere on the rivers of Brazil. He had never watched the lanterns at the time of the full moon; when he remembered it was always the dark of the moon or beyond the tropics. Yet the idea of the moths in the high darkness, straining upward, filled him with longing, and at these times he would know that he had not found what he was looking for, nor come closer to discovering what it was.

Across the table the whore, uncomprehending, searched his face for a clue to something, anything at all. *"Qué pasa?"* the whore said, looking away; she expected and received no answer. *"Qué pasa?"* the whore sighed.

The taverna called La Concepción sat back from the mud street, behind a yard of beaten earth and mango trees; most of its customers sat at wooden tables in the yard. The loud radio competed with a dice game, in which the dice cups were banged down as violently as possible upon the table, accompanied by hoarse shouting from the player; this game was a constant from noon to dawn. The radio, with the tumult of the gambling, was more than a match for the voices of men,

At Play in the Fields of the Lord

dogs and roosters which, mixing freely in the yard, fought for a hearing.

Drinking in silence at his table, he felt cut off from all the rest, as they were cut off from one another. Men moved like shadows in this cave of noise, while outside them, outside the glare, stirring the black leaves, hung the great hungry silence of the jungle. The people clung like moths to the wan light.

"Qué pasa?" the whore said again.

The alcohol, which at first had bathed his skin in a glow of peace, now made him restless, and his restlessness made her nervous. He reached out and took her hand, and she subsided. It was still early, and somehow he would have to pass the rest of the evening, for he had slept most of the day. He had had this woman quietly and quickly, and because he made no more of it than it was, the woman liked him; she tried to communicate her own loneliness and even a haggard femininity. He had listened politely, but now his silence had defeated her and she would go.

"Hasta luego, hombre," the woman murmured. She was still searching his face, like someone awaiting word.

"Hasta luego," he said.

So long as he kept moving he would be all right. For men like himself the ends of the earth had this great allure: that one was never asked about a past or future but could live as freely as an animal, close to the gut, and day by day by day.

1

At four miles above sea level, Martin Quarrier, on silver wings, was pierced by celestial light: to fall from such a height, he thought, would be like entering Heaven from *above*. The snow peaks of the Andes burst from clouds which hid the earth, sparkling in the sun like gates of Paradise, and the blue dome of the mountain sky was as pure as the Lord's pain. Where the clouds parted, it was true, dark lakes reflected wild demonic gleams, but the red roofs of the villages on the lone road traversing the sierra were signals of sane harmonies, good will to men.

Quarrier, at his window on the firmament, could barely restrain a warble of pure joy. Instead he whistled tunelessly and hummed, until his wife, in the seat behind him, told him that he sounded like a kettle. He stroked the head of his little boy, whose nose was pressed into the fog made by their breaths upon the glass. The snow fields had scarcely passed from view when Billy Quarrier first thought he saw wild Indians and jaguars and anacondas. "Look, look, Pa! Right down there!"

"Where does he come by such outlandish notions?"

Martin turned around and gazed affectionately at his big wife; his wife amused him. Her pale face looked lye-scrubbed, and a sour expression camouflaged native handsomeness, as if this character, like her humor, was something to be suppressed. To cheer her, he made his joke about a heavenly descent, and laughed when she

3   *At Play in the Fields of the Lord*

would not laugh. He said, "Now sweetheart, there *are* jaguars and anacondas here, that's all." Kneeling on his seat, hands resting on its top, he loomed above her, anxious to interest her in all the information with which he had prepared himself. But she was not an easy person to reach out to, and he drew back a little when her hand dropped, out of habit, to tug down the hem of her dress. "Many of these tribes consider the anaconda their ancestor," he said. "They think their shaman is a jaguar—I mean, that he can become a jaguar at night."

Hazel shifted fretfully. Look at him kneeling on his seat! Why does he *kneel* like that?

"Shamans," she said. "That's why the Lord has sent us here, to rescue these poor heathens from such darkness." When he smiled vaguely, turning away, she said, "You shouldn't have filled your own head with such fiddle-faddle, let alone an innocent child. All he can think about are savages and these awful snakes and jungle animals." She tried to smile at him, to show that she was not quite serious, but she could not; the airplane had made her feel much too upset. Nevertheless, it seemed appropriate that they should undergo some sacrifice and even hardship in the performance of their Christian duty, and she was therefore content to enter a terrain so remote from the green bright plains of North Dakota, where Satan, as her father said, "had been run clean 'cross the county."

The high peaks of the cordillera fell away, marching down the southern sky toward Tierra del Fuego; the plane lost altitude. Brown wastelands of the alpine tundra surged in the cloud plateaus, and far lone huts, untouched by sun, looked uninhabited. The sky lakes of the glaciers turned dull-green, then black, and the white overcast turned gray; clouds gasped up out of sudden chasms, swirled from the earth like vile subterranean vapors. Tundra gave way to chaparral, and chaparral to the trees of the high forest. The dark vapors forsook the trees and, drifting, touched the plane; a vulture tilted outward and away.

Now the airplane plummeted and slid down the

east slope of the sierra. Hazel Quarrier moaned, and her husband went back to her and took her hand. The mists swarmed past the window and the cabin darkened; lights, flickering off and on, bounced and shuddered with the plane itself, which roared confusedly in its descent through the updrafts of the cloud forest.

Then the window cleared again. They had forsaken the realm of sunlight for a nether world of dark enormous greens, wild strangled greens veined by brown rivers of hot rain, the Andean rain, implacable and mighty as the rain that fell on those sunless days when the earth cooled.

Madre de Dios, already in view, formed a yellow scar in the green waste. With its litter of rust and rotting thatch and mud, the capital of Oriente State resembled a great trash heap, smoking sullenly in the monotony of rivers.

The three Quarriers at their plane windows were taken aback by the grim prospect; even Billy could not mistake this devastation for an Indian village. The DC-3 slid out into its turn, over the river front, where derelict craft, misshapen and unpainted, nuzzled the bare mud bank; the heat of the place rose to engulf the plane.

Now a few figures came in sight. They stood like sentinels, as if transfixed by a sudden cataclysm. The mud streets, of a yellow-orange color, deeply rutted, were barren of all life but pigs and vultures and a solitary dog. Then these too disappeared, and the mud airstrip, parting a rank depressed savanna, swung into their view. A light plane and an old Mustang fighter were parked at its edge; the fighter plane was belly-deep in weeds.

Quarrier rearranged his legs so that his knees, in the event of crash, would not bend in the wrong direction. They were certainly a long way from North Dakota, as Hazel had said. Except for their term at Moody Bible in Chicago, they had scarcely set foot out of the Dakotas in all their lives until a month ago, when they had gone to Florida to catch the freighter. And here they were, thousands of miles from the clean kitchens and church suppers of home, ending their second airplane ride, not at the county airport but in a steaming jungle town on the banks of the Río de las Ánimas—River of Souls! Such names were common in these parts, and sooner or later Hazel would horrify herself with the translations.

The people and dogs of Madre de Dios awaited them. There was no road into the jungle, and this plane, which crossed the Andes twice a week, was the sole evidence of an outer world. Men and dogs in the foreground, women and children to the rear, they stared at the old machine as it lumbered to a halt. The men looked of a size, and in some hangdog way identical: small brown mustachioed halfbreeds, barefoot, in pajama tops and ragged pants and floppy sisal hats. The women, in gingham, were more various and more washed-out; the children were in rags. All stood in ranks behind a large pale man with a pistol on his hip, a small pale man in the white cassock of a priest, and a blond man in a rich blond beard, shorts and short-sleeved flowered shirt; this man stood with feet apart, strong fists on hips, and a fine smile on his sunburned face. All three wore shoes. The Quarriers recognized the blond man, from his picture in *Mission Fields,* as Leslie Huben.

Quarrier stared at Huben out of his small window. When the man grinned lustily and waved at them, he grinned obediently and waved back. Then he took off his glasses and wiped them with his handkerchief, wondering how much the other knew about him. When the cargo door swung open and Huben strode forward on brown legs to pump their hands, Quarrier watched the awe appear on the faces of Billy and Hazel.

Huben introduced the "Mart Quarrier Family"— Hazel glanced sardonically at her husband and blinked her eyes—to El Comandante Rufino Guzmán, the prefect of Oriente State; this imposing man, in a tieless white shirt buttoned to the throat, was the first prefect the Mart Quarrier Family had ever beheld. He addressed them in a loud and worldly manner, responding to Martin's *"Buenos días, señor"* with "We arr es-spik Ingliss here!" To Hazel, bowing formally, he spoke Spanish in a courtly manner, in no way abashed by his unshaven face, his open fly and a strong breath of aguardiente. "Pleased to meet you, I'm sure," Hazel Quarrier said, her fingers fretting on her purse. Then Martin Quarrier, last in line, took the official hand of welcome. It felt like loose stones in a damp rubber bag.

The scene was observed with apparent approval by the small priest, who had not been introduced. He stood at the right hand of the Comandante, and it was now clear to Quarrier that while Huben and the priest both accompanied the illustrious Guzmán, they were not themselves on speaking terms. Quarrier wondered if this small man in his white cassock was the Black-robed Opposition whose fearful defeat at the hands of Huben had been recorded in *Mission Fields*. Under the keen eye of the Enemy he felt more and more uncomfortable—far more uncomfortable, it was plain, than the neglected party, who was, if anything, amused. And his discomfort knew no bounds when the priest suddenly smiled at him, and extending his hand said, "Xantes."

Martin said, "Howdy. Martin Quarrier. This is Mrs. Quarrier, and this here is my son, Billy. Billy, this is Father Xantes." Because he was uneasy, his words sounded stiff and wooden to him, and he watched with relief as Hazel, carried away by all the protocol, accepted the Catholic hand.

Hazel said, "How do you do, I'm sure."

Leslie Huben said, "Pardon me, folks. I should have made the introduction."

Billy Quarrier said, "Hiya, Father. Ever seen a Niaruna Indian?"

And the Comandante said, "Ha, ha, ha, ha." He did not laugh these sounds but spoke them: "Niaruna! Ha, ha, ha!" The outburst seemed to Quarrier so arbitrary that he had to smile, but when he saw that the priest was smiling, too, and that Huben watched them both, unsmiling, he turned his head away as if to cough.

7   *At Play in the Fields of the Lord*

Past Huben's head, across the strip, he could read the lettering on the small planes. The tail of the fighter was inscribed:

FUERZAS AÉREAS

and on the pocked fuselage of the light plane was scrawled:

Wolfie & Moon, Inc.

Small Wars & Demolition

The doors of this plane were both wide-open, as if its occupants had abandoned ship before it had stopped rolling, and rushed off into the jungle without even bothering to turn off the ignition. He smiled again. Huben was following his gaze; in the hot gusts, the hair at the crown of Leslie's head rose like a crest. Hazel wigwagged her husband in warning, hat feather trembling. The world awaited him. "Well, I mean, it's all so strange," Quarrier blurted; then the laughter came and he squawked hopelessly, like a chicken. "That little plane . . . I mean, small wars!" He struggled to compose his face. "Are they Americans? Is it a joke?" He laughed again.

"Martin!"

Quarrier glanced back at the tattered plane. It was giving off troubling emanations—not the outlaw craft itself, but something wild and humorous and free that was suggested by that rough red lettering. Suddenly he felt depressed, as if he had entered a cold air pocket, but the moment passed and he felt fine again.

"Martin! What *are* you staring at? My goodness!" She had not meant to sound so peevish.

His head half turned in the weak sun, he regarded her questioningly, a stumpy man in a baggy suit; his glasses, thick and rimless, blurred his gaze and made him appear irresolute. Staring at his huge forehead and thin limp blond hair, at the red skin of his face and

8

neck nicked by quiescent acne, Hazel was struck by his fierce ugliness, and wondered for the thousandth time how Billy could be so beautiful. She inspected her son, who was loitering right next to the Comandante's leg, admiring the pistol; to spare Billy that raw look his father had, she left his hair long on the forehead. In his red tie and small white shirt he looked just like a choir-boy on Christmas cards.

She reached and patted Martin on his breast pocket and turned away from him, aware that he still gazed at her. "Oh, that airplane scared me so," she said, not looking at him.

She was ashamed of noticing his ugliness. Yes, she instructed herself, we are surely entering the realm of Satan; we must prepare every defense; we must . . . Why, take Madre de Dios! Just imagine giving such a name to *any* place! That's those Catholics for you! Billy had told all his friends in school that he was off to Mother of God. Martin had laughed, but suppose some Catholic had come along and changed the name of Chippewa Flats to Mother of God, North Dakota?

Despite herself, this idea made her giggle. Well, it isn't funny, Hazel Quarrier; no, it isn't. Frowning, she spanked and tugged her skirt, as if to prepare it against foreign matter.

Now young Mr. Huben had taken her husband by the elbow and led him off; she followed them promptly, clutching Billy by the hand, and behind them came several desperadoes in old pajamas, carrying the luggage. The little priest trailed the party, an amused expression on his face, his hands folded behind his back. Every few minutes Hazel turned and frowned, to show these men that she was on to them and that any attempt to rifle a bag, much less make off with it, would be dealt with harshly. But the halfbreeds were not laughing or conniving; padding hurriedly on their bare feet, they looked less murderous than thin and tired.

Ahead of her, the sweat stains grew under the arms of Martin's jacket; typically, he had forgotten his summer suit and wore the Sunday serge of his own cli-

9   *At Play in the Fields of the Lord*

mate. Beside him, Leslie Huben walked with springy step; she regarded the man's abbreviated garb, his long bare legs, with mixed emotions. The God-given beauty of Leslie Huben made her feel defensive about Martin; she was not certain how she should react to Huben's "modernism," to the brown legs and hula-hula shirt.

In the New Fields Mission, this young man was already a legend. A former star in college basketball, he had been called from a lucrative job in the real-estate and insurance business to emulate St. Paul: *"Be ye followers of me,"* he had told the Tiro Indians, *"even as I also am of Christ."* This moving event had been described in his first letter to *Mission Fields,* the monthly publication of the New Fields Mission. He became a regular contributor, and his fervent accounts of the dark jungle won high praise. Soon he announced his intention of carrying the Word to the savage Niaruna. "I am enjoying the profits of a business deal I entered into with the Lord," he wrote in the May issue. "Invest to Gain. The Lord has impressed upon Andy and the Undersigned the command to Go." Andy was Huben's pretty wife, by far the prettiest face in the pages of the magazine, and there were those faint hearts among the readership at home who wanted to stay Leslie and Andy from trying to contact this fiercest of all peoples in the jungle. *Mission Fields* exhorted its readers: "Pray much for Leslie and Andy Huben in their brave efforts to call the Niaruna unto the communion of Jesus Christ. Let your hearts be with this young couple in Jesus, for a greater harvest of souls in the days ahead." In the August issue Huben thanked his sponsors for their prayers: "The Lord has surely opened up this work: our Uyuyu has renounced his contact with the darkness and corruption of the Opposition, and *this very day* has led a band of Niaruna to our door! We have thrilled to see this fellow Uyuyu grow so rapidly in the Lord . . ."

Despite Huben's modest tone, it was quite clear that he had not only contacted the Niaruna but had administered a stinging defeat to the Forces of Rome. Funds were found almost immediately to sponsor another missionary pair to help him; as Huben wrote gratefully at Christmas, "A tremendous outward evidence of the Lord's working things out to open the doors to this tribe was the sending of the Mart Quarrier Family. The day that we meet this fine Christian couple at the jungle airstrip will surely be a glad, glad day for Jesus!"

Peering about her at the scraggy lots walled in by jungle—why, it was just like living in a hole!—Hazel recalled with slight discomfort this first mention of themselves in print. She was glad of Martin's opportunity to work with such a man, yet afraid that Leslie Huben might not understand him. Martin's history of failure was as notable as Huben's swift success—suppose this little Mrs. Huben gave herself airs? It would be too mortifying! And all the worse because Martin was a missionary son of missionaries, an honors graduate of Moody Bible, and Leslie's senior in experience by many years. Despite his record, he was generous and industrious and very bright—perhaps *too* bright; could that have been the trouble?—and it did not seem fair that he had been transferred after ten long years at the Sioux mission, and just when he had shown some progress. Why, some of those poor people were still called "red niggers" by the ranchers, and had been living in junked automobiles when Martin got there!

Well, the Indians had been ungrateful when it came time for conversions, that's all there was to it. They were like all reservation Indians, as people said—too proud to work and too proud to take. Leslie Huben would have done no better.

Although the morning was still new, the heat had settled for the day, a humid breathless heat that seeped from the green walls, from the pale mists. That plane trip had exhausted her. As they neared the village outskirts, her nostrils were assailed by drastic odors: the redolence of tropic plants which filled the yards: sweet whiffs of pig dung, garbage and strange cooking; the

11   *At Play in the Fields of the Lord*

reek of stale water and excrement from weedy ditches; and an overlying pall that smelled like vomit, which Leslie said came from the sawmills on the river.

Billy had fallen far behind, attended by dirty-looking children and a yellow dog beset by mange. The children tugged at Billy's shirt, saying, *"Ay, gringuito —qué tal? S-ss-t! Gringuito!"* Fearing nameless infections, she wanted to slap them away, but Billy accepted their attentions cheerfully. Billy said, "You kids ever seen any Niarunas?" and they jeered at him, mimicking: "Yoo kit ever sin Aniaruna?" Billy laughed with the children, though soon he came running and took her hand, smiling up at her in a bewilderment that wrung her heart—how could they have brought a child to such a place! But a moment later he was cheerful once again. "Ma, did you like Father Xantes too? I think the father is a very interesting person." She did not bother to point out that the interesting person, who was still trailing them, had not opened his mouth in front of Billy except to pronounce his name.

The children ran to alert the streets, but the dog still followed her and Billy. He announced that he had named the dog New Walter, in honor of a friend in North Dakota named Walter Hubbell. Then Billy ran off into an alley, followed by the dog; the animal dodged a kick or two and caught a third. She hated the cheerful cruelty in the faces, the laughter as the dog, legs tangling in its haste to round the corner, fell on its chest and yelped. She hurried after Billy, hoping that Martin would see them disappear and wait for her.

By a small fire, three Indian women in coarse blouses of soiled cotton, black wrap-around skirts, nose ornaments and ankle thongs were cooking some sort of mealy cakes laid on the embers. They were attended by two men in ragged store clothes. One of these men, very drunk, was lying on his side, his head clutched between his hands, while his companion, swaying weakly, was urinating on the ground just behind the women. The women paid no attention to either one; they gazed impassively at the child and at the large white woman following him.

"Niarunas!" Billy said. "See them? Niarunas!"

A townsman, passing, laughed contemptuously. *"Niarunas!"* he said to Hazel. *"No son Niarunas! Son indios mansos, son Mintipos."* This halfbreed was drunk also; he leaned over Billy, shouting, *"Ay, chico? No son Niarunas, entiendes? Los Niarunas son salvajes, indios bravos. Éstos"*—he pointed—*"son indios mansos."*

The Mintipo man turned the arc of his urine in a slow circle, and regarded the halfbreed with a grin of fear and anger. His face was swollen and his eyes yellow. Thickly he said, *"Y tú? Mestizo."* Almost falling, he gestured violently at the gathering onlookers, while his women stared into the fire and his fallen friend clutched his head still tighter and drew his knees up toward his chest. *"Caballeros,"* he jeered. *"Caballeros mestizos."* He pointed at the dog. *"Otro mestizo,"* he said. When he clutched at his crotch and shook it, Hazel dragged Billy away, and the people laughed, not at the Mintipo man but at the gringos.

"Dead drunk! And at this hour of the morning!" Hazel Quarrier exclaimed; she felt slapped across the face. But her remark struck her as silly and scared—not that she would have described herself as "sensible and effectual and courageous," yet she knew she was regarded in this way by those who knew her on her own home grounds, where good sense and diligence and moral courage meant something. In this place such qualities must be totally unfamiliar, much less effective.

"What does *mestizo* mean?" Billy asked her. "That Indian guy called Walter a *mestizo.*"

"I suppose he meant 'mongrel,'" Hazel said. "Now come along."

Billy looked down at the dog with new interest. "He's a real mongrel?" he said. He fell to his knees to pat the dog, which shied sideways. "C'mere, Walter,"

13   *At Play in the Fields of the Lord*

Billy said. "I thought you were an Indian dog. I never even *heard* of mongrels." When the dog came up on its belly, whining, and Billy pressed his face to it, Hazel yanked him to his feet—what could she be thinking of, letting the child play in this filthy street, with vultures and pigs and diseased dogs! In a place like this, for all she knew, human beings could catch hog cholera. She would have to be constantly on guard. When Billy clutched at Walter, she drove the dog off with her foot.

At the mouth of the alley the little priest watched over them discreetly, his arms folded behind his back.

She had not recovered when, at the next corner, they were accosted by a bearded man with huge dark glasses and a gold earring; he had a henchman in attendance, and like everyone else in this awful place, he was intoxicated. At the sight of Billy his beard cracked wide in a leering grin; lurching backward, he raised his arms. "C'mere!" he said, and Billy, churning forward, hurled himself onto the man's chest, crying, "You want to look at Walter? This is my dog Walter!" The man tossed him up into the air, laughing insanely. "Wall-ter," the man babbled, "Wall-ter! This is beautiful, man! So how's wit' you, Stud? How's things in the old U.S. and A.?"

Hazel did not realize at first that the man was talking English. She was tempted to declare aloud, Some people don't care *how* they go about the streets! And if the ruffian responded rudely, as he must, she would then say, And you call yourself an American! Humph! The idea of saying things like this amused her and she looked forward to the exchange, but just then the man's companion said something she did not catch. The bearded one lowered Billy to the ground, eying her the while in an evil and suggestive manner.

"Oh yeah," he nodded. "The God Squad, huh?" He had his hand on Billy's shoulder; when Billy retreated toward his mother, the hand fell disgustedly to his side.

"You're a very rude man," Hazel said. "And you call yourself an American! Humph!" But as she passed, her eye was caught by the face of the other man; though his face was calm, his cold eyes chilled her to the soul. Even worse, he had sniffed out her private joke and—why, look at that—he was winking at her!

"American!" the bearded man called after her. "So who's American? They slung us out!"

"Do you think he's a pirate?" Billy said to her. "He was wearing an earring, did you see it, Mom?"

"Your countrymen," a soft voice said. "It is amusing, no?"

Glancing back, she saw the priest, who smiled at her as if he approved, not only of her joke, but of the general fact of her existence. She hurried on. Had she imagined it, or had this man winked at her, too?

Why were people *winking* at her? She was close to tears. Her heart was pounding, and the sawmill smell and the clinging heat, stoked by her anger and exertions, made her discomfort ever more acute.

The people in the street stared at them, pointing; the gringos were admired lavishly, aloud. She tried to smile at them, and look with an interest at their town, but the repetitious litter of poor shacks, the beaten citizenry and scuttling children, the shop windows, few and filthy and filled with garish imitation goods, the mud and vultures and the smell reminded her of the slum outskirts in the southern towns which she had glimpsed from the bus to Fernandina, Florida, two months before. The sad brown eyes, the gentle whispering enmeshed her; never had she felt herself so enormous, such a freak. The swarming vultures with their naked heads and pale white ghostly legs filled her with loathing; the village whined with flies. She thought, But *everything* is dirty; there is nothing clean here, *nothing*. Her body was sweating more freely than she had thought possible; she was startled by her own plenteousness, and felt afraid.

Just as the hotel came in sight, the one car in Madre de Dios came up from behind, driven by a soldier in green uniform. The car rolled and slid on the muddy ruts, and although El Comandante smiled at her in a courtly manner, no offer was made to rescue her from the open road.

Nor did solace await at the Gran Hotel Dolores, in which all of the heat and bad smell and corruption of Madre de Dios seemed to collect. The toilet alcove —no real toilet, but a stand-up, or rather hunch-down, arrangement housed in a rickety courtyard shed— brought on the tears that she had held back all morning, so that she cried unrelievedly even as she relieved herself.

Why have we come here? she cried silently. What am I doing in this awful place?

Jesus said: *In the world ye shall have tribulation: but be of good cheer; I have overcome the world.*

Remembering this, she felt a little better.

2

"Open letter from the fields of the Lord:

"The Martin Quarrier Family has arrived! Pray much for His servants Martin and Hazel Quarrier, pray much for the Undersigned and his wife, Andy, who must try to take His Word to the savage Niaruna, for this work will surely be difficult and dangerous. All your prayers are needed, for Satan is marshaling his forces and the Opposition is ever ready to take over at our first misstep.

"Since I last wrote, the Lord has heeded all our prayers, and work proceeds very well among the Tiro and Mintipo—all our jungle tribes, in fact, except the Niaruna, who, as you know, were first contacted by your correspondent and are therefore closest to his own heart. These Indians are still wild and savage and go naked and drink intoxicants called Masato and Nipi, which is also known as Vine of Death, and live in a state of total barbarousness and filth and sin. Less than a year ago, these same savages killed an agent of the Opposition, by name of Fuentes. If you could see these poor lost souls, you would realize how confidently Satan still walks

17   *At Play in the Fields of the Lord*

among them, and meanwhile all the men still get disgustingly intoxicated, falling down finally in a stupor.

"On my first trip up the Espíritu, as I wrote before, I left Andy behind in Remate de Males, in case something went wrong, but now that Martin is here and the contact is made, we have decided to take the girls in with us, and Billy Quarrier, too, as there is no mission school this side of Cochabamba, in Bolivia.

Let not your heart be troubled, neither let it be afraid (John 14:27).

"We surely thank the Lord for His new outboard motor, that He entered into your hearts and made you generous: *But my God shall supply all your need according to his riches in glory by Christ Jesus* (Phil. 4:19). We will pray for all of you here in *the uttermost part of the earth* (Acts 1:8), for now the Word may be speeded all the more rapidly into these dark rivers where the souls of the lost cry out to us: Come save us! We are headed straight for Hell!

"Before we are through, we hope to have an airplane survey, so that we may hunt out the last lost soul in this great wilderness. Not one will escape the great net of our Lord! *For some have not the knowledge of God: I speak this to your shame* (I Cor. 15:34).

"The Lord has again impressed on us the great importance of the Niaruna work being built of God. The Lord willing, when you hear from us again we will be able to report that all your prayers for the souls of the Niaruna and the work of His servants have been heeded.

"Yours for a greater harvest of souls in the days ahead,
"LES HUBEN, *Madre de Dios*"

After reading his letter aloud, Leslie led them in a hymn. The two couples were seated facing one another on the twin beds in the Hubens' room, where the arrival of the Quarriers had been celebrated with orange drinks called *gaseosas* and informal prayer.

Now Leslie cried out gleefully, "If you think this is bad, folks, wait till you see Remate. Why, Madre is a paradise alongside of Remate." Remate de Males, farther upriver, was the nearest trading post to the new mission. "It's like going," Huben said, "from Purgatory straight to Hell."

"My land!" Hazel said. When her husband glanced at her uneasily, she smiled a tremendous party smile at Andy Huben.

Andy Huben, smiling back, gazed at both Quarriers a moment before she raised her glass. "Welcome to Madre de Dios," she said.

Andy Huben's voice was one of the loveliest that Martin had ever heard, low and gentle and a little hesitant, a little sad even, yet at the same time clear and peaceful; it had a quality of childlike wonder. With that look of surprise and the two neat buckteeth that just touched her lower lip, she reminded him slightly of an Easter rabbit; her clear face combined an air of innocence with something as saucy and irreverent as a hot cross bun.

"As I wrote in my last epistle," Leslie said, "the Lord surely gave us the command to Go when He sent down the Mart Quarrier Family."

"Well, the Mart Quarriers are here, and they mean *business!*" Hazel cried, with a wild look of suppressed laughter.

When Martin tried to smile, Andy smiled also, slipping her hand through her husband's arm. "We're awful glad you Mart Quarriers have come," she said, to warn them of her awareness of their joke.

"Not that Mart here and I are going to see eye to eye on every little thing!" Leslie slapped Quarrier on the knee. "But maybe until you kind of get the feel of

19   *At Play in the Fields of the Lord*

things, Mart, maybe you'd better talk to me before you say anything like you did to the Comandante."

Hazel said, "Oh Martin, we just *got* here."

Andy Huben said, "Mr. Quarrier was in the right."

"Are you sure you know what we're talking about, Andy? And anyway, use Mart's first name; we're all going to have quite a beautiful Christian fellowship before we're through."

"Perhaps I was mistaken," Quarrier muttered. He explained to Hazel what he had learned from Huben: that the Comandante had become increasingly impatient about the Niaruna, due to pressure put upon him from the capital to establish colonies and develop a lumber commerce in their lands, and to consolidate with garrisons the common frontier with Brazil; he felt that he had been patient to a fault with the missionaries' attempts to make peaceful contact with the tribe, but since no real progress had been made, stronger measures had become necessary. The Niaruna themselves had forced his hand, he said, with their raids upon the peaceful Tiro and on the settlement at Remate de Males.

"Now you have to admit, Martin," Huben said, "that Rufino is in a tough position with the government. And just remember that without his good will no Protestant mission would be allowed to work here. After all"—he turned to Hazel—"Rufino is a Catholic."

"My goodness," Hazel said, "a Catholic! Imagine a Catholic helping out in the Lord's work!"

"He's a very practical Catholic," Andy Huben remarked. "He thought that Leslie might open up that country faster than Padre Xantes, who is getting old and has no help."

"Then he's a *good* Catholic," Hazel declared. "I don't know which is worse, a bad Catholic or a good one!"

Leslie Huben laughed with the rest, but at the first opportunity he said, "Whatever he is, he's on our side.

20

I worked hard to get him there, and I intend to keep him there."

"Oh Martin, really," Hazel said, "why don't you listen to Mr. Huben—"

"Leslie," Leslie said.

"—listen to Leslie!" It seemed to her that his beard made Leslie look rather naïve. She smiled unhappily toward the Hubens, taking Martin's arm. "He's such a stubborn man," she smiled. "Yet you say, Mrs. . . . Andy . . . that he was in the right."

"He can be morally in the right," Andy Huben said mildly, "and still be mistaken."

"Oh, I don't understand how *that* can be, I'm sure!" Hazel lifted both hands to her collarbones, begging the embarrassed Hubens to forgive her for her old-fashioned notions. "Well, you can't teach an old dog to suck eggs," she told them.

Martin broke in to remind her that she did not even know what he had done. He told her that he had encountered the Comandante in the afternoon, and after an elaborate exchange of civilities had suggested to Guzmán that an armed attack on savages, except in self-defense, was against the national law. The Comandante had taken this reminder as a threat and had become angry.

Hazel Quarrier groaned, and Huben shrugged hopelessly, trying to smile. "What a fellow!" he said. "He hasn't been here a single day, and he knows the law better than the Comandante!"

"It's a well-known law," Quarrier said. "They even mention it in the tourist literature."

"One of the first things you'll have to learn, Martin," Huben said, "is that here in the jungle, there *is* no law." He had jumped up and was pacing around the room. "Why, slavery is against the law, and half the people in this town are slaves! The good Lord knows that slavery is an abomination in my sight, but the fact is that slavery is very difficult to control when the Indians themselves practice it, not only with their captives, but by selling their own children to other tribes. Why, Martin, there's hardly an Indian in this settlement who isn't enslaved by *somebody!*"

"And Guzmán?"

"What about him?"

"Your Mintipos say he profits from the slave trade."

"Do you have proof?" Huben placed his fingertips together. "Now you be careful, Martin. If we don't have Rufino's cooperation we're going to be in trouble."

"If we condone human slavery, we'll be in worse trouble still."

Huben shrugged him off. "Look. There's a law here against holding an Indian to any debt he can't work off in a week—that law is a local joke. When you told Guzmán he is breaking the law, I'm surprised he didn't laugh in your face! The Comandante *is* the law here in the jungle, he takes the place of God Himself!"

Hazel gasped. "Really, Mr. . . . Leslie," she began. "You *do* have a free-and-easy—"

Quarrier grasped her firmly by the arm and she subsided. "Then what did he mean," he said to Huben, "when he said he had no intention of breaking the national law?"

"I know exactly what he meant," Huben said. He paused. "He has an old army plane out at the airstrip, but it doesn't work, and its pilot has been transferred. He can't call in another one without drawing attention to what he wants to do."

"There were two planes at the strip," Quarrier said.

"That's right," Huben sat down again. "Remember when you asked out there about that other plane?" He jerked his thumb, then narrowed his eyes and lowered his voice. "Two Americans. They live right down the hall. They turned up about ten days ago, before we came up from Remate, and Andy says she thinks one of 'em might be pretty notorious; he looks like some feller that had his picture in the paper back home!" Leslie smashed his fist into his palm. "Anyway, they're the blackest kind of sinners—drunkards, fornicators, killers. Yes, they're killers, mercenary killers, no better than those who nailed our Lord upon His cross!"

"Jumping Jehosophat!" Hazel cried, placing her hand on her cheek; she winked at Martin in full view of Andy. He knew that she was punishing him because Andy was pretty, and he tried to distract attention from her. He said, "Where did they come from?"

"Bolivia, I think. There's been another revolution there. Anyway, they've hired themselves out to Guzmán—this is just the chance he's been waiting for."

"But somebody will report this!" Quarrier said.

"Who will? Nobody will. And even if they did, they would not be believed. And even if they were believed, Guzmán might be embarrassed, but his action would be approved. I tell you, Martin, the government wants those lands developed. So who's going to report him? Nobody will. Nobody gets in that man's way!"

"Martin will," Hazel said. "Won't you, Martin?" Her tone was so cold, her voice so very different from the flustered voice of a moment before, that the Hubens stared at her.

"I don't know yet," Martin said.

"Why, I saw those men this morning, in the street!" Hazel acted flustered once again. "And they're even more black-hearted than you say they are!"

In an early light as clear and warm as melted amber, Quarrier would set forth with Billy to look at Indians in the market place, or to walk the river bank, keeping a sharp eye out for jaguars and anacondas, or to take a boat across the river to the jungle on the far side. There was so much to do. Yet in the end nothing happened; they never found what they were seeking. Even Billy tired quickly once the sun had leaped clear of the trees; the sun grew swollen, lost its outline, turning the sky from limpid blue to dull cooked white, like a gigantic frying egg, until the sun itself turned a sick white, in a white sky.

Though it was still early in the morning, they would retreat into the Gran Hotel, with its slow creak of ceiling fans and dusty purr of frazzled chickens in the kitchen court. In the bar of the hotel, the people sat all day waiting for rain to cool the air, and when the rain came, every afternoon, they waited for it to clear. The missionaries felt uncomfortable in the bar-salon and did their sitting in their rooms. They were waiting for supplies to come, and meanwhile they sweated like the damned, and sipped on orange *gaseosas* and prayed prayers.

For three days now, in time of worship, Andy's right knee and his left had touched, and he was straining to touch knees again when the brutal shout of the gross bearded outlaw pierced the thin ceiling from the bar below; all four stared at one another, tense with dismay. Only the moment before, Leslie Huben had said, ". . . and we pray for the Niaruna, O Lord, that they may come to know Thy great love and the blessings of a Christian life in Thy sight and the joy of the hereafter in Heaven above—"

"—AND BLOW THEM LITTLE BROWN PRICKS TO KINGDOM COME—"

"Amen." Leslie, startled, concluded his prayer by mistake.

In the silence Martin thought, Can God be laughing at us? He really meant, laughing at *me,* for he realized that none of the others had grasped the juxtaposition of *Heaven* and *Kingdom Come,* nor even the obscenity, but only the dreadful callousness of that man's exclamation mounting from the lower regions. It was left to him, Martin Quarrier, to see the lurid irony of the timing. Why had he seen it? And why—since the event was circumstantial, after all—had his first thought been that God was laughing?

Or had the Lord intended that hellish cry to draw his attention to his own behavior; for an instant his leg

24

had actually been pressed to hers, because Andy had swung half about, and gazing straight through him, blind to his confusion, said, "May God have mercy on his soul."

"Amen," her husband said again.

"No," Hazel said. She had started up like a goaded beast, then sank back heavily once more, her shoulders slumped, her ears protruding through her hair; her bun, ordinarily immaculate, had collapsed since their arrival, and reminded her husband of a loose rat's nest he had once found in the barn. "Sometimes we ask too much of Him. Our God is a just God, and He will strike down such iniquity with His terrible swift sword!"

"On Judgment Day, perhaps," Quarrier said. He rose and went to the window. In his guilt he did not wish to look at Hazel, who wore high sneakers and a big print dress with hearts and bright red roses on a shiny background; his guilt made him feel irritable.

Huben jumped up and walked the room, up and down, his eyes upon the floor. "I'll be franker than I was the other day, Martin. If the Niaruna *can* be cowed a little, they will be softened up for an outreach of the Word, and this will make our work—yes, *your* work too, Martin, don't look at me like that—a darn sight easier. Don't you forget that the Opposition is just lying in wait to see us lose the advantage I have won in Jesus' name."

Quarrier said, "It is our responsibility to try to stop him—"

"It is *not* your responsibility. It is *my* responsibility."

"Yet you don't accept it."

"I beg your pardon." Huben stopped short in his pacing. "Now you be careful, fella. We have other people working with the Tiro and Mintipo in this area, and I can't, I *won't* jeopardize those fellows for your sake—"

"I certainly understand that you can't jeopardize the other missions, so what I'm after here is permission to talk to Guzmán again on my own responsibility—"

"No," Huben said. "You've caused enough trouble already. I'm sorry, Martin, but I forbid this."

"I'll talk to the Americans then."

Huben shrugged. "Go ahead. You'll get nothing but jeers from men like those."

"They are devils," Hazel muttered. "The limb of Satan. That hairy one—he could pass for a devil himself! And that other one—I've never seen a face like that in all my born days. That man has looked Satan straight in the eye!"

"I don't know," Andy said slowly. She had moved across to Hazel, who had never once lifted her eyes from the hands clenched in her lap, and now she put her arm around Hazel's shoulders. "That second man, I saw him in the corridor. Maybe Martin could talk to that second man."

"Yes, I'll try." Quarrier turned his gaze from Leslie to Andy. "What does he look like?"

"You must have seen him in the hall. In a strange way, quite an interesting face. Dark, a little hard. Indian blood. And he always wears a dark blue neckerchief round his throat."

"What makes you think he's Indian?"

"Oh Andy!" Leslie snorted. "She's got this idea that this Moon fellow comes from up our way. He looks more like some kind of an Italian to *me*."

"I *know* he's an Indian; he's part Cheyenne." Andy got up and walked about the room. "I knew I'd seen that face before, and when I learned that his name was Moon, I was certain of it." She turned and looked at her husband. "He's from our mission schools, somewhere up in the Northwest."

"That *hairy* one?" Hazel, distracted, was gazing out the window after Billy, who was playing in the streets. "That hairy one never came from our *Sioux* mission, I'll tell you that much!"

"No, no, the other man."

26

"Andy, honey, just because this fellow looks a little Indian—"

"I told you, he's part Cheyenne or something; anyway, he's from the reservations. And he was bright, and he had a fine war record, and he was a Christian, so they decided to make an example of him, don't you remember? Years ago. He was the first Indian from the missions to go to the state university—Somebody Moon. There was a lot of talk about it. I remember, because my dad was all excited."

"But you were only a child!" said Leslie, frowning.

"Yes. I was only a child, but I cut his picture out of the paper and even kept it in my room. I felt sorry for him, I don't know why. I mean, I guess I felt sorry for *all* Indians, the way we treated them. And especially the Cheyennes—the first time I read about that journey from that Oklahoma reservation, all the way north across Kansas and Nebraska and South Dakota and on into Montana, and getting shot down by those stupid, stupid people just because they wanted to go *home,* I cried all night—it makes me cry right now!" She laughed at herself, for angry tears had risen to her eyes. "So anyway, I prayed for him."

"Dull Knife's people," Quarrier said.

"Martin knows all about Indians," Hazel said in a flat voice. It seemed to her that her husband, in the past years at the Sioux mission, had grown more and more indecisive, masking a loss of evangelical zeal with his "respect" for the Indian culture; how was he ever to redeem a people whose religion seemed to him so beautiful? It was her theory that his fascination with the tribal sacraments, the respect he paid them, not only impeded the harvest of souls but was downright disrespectful to the Lord. Martin claimed that his gradual methods laid a better foundation for true faith than quick conversion, but his dogged adherence to these methods was the sin of pride.

"Well, a lot of my mother's people were massacred by Sioux in Minnesota, so our family isn't quite so sentimental as Andy's is." Leslie looked impatient. "You mean this Moon got his picture in the paper for going to the university?"

"Well, yes. And again for being thrown out of it, just before graduation. A lot of folks hollered, 'Darn drunken Injuns!' but they were pleased it happened. And then a third time when he was sentenced. Only he never came home again—they never caught him."

"A criminal!" cried Hazel, who had never seen one. "I might have known! And a backslider, at that!" When her husband smiled, she immediately looked cross; this was a rule of her game.

"Well, it wasn't all that simple." Andy seemed sorry that she had brought it up.

"I think I *do* remember," Quarrier said. "Somebody Moon. I certainly do remember. He assaulted somebody, stole his money—don't you remember, Leslie? It was in all the mission newsletters for months." He rose and started for the door.

"At that time, probably," Leslie said, "I had not been called by Jesus. Anyway, it just goes to show you what you're up against. A man like that will only mock you."

"Be ye not unequally yoked together with unbelievers," Hazel intoned as her husband went out, *"for what fellowship hath righteousness with unrighteousness?"*

And what communion hath light with darkness. II Corinthians, Martin thought as he went down the stairs. He had never dealt with this aspect of his work, the hostility and jeering, the contempt. How strange that the contempt should be so frightening—as frightening, yes, as the danger from the savages . . . Well . . . He drove himself along the corridor, determined not to reconnoiter but to make a firm entry and demand an audience.

In the door to the bar he collided with Padre Xantes. The priest smelled of liquor but was otherwise composed. "Good evening, sir," he said to Quar-

28

rier. "You are looking for the bar?" And he smiled pleasantly at Quarrier's consternation.

Quarrier grinned, frowned, said "Excuse me," said "Good evening," and finally in a fit of nervousness and impatience extended his hand, which the padre took, and to his dismay, did not release. They struggled silently in the passage.

"Why do you hate and fear us so," the padre said, "when all we feel towards you is mild astonishment?"

Still smiling, Quarrier thrashed politely, desperate to free himself. This is absurd, he raged; why does he cling to me?

Over the padre's shoulder he saw Huben's convert, Uyuyu, who skulked past them, hissing, *"Buenas. Buenas noches."* The padre said, *"Sí, sí,* poor Uyuyu. Such a promising boy!" He gasped for breath, but still he clung to Quarrier like a blind man. *"Sí,* I raised him myself in the mission, raised him a pure *católico,* and now he is—eh? What is he, this Indian we have fought over? A Protestant? Do you believe so? Is he neither? Is he both?" The padre stopped smiling; he gripped Quarrier's hand in his bony fingers. "Answer me, Señor Quarrier. Do you think *he* knows the difference?"

Later Quarrier wondered at that last remark; did the priest not mean, "Do you think *He* knows the difference?" How false and cynical, if true—did it betray a papist lack of faith in their own dogma? He should not have talked to the priest at all. Just at that moment he broke loose—or rather, the padre threw his hand away, casting it up into the air as if setting free a dove.

3

Wolfie wore habitually, even at night, a black beret, outsized dark glasses, the green fatigues of one or more foreign armies, and a gold earring in his left ear. He had been talking loudly when he lost his footing in the slime and fell, and because he was drunk he continued talking in mid-air and while still on his hands and knees, as if nothing were amiss. He was still speaking as he rose. He was a broad squat powerful man, with big loose hands and a big shaggy head, a chest like a nail keg, and small feet, and he was tightly sprung; one had the impression that Wolfie, fitted out with rubber soles, could bound five feet straight up into the air from a standing position.

"How come he wants to see us!" Wolfie shouted; they had been summoned by a soldier to an audience with El Comandante. "There ain't enough bread to pay this Guzmán, anyway!" When Moon did not answer, Wolfie said, "Look, we got thirty-four pesos and we was into him for more than that ten days ago. And I ain't goin to no calabozo, never again, not in this town and not on this whole lousy continent. I'm very particular about the pens I go to." He stopped short in the street. "Remember down in Paraguay? Like, that food, man. Are you kiddin? That's *food*? And also those are very unhygienic conditions, not to mention stink. It stinks in there worse than it stinks out here." He drew in a violent breath of the sweet jungle night.

"Phoo!" he said. "This jungle! How can you stand it—you depraved or what? I mean, this is where God *farted*."

"It smells to me like the night was full of flowers."

"Oh man," Wolfie said. "Flowers. Flowers, he says. Oh man." He walked on a little way. "Lissen. I am very serious," he resumed. "I don't dig this jungle scene. I wanta split, and we ain't got bread enough to gas up the lousy aircraft. I am being very serious with you. If there ain't a solution around here pretty fast, we're screwed."

"That's right."

"And when you showed him them river diamonds, he told you they looked phony."

"All diamonds are white, says the Comandante."

"I tell you what I think. I think this Guzmán, he's gonna hang in there a little more and then he's gonna grab the aircraft."

"That's what I think too."

"Well, we ain't gonna take the screwin lyin down."

"We'll have to take it standing up then."

"Yeah, yeah, so all right. So I'm gonna send a letter to the American ambassador and sign it 'An Outraged Citizen.' What do you say to that?" Wolfie shadowboxed, punching and snorting in the open street, but almost immediately gave it up. "Okay, never mind, don't talk to me, I forgot Cuba. So we lost our citizenship—that was my fault?" He shook his head and sighed, then laughed. "Old Wolfie," he said, "the Wandering Jew. Only why in Christ did we wander into this place for—it wasn't funky enough in all them other jungles? Why don't we ever wander along the Riviera, maybe? *La dol-ce vita,* right, Lewis?" He sighed mightily, enjoying himself. "And just to think, only twenty years ago I was Fat Morty, the best kid on the block. I took my bar mizvah and I never ate goy dreck, and I was goin to be, like, a Talmudic *scholar*. And now I'm the Man without a Country. There ain't no justice, right, Lewis?" He grinned. "I got an idea, Lewis. If we go to the calabozo, we might as well go there flat, because they'll grab the thirty-four anyway. So first we're gonna go back to La Concepción, Lewis, and have a little drunk for ourselves, all right, Lewis? . . . I said, all right, Lewis?"

"Afterwards," Moon said.

The Gran Hotel Dolores was a structure of twelve rooms; except for the church and mission of the Iglesia de la Virgen, it was the largest building in the settlement, and the only one besides the sawmill which was roofed with tin instead of thatch. The hotel had been erected in the great era of the rubber boom, in anticipation of a prosperity that came but did not remain; it gave shelter to transient timbermen and plantation *patrones,* to explorers investigating the wild tribes and rivers of Oriente State, and to missionaries, as well as to such rare visitors as the state's political representatives in the capital.

The hotel bar, which occupied one flank of the whitewashed lobby—dining-room—salon, was the center of Madre de Dios, for the rest of the settlement, unequipped with generators, was plunged into darkness by the jungle night. Hence the people were drawn like insects to its light. Those with money and those who had spent money at the Gran Hotel in the recent past congregated inside, while the rest gathered on the sidewalks, content with the glow from the large windows in the white plaster wall. Here, as the evening passed, they might speak softly or sing; the townsmen at the tables inside sang rarely and spoke loudly. Having neither glass nor screen but only large wooden shutters to be closed in time of storm, the windows were used periodically for sudden entry and exit. The bar was located on a corner, and since its two doorways serviced each of the only two streets in town, the clientele commanded a view of almost everything of importance that took place in Madre de Dios.

A further attraction of the Gran Hotel was a radio that played full blast all day and night, as if—since all jungle radios were overpriced—its listeners were entitled at the very least to all the volume it was able to deliver. The radios were cheaply made, and since it was never certain that, once silenced, one would ever speak again, and since there was no one for two hundred miles who could repair it, the usual practice was to turn it on immediately upon purchase and leave it on for the rest of its natural life. Once dead, it remained in its place of honor forever: a mute radio, all set about with Spanish doilies, artificial flowers and a hand-tinted portrait of the Virgin Mary, was in Madre de Dios a symbol of prestige. Behind the bar of the Gran Hotel two dead radios flanked the live one.

These were but a few of the unusual features which made the bar of the Gran Hotel Dolores the heart of this jungle capital, and it was to this place that there came each night, in a private car with a soldier-driver, its proud owner, El Comandante Rufino Guzmán. Since no road in Madre de Dios went farther than the airstrip, the car, brought in by lumber raft, was used almost exclusively to conduct El Comandante between his house at the army post and the hotel. El Comandante invariably sat himself behind a table in the corner, opposite both doors and beneath the enormous fan. Here his townsmen could come to him as to the Judgment Seat, and here he could witness and preside over almost everything that took place, not only in the bar itself, but in his entire kingdom.

On this February evening one of the two Americans who had sat down with Guzmán stood up almost immediately and walked about the room; he returned to the table but did not sit down again. In the two weeks since their arrival in Madre de Dios, Moon and Wolfie had put on a bold face, ordering the best that the Gran Hotel Dolores had to offer, but the Comandante had not been taken in, and now he was baiting them at his leisure. Collecting their passports that first day, he had grinned in a way that had alerted them to the dimension of their predicament, saying, "Of course the *señores pilotos* are very welcome in my humble city; it is only a formality, and soon the *pasa-*

portes will be returned." Wolfie, thinking to put this greaser at his ease, had yelled out, jerking his thumb at Moon, *"Amigo mío* him also heap big *indio!"* The Comandante, who was not an *indio,* had gazed briefly at Moon, a gaze that made Moon coil and stiffen; he had not returned the papers, and meanwhile their bill at this hotel mounted remorselessly.

Now he pointed at Moon's chair, as if Moon, standing, made him nervous.

Moon remained standing, hands in pockets.

The Comandante took note of this small rebellion; he lifted the glass, poured the liquor down his throat like a man filling a hole, and blew the air back out at Moon in a huge belch, as if to send him flying from his sight. The people in the bar sniggered expectantly, nudging one another. They watched the Comandante wipe his mouth with the back of one hand and with the other signal for another drink. Over the back of the wiping hand, which he held for a long time at his mouth, his eyes were hard as points.

Inexplicably, Rufino Guzmán laughed: "Ha, ha, ha, ha."

"This is some terrible kind of a jungle *beast,"* Wolfie observed, sincerely impressed; he hitched forward in his chair to stare more closely at the Comandante.

In this place, all but isolated from the world, the big pale man beneath the fan was the natural enemy, and their enmity was an old one; Moon reacted to his gaze with the clutched fear and hatred that he had once felt for the county sheriff. Though he kept his expression blank and casual, it was all he could do to face him. They had met on all the earth's frontiers, in all its jungles; this was the strongman unrestrained, the incensed executor of his own law, swollen and jovial with power.

The Comandante was a massive man, quite unlike the small brown halfbreeds of his town, a big thick man with a pale thick unshaven face. He had a coarse small crown of hair, more like a tuft, and a tight pot-

34

belly like a swallowed ball. Ever since Wolfe had boasted of Moon's Indian blood, the Comandante had called Moon *piloto* with heavy sarcasm, in a way which suggested that Moon's status as *señor piloto* was a tremendous joke. So intent was Guzmán on conveying disdain for Moon that he addressed all his remarks to Wolfie, even though Wolfie spoke almost no Spanish. In this way Moon was made to serve the white *caballeros* as interpreter. Wolfie was quite oblivious of this situation, and for the moment it amused Moon to pretend that he was oblivious of it also.

"How long do you plan to be our guest in Madre de Dios then?" the Comandante said to Wolfie.

"Bueno," Wolfie said. "Right, Lewis?" Behind his hand he said loudly, "I'm just kind of stringin this beast along."

"We will leave when you return our passports," Moon said, after a moment. The United States had revoked their passports *in absentia;* there was no sign on the documents themselves.

"But of course, and I will be delighted to return the passport of the *caballero"*—Guzmán bowed to Wolfie—"when the *caballero* regulates his accounts at the hotel. I am an understanding man. I do not even ask you why you have no visa for this country, or inquire where you have come from. On the other hand, I am not stupid. Your airplane is full of armaments. It has bullet holes in its wings. I *know* where you have come from. And I also know that if I send you back there . . ." He smiled broadly. "You chose the wrong side, no?"

"Caramba!" Wolfie said, judicious. "How'm I doin, Lewis?"

Moon said, "We have no money, and apparently there is no work we can do here."

The Comandante nodded. "I much regret it, of course, but even if there was work that you could do, I am not empowered to issue work permits to foreigners. I am sure you understand my position."

"You own the hotel, you own this town. We are

living at your expense; therefore we figure you have something in mind."

The Comandante sighed. "If you cannot regulate your accounts in a very short time, you will force me to confiscate your property."

"The airplane."

"The airplane. Precisely."

"And you know what the plane is worth."

Guzmán grinned. "As a matter of fact, I do. I have made inquiries."

"We are American citizens. Suppose we complain to our ambassador?"

Guzmán grinned still wider, a grin that shot straight back along his jaw without curling upward. "I beg of you," he said, "please do so. Your embassy will advance you funds and you may regulate your accounts, no?" His tone changed, and for the first time he spoke to Moon directly. "I have been waiting for you to do this, *piloto*. Why have you not done it, eh?" When Moon was silent, he continued, "Because you do not wish to do it. Because you are fugitives, perhaps, or criminals." He banged both hands flat upon the table. "All the more reason why I must protect my country!" He waved his hand toward the door, dismissing them. "I will give you three more days," he bawled, and jammed his face into his glass again, surfacing a moment later with a blast of air.

"Hey, *momentito*," Wolfie said. "Hey, Lewis, remember what we heard about them Indians?"

"Guzmán," Moon said.

The man whirled on him. "Mestizo! You will call me Comandante Guzmán!" he shouted. "Be very careful! I can send you back where you have come from, do you understand? And there you will be shot!"

Moon was listening to his partner, his face expressionless. Then he said to Guzmán, "It is your job to develop this region, no?"

"Eh?" Guzmán placed his fingertips on the table, as if about to spring. "What is it?"

"The Niaruna are still not pacified, and the news

36

is getting out, and yet your hands are tied because the law prohibits you from sending your soldiers in to kill the Indians."

Guzmán nodded, looking carefully at Moon. "I am quite able to take care of our poor Indians."

"We were just thinking that a foreign plane loaded with armaments . . . ? On its way elsewhere . . . ?"

Guzmán kept on nodding. *"Claro,"* he said. *"Sí. Claro."*

Later, on their beds upstairs, they discussed it further. They were both irritable, Wolfie because he felt Moon had not really told him what had been decided with the Comandante, and Moon because he did not want to think or talk at all. He lay on his back and stared at a huge moth pasted on the ceiling.

"Lewis," Wolfie said. "I ain't as stupid as I look, so level with me. Something happened there right at the end, I seen his face." He heaved over on his side. "That bastard's got a plan he didn't have before, now ain't that right? He kinda likes the Old Wolf's idea about goin out and leanin on them poor motherin Indians we heard about, the ones that's buggin him out to the east. Right?"

Moon was silent.

"Oh that murderin bastard," Wolfie said. "Like, shame on'm." After a while he said, "Listen, Lewis, I don't blame you, not wantin no part of this. I don't *blame* you, only did you stop and think, if *we* don't do it, somebody else's goin to, and if we *do* do it, we don't have to make no direct hits, just maybe like a little napalm upwind, know what I mean? Just run 'em the hell out of there."

"Um."

"Well, there's always the diamonds, Lewis."

"Yeah."

"These greasers run a lousy jail, Lewis, and how about the aircraft? And also, these Neo-rooneys ain't real Indians, Lewis. They ain't like Blackfoots or

Apaches or Cheyennes or nothin. They're just a bunch of starvin jungle rats, just like you told me. This is *South* America, remember? It ain't like they was your own people or nothin. So maybe you could kind of think of it like a *mercy* killin, huh, Lewis?"

Wolfie cocked his hip and cheerfully broke wind. "I said, huh, Lewis? You ain't startin to go soft on me, I hope?"

Moon was staring at the moth so hard that it blurred and became two.

He was still irritable when Uyuyu knocked on the door; he snapped it open, and the Indian leaped back toward the stairwell. In the cheap red shirt that the missionaries had given him, Uyuyu's neck looked thin, and his face twitched in his attempts to smile. This Indian happened to have a bright red shirt with bright blue rockets on it, but otherwise he was identical to his counterpart in every frontier river town from Puerto Maldonado in Peru to Pôrto Velho in Brazil, from Riberalta in Bolivia to Bahía Negra down in Paraguay: the native with the bright smile and the Christian humility, the sharp eye and the crucifix. Moon demanded, "Did you bring it?" He did not know which gave him most shame—the stupor of the Indian defeated by the white man, or the hunger of the convert like Uyuyu, with his base imitations of the white man's way.

Another door opened down the corridor, and a girl appeared in a shaft of light. She closed her door and came toward them. Uyuyu tried to slip past Moon into the room. Perversely, Moon deterred him. Uyuyu was still pushing gently as the girl approached the stairs. She greeted him—"Uyuyu, *buenos días*"—and smiled inquiringly at his discomfiture. Glancing at Moon, she nodded politely, then looked carefully again. She was a small girl with straight brown hair to her shoulders and a clear open face, sunburned, in hide sandals and a dress of pale blue faded linen. Moon' had noted her nice legs while waiting to see her face,

38

but it was the face that struck him. The skin was warm and clear and the mouth full—the line of the upper lip was a soft arch and white teeth touched her lower lip in a wistful way. So certain was he that she smelled good that his belly glowed and tingled, and at the same time he was overwhelmed by nostalgia for something lost. Frantic, he cleared his throat. She was turning toward the stairs. "I don't guess we've met before," he said.

She gazed directly into his face. "No," she said, "no, we haven't." She went on downstairs.

"Misionera," Uyuyu said, grinning tentatively. The Indian was prepared to speak of her with reverence or obscenity, according to the whim of his new master, but Moon only scowled at him and sent him off; Uyuyu was to seek out his friend, the *ayahuascero,* and bring Moon a fresh bottle of the drug by the next evening.

Moon went back into the room. Wolfie lay flat out on his bed, his beret propped on his huge dark glasses, his gold earring on the pillow, snoring. At the rust-flecked mirror on the fly-specked sink Moon curled his lip at what she must have seen. Once, at a police hearing, he had heard a tape of his own voice, and the sound had seemed just as foreign to him as the face which now confronted him: a lean face, yellow-bronzed with sunburn and malaria, carved close around high cheekbones and an Indian's broad mouth, a weathered face, so set in its expression that the dark eyes seemed to burn through a leather mask. The face was capped by a hood of blue-black hair as thick and solid as a helmet—a bad head, he thought, a *dirty* head, as the French say. It looked too big for the body, though the body was strong and quick enough— or had been before he had worn it out with lush and tail and junk, and now malaria. Well, he was scarcely a parfit gentil knight; as Wolfie said, he looked like some Hollywood Geronimo trying to kick a ninety-dollar habit.

Moon toppled backward over the end of his own bed and blew a long sigh at the ceiling. Wolfie was sighing, too.

"I've had a hard-on for three days now," Wolfie said. "You think I ought to consult my physician?"

And they lay there laughing for a long time, Wolfie hiccuping for joy, while the vultures circled in the dull gray sky beyond the window, crisscrossing the black crest of jungle, and the enormous moth on the ceiling gazed down upon them with the white eyes on its wings. And then Lewis Moon sat up again and brought both feet down hard on the floor between the beds.

4

On their way downstairs they were intercepted by the Comandante, who bought them a drink. Moon emptied his glass and banged it down on the table between himself and Guzmán, contemplating his host until the latter, caught by the sound in mid-pontification, withheld a frown, smiled that long smile that seemed to move straight back instead of moving upward, and asked Señor Wolfie if he and his . . . friend? . . . would not have another. Moon raised his eyebrows, shifting his gaze to a fourth man who had joined them at the table.

"I would be happy to join you," the priest said in English; he had come in late. He smiled, affecting innocence of the Comandante's irritation, and bowed almost imperceptibly to Moon. He was a small spare figure with a shrewd frugal face and stiff white hair standing straight up on his head, and this evening, despite the heat, he wore his black robe and a crucifix on a long chain.

More drinks came, and still more drinks, and the Comandante paused briefly in his discourse to display soiled photos of his forlorn fat wife, taken head on, at attention—Señora Dolores Estella Carmen María Cruz y Peralta Guzmán, he proclaimed—and of his son Fausto, whose head at this moment was just visible behind the bar. El Comandante did not dispense salaries to strangers.

41   *At Play in the Fields of the Lord*

"The Indians, in my heart I love them, they are my brothers, but this great land must be made safe for *progress* . . ." Guzmán had already made his point obliquely, confidentially, demanding and eliciting an occasional *"Sí, claro"* from Moon and from the padre; swollen with drink, he was now prepared to start again. Even Wolfie, who had caught little or nothing of the address, sensed that they were in for a reprise. "Oh man," he groaned, and rolled his eyes. Clearly, he felt that an interjection in another language could scarcely be taken amiss—or not, at least, by a drunken greaser. And it was true that in an access of self-hypnosis, El Comandante continued to speak with furrowed brow, his eyes shut tight in psychic pain; he seemed oblivious of them all.

Los indios, quiero decir, los salvajes bravos—"

Wolfie whistled. "Even him payin for the drinks, it *still* ain't worth it. I mean you boil down all this gas he's blowin which I don't even understand a word of it, and what he still wants is that we swing out there and blast the crap out of the redskins, right?"

Moon nodded, and the padre's smile flickered a moment, like a tic.

"Jesus, why don't he spit it out then?" Wolfie said. Then he yelled, "Get your ass out there, boys, and blow them little brown pricks to Kingdom Come!"

The silence that followed caused all three to turn toward Guzmán. He had stopped talking some time before and was watching Wolfie with a hatred so huge and silent that it bathed the entire room in apprehension. The faces gathered swiftly in the windows.

Wolfie nodded his head, impressed. "Look at them eyes," he said. He kept on nodding. "Like he don't understand a word I said and this jungle beast wants to massacre the poor old Wolf." To Guzmán he said, "What are you, some kind of an anti-*See*-mite?" And he laughed into Guzmán's face, in honest delight.

Moon caught a glint in Wolfie's eyes which, coupled with the cheerful tone, meant that his partner

42

wished to fight. And Guzmán himself, who had also attained that plane of drunken perception on which all languages are understood, turned his gaze from Wolfie to Moon and, making no headway, to Padre Xantes; the priest lowered his eyes, though calmly.

"Bueno," said Guzmán ambiguously, and cleared his throat. The padre, chin on chest, nodded minutely.

"No bread, no bombs," Wolfie told the Comandante. "You got that, Duke? So let's cut out, let's go get laid." Jumping to his feet, he clapped Guzmán on the shoulder; Guzmán's hands dropped down below the table, and Moon's own hand slid inside his shirt. "How about that, Stud? *Chicas? Mujeres?"* The hands appeared again, first Guzmán's, then Lewis Moon's, and were placed carefully on the table edge. Moon almost said, "He's got a knife," but watching Wolfie, he knew he did not have to.

Guzmán decided to smile. The smile slid back along his jaw, more like a split. "Gurls," he said. *"Woo-*mans." He laughed: "Ha, ha, ha, ha." It occurred to Moon that Guzmán was the only man he had ever heard who actually said "ha, ha," when he laughed, heavily and separately like that: "Ha, ha, ha, ha." While Guzmán laughed, he stared at Moon. *"Indio,"* he said. "Ha, ha, ha, ha."

Moon did not join them when they left. He sat quietly, facing the padre, and after a while the priest lifted his head and returned his gaze. "You think I am humiliated, do you not?" the padre said.

"Why do you care what I think?"

"You don't answer my question."

"It's not my problem, Padre."

"I am humiliated, of course. It is humiliating to have to sit here and listen to cold plans for taking life and know that one will not raise a hand to stop it."

"Why do you sit here then?" Moon said.

"I was told to come. Our Comandante intends to break the national law, which forbids the killing of Indians except in self-defense. But as long as he com-

43   *At Play in the Fields of the Lord*

pels the representative of the Church to give tacit agreement to what he is doing he can always spread any blame so thin that—"

"Yes, I guessed as much. I asked a stupid question."

"The question you intended to ask, señor, is how a priest such as myself, willing to sit here and drink with villains, may call himself a priest. But is he then to turn his back on the other tribes who need his help, to abandon the work that *can* be done, to do nothing but creep about an empty church? For that is the alternative, should one contest the word of El Comandante. And so I must choose what seems to me the lesser of two sins, and pray for forgiveness in the eyes of the Lord."

The priest stood up. "I suggest," he said "that you and your colleague must do the same." He bowed very slightly. *"Buenas noches."*

"Buenas noches, Padre."

Xantes hesitated.

"What kind of men are you? Could I plead with you? No! And if it is not you, then it would be somebody else."

"That's right. You're not a stupid man, Padre."

"Quite true. I am the only man of—is it this word? —*sensibility* in the entire state of Oriente; that makes me *some*body, no?" He paused. "And who are you, Mr. Moon? *Are* you anybody?"

Moon looked at him; he had been taken by surprise. "Me?" he said. "Why, I am the great halfbreed of the world." He paused and drank; the priest awaited him. Moon seized a fold of his own skin. "The color of modern man! In a few centuries everybody is going to look like Lewis Moon." He burst out laughing.

"You are not truly amused," the padre told him coldly; Moon stopped smiling. "You did not answer my question—*who* are you, Mr. Moon? I did not ask *what* you were." Xantes considered him a moment; they nodded at each other. "You are an educated man. In the times we have talked, I have found it entertaining. It is too bad we work against each other, no? In a stupid world?" He bowed.

Moon rose drunkenly and returned the bow, lifting his glass, but the priest, in elegant distaste, paid him no heed. For all his drink, he was as ascetic and erect as he had been three hours before, though he had to shuffle now to keep his balance. Turning slowly at the door, he contemplated Moon for nearly a half-minute. "These Indians that you wish to kill . . ." A faint smile emerged on his face, and he nodded his head up and down, up and down. "Yet it appears that you are part Indian yourself, señor?"

Moon was silent.

"How sad," the padre sighed. "Does it not strike you as rather *sad,* señor?"

Then he was gone. Moon sat down heavily. His ill humor was compounded by the appearance of Uyuyu, even though it was Uyuyu whom he awaited; the very sight of that red shirt annoyed him. The Indian must have lurked outside until Xantes departed, not wishing the priest to learn of his business with Moon. And since Moon did not feel guilty, Uyuyu's guilt annoyed him further. According to Xantes, Uyuyu had come to Madre de Dios in search of an education so that the Indians of the Remate de Males region would be less easily cheated by the traders. He had sold his service to the priest, who taught him to read and write, and he became a fanatic Christian: within the year, Xantes had made him the mission teacher at Remate. But when his Catholic prayers for his people went unheeded, Uyuyu had switched to the Protestant prayers of Leslie Huben. He had also applied his education to the exploitation of the very people he had set out to defend, and was now so little at ease with himself that as he approached Moon's table, his grin and grimace were not readily distinguishable. But he had brought it, a large wine bottle full of the thick brown fluid called *ayahuasca,* which he placed on the table, patted, and relinquished.

"Uyuyu. *Ésta muy fresca,* Uyuyu, *no?*"

"Muy fresca, señor—ayahuascero amigo mío."
The Indian backed out of the room. The distemper in his narrow face reminded Moon of James Mad Raven, one of the last full-bloods on the reservation. James Mad Raven had called the halfbreeds "white trash" because the halfbreeds, in recent years, had taken to calling James Mad Raven "nigger."

Up in Barbados lived a big brown nigger girl in a big plain dress with a round white collar. Moist-voiced and obscene, with a languorous warm tongue and a breath of candy, she had tried hard to evangelize him, wagging an earnest finger with one hand while with the other she explored his lap under the table.

She was an Anglican, very devout. "Mahn, you got to *know* Jesus. And how you gone know Jesus if you wuh-shipin dat May-ry?" It did not occur to her that someone who was not Anglican might not be Catholic either. When he said nothing, she had mourned a little. "In de day, you see, it be all right, but in de night, mahn . . ." She sniffed painfully. "De single life, doss de way it go." This big sweet girl took him home with her to a world of chickens and poinsettias. *Now what tam you mus go, sweet honey. Coss when you go, you woan com bock.* In the morning, her little boy clung to him all the way to the bus back to the port, calling out joyfully to children who jeered him, "See mahn deah? He fath-ah to *me!*"

Wistaria, that was her name. Wistaria dancing naked in her cottage. Wistaria, who cried when he went away, was the only one he could remember.
De single life, doss de way it go.

In the bar the atmosphere had changed; a dim figure had moved into the corner of Moon's consciousness. Turning his head very slightly, he saw a man poised in the doorway. It was a gringo; in the remote corners of the world the short-sleeved flowered tourist shirt, the steel-rimmed glasses, khaki pants and bulldog shoes had become the uniform of earnest American enterprise. Moon recognized the man as the new

46

missionary. His head was cropped too close, so that his white skull gleamed, and the red skin of his neck and jaw was riddled with old acne; his face was bald with anxiety and tiresome small agonies.

Coming up to the table, the missionary bumped nervously into a chair; it screeched on the tile floor. *"Buenas noches, señor,"* he said. *"Puedo sentarme?"* He sat down on the edge of the chair.

Raising his eyes without raising his head, Moon contemplated him while he rubbed his ear, which was already numb with drink. After a moment he said, "Why don't you sit down at my table?"

"I have," the man exclaimed, flushing. "I mean—" he stood up, knocking the chair backward. "I didn't mean—" He restored the chair. "It turns out we're both Americans! Imagine! I mean, the way you dress and all, someone could take you for—"

"—a gook, a wog, a spic, a spade—"

"Excuse me? No, a local fellow. Of the town."

"Because of my clothes, you mean."

"That's right."

"And because I look like all these local half-breeds, these mestizos."

"Well, yes, in a way," the man said, gazing frankly at Moon's face. "Look, I was just trying to get acquainted. I knew all along you were Mr. Moon."

"Well, I know who you are too, friend, and if you sat down here to save my soul, forget it."

"How could you tell I was a missionary?"

"Are you serious? How do you tell a hunchback or an elephant?" Moon whistled in derision.

"I don't understand why you're so angry—I just got here!"

"All halfbreeds, as you must have heard, are violent and treacherous, especially when under the effects of alcohol."

The man laughed aloud, controlled himself, and sighed. "Personally, as an American, I'd be very proud to have Indian blood. I think most Americans would be proud to have it."

"They would, huh?"

"I should think so."

"How much Indian blood would most Americans be proud to have?"

"Oh." The man sighed again and shook his head. "But you've done all right, it seems," he said, unruffled. "Probably your education is better than my own."

"Probably. I'm very well educated." Moon, nodding, finished his glass. "When you walked into this room just now, you not only knew my name was Moon but you knew that I was educated. You knew exactly who I was, isn't that right?"

The missionary tried to bluster, then waved his hands and groaned.

"*How* did you know?" Moon said.

"It was just that Andy . . . Mrs. Huben . . . she remembered reading something . . . she was very sympathetic with your position."

"She was, huh? Let me ask you another question."

"Why, certainly."

"How would you like a short kick in the nuts?"

The man stood up.

"Sit down," Moon said, taking his arm. "They say that Indians can't hold their firewater." He grinned stupidly, and the man sat down. "Last question," Moon said. "How would you like me to marry your sister?" He burst out laughing, leaning back in his chair, hands in his pockets.

"I would like to ask *you* a question," the man said. When Moon only shrugged, he said, "With that education and everything, how did you end up in Madre de Dios?"

"Why, I'm a missionary," Moon said. "I'm at work in the fields of the Lord. *Go ye into all the world, and preach the gospel to every creature.* Mark, Chapter 16, Verse 15. You want to get preached to?"

The man looked angry but said nothing.

"You don't believe I'm a missionary?"

"Of course not."

"Are you calling me a liar?"

The man said, "I deny your right to speak this way, even in jest, because you're not a missionary. You are a vicious, drunken man, and a blasphemer." He mopped his face, very upset. "The Niaruna you intend to murder are the ones I will be working with. I mean to go to them whatever you people do. If you bomb them, machine-gun them—"

"It will make things hot for you, is that right?"

"I wasn't thinking about that—"

"Better start right now, then."

"I've thought about it. I have a wife and child."

"You have faith in the Lord, don't you?"

"There are limits to what we can ask of the Lord's mercy."

"Well, I never thought I'd live to hear one of you fundamentalists admit *that*. Look, what are you hanging around for?" Moon said. "Why did you sit down here in the first place?"

"When I say unto the wicked, Thou shalt surely die; and thou givest him not warning, nor speakest to warn the wicked from his wicked way, to save his life; the same wicked man shall die in his iniquity; but his blood will I require at thine hand!"

"Okay, I'm warned." Moon gazed at him. "You have faith then."

"Yes, I do."

"When you are out there in that forest, with the savages behind those trees—how much faith will you have then?"

"In God?"

"In your own faith."

The missionary began to speak; he faltered and stopped short.

"I'll bet you've asked yourself that very thing quite a few times. Let me ask you something else. Did you earn your faith, or were you stuffed with it, like a big turkey?"

"My faith is a question I'll have to work out without your help." The man got slowly to his feet. "I wanted to talk to you, Mr. Moon, but I see it's impossible. Perhaps you could tell me where I could find your partner."

Moon picked up his glass and drank. "You want to see Wolfie, you'll find him at the cat house. Only he hates being interrupted while he's in the saddle, so while you're waiting you can screw one of the pigs." He finished his drink and stood up. The serenity in the missionary's face incensed him; yet he wondered if he really knew what he was angry at. Was it the distemper he felt whenever he had talked too much, or was it only that flat ugly voice of Western white America that to this day he could not hear without a twitch of shame and hatred?

One time, drunk, he had taunted his father for volunteering as a soldier in World War I, taunted him as a mongrel white. Alvin Moon had whipped him so badly that he had finally drawn a knife. They were in a saloon, the first and last time they ever had money enough to get drunk together. Alvin Moon told him to put down the knife, and he had done so without blustering. They returned to their bar stools and went right on drinking. After a while, when the onlookers had gone, Alvin Moon said, "That meanness." He had it all thought out. "You tote that there meanness around with you just like you tote that big heavy old-time war knife that the old men give you. There ain't no real use for a knife like that no more."

To the missionary he said, "South Dakota? Or Nebraska? New Tribes Mission? Far Tribes Mission? Or S.I.L.?"

"North Dakota. Far Tribes Mission." He paused. Well, Mr. Moon—"

"Lewis Moon." He gave his hand.

"My name is Martin Quarrier."

"Well, Martin, you got the call, is that right?" He closed his eyes, resting his face in his hands. "Care for some *ayahuasca?*"

"If that stuff's *ayahuasca,* you better be careful.

50

That's a poisonous narcotic drug. The Indians call it nipi. Why, it gives you hallucinations! It can kill you!"

"That's right," Moon said. "Care to try some?" He sat back, stretched his arms, and sighed. Without bringing his arms down he opened his eyes and looked at Quarrier. "What can I do for you?" he said.

"I've heard what you men are going to do. I hoped you would tell me it's not true."

"To tell a lie," Moon told him, "is a sin."

Quarrier's laugh, though genuine, trailed off into a squawk of desperation. Moon laughed too, in drunken glee. "This Indian, Uyuyu—Is it true that he's working both sides of the street? I mean, I was talking to the padre. Uyuyu's a Protestant *and* a Catholic, isn't he?"

"Do you mean that Indian who was just here? The one we call Yoyo?"

"Yeah—Yoyo." Moon laughed softly, steadily. "That's beautiful."

"Yes, he's been both."

"What is he now, a Seventh-Day Adventist? A Jew, maybe?" Moon frowned. "Forget it, man." He waved Quarrier off, or rather, Quarrier's expression. The steady stupid honesty of the man's face annoyed him; he felt somehow exposed. "Yoyo," he muttered. "That's beautiful. Who thought of that?"

"Andy—Mrs. Huben. Leslie's wife."

"Oh yeah, the one who sympathizes with my position. So that's Leslie's, huh? The pretty one."

Quarrier nodded, flushing.

"Yours is the big girl, with black hair."

"Yes."

"You think Leslie's little wife is pretty, too, I bet." He studied Quarrier, then made a guess. "You think you're in love with Leslie's wife, is that right?"

Quarrier started to protest but was too upset to find his words. His face lost color.

Moon heard his own voice say, "You screwed her yet?"

"You coward!" Quarrier stood over Moon, holding his fists up like a child holds up two broken toys. Tears came from behind his glasses and rolled down his cheeks. "You have a demon. You're a drunken coward!"

Moon laid his hands flat on the table. "I guess you could say that, all right," he said. "I guess you could say that." The rage had collapsed, subsiding in a sour self-dislike. His peaceful admission took the other man aback; Quarrier stood there, fists still clenched, still crying, as if behind those heavy lenses his eyes had melted.

"Your fists are clenched," Moon observed quietly.

"Well, come outside! If you are man enough!"

The naïveté of this jibe pained Moon worst of all; in the excess of his spleen, he longed to slug this stupid-looking hick in his thick glasses, but he made himself say, "I am not man enough," and not only that but—lest the missionary imagine that he was being treated with contempt—"I am too drunk." And finally he said, "I'm sorry. Please sit down."

"You mean you're just going to sit there and let me call you a coward?"

"You'll get tired of it after a while," Moon said.

5

Wolfie and Guzmán were fighting to get through the door together; each dragged after him a giggling and frightened girl. Neither girl had left puberty far behind, and each had the small potbelly and high wide breasts, the flat face and delicate limbs of the jungle Indians. The pretty one wore her black hair pulled behind her ears, showing cheap earrings, and her bright red dress was tight; when Guzmán brought her to the table she winked at Lewis Moon, and slowly stuck her tongue out.

"*Se llama* Suzie," Guzmán said. "*Qué quieres aquí?*" he jeered at Quarrier. "*Misionero! Misionero* want woo-mans!" But when Quarrier glanced at the girl, then back at Guzmán, the Comandante removed his hand from her behind and placed it over his heart. It was not to be thought, he assured the room at large, that the girl was for himself; El Comandante Rufino Guzmán, as the world well knew, was the honorable husband of the beautiful Señora Dolores Estella Carmen María Cruz y Peralta Guzmán. The *indio* girl was for the North American mestizo, Señor Moon. At this Suzie giggled, stroking Guzmán's upper leg. She too was very drunk. "Rufi-*ni*-to," she said, and winked at Moon again.

But Moon and Guzmán paid no attention to her. The Comandante was smiling triumphantly at Moon, and Moon smiled back at him until the Comandante, looking confused, stopped smiling and began to glare.

Moon thought, Well, there's going to be trouble. Any time now. Casually he checked Guzmán's hip; the pistol belt was missing.

At the bar Suzie's friend had broken loose from Wolfie, who was addressing her affectionately as Fat-Girl; with his beard and beret, his loud meaningless sounds, his erect cigar and huge dark glasses, he had frightened her out of her wits. She had an open stupid face, with pockmarks and missing teeth, and was barefoot beneath her printed frock of mission gingham. Nevertheless, seeking to emulate her friend as well as to better her own lot, she addressed herself to the third gringo. Arms straight at her sides like a child reciting, she smiled and winked, stuck her tongue out very slowly, and said to Quarrier, "Ay yam Mercedes. Ay yam vir-geen."

"Ha, ha, ha, ha," cried El Comandante Rufino Guzmán. "*Misionero* luff Indio gurls! Ha, ha, ha, ha!"

Moon gazed solemnly at Guzmán, then bent his head and began to laugh, and Wolfie, rushing up with his cigar and giant beer bottle, saw Moon laugh and began laughing too. He sat at the table, grabbed his Fat-Girl onto his knee and howled until the tears came, out of sheer empathy. After a time he subsided into spasms, snorting and crying, as the laughter rose and burst in high little sounds out of his nostrils: *snee, snee, snee, snee.* From along the bar and at the windows, beneath the display of hand-tinted Virgins and flamenco dancers on *aguardiente* calendars, soft-drink signs and plaster crucifixions, the laughter clattered without mercy. Sweet Suzie laughed straight into the face of Moon, her dark eyes mirthless, and fat Mercedes, who imagined that she was the mother of the joke, laughed modestly as best she could, for on Wolfie's knee with both of Wolfie's hands clasped hard upon her breasts, it was hard for a girl to get a breath. Moon recognized her as the girl who worked in Guzmán's kitchen. He smiled at her sympathetically, in response to which she winked at him again, and again stuck her tongue out.

"Ha, ha, ha, ha," shouted the Comandante, hurling himself backward; he believed himself to be the witty one. *"Snee, snee, snee, snee,"* the Old Wolf whimpered, doubled forward. Yet Guzmán, surrounded by laughter, laughed alone; and as for Wolfie, at no time during his entire seizure did he know or care what he was laughing at.

"This is a madhouse," Moon said approvingly to Quarrier, who looked like a man on whom the sky was falling.

Suzie, following Moon's gaze, leaned back and nestled her elbow in the missionary's groin; cocking her head far backward so that she stared straight up into his face, she cried out the identical words that Mercedes had spoken with such success a few minutes before. She kept her head that way for several moments, frowning when her remark was disregarded, and at the same time aware that something better was afoot: for Quarrier, who had jerked back from her elbow, was helplessly peering down into her dress. The girl raised her hands beneath her breasts until they swelled like buttocks in the neck of her dress, and said to Quarrier, *"S-ss-t, s-ss-t, misionero, s-ss-t!"*

Recoiling, Quarrier uttered a little cry. His sweating tormented head swung back and forth, back and forth. "What do you seek here?" he said to Moon. "What are these lost souls laughing at?" Moon took his wrist and pulled him down onto the bench beside him. "Be quiet," he said, "you're not here to save us." But Quarrier persisted, waving his free arm about. "You are lost souls, can't you realize that? You have Satan in you, every one of you!"

Moon squeezed his wrist so hard that the man faced him in surprise. "She's got nice tits," Moon said, "wouldn't you say?" Quarrier opened his mouth, then closed it, reddening so violently that his whole face seemed to swell. Moon said to him, "Now listen, friend, you're welcome here, but never mind the Gospel lessons."

But Wolfie, in violent antipathy to Quarrier, was repeating, "What are they *laughin* at, he says! What are they *laughin* at?" louder and louder; then he reared up in his chair, shoving his Fat-Girl aside. "What are you, some kind of a religious *fanatic* or somethin? You don't like people enjoyin theirselves, or what?" He smashed his fist on the table. "At least that Catholic, at least he'd take a *drink* with us, for Christ sake! Hey"—he turned again to Moon—"hey, Lewis, you remember them big spade girls we had in them rum-and-drums up in Barbados? Did I ever tell you them whores was devout *Catholics,* for Christ sake—*and* Protestants? And I bet every humpin one of them, Catholic and Protestant, had the clap."

Now what tam you mus go, sweet honey. Coss when you go, you woan com bock.

"I was in Barbados once," Quarrier said. "On a freighter. We came down here by freighter from Fernandina, Florida. In Barbados my boy Billy and myself went up the street and had ourselves a very nice chicken chow mein dinner."

Now that, thought Moon, makes *two* sad things that happened in Barbados.

Wolfie winced. "Oh man," he said. "Lissen. Where was I? Oh yeah, I was gonna say, like where the hell do you get off tryin to tell us about sin? That's what you're hangin around for, right?"

"Yes," Quarrier said, and Moon watched Wolfie twitch under the steady gaze that the missionary fixed upon him.

"Well, you got nothin to look so holy about, am I right, Lewis?" When Moon said nothing, Wolfie turned back angrily to Quarrier. "You and them Catholics both. Some *holy* men! All this lousy backbitin and knifin over people who maybe they don't want no part of *neither* of you; well, maybe you ought to think of *that* before you come sneakin around here criticizin!

56

Maybe them people are better off bein run back into the jungle where they got a little human *dignity,* for Christ sake, and not where you bastards can make beggars out of them, not to mention all the booze and slavery and syphilis"—Wolfie jerked his thumb at his female companion—"that comes after. How long do you think them Neo-rooneys are gonna last once you've softened them up for all these jungle cons?" He jerked his thumb at Guzmán. "Ten years? Thirty years, maybe?" His voice rose. "So don't come runnin to us about our business. 'Physician, heal thyself'— right, Lewis?"

"Fa-Cry-sek," the Comandante said. "Fa-Cry-sek."

"Rufi-*ni*-to," complained the whore called Suzie. *"Silencio! Nosotros hablamos inglés.* We arr es-spik Ingliss!"

To Wolfie—though looking straight at Quarrier— Moon said, "You forgot the part about robbing the Indians of their own culture and then abandoning them"—he raised his voice in mock outrage, as if he were making a speech—"leaving them with nothing strong enough, neither their old culture nor a new one, to support them against the next group to come along."

"Oh yeah," Wolfie said, "that's right. Neither their old culture or a new one," he yelled angrily at Quarrier, "and then you come runnin to us about our business. Well, all I can say is, 'Physician, heal thyself.' "

Quarrier said mildly, "They say that every sin has its justification in the mind of the sinner."

Pleased that he had acquitted himself so well, Wolfie had leaned back in his chair, relighting his cigar; now he slammed forward once again.

"Jeez! You're a smug sonofabitch, now ain't you!" he said to Quarrier. "And I'll bet that kid of yours you mentioned a minute ago, the chicken-chow-mein eater, for Christ sake—I bet you already made another smug sonofabitch out of that kid already, am I right? Well, let me tell *you* somethin: I never sinned in my whole life—I don't *believe* in sin!"

"Smuk snuffa-bits," Guzmán repeated. "Smuk snuffa-bits. Ha, ha, ha, ha."

Quarrier opened his mouth to speak, then closed it.

Moon got to his feet and made his way around the table. Behind him he heard Wolfie say, "Well, it just so happens I *seen* your kid, I run inta him on the street. Don't get me wrong, he's a real nice kid, Reverend, no shit. Listen, Reverend, you ain't really a *bad* sonofabitch or nothin. It takes all kinds to make a world, know what I mean? Know what I mean, Reverend?"

Holding his breath, swaying drunkenly beneath a bulb which illumined little more than grime and moisture, Moon stared awhile at the cement wall; it took just such a hopeless international latrine in the early hours of a morning, when a man was weak in the knees, short in the breath, numb in the forehead and rotten in the gut, to make him wonder where he was, how he got there, where he was going; he realized that he did not know and never would. He had confronted this same latrine on every continent and not once had it come up with an answer; or rather, it always came up with the same answer, a suck and gurgle of unspeakable vileness, a sort of self-satisfied low chuckling: Go to it, man, you're pissing your life away.

Standing there, swaying pleasantly, he grinned. I do not care, he thought. I no longer care. If I can just stay where the action is, I never *will* care, never again.

In the dark corridor leading back into the bar-salon, Guzmán's son Fausto lay in wait; he swung open a door for Moon's inspection. Inside was a table and a cot; there was no window. *"S-ss-t, señor, s-ss-t."* The boy's eyes flashed; he pointed vigorously at the door to the bar, through whose glass pane the head of fat Mercedes swam in a garish light. Then he pointed at Moon, then at the bed. When Moon only shrugged, Fausto scuttled ahead of him to the next

58

door, jerked his thumb at it and grinned. There were murmurings within. Bending forward a little, the boy made a basket of his arms and then, rolling his eyes, moved his hindquarters in and out spasmodically, in the manner of a dog.

Moon entered the bar, disregarding the urgent tugging at his sleeve. As he suspected, it was none other than the perfidious Wolfie who was missing. Moon found himself face to face with the fat girl in mission gingham, who stuck her tongue out very slowly.

"We arr es-spik Ingliss," said the Comandante. He looked disgruntled, and was scratching his armpit inside his shirt. Across the table Quarrier was still present, his hands clenched on his knees, his face pale and rigid behind the dull thick lenses.

"Okay," Moon said. "The pen of my aunt is on the table."

"You fren fock woo-mans," Guzmán retorted. He was glaring at Moon with an artless hatred that grew with every drink. When the fat girl reached over and stroked his arm, he drove her off with a backhand blow across the breasts. *"Vete al diablo!"* commanded El Comandante. "We arr es-spik Ingliss!"

Quarrier said, "Did he tell you he'd stolen my letter to the government about his methods with the Indians, in which I reported that he makes money in the slave trade? Because I've learned just that from our Mintipo believers here in town."

Moon put his glass down. "You just got here a few days ago, isn't that right?"

"That's right." Quarrier nodded up and down, aggrieved. "That boy Fausto showed him the address, and he read my letter and then tore it up, right under my nose."

"Send another letter," Moon advised him. "This time accuse him of tampering with the mails." He shook his head. "Take it from me, you're a born loser."

After a pause Quarrier said, "Do you really think attacking the Indians is going to pacify them?"

"No," Moon said, "but killing them is." He

reached over and seized Wolfie's abandoned glass and drained off what was left in it. Wolfie came and signaled to his Fat-Girl. "That Suzie of yours, for Christ sake," he complained to Moon. "She's too damn drunk to move." Mercedes got up and wandered toward him, clutching her arms to her hurt breast and glaring over her shoulder at the Comandante, who was drinking even more heavily than before. He glowered evilly at Wolfie and the girl, nodding his head as if to indicate that a moment of dreadful reckoning was at hand. When Wolfie yelled at him, "So what's with you, you spic sonofabitch!" Guzmán gulped at his beer, protruding his lower lip at Moon and expelling noisy puffs of air, like a blowing horse; after a time he disappeared toward the latrine.

The place had emptied; Fausto was sleeping behind the bar. An occasional head poked furtively through the door, but the window clientele had vanished. Somewhere a rooster crowed, and a pig snuffled in the mud street; a light of the oncoming jungle dawn soured the bad light in the room.

Quarrier tried doggedly to interest Moon in the Niaruna, showing him a crude dictionary compiled by Huben and Uyuyu. "They seem to use the same stem for verbs and nouns and adjectives, with just a change of affixes, and they have genders, and their second-person pronoun is *ti*. All this suggests an Arawakan stock, the only one in this region. Perhaps you know that some tribes in our own South may derive from the Arawak as well. And I remember something else: the Sioux word for the Life Force, the Great Mystery, is *wakan;* in certain jungle tribes a word of quite similar meaning is pronounced *waka!*"

"The Great Mystery, huh?"

"You probably know much more than I do—"

"You are trying to tell me that there are similarities between the Plains Indians and these Indians we are going to bomb, isn't that right? Well, there were much greater similarities between my people and the Crow, between my people and the Shoshone, and even

60

when the one real enemy was the white man, we killed Crows and Shoshones whenever we had the chance."

Moon was silent for a time. Then he said suddenly, "I know all about you, Quarrier. You're a pain-in-the-ass type, a nosy . . . Listen, we had one just like you when I was a kid, always appealing to our primitive nobility. He was all read up on the proud Cheyenne in paint and eagle feathers, and all he found was a pack of ragged halfbreeds chewing dog meat. 'Can't you see we're trying to *help* you people—?' Christ! The Indian didn't *need* help until the white man came along, and here was this poor sonofabitch looking for *gratitude*—"

Then Wolfie shuffled in, swollen and sobered, one hand scratching his chin bristles, the other still fumbling with his trousers. Behind him marched Mercedes, looking put upon; haughtily, arms still straight at her sides, she went on out the door into the street, like a huge toy. Wolfie glared sheepishly at Moon. "Lousy," he said, and coughed and spat. "I mean, that was *really* a nowhere hump. Nowhere at all." To Quarrier he said, "You got a wife upstairs here, right? You people *screw* at least, I hope. So keep your eyes to yourself."

Quarrier rose without expression and went out toward the latrine.

"Well, I'm glad you *got* one, anyway," Wolfie called. When Quarrier was gone, he said to Moon, "You dig that guy, huh?"

"He's all right," Moon said. "He's better than most of them; at least he's not stupid."

"He's not, huh? You mean he just *looks* stupid. He just *acts* stupid." Wolfie, scratching, sounded like a pig on a dry fence. "So where's the treacherous greaser?" But even as he spoke the door opened and the Comandante appeared. He too looked angry, and he yelled violently at his son Fausto, "Son of a cow! Close the doors, close the shutters, before the Gran Hotel Dolores is stolen out from under you!" And the boy, jolted from his sleep, dropped down behind the bar in case something was hurled at him, then darted out at the far end and scurried to close the doors.

The Comandante pitched over to the table, where he drank down a half-bottle of beer at a single draught. When he came up for air he was breathing hoarsely. His color was bad and his fly was open. "We arr es-spik Ingliss," he gasped finally at Moon, then nodded craftily toward the room in the rear. "*Piloto,* you wan focks woo-man, no? *La chica* Suzie—drunk! Ferry drunk!" He raised both hands to the side of his head to indicate that the girl was unconscious. "*Ahora*"—he pointed at the door—"you focks Indio gurl, *vamos,* no pay *nada.*" He raised two fingers, grinning triumphantly at Moon, his gold tooth gleaming. "Indio boy," he said, "fock Indio gurl, no pay *nada.*"

Moon grinned back at him. In a flat voice he said, "The Comandante is a dirty pig. *Un maricón sin vergüenza.*"

A moment later, he lay flat upon the floor. Guzmán had taken a large beer bottle by the neck and whipped him a backhand blow along the skull; he stood over Moon, holding the bottle by the neck. Quick as a snake, Moon thought, quick as a snake. The bottle was not broken, so at least he was not cut. A fractured skull, maybe. He gazed peacefully at Sheriff Guzmán from the floor. If you don't kill me now while you have the chance, he thought, you're going to regret it.

An arm appeared around the Sheriff's neck, and a wild hairy face over his shoulder; both disappeared from view. A woeful crash, a roar of animals, and the light on the ceiling spun; the end of the world has come at last, he thought, we have collided with the moon. And he sank away into oblivion. When he came to again, there was a kind of silence, the only sound a breathing and a scrape of feet; he sat up, hauling at the table leg, and stared at the scene before him. Wolfie and Guzmán were each using one hand to hold their pants up. They were circling in the center of the room, and in the free hand of each of them was a knife. Behind Wolfie, also circling, was the wretched Fausto, clutching a bottle.

Moon said, "Hey, Wolf—"

"I see him," Wolfie said, his eyes fastened on Guzmán. "I see the little lad. And the little lad gets one step closer, he's gonna get his throat cut." Wolfie had now secured his pants, and his free hand was extended out behind him toward the boy. He did not stop moving, but kept circling, circling, knees bent, in a kind of squat; as he passed the table he seized a bottle by the neck and broke it in half—*crack*—on the table edge, and kept moving. Now he had a weapon in each hand. Passing, he said to Moon, "How you doin, kid?"

"Give me your knife."

"No, no," Wolfie called back over his shoulder, "no, no. This one is mine. He pulled the knife on me, not you." The next time around he said, "And anyway, you ain't no knife fighter, baby—he'd take you." Moon struggled to his feet, hanging on to the table, then crashed back clumsily off the bench against the wall. "No, no," Wolfie murmured next time around. "This one is mine, baby, this one would take you."

Though Moon's eyes had cleared, his body was still paralyzed. He watched Wolfie with a vague dispassionate admiration for something done professionally, with grace: the flowing movements of the man, the sure feet flat to the floor for balance and silent as on tiptoe, the swift strong gliding legs, the big delicate hairy hands loose at the wrists, the long knife held out like an offering, blade flat, to pass more easily between ribs . . .

Guzmán bellowed at his son, "Fausto, Fausto! *El otro! Mátalo!*" Moon sat with his feet straight out and his palms on the bench and watched the frightened boy coming to kill him. In his daze he was struck by the wide dark eyes, the wide agonized mouth like a hole—*crash*—a spot on the wall and falling glass and the boy broke away with a little screech, dropping his upraised weapon, for Wolfie had whirled and whipped his jagged bottle at the boy's head. Guzmán broke to lunge and slash at Wolfie, who turned under and out and away so easily that Guzmán stopped short and dropped his arm in surprise and—yes, Moon thought, yes, there it is, the good old fear.

He had seen Wolfie's knife come out before and he was sorry he had missed the moment this time, for it was one of the prettiest things that he had ever seen. It was like the first electric movement of a dance: the draw from inside the shirt was too fast for the eye, so that the forward and outward motion of the blade as the hand unfolded seemed slow-motion by comparison, and lethal because it was so graceful and unhurried, like a ritual performed many times over. Guzmán could not have watched this movement closely or he would have quit right then and there.

The boy whimpered, coming up again with his bottle, but he was no longer in the fight.

Wolfie sensed all of this and grinned, moving in closer, for Guzmán's step had straightened. The big man, until now as quick as Wolfie, was moving slowly, his legs stiffening; in a moment he would lose his nerve and freeze—and then, Moon thought, your only chance is to make your move or run before you freeze. Moon watched the pale unshaven face with distaste for what now must happen, but without pity.

Wolfie had not yet made a pass, though he had feinted once in play and laughed when his foe leaped back; the intense happy grin on Wolfie's face parted his beard. That was the terrifying thing. Moon knew now what Wolfie had known from the beginning: that the outcome had never been in question, not even when there had been two against him. It was the big man's sudden awareness, not of Wolfie's awesome skill but of his still more awesome and implacable assurance, that had shaken his nerve beyond repair.

"Villians!"

Well, Moon thought, did *I* say that? He turned his head. Quarrier stood there in the door leading to the latrine, the near-naked body of the small Indian girl in his arms and on his face the ultimate outrage of Jehovah. Quarrier, mouth open, glared at the shambles of the room in disbelief: the knife fighters and broken bottles, the cringing boy, the torpid Moon.

Wolfie had halted in mid-stride to stare at Quarrier. Moon yelled a warning and struggled to his feet. In the same second Wolfie ducked so low that his fingertips grazed the floor, and came out and up again, knife erect. Guzmán tried too late to stop his lunge; as he fell, he rolled sideways with a grunt, casting away his knife, and when he struck the floor, yanked his knees up to his stomach and his arms up to his face: *"Misericordia!"*

Wolfie stared at him, his own knife shivering; then he whirled and rushed at Quarrier, shoving the knife point at his face. "You stinkin bitch! Didn't I tell you keep your nose out? Did I or didn't I? You spoiled it, you gone and spoiled it." He actually stamped his foot. "Jesus!" he shouted. And he drove his knife so hard into the table that the wood split.

Sensing that Wolfie had lost interest in him, Guzmán scrambled for his weapon, then leaped to his feet in fighting posture, bounding and circling and bellowing with rage. In terror of his father's ferocity Fausto screeched, "Papá, Papá!" But Guzmán had the wit not to catch Wolfie's eye, addressing himself instead to Quarrier.

"Hah, *evangélico!* Hah, *estúpido!*" And he pointed his knife at the girl. Quarrier tried clumsily to pull her skirt down—she was naked underneath—but since the cloth was bunched against his waist, he failed. He lowered her feet to the ground and the skirt fell. "Hah," Guzmán cried again, smiting his palm to his forehead, *"evangélico! Evangélico* fock Indio gurl!"

"Yeah, how about that?" Wolfie murmured. "How about that?"

"No," Moon said, "he didn't do that." He remembered how the missionary had stared down the girl's dress. "Don't be stupid, Wolf."

"Stupid!" Wolfie grunted, nodding his head. "And this to the guy that only just saved his life." He slumped angrily into a chair.

The Indian girl had come around. She sat alone against the wall under a yellow bulb, as if in wait for someone to come and tell her where she must go. Hands pressed like fig leaves to her crotch, she stared dully at the men, uncomprehending. With her lipstick and earrings gone, she was no more than a child.

Quarrier stood at the table. The girl had been sick on his sleeve and he smelled bad. He said to Moon, "Do you realize what these evil brutes have done? Do you care? I don't know what to say to you—"

"Don't say nothin then," Wolfie told him. He shouted suddenly at Guzmán, "You want us to fly tomorrow, prick? Because if you do, you better get our papers set."

Guzmán, once he had understood, roared angrily in acquiescence. He drove the Indian girl out the door into the dawn and his son after her, fetching the latter a slap across the head. "Son of a cow," he bawled, "go home to your poor mother, Doña Dolores, and tell her that her husband, El Comandante Don Rufino Guzmán, has set out on his journey to the *casa!*"

Quarrier spread his arms in a gesture toward the room which, with the shutters closed, had become dense with smoke, and stank of sweat and spilled cheap beer and breathing. "How did I get myself in such a place . . ." He shook his head.

Moon took his bottle of *ayahuasca* and moved toward the stairs. "I told you, friend," he said, "you're a born loser."

"Ain't we all," snarled Wolfie, "ain't we all."

6

It had been the confrontation with the padre, he decided, that had set in motion that series of grotesque events. And though the episodes had been the fault of Guzmán and Wolfie, the man who had upset him most was Lewis Moon. *She's got nice tits, wouldn't you say:* Aow, how that phrase still twisted him! Moon had faced him with his own perfidy, his longing for another man's wife, and even worse, a sinful lust for women in general, including the poor little Indian believer. He could not excuse this on the grounds that Hazel had been cold to him, for to his astonishment her growing terror of this place, her disapproval of his every action, had been accompanied by wild, sobbing desire which had shocked him mightily, not only because it was so unlike her, but because of its greedy and insatiable nature. Perhaps he should send her home from this jungle that deranged her so. But she had no memory of her night fevers and refused to discuss what she considered his false concern for her. Except to accuse him of consorting with killers and harlots, she had scarcely said a word to him since they came to Madre de Dios. She had become so dogmatic since leaving home, so frightened! Yet even back in North Dakota, it had been difficult to persuade her to learn a little Spanish, for wasn't Spanish a Catholic language? Had Hazel been reared far away from the Protestant heartland of the Great Plains, she would have made a redoubtable

Catholic or even Communist; it was the dogma that attracted her, the security of righteousness, for she felt no need to understand her faith.

Yours is the big girl, with black hair. How careless that had been, and yet how mortally insulting, not only to himself and to Hazel but to all women. What sort of man was this?

He had almost given up on Moon as a cold sinful killer, a man who thought and spoke, when he spoke at all, in short quiet starts of violence. And it was just after he had asked if attacking the Indians was going to pacify them, and Moon had said, *No, but killing them is*—and to think that, startled by such dreadful cynicism, he had almost laughed! He had to get hold of himself!—that Moon, blaspheming, seeking to corrupt, had nonetheless spoken to him with passion, and in warning. Why did moral judgment of this man seem beside the point; could it be that Moon was fatally damned, beyond redemption? He had never heard of such a thing.

You're a devil—a true devil! To try to corrupt—

If I can corrupt your faith, it smells already to high heaven, right? Moon had leaned forward, feeling drunkenly for his words. *You look frightened, Mr. Quarrier. But you warned us a while ago that we would go to hell, so I am warning you*—he laughed—*that you are there already. You're in the jungle now, up to your fat God-fearing ass, and in the jungle the game gets a little rougher.*

You're very drunk. Why, you're not even making sense!

Perhaps I'm not. But I see that you understand me.

When Moon had gone off to bed, he and Wolfie were left staring at each other across the wreckage of the evening.

"Moon? So how do I know about Moon—I mean, he's only my *friend* and I *still* don't know'm!" Wolfie waved Quarrier away. "Like, don't bug me, Reverend. You don't get to *know* guys like Moon, for Christ sake,

68

they don't stand still long enough. You either swing with'm or you don't, that's all."

But in a little while, more quietly, Wolfie began to talk again. "I don't know why I even *tolerate* this madman, you know it?" He shook his head. "There's this kind of very way-out cat—like you run inta him all over the world, and each time he looks different and each time he disappears, but always I know I'm goin to run inta him again, because the guy is on the road, he's always on the road, and he's got nine lives and nine names and nine faces. Only this one, this Moon, he's different. I run inta him in Israel, and since then we been to Cuba and all over. Like in some way which I am too stupid to figure it out, he's beautiful, see, and also he's mean as catshit. They don't come no meaner than Lewis Moon, and you never know when he's goin to be mean or when he's goin to be beautiful. He always cons you; sometimes I think—in *his* mind, understand? —there ain't no difference."

Wolfie glanced up. "I mean, you seen how quiet he is? Well, that quiet sonofabitch is also the angriest sonofabitch I ever knew. He'd give you his last dime one second and break your neck the next, and you'd never know why he done either one."

According to Wolfie, they had lost their American citizenship for fighting in the armies of foreign countries; their plane they had stolen in Cuba, and they had come with it to South America via Hispaniola, Barbados, the Windwards and Venezuela. Lacking visas, they stayed away from the big towns on the coast and worked the back country. In Cuba, Wolfie had taught Moon to fly; Wolfie was also a mechanic. They had banged down the continent to Tierra del Fuego, where they had made big money bombing out a rash of oil-well fires.

It was on the strength of this feat that Wolfie had painted on the fuselage *Wolfie & Moon, Inc.—Small Wars & Demolition.* In Paraguay they had operated two new bulldozers that no Paraguayan could run, and had torn up the landscape near Asunción more or less at will until the day when Wolfie was slapped in the face by a low branch of a huge tree; he had battered the giant to the ground, demolishing the new bulldozer in the process. He was freed from an ancient jail by Moon, who destroyed it with the remaining bulldozer —"I wake up and there he is, right next to me, yankin on the controls!"—but they were caught immediately. They were on the point of being shot, Wolfie was certain, when Moon handed over to the guards some river diamonds he had once picked up in Venezuela; they took off in their plane that night and crossed the border into Bolivia.

In Bolivia they had settled for a while, flying for the new revolutionary government, and then for the still newer revolutionaries who took over in Santa Cruz de la Sierra. With the defeat of the latter, their luck ran out; in haste they had flown to Riberalta in the Beni, where their last money had gone for a tank of gas. That same day they had crossed the border.

"Moon's been all over this lousy continent, you know, on *foot,* for Christ sake. Took him three years, and all he's got to show for it is malaria." Wolfie shook his head. "Like I says to him, Lewis, like what are you, some kind of a *mas*-o-chist or what? Like, there're *jag*-you-ars here! Not to mention all them *serpents,* Lewis, and tarantulas and crocs and vampires and poison arrows. Whatta you got, I says to him, some kind of a *hang*-up about this place? I says, Gimme Frisco or the Village any time, that's the Old Wolf's kind of jungle!"

Wolfie looked restless; he needed to talk and was prepared to talk too much. Quarrier noticed how careful the man was to establish his expertise in regard to Moon—a kind of possessiveness, a proprietary interest, as if Moon were some easily recognized and very valuable phenomenon that others might try to steal.

"Oh, I don't mean I ain't *heard* things," Wolfie confided. "Like, in Cuba, I ran inta some guy who knew a guy that said he done time with Moon, you know, in stir; if you wanna know what for, don't *ask*

70

me. And once I seen he had some kind of a union card, and it turns out he worked over in New York with them Mohawks or Mohicans or whatever the hell they are that work on the high girders in them new buildings. After that, he was in the merchant marine, and one year he jumped ship in Maracaibo. He got up in them rivers and got hold of a big haul of them river diamonds some way, and that was all the stake he needed. He bummed around this continent on foot —like one little knapsack. Even the handle of his razor is sawed-off; it fits inta a match box, for Christ sake!" Wolfie laughed. "He learned long ago to travel light, and he never give up the habit; he don't own nothin and he don't want to. Once I asked him what the hell he thought he was doin down here, and he told me he was huntin for wild Indians. He said there was horse Indians in Patagonia that fought with the goyims just like on the Plains, but they was all on reservations, and the Indians down there in Tierra del Fuego were all gone. The mountain Indians, he said, were nothin but tame diggers, and from what he heard about the jungle tribes they were nothins—little rats, like, sneakin around the swamps. Right about then, he got bad dysentery and malaria, so he grabbed a ship out of Callao, west for Hong Kong."

Wolfie got up and scratched himself all over with both hands. He was tottering, and placed one foot slightly ahead, to maintain balance. "Don't you go tellin him I told ya nothin, because I don't really *know* nothin; I only picked up a little here and there, from things he said." He blinked. "Where was I?" He frowned at Quarrier. "Oh yeah. So don't go gettin nosy."

Quarrier stood, but Wolfie waved him down again. "What *are* you?" he demanded. "Hyper*thy*roid?" He shook his head again, astounded at his own patience with the world. He whistled a little, his head nodding. Quarrier was listening for his snore when Wolfie said, "For all he says about himself he might as well have come from Mars, only I happen to know it's out West somewheres—he's part Indian. His father was half-breed Cheyenne Indian and French Canuck, his mother halfbreed Mississippi Choctaw, which prolly this makes him some nutty kind of a Negro. But it don't matter where he comes from; like I was sayin, a guy like that is always on the road, like he was condemned to it. I been around a lot—I mean, I ain't like him or nothin, I ain't no drifter—and I run inta other ones just like him. He don't belong nowhere, he's like a house cat somebody runs out on, you know, like turns out at the edge of some woods: he don't belong where he comes from and he don't belong where he is, so he keeps movin, and soon he's a wild animal that you don't never tame again."

"But you," Quarrier said. "You're going home."

"Yeah," Wolfie said tiredly. He slumped back against the wall. "I mean, I been just about everywhere, I seen enough of life. Some one of these fine days I'm goin home. I even got a wife and boy home, see."

"You do?"

"Well, kind of. Azusa's common-law. Azusa and Dick the Infint. We named the infint Dick."

"You mean Richard?"

"No. Dick. We named the infint Dick." Wolfie shrugged. "For some goddamn reason when I say that, Lewis always laughs."

"But tomorrow—today, I mean—you're going to go out and bomb those innocent—"

"Oh, man." Wolfie stood up. "You know? Like, cool it. According to what this Guzmán says these Neo-rooneys been massacrin for thirty years. That makes them bloodthirsty savages, don't it? And anyway, this Guzmán, he's got us by the balls." He stared appraisingly at Quarrier. "You ain't a bad guy, Reverend. You come to Frisco, Reverend, you look me up. In Sausalito or any of them North Beach expressos, they all know me. If they let me back in the good old U.S. and A., that is. You just ask for Wolfie." He stuck out his hand.

"All right," Quarrier said. "My name is Martin Quarrier."

"Pleased to meetcha," Wolfie said, "I'm sure."

Quarrier was at the airstrip the next morning when Wolfie & Moon, Inc., went to work. The airplane had already been gassed up, although as a precaution the Comandante still held their passports. Moon's whole face was swollen from Guzmán's blow, and his grin was painful. He nodded to Quarrier, but Wolfie, who looked terrible, had apparently forgotten their new friendship, and responded to Quarrier's "Good morning" by spitting noisily on the ground.

"You're going ahead with it then?" Quarrier said.

Moon said, "The bombardier here couldn't hit Bolivia today, much less a village."

"So how come you dragged me out here?" Wolfie said. "The way you fly even when you *ain't* got no hangover, I'm lucky to get back alive."

"The fresh air will do you good."

"Fresh air, my ass!" Wolfie was sweating violently in the dank heat. "There ain't a breath of fresh air in this whole miserable continent."

"Please don't do this," Quarrier said.

Without answering him they climbed into the plane. Moon waved enigmatically at Quarrier as the engine noise exploded. The plane jounced and wobbled to the end of the runway, where it roared a moment, shaking like a leaf; then it spun around and came back down the strip, bounding the ruts and depressions like some huge ancient bird seeking to get aloft. The wheels had scarcely left the ground when it curved away; by the time it cleared the trees, it was already headed eastward.

When the silence had settled down again and the loiterers had begun to drift away, one man remained.

"Ah," the priest said. "Good morning, Mr. Quarrier."

They did not attempt to cross the strip of ground between them.

"Good morning, Padre," Quarrier said, starting away.

"Have you thought over my question?"

"What? I mean, *what* question?"

"It's quite simple. I asked you, do you think *he* cares?"

"Do you mean Yoyo?"

"Why, but who else— Oh yes, oh yes, I see!" The padre actually clapped his hands. "Very good, Mr. Quarrier! Excellent! Bravo!"

Quarrier had started back toward the town and Xantes kept pace with him, remaining on the far side of the road. They went along slowly in the heat. Quarrier was amazed; this man was laughing at him! "I don't want to discuss this with you," he told him finally. "I don't understand why you talk to me at all."

"We have a common problem: the Niaruna."

"The Niaruna are no longer your concern."

The priest raised his eyebrows. "On the contrary," he said. And he stepped firmly in front of Quarrier, blocking his path. He told Quarrier how his colleague, Padre Fuentes, had been killed by the Niaruna on the very site on the Río Espíritu where Leslie Huben had since established his own outpost. "The Indians," Xantes remarked, "think it demeaning to harvest crops from a *chacra* cleared by other people, but apparently Señor Huben does not share this view." Before Quarrier could defend Huben, the priest had passed on to an account of the martyrdom.

There were two nuns with Fuentes, and all three were taken alive; the sisters were later returned in a barter deal arranged by Yoyo, in which two women of Huben's tame Niaruna band were delivered to the savages. By this time the sisters had been martyred so decisively and so often that both preferred to give up Indian work and return to their convent in Spain. "This convent is built," Padre Xantes said, with a sad smile, "in the manner of a citadel—impregnable."

According to Yoyo, the martyrdom of the Dominicans had commenced on the trail leading eastward from the mission. Had the Indians understood the true nature of poor Fuentes, his death might have been more prompt and even, perhaps, more merciful. But they imagined from his cassock that he was female. "They had not got far into the jungle when it came into their heads to rape my poor *compadre*. Imagine their chagrin! *Pues,* to make this *historia* a brief one, they became angry at the deception and beheaded him. We found the body eight days later."

The priest stared coldly at Quarrier, who stared as coldly back. It seemed to him that this curious man had actually taken relish in the telling.

"You will now see," Xantes remarked after a moment, "why I am presently at a disadvantage in regard to the Ñiaruna. I have written for a replacement for the good Fuentes, but the record of the Niaruna does not inspire many volunteers. You will also see why I consider the Niaruna my concern. Why, *all* the jungle peoples, and the mestizos too, and the *patrones* and even Guzmán, our magnificent Comandante—and yes, even yourself, even *yourself*, Señor Quarrier—are my concern. Good day!"

And the little Dominican, bowing, hurried on ahead of Quarrier on the bare path beneath the bare brown sky, his frail body struggling in his heavy cloth, his thin head bobbing.

Quarrier spent the morning in the dining room, at work on Huben's Niaruna dictionary. While he knew that it was important that he do this, he was extremely restless, and was constantly distracted from his work by the random complaints of fat Mercedes and by the thin fatalistic townspeople, pigs, children, vultures and indentured Indians who paused before the window. He was plagued by worry about Billy, about what might befall them in the months ahead, about the stranger who passed her days on the other bed—the stranger for whom, he kept reminding himself, he was responsible. But more often he thought about Andy Huben and the fact that at a time of terrible peril he was sinfully at-

At Play in the Fields of the Lord

tracted to her. At these times he would groan aloud, causing Mercedes to glare and snigger.

Twice that day Guzmán himself came by to check the hotel accounts. Each time, seeing Quarrier at the table in his salon, he winced and snarled and cleared his throat with violence as if, had it not been his own hotel, he would have liked nothing better than to spit copiously upon the floor.

Quarrier had placed his chair so that he could see the hallway and be sure to intercept Wolfie and Moon when they returned to the hotel. However, he soon fell asleep, doped by the sun and the drone of flies; he awoke sometime later at the roar of a plane and the sound of running feet.

In the street, people were standing in the mud, staring upriver. From out of the haze came the growl of a small airplane, invisible, and then the growl rose to a shriek as the plane plunged toward the earth. For a moment, over the edge of town, a bruise formed in the haze, and then the plane burst through at a dreadful angle, seeming to plunge into the trees upriver. But its roar continued, reverberating wildly in the forest; a few seconds later it rose once more, too steeply, into the overcast, its motor dying to a point no longer audible. Then, incredibly, it dove again. After this dive—the third, according to those in the street—it leveled off and headed for the airport; the people, wringing their small hands, ran out to meet it.

When the fliers appeared at the hotel, Quarrier set himself to question them. But Wolfie looked sick and exhausted, and though Moon's face was composed, his shirt front and throat were heavily caked with blood. Moon scarcely nodded at him. "Nice country," he remarked, and went upstairs.

Toward evening Quarrier cornered Wolfie, who was in evil humor. They had not yet attacked the Niaruna villages, Wolfie said, but he refused to say anything else. Moon was already under the effects of *ayahuasca*. "If you got any idea you want to talk to Moon, forget it. Like, don't *bother*. He drunk enough to turn

76

on a rhinoceros. I seen him flip on this Indian soup before, down in the Beni. It's like I told him after: Lewis —he don't like being called Lew, see, only Lewis, which this is some goddamn *family* name or other, so I call him Lewis, for Christ sake—Lewis, I told him after, like make it with *pot*, Lewis, or hash, man, or peyote, you can even *shoot* it if you wanna, jam the needle right inta your miserable *brain*, Lewis, only just lay off this jungle junk, this Hiawatha. I mean, who needs some kind of a *loo*-natic around, who needs it? And you know what he says to me? Lewis, I mean, this crazy Lewis says, *I* need it; it allows me to *see*. You're outa your fuckin mind, I told him."

To Quarrier, Wolfie's idiom was so outlandish that he might as well have listened to a savage; the waving hands, the cries and grunts made the problem very similar. Although he got the gist of the speech before it ended, he was wincing and frowning so violently in his concentration that Wolfie himself recoiled in alarm.

"Look out! Back up!" he cried. "What's the matter, you gonna puke or what?" He started away, then turned back, furious. "Jesus, here I'm tryna tell you somethin which this is for your own good, and what do you do—you gawk at me like it was *me* that was the lunatic, not you guys." He stomped into the bar, still shouting. "You're livin in Nutsville, Pancho, take it from me," he told the bar man, who crouched back in terror against the bottles; Wolfie, who claimed to be incapable of telling foreigners apart, had forgotten that he had tried to kill this boy the night before. "Another nut!" He smote his brow. "Another one!"

Quarrier looked up to see Hazel, drawn from her room by Wolfie's uproar, staring at him in horror from the stairwell. She looked like an old woman.

"You're laughing," she cried. "How can you laugh? Are you insane?"

7

They picked up the Río Espíritu at Remate, and followed it north and east. By airplane the distance was not great, for Moon did not follow the serpentine river but swung across the bends. They crossed several Tiro villages; some of the Indians scattered into the forest while others ran out into the yard between the huts to stare at the terrible bird. Then for a long time there were no signs of life, only the dark green of the canopy and the glisten of black water in the swamps and wormy creeks. Soon the Espíritu itself was no more than a creek, and now an unmapped river came into view, unwinding eastward; the headwaters of the rivers were no more than three miles apart, though they flowed in opposite directions. On the bank of the unnamed river, back a little distance from the bank, there appeared a deserted village.

Moon swung over it in a low glide. The village had not been abandoned but evacuated: a wisp of smoke and the Indian dog that scurried across the open yard confirmed this. One small incendiary, he thought, will take care of this whole outfit.

They circled back to the Espíritu and this time found the mission settlement: two large huts and a wooden cross. They must have passed right over it, and it was easy to see why they had missed it, for in the short time since Huben left, the jungle had reclaimed it. The huts were smudged by vines and leaves, their outlines blending with shadows, and the yard itself was a tumult of green strands and infestations. The wooden cross had been seized by a thick liana and was tilted crazily, about to topple. A damp miasmic heat seeped through the plane each time they neared the ground, and the ground steamed softly in the morning light, as if the earth were cooling still in some primordial gray morning.

The scene was so infernal that even Wolfie, startled from his doze by Moon's maneuvers, spoke in horror. "Whatta these Indians *got?*" He coughed, in pain. "Some kind of a emotional *involvement* with this place?" At a loss as to where to spit, he swallowed, wincing. "Oo," he said. "Like, I'm dyin, man." He reached behind him to unstrap the crate that held small incendiary and fragmentation bombs. "This ain't gonna be no bombin, man. This is what you might call *pest* control."

"Go back to sleep," Moon said. "There's nothing to bomb yet."

Wolfie settled back, clasping his hands on his gut as he closed his eyes; he blew a loud sigh through his lips. "There ain't, huh? Well, if I had bombs and time enough, I'd bomb this miserable jungle from end to end. I mean it. It gives me the creeps, I don't even like to look at it even." He sat up again and stared at it. *"Whee-oo!"* he said, and shook like a wet dog. "So why don't we unload a few of these highly dangerous explosives and cut back to Madre and grab the bread and split?"

Moon left the mission area and moved back up the river to the empty village and circled it at a distance; in comparison with the mission station, the yard was brown and bare and the thatch clean.

"All right, Lewis, maybe you don't wanna bomb no Indians, is that what you're sayin? Who needs it, you're askin me. What'd these noble redskins ever do to us, right? They're only just another minority group, right? So that's exactly what I'm tellin you—it don't matter where you drop the bombs, you can drop 'em in the river for all I care, or right on their lousy heads, that's beautiful too, but anyway, like it don't matter— let's just *drop* somethin in case this Guzmán got his nose inta this crate and counted, and then we waltz back to Madre havin done our duty fait'fully; and by tomorra night, man, we're outa the jungle, we come up for air . . ."

Getting no response, Wolfie sighed with disgust and subsided once again, eyes closed. Moon scarcely noticed him. He was intent on the still, silent clearing, the silent watchful waiting, as tangible as blood—he could feel it right through the noise and vibration of the plane. Unlike the Tiro, the fierce Niaruna were terrified. These inner rivers were narrow and winding, so that the pontoon planes used in the jungle could not land on them beyond Remate; the chances were that the savages hidden in the trees below had never seen a plane in all their lives. The rain forest of the Niaruna lay at the farthest eastern reaches of the country, and part of it was thought to cross the disputed frontier into the jungles of Amazonas. The only scheduled flight within five hundred miles was the plane that came twice each week to Madre de Dios and returned across the Andes.

He circled closer, banking low; he could scarcely hope to glimpse the Niaruna, and he was about to climb again when he saw what he had come down to this continent to see. A naked man appeared at the edge of the clearing, and stamping violently on the ground, raised a black bow. Moon did not see the arrow until it hung suspended for an instant at the top of its arc: a gleam of blue-and-yellow feathering, like a small bird, a turn of dull light on the cane shaft . . .

". . . like, one problem," Wolfie was saying, "was gettin her to be, you know, like *in*timate. Man, I tried everythin, even daisies. Finely I grabbed her hand and *put* it there—it didn't take. It got to be this kind of a joke: her sayin she would never touch me, I was too funky, man, I was not her type, Azusa said. Well, I was kind of, you know, like in*trigued*. So I got her to promise just one little thing: If you ever touch it, Zoose, I says, just even once, then we go all the way—right, baby?"

Until this moment the only Indians that Moon would acknowledge were the old men of his childhood who had survived the long wars with the whites on the Great Plains. Most were reduced to the white man's denims and were grateful for rolled cigarettes and sweet canned foods, but one of these old warriors, steadfastly scorning the government dole, had lived out his stubborn life in a small cave. This old man spoke often of Charles Bent, the halfbreed Cheyenne son of Trader Bent of Bent's Old Fort, down on the Arkansas, whose rage had only found relief in violence. Charles Bent, or so the legend said, had escaped the slaughter of Black Kettle's unsuspecting people at Sand Creek, and after that had tried to kill his own white father. With his young warriors of the Dog Society, Charles Bent had waged revenge so cruel and savage that the Cheyennes themselves, the Race of Sorrows, who had suffered more death and betrayal from the whites than any tribe on the Great Plains, had turned their backs on him. But a few Cheyennes still knew Bent's name, and Moon, peering into the bright mad old eyes of this ancient cave dweller, caught a brief flicker of that lunatic rage that closed the heart and snapped the teeth shut like a trap, and caused a man's whole head and frame to shudder.

This old man's son, named James Mad Raven, after years of apathy and sullen silence, had performed the outlawed Sun Dance all alone. Leaning back at the end of a lariat run through his breast skin with a harness awl, he circled a dead tree by the trading post, a whiskey bottle in his hand. Then the skin tore and he fainted. At the request of the missionaries, he was seized and jailed, and he died in jail of the shock and pneumonia brought on by his ritual wounds. Lewis Moon had watched the Sun Dance of James Mad Raven, had seen him lying stunned beneath the sky in greasy dungarees and sateen cowboy shirt with fake

81 *At Play in the Fields of the Lord*

pearl studs, and old black broken street shoes, without socks.

The old men had known something that their heirs would never know ever again. Because they were pleased by the boy's interest, they talked in front of him for hours on end about the last great councils of the Chis-Chis-Chash, as the Cheyennes called themselves, when Two Moons and Dull Knife had joined forces with Gall's Uncapappas and the Oglallah Lakota of Chief Crazy Horse against the troopers. Before the great victory at the Greasy Grass Creek, they had numbered fifteen hundred lodges, and the smoke of their fires had shrouded the blue sky of the high plains. That was the boy's regret: the loss of this vast triumphant sight, the thousands of campfires and ponies galloping and colors and buffalo meat and smoky smells and wolf howls and wild yelling.

There were wild tribes in Paraguay and in Bolivia and on the rivers south of the Guianas, but he had never reached them. And once there had been wild horse Indians—the Araucanians and Tehuelches—in Patagonia, but he had arrived there a half-century too late; as in the case of the Plains tribes, the few thousand remnants had been penned up on reservations. He had wandered down to Tierra del Fuego and stared into the face of the last Yahgan left on earth.

The bright shimmer of the arrow, the lone naked figure howling at the sky—it had been years since he had grinned like that, with all his lungs and heart; he actually yipped in sheer delight. Now he had sensed something unnamable and always known, something glimpsed, hinted at, withheld by sun and wind, by the enormous sky . . .

"What are you, *air*sick? You got this awful look on your face, you're makin noises!" Wolfie shrugged, and clasped his hands behind his head. "Anyway, Old Azusa knew that I meant business, see, like she grown *wary*. And I was gonna give up hope on her, and was kickin myself for gettin hung-up on a chick that was sexually disturbed, when one night we was sittin in this art film, eatin popcorn outa the same box, and she says, Did you find the prize yet? This popcorn got these little prizes, see. Well, like *in*stantly I get this beautiful idea from this joke that I heard once, but beautiful, the answer to a maiden's prayer. As usual I had, you know, this erection, so quick as a mink I work a hole through the bottom of the box, with my fingers, I mean, and in*sert* it, you know, all sweet and innocent, nestlin right up amongst these *pop*corns, dig? Then I whispers, No, Zoose, dear, I didn't find it yet, I'll race you. Well, Old Azusa digs right in—she's still watchin this *art* film, see—and *whammo!* What the hell kind of corn d'you call *this?* she yells. It's *livin!* That's the prize, I says to her, that them popcorn people laid on you, like maybe it's some nutty kind of a *pet.* Well, you know, man, that crazy chick—once she got *hold* of it she never let go for a week, and it was exactly nine months after this art film that we gave birt' to this *in*fint which we named it Dick . . ."

The lone man was still leaping in the clearing. Three more Indians ran forward as Moon banked around, but they did not raise their bows. Crossing again, he saw them struggling with the bowman, trying to drag him back into the forest. They succeeded, for a moment later the clearing was as empty as before. On the next pass he went into a dive, so low that he had to yank back on the stick to clear the trees again. This time, glancing back as he banked away, he saw the Indians, a band of thirty or more, appear at the edge of the clearing, running and gesticulating at one another; several men tossed their bows to the ground. When he passed again, they fell to their knees, staring straight up at him, and clasped their hands upon their breasts. He came in lower to make certain, the shadow of the plane like a black hammer on the clearing; when the shadow crossed them, they broke and scattered off into the forest.

Wolfie, who had reared up when the plane dived,

missed what Moon had seen; he had heaved joyfully around and wrestled a bomb out of its nest, and by the time he turned back again and set to work removing the panel on his side window, he saw only the Niaruna's final flight.

"Now you're swingin, man," he said. "Anyway, they ain't nothin but a bunch of Jews." Taking Moon's silence for surprise, he laughed. "What are you, ignorant? This is the Lost Tribe of Israel, man, ain't you heard that?" He hooted gleefully. "And now is *their* turn to get persecuted, just in case they forgot how it was back there in Tel Aviv."

Moon laughed. "Put that stuff back," he said.

"Don't put me on now, Lewis." Still struggling with the window, Wolfie gazed at him suspiciously. "Bombs away, man, if I can get this mother open long enough—some *bombin* plane, that's all I gotta say. Why in Christ did we steal *this* for?" He paused a minute, wheezing. "Where you goin? Come on, man!"

Moon said, "I didn't see you getting set, or I would have told you we didn't need it." He had swung wide of the village, and was headed back downriver.

"Didn't *see* me? Like, man, I am seated *next* to you, man, in the adjoinin seat. What are you, farsighted?" Wolfie returned the bombs to their crate; he was grunting angrily. "You woulda thought you woulda *smelt* me, at least, with this lousy jungle sweat I'm workin up. Every time I raise my arm, I knock myself out practically. This Christly jungle!" He swore and muttered for a while, but by the time he turned around again to stare balefully out across the jungle, his voice had lowered and turned cold.

"Look," he said, "you better answer me. I'm sick of clownin, Lewis, you're gonna push me too far. I ain't noticed you hesitated to get blood on your hands when the price was right, so come on, explaina me, what is it? You dig Indians but not spades, is that right? And them Cubans, which is half-spic and half-spade and half-Indian too, from what I hear—you don't mind bombin *them*." He heaved around. "But Indians, never. Them little brown nudes down there that are prolly cannibals and I don't know what else, no dice, not them!"

Wolfie was panting. When Moon remained silent, he looked confused. "Jesus! So just don't push me too far," he said. "Oh yeah, where was I? So I want you to explain to me."

"It sounds like you're explaining something to *me*," Moon said.

Wolfie nodded. "You're kind of a smart-ass sometimes, you know that, Lewis? I was just rememberin last night, the way you told me I was kind of stupid sometimes. You don't even think you hafta bother explainin nothin, because Old Wolfie is stupid and ignorant, right? A kind of a clown you keep around for kicks. You think all you gotta do is say, So Wolf, forget it. Well, a lot of people would say that Lewis Moon is a cold-hearted communistical murderin sonofabitch, you know that, don't you? A bum. That you never been off the road in your life and wouldn't know how to make a honest buck, so you kill for money. A lot of people would say that, Lewis."

"A lot of people would," Moon agreed.

"God, you're just so sweet and cool, now ain't you? Christ!" Wolfie drove his fist so hard against the side of the plane that the fuselage quaked. "I had enough of this! How in hell did I get tied up with a cat like you in the first place, that's what I wanna know. Well, listen, let me tell you somethin, college boy, who was it taught you to fly? You ain't so smart as you think, when you got to learn your livin from *me*. And another thing, before I hooked up with you I wasn't nobody's sidekick, everybody else was *my* sidekick, it was Wolfie-and-his-friends wherever I went, and what I wanna know is, what did you do for a patsy before I come along? You have some kind of a congenital idiot, or what?"

"Let's see now. There was Kublai Cahn, he got

shot down in the Negev. Or was that you? With those rabbi beards," Moon said softly, and smiled at Wolfie, "it's hard to tell you Jews apart."

Wolfie's knife was out so fast that Moon raised his eyebrows, impressed. He shifted his head minutely, for the tip of the blade was against his throat, under his chin; it had broken the skin, and he felt a warm trickle slide down to his collar.

"I had enough, Moon, like I told you." Wolfie's voice was thick and quiet. "When you get to Madre, you better put down nice and easy."

Staring straight ahead, Moon considered his situation. He had about eighteen minutes before he would drop in for a landing, and that was probably not sufficient time for Wolfie to cool off. Very gradually he eased off course.

"Straighten out. South-southwest 183 degrees."

So . . . Moon shrugged and grinned, and the grin spread quickly across his face; he knew he must not laugh, but he could not help himself. Already his body shook, and then his mouth fell open with the laugh and the knife cut him again.

"Don't laugh," Wolfie said. "Because I ain't laughin and I ain't kiddin."

Then the pain overtook Moon and he stopped. The whole front of his shirt was damp with blood.

Wolfie said coldly, "You're a fuckin maniac, you know that?"

Moon held his head as still as possible. In the near distance he could see Madre de Dios, the smoke of the lumber mill and the hot glaze on the tin roofs.

After a while he said, "So you're going to stick me."

"When we get in. I don't want you bleedin all over my aircraft." He forced Moon's head back slowly on the knife tip. "There ain't much I'd put past you, but Jew-baitin! It's okay for a Jew to be a anti-Semite, but not no goyim bastard like you."

Moon glanced at him quickly; he caught the faint

humorous flicker before Wolfie could suppress it. "Not that that's the only reason," Wolfie snarled.

"Did you see that guy shoot an arrow at the plane?" Moon considered knocking Wolfie's arm away and throwing the plane into a roll. But though he had little to lose by this maneuver, he had nothing at all to gain; Wolfie would kill him with the first reflex. Then he heard Wolfie's voice again, and from its tone he knew that he had won.

"That's a reason *not* to bomb? Are you outa your mind, Moon? You really mean you'd cop out on our only chance because some lunatic of a Indian is nutty enough to shoot an *arrow* at us?"

And though this was exactly what Moon did mean, he now turned his head and gazed coldly at his partner. He was sorry that he had pleaded, however obliquely, and now that he had gained an edge, the knife point at his chin infuriated him.

"Don't try to understand anything," he said. "Just put that knife back and shut up." And he thought with a wild icy glee, Now you've done it. Now you've done it.

Wolfie forced his head back once again, drawing new blood. "C'mon, set the plane down. This can't wait."

"Suppose I don't."

"I'll give it to you here. I can fly this thing too, remember?"

Moon jammed the stick forward and tipped the plane into a dive. Before they gained speed he yelled, "If we still have wings when I pull her out, you drop that knife out the side window, okay, kid?" And gritting his teeth against the pressure in his chest he sent the plane howling down at the green chaos, the treetops spinning and the brown river leaping upward and out to the side—an orange slough, white birds like giant flowers, green—hauling back again, eyes shut, and the pain of terror like hot wire in his chest—he had cut it too close—then a rush of leaves, the nose of the plane against the sky: Wolfie's livid face intent on him, teeth bared, Wolfie bracing himself with his feet, keeping the knife neatly in place with his left hand while with his right he hauled instinctively at his own wheel; in a moment he would try to kill Moon and take over the dual controls. But on the rise, the plane snapping and shuddering like a kite, Moon rolled it violently to the right, knocking Wolfie back, and plunged again, at the river this time, pulling out of the dive a few yards above the water, to roar along beneath high branches, so that for a moment of horror it seemed as if they had entered a tunnel of swarming green; then he broke for the sky again, climbing steadily at an angle so steep that Wolfie, seeing that a stall was imminent, did not make his move.

Wolfie tried to shout, and when he found he could not speak, removed the knife from his companion's throat and tapped a small metal plate on the controls, the manufacturer's plate that read, THIS AIRCRAFT NOT CERTIFIED FOR ACROBATICS. Then the colors of oblivion whirled about their heads, and when they came out again Wolfie did not raise the knife. He was shaking his head sadly; the rage that had filled the tiny cabin shrank to an injured muttering. He had trouble clearing his throat. "You wanna commit suicide is fine by me, only just swing past Madre first, and let the Old Wolf bail out." He reached back and stroked the parachute behind the crate. "I ain't like you. I ain't mad at life, Moon. I ain't got no lousy death wish." As he spoke he toyed with the side window, but his hand shook so that he was helpless. He did not seem to notice that Moon had leveled off and was flying normally. "This knife always brought me luck," he said. "I had it made up special one time, down in Mexico."

"Keep it," Moon said. His heart was pounding so that he felt sick, and his legs, like two plastic tubes of water, were all but useless on the pedals.

On the airstrip at Madre de Dios they sat stunned in the plane for several minutes, unable to move. The people gathered around the plane at a little distance, the barefoot men, the barefoot women, the dogs and children, all of them remorseless in their curiosity. "Do not feed the lunatics," Wolfie said. Although neither of them thought this very funny, they began to laugh loudly and violently, until the tears poured down their cheeks. Not yet able to face each other, they sat there shoulder to shoulder in the stifling heat of the small cabin. The bystanders withdrew a little, and they laughed a little harder; then, as suddenly as they had begun, they stopped laughing and crawled out of the plane. In silence they refilled the empty tanks by siphoning gas from the drums on the rickety platform, then locked the cabin, and in the haze of the dead sun, staggered off toward the town. The people, who had sighed and poked one another at the sight of Moon's bloody throat, fell into line behind them.

Moon searched for a way to make amends. Because he was still angry about the knife, he started by saying sourly, "So you think I'm an anti-Semite, huh?"

"Nah, not really," Wolfie said. "You're anti-everything. But I'm an anti-goy, confirmed, for life. Everybody knocks the Jews, but it's hard to find a Jewish lunatic."

Moon grinned, but Wolfie's own smile was dispirited. He walked stiffly, in a kind of shock, and his face was sad. For the first time that Moon could remember, his partner did not feel like talking, and as his own head began to clear, he realized that Wolfie's terror in the plane had been fed less by fear of death than by bewilderment at Moon's contempt for both their lives, by the threat of a totally meaningless end. When Wolfie had recovered from his shock, from his fatigue and hangover as well as from the experience of the morning, he would deeply resent what had been done to him and especially the careless way in which Moon had told him that he could keep his knife. Eventually he would doubt that he had ever seriously intended to kill Moon, and that Moon had known this all along and had humiliated him anyway. Then he would question his own courage and find some excuse to prove it, and the only proof would be the death of Moon.

Even this one, Moon concluded, glancing at the violent man beside him. Even this one must be handled like a baby.

His mind strayed back to the strange sights of the morning; he wanted to think about what he had seen and why it had so excited and unsettled him. To Quarrier, who stared at his bloody shirt from the salon doorway, he refused conversation, saying enigmatically, "Nice country," and continuing upstairs.

Wolfie lay down on his bed without taking off his boots and fell asleep, a surprised expression on his face, mouth slightly open, and the handle of his knife protruding like an iron nose between the buttons of his twisted shirt. Moon sank down slowly on the edge of the other bed and contemplated the round face and the roistering beard, the inseparable earring and dark glasses and beret like grotesque toys, the knife made specially down there in Mexico. In all the time that he had known this man he had never seen that knife before when it was not in use, and the fact that Wolfie had gone to sleep without sliding its sheath beneath his arm was the bleakest evidence of his defeat and new dependence.

He reached across and removed Wolfie's beret. Wolfie's hand flicked toward the knife, stopped, settled back upon his stomach. He sighed like a sleeping child. Moon nodded in regret. From now on, in some way, he was responsible for this human being; the partnership was over. And though he knew that this new relationship could have come about at any time in their common past, he was sorry that it had happened. Since he himself would refuse responsibility for this man—for any man—he and Wolfie had better part company, and the sooner the better. He made the decision without turmoil; he had made it before with other men and with twenty years of women. But the decision did not spare him sadness. A fine old kind of friendship had been killed, and a fine old freedom.

How often in life, it seemed to him, he had come to this place before.

He lay back on his bed and closed his eyes. He would go again to where men shot arrows at airplanes, but how, or even why, he did not know.

8

A dog turned in its circle and lay down in the shade, and a vulture swung up and down in a short arc above the jungle, as if suspended from a string. In the heat of the siesta, the street below was hollow as a bone.

He took the cork out of the bottle, and holding his breath to kill the bitterness, drank off half the brown fluid in a series of short gulps, gargling harshly when he was finished and spitting the residue into the street. The aftertaste made him gag. He sat down on the window sill and in a little while the nausea receded, leaving only a thick woody taste and a slight vagueness.

A half-hour passed. Maybe the Indian had watered the infusion. A voice in the salon below sounded remote to him, and he nodded; he was on his way. A little more *ayahuasca*, Mr. Moon? He took up the bottle and drank off another quarter of it, then set it down very slowly. You've made a bad mistake, he thought; already he knew he did not need it. The effects were coming very suddenly, and he stood up and stalked the room. *In overdose,* he had read somewhere, *the extract of* Banisteriopsis caapi *is quite poisonous and may bring on convulsions, shock and even death*.

How silent it was—the whole world was in siesta. He glanced quickly out the window, to take time by surprise; the dog slept soundly, and the vulture still swung up and down its bit of sky, dark as a pendulum. From the far end of the street, a solitary figure was moving toward him, down the center of the street—the last man on earth. There you are, he thought, I have been waiting for you all my life.

Now he was seized with vertigo and apprehension; his heart began to pound and his breath was short. He went to his bed and lay down on his back. He felt a closure of the throat and a tension in his chest, a metal bar from chin to navel to which the skin of his chest was sewn. Breathing became still more difficult, and a slight pain in the back of his head became a general, diffused headache. He turned cold and his teeth chattered; the hands pressed to his face were limp and clammy.

I am flying all apart, he thought; at the same time his chest constricted ever more tightly. *Let go,* he told himself aloud. *Let go.*

He rolled over on his side and blinked at the other bed. The man on the bed retreated from his vision, shrinking and shrinking until he was no bigger than a fetus.

Color: the room billowed with it; the room breathed. When he closed his eyes, the color dazzled him; he soared. But there was trouble in his lungs again, and his heart thumped so, in heavy spasmodic leaps, that it must surely stall and die. He broke into a sweat, and his hands turned cold as small bags of wet sand . . .

He sat up, aching, in a foreign room. He could breathe again, although his heart still hurled itself unmercifully against his chest: how thin a man's poor chest was, after all; it was as thin as paper, surrounding a hollow oval space of wind and bitterness. *Thump, thump-ump, um-thump;* it would crash through at any minute, and what then? Do I greet it? Introduce myself? How long can a man sit holding his heart in his hands?

Or was that thump coming from elsewhere? The thump of a bed—were the missionaries making love? The male missionary making love to the female missionary? The Courtship of Missionaries: the male missionary, larger and more splendidly plumaged than his shy dowdy mate, hurls his head back joyfully and sings "Praise the Lord," upon which he rushes forth, tail feathers spread, and mounting in a decorous and even pious manner, inserts his tongue into her right ear . . .

You are the Lost Tribe of Israel, and therefore you must pray especially hard, for the Lost Tribe of Israel is under God's everlasting curse. Do you understand? Why don't you answer me? What is the matter with you children—do you wish to remain accursed? Now you answer me, Lewis Moon, or I'm going to beat you. Lewis? Lewis!

Now his body cavity felt hollowed out as if cold sterile winds were blowing through it . . . loss, loss, loss. *Loss.*

Look into the sky and think of nothing, said Alvin Moon "Joe Redcloud," *but do not look into the sun, for the sun will blind you. Face east on the first day, south on the second, west on the third, north on the fourth, until you are at the center of the circle, and then you will know the power of the world.*

After the first day his stomach hurt and he felt foolish, all alone on a rock lookout above a river bend of box elder and cottonwood; all that night he shivered. He was not like the old men, nor even like his father; he spoke American and raised the American flag at school; he wore blue jeans and looked at magazines in stores and stood around outside the movie in the town, searching his pockets as if he had real money; and he did not believe in visions. Like all the children, he killed his hunger at the mission house on Sunday and afterward felt ashamed. Once he went hungry, telling the missionary that Cheyennes never ate on Sundays.

He remained on the rock a second day and a second night, just out of stubbornness, and because he was proud of the rifle that Alvin Moon had laid beside him. No bear nor cougar came—the animals would not bother him, his father said, if he sat still—and on the third morning he did not feel hungry any more and sat there motionless, letting the sun and wind blow through him. He was as firmly rooted in the ground as the young pine. By afternoon he was growing weak and became filled with apprehension: something was happening. The jays and squirrels had lost all fear of him, flicking over and about him as if he had turned to stone, and the shrill of insects crystallized in a huge ringing silence. The sky was ringing, and the pine trees on the rocks turned a bright rigid green, each needle shimmering; the pines were ringing and beside him a blue lupine opened, breathing. Then the river turned to silver and stopped flowing. The jays trembled on the rock, their eyes too bright, and the squirrel was still, the gold hairs flowing on its tail. He stared at the enormous sky, and the sky descended and the earth was rising from below, and he was soaring toward the center—

Then, in the ringing, far away, rose a flat droning. The airplane unraveled the high silence as it crossed the sky; it disappeared without ever appearing, and when it had gone, the sky no longer rang. He sat a long time on his rock, but the sky had risen, leaving him desolate.

Light-headed, he went down to the river, where he drank. He found mushrooms and fresh-water mussels, and some berries, and when he had eaten he laughed at his three-day vigil, pretending that he did not feel a dreadful sorrow.

On the fourth day, waiting for Alvin Moon to come, he hunted. He killed a wild goose on the river, and boasted of it to his father.

His father gazed at him. *And where is the goose,* his father said.

I could not reach it, the boy said. *It came so close, and then it drifted far away.*

He reeled from the bed and drifted to the window, but the figure coming down the street was gone; again he had missed some unknown chance. The street was

95   *At Play in the Fields of the Lord*

void, a void, avoid. Dog, heat, a vulture, nothing more. A dog, a vulture, nothing more, and thus we parted, sang Lenore.

Singing. Somewhere, somewhere there was singing. His whole body shimmered with the chords, the fountainhead of music, overflowing. The chords were multicolored, vaulting like rockets across his consciousness; he could break off pieces of the music, like pieces of meringue.

You're sleeping your life away, he told the dog. Do you hear me? I said, Do you hear me?

Meri-*wether*, Sheriff Guzmán said. *That's some name for a red nigger, ain't it? You're the smart one, ain't you kid? Ain't you supposed to be the smart Cheyenne? Done good in the war, and now they gone to send they little pet Christ-lovin Cheyenne to college, ain't that right, kid? Well, kid, if you're a real smart Injun, you won't even go and look at me that way, you'll keep your Injun nose clean, kid.*

Oh, to be an Indian! (Now that spring is here.) Big Irma: *Be a good boy, Lewis. Do not fight so much. You come back and see us now.* Alas, too late—the world is dead, you sleepyhead. The Inn of the Dog and the Vulture. There are voices, you see, then singing voices, then strange musics, hollowed out, as if drifted through a wind tunnel, these followed by a huge void of bleak silence suggesting DEATH

THE STORY OF MY LIFE, by Lewis Moon.

Now . . . something has happened, was happening, is happening. BUT WILL NOT HAPPEN. Do you hear me? I said, DO YOU HEAR ME?

A softer tone, please.

To begin at the beginning: my name is Meriwether Lewis Moon. Or is that the end? Again: I was named Meriwether Lewis Moon, after Meriwether Lewis, who with Lieutenant William Clark crossed North America without killing a single Indian. So said my father; my father is Alvin Moon "Joe Redcloud," who lived up on North Mountain. Alvin Moon still traps and hunts, and in World War I, when still a despised non-citizen, exempt from service, joined those 16,999 other Indians as insane as himself who volunteered to serve in World War I. Alvin Moon is half-Cheyenne; he went down South when he came home and took up with a Creole Choctaw woman named Big Irma and brought her back up to his mountain. The worst mistake that Alvin Moon ever made was trying to educate himself; his information about Lewis and Clark was the only piece of education he ever obtained, and it was wrong. He used to joke that he couldn't educate himself unless he learned to read, and how could he learn to read if he didn't educate himself? So he left off hunting and trapping and came down off his mountain and took work near the reservation to keep his children in the mission school, to give them a better chance in life.

I ain't got nothin, said Joe Redcloud, and I don't know nothin, not a thing. And the hell of it is, I broke my back, paid out every cent, to keep them kids into that school, and now they don't know nothin, neither, only Jesus Christ. Now ain't that somethin? They sit around here thinkin about Godamighty, I reckon, while they're waitin on their gover'ment reliefs.

All but Meriwether Lewis.

Again: my name is Lewis Moon, and I am lying on a bed (deathbed?) in a strange country, and I hear eerie voices and a crack is appearing on the wall, wider and wider, and the bulb in the ceiling is growing more and more bulbous, and will surely explode—a crack (of doom?) of lightning down the walls.

The extract of B. caapi is a powerful narcotic and hallucinogen containing phenol alkaloids related to those found in lysergic acid, and whether or not it finds a respectable place in the pharmaceutica of man, it has held for unknown centuries an important place in the culture of Indian tribes of the Amazon basin. At the time of my experiment I was lying in a narrow room with a corpse in the next bed, with God, a vulture and a dog as witnesses, wishing that Marguerite were here. Marguerite. I wish to tell Marguerite that the reason I

At Play in the Fields of the Lord

did not make love to her that time in Hong Kong was not because I did not want her but because I had reason to believe that in the late, low hours of the week before, I had contracted a low infestation. I did not know Marguerite well enough to give her crabs—you understand? Marguerite had alabaster skin, triumphant hair, and an unmuddied soul, and a swinging little ass into the bargain.

You listen to me, Meriwether Lewis: what the hell you sass that Sheriff for? He mighta kilt you. You stay clear of whiskey, then; long as you can't stay out of trouble, you ain't welcome back. And don't you show your Mam that bad face, neither; I whupped you plenty times before, and I'll whup you again, hero or no hero. Alvin Moon "Joe Redcloud" said, *You're all your people here got left to count on. You go get that education, hear me now? And then you come on home and learn it back to us as best you can. Because the way things are goin they ain't no hope for none of us, lessen we don't get somethin learned here to us pretty quick.*

I have opened my eyes again, to shut off all that blue. Color can threaten, overwhelm, whirling like that —an ant in a kaleidoscope might sense the problem. But out here the bed shudders, the chair sneaks, the bureau budges; they back and fill, about to charge. From above the bulb socket descends like a falling spider, leaving the bulb behind.

B. caapi, *which is named for the* caapi *of certain Brazilian Indians, is also the* camorampi *of the Campa, the* natema *of the Jivaro, the* ayahuasca *or* haya-huasca *of the Quechua-speaking peoples, the* yage *of Ecuador, the* soga de muerte *of most Spanish South Americans, names variously translated as "Vine of the Devil," "Vine of the Soul," "Vine of Death": the Spanish term means literally "vine rope of death," the* soga *referring to the jungle lianas used commonly as canoe lines, lashings, ropes, etc. In addition to certain medical properties, the vine can induce visions, telepathic states, metaphysical contemplation and transmigration; these*

conditions are used by the Indians for the reception of
warnings, prophecies and good counsel. Among many
tribes one purpose of the dream state is identification
of an unknown enemy, and the use of it is thus related
to the Jivaro practice of taking tsantsas, *or shrunken*
heads . . .

I am cut off, I feel both silly and depressed; it is
the solitude, not solitude but isolation . . . Death is the
final isolation, but from what, from what?

I am trying to reach out to you, but I do not know
who you are, I cannot see you. I only feel your presence
in this room. Perhaps . . . I wonder . . . are you inside
me? And if so . . . Now listen carefully: There is a
lost reality, a reality lost long ago. Are you in touch
with it: can you tell me—did you see?—the man with
the blue arrow—

Or . . . or are you the figure in the center of the
street? So you came here, after all! Can you hear
me? I said, CAN YOU HEAR ME? CAN—YOU—
HEAR—ME!

I cannot reach him through the sound and silence,
distant sound and deepest silence, like a thick glass
barrier between the world of the living and myself, as if
I were wandering on an earth which had suddenly died,
or in a Purgatory, myself already dead.

There is something that you have to understand.

Now look what's happening—can you see? It's
Him, the Dead Man. Resurrection. Rising out of bed.
Not suspecting that I am already dead, he will attempt
to kill me.

He speaks: *StopshoutinforChristsake!*

Here he comes, intent on the kill. He has broken
the glass wall. He drags me across the room. He has a
costume, he is all dressed up like a soldier of fortune,
he is very hip; but see the rosy cheeks behind that
beard? An enormous child!

"You are an Enormous Child!"

Nevermindmejustlookinthemirra! *Whatareyou-*
somekindofaaddictorwhat? Gowanlookatyaself!

See that pale face in the glass! The face is rigid,

and the eyes are dark and huge. Over the left eye drifts a dark shadow, like a hand. There you are, I see you now, and the bearded man, your warder.

He knew his lucidity could not last, and because he had taken too much, he dreaded going under again, and he started to ask Wolfie for help. "Hey," he said. But he could not ask, he had never asked in all his life, and even if he asked, what could poor Wolfie do? There were no sedatives in Madre de Dios; sedation was superfluous in a graveyard. He pushed away and tottered toward the window, where he fell across the sill. The dog and the vulture were gone. The light was tightening in the way it always did before the sudden jungle night, and down the center of the street a solitary figure walked away.

The bottle stood upon the sill; he drank it to the bottom.

He felt like crying, but did not. He had not cried in twenty years—no, more. Had he ever cried? And yet he did not really feel like crying; he felt like laughing, but did not. Stalking Joe Redcloud's shack as twilight came, he waited to be called back, beaten, and forgiven, but with the clear prairie darkness came the knowledge that the call would never come, that the days of tears and comfort had come and gone before he had realized they would ever end. Dry-eyed, enraged, he crouched in the sagebrush for a little while, and then moved off like a lean yearling grizzly driven snarling from the cave, feeling very bad and very good at the same time, and spoiling for a fight.

He crouched beside the window sill, his back to the world without, and far away he heard them coming, the marching of huge nameless armies coming toward him, and once again his hands turned cold. He felt very cold. On the wall of the room, over the door, he saw a huge moth with a large white spot on each wing. It palpitated gently; he could hear the palpitations, and the spots were growing. And there was a voice, a hollow voice, very loud, and very far away, calling through glass, and there were hands on him and he was shaken violently. The voice rose and crashed in waves, rolling around his ears; it was getting dark.

NowlistenI'mgonnatellGuzmánweflytomorrowaw- right? AwrightLewis? I saidAWRIGHTLEWIS?

He looked at the man and the man's head, fringed with hair; the head shrank before his eyes and became a *tsantsa*. He could not look, and turned away. A figure crossed his line of vision, moving toward the door. The door opened and light came in. The voice said *Thisis- nowheremanI'vehadenough.*

Don't go . . . I need . . . Don't go. I need . . . But he could not hear his own voice, and he could not have said just what he needed. From over the man's head the large white eyes of the moth observed him; they pinned him, like incoming beams. The music crashed, the wave . . . The door was dark again. He pushed himself to his feet and stared out of the window. The dark was rolling from the forest all around, and the sky was so wild as the sun set that it hurt his eyes. He reeled and fell, then thrashed to his feet and fell again, across the bed, and was sucked down into the darkness as the music burst the walls and overwhelmed him.

His body diffused and drifted through cathedral vaults of color, whirling and shimmering and bursting forth, drifting high among the arches, down the clere- stories, shadowed by explosions of stained glass. In the dark chapels of the church was a stair to windy dun- geons, to colors rich and somber now, and shapes emerging; the shapes flowered, rose in threat and fell away again. Fiends, demons, dancing spiders with fine webs of silver chain. A maniac snarled and slavered, and rain of blood beat down upon his face. Teeth, teeth grinding in taut rage, teeth tearing lean sinew from gnarled bone. Idiocy danced hand in hand with lunacy and hate, rage and revenge; the dungeon clanked and quaked with ominous sounds, and he kept on go- ing, down into the darkness.

Snow, dawn, black aspens. The creature rose at the boy's coming and somersaulted backward, whining and snarling, the trap clatter muffled in white silences; whiteness; the blood pools colored black, the tight-sewn cold.

A great head, and yellow eyes too big for Coyote —the last wolf in the mountains, the first and only wolf the boy had ever seen. He had no rifle. The old wolf leaped, to drive him back, and fell forward on its muzzle, which rose white-tipped from the snow; its tongue fell out. The icy steel worked tighter on its fore-leg, and the pain confused it, for it looked aside and wagged its tail a little, shivering. Then, just once, it howled a real wolf howl, pure as the black air of the mountain forest. Then it lay down. It had been gnaw-ing on its foreleg, just above where the trap had snapped, and now it began again, whining and snarling at its own agony, at the stubbornness of its own bone which held it earthbound. The mad yellow eyes watched him, the taut muzzle, the purplish curled gum, red teeth, the jaw; the scrape of teeth on living bone made him cry out. The ears flicked forward, but the gnawing did not stop.

When he came close, it sprang sideways; another such spring might free it. He drew back, frightened of the mad wild yellow eyes.

The sun rose to low banks of winter clouds; the day grew cold. He cut a sapling and carved a spear point, long and white; confronting the wolf, he drove the raw white wood into its chest as it came up at him and fought to pin it to the ground and grind the pain out of it. But still it fought to live, dull heavy thumps in the white flying powder; a blood fleck seared his lip—the wolf was snapping at the place where the stake pierced it. Shaken free, he had fallen within reach of it, but the stunned creature only raised its bleeding teeth from its own wounds and stared at him and past him, blinked once at the dying winter world, in daze, and lay its head upon its forepaws, panting.

He opened his eyes, gasping for breath; he drifted

downward. Once the abyss opened out into air and sunlight, but there were papier-mâché angels, and again he broke off chords of music from the air like bits of cake: the Paradise was false and he went on. A spider appeared, reared high over his head, then seized, shredded and consumed him. Voided, he lay inert in a great trough, with molten metal rising all about him in a blinding light. SO THIS WAS BRIMSTONE. The missionary's pasty face peered down at him over the rim: *This is a proud day for the mission, Lewis, and a proud day for your people. We all count on you.*

Eyes. Eyes. He struggled to free himself, but the stake held in his heart, the hole in his heart; even breathing hurt him, even breathing. He clawed at his own chest to ease it. If only he could get that pain out, then his heart would bleed his life away, but gently.

A road of trapped insects, flies and bees, and he among them: mad drone and bugging and brush of hairy, viscous legs scraping toward remote slits of air and light, of acrid insect smell, of flat inconscient insect eyes, unblinking, bright as jewels, too mindless to know fear, oh Christ, how mindless. Humans . . . A human mob, pounding its way into the bar, in search of—what? It did not know. It had no idea what it was hunting, but was hunting out of instinct, with myriad flat insect eyes, trampling everything underfoot; he shook with fear. Like a rat he was, a famine rat of broken cities, a quaking gut-shrunk rat, scurrying through the wainscoting of falling houses. His skeleton flew apart, reassembled in rat's skeleton; his spine arched, the tiny forefeet and long furtive hand, the loose-skinned gassy belly; he poised, alert, hunched on his knees upon the bed, hands dangling at his navel, long nose twitching. In the mirror across the room he saw the hair sprout on his face and the face protrude.

He found his way across the room and stared so closely into the glass that his nose touched it; he watched the face wrinkle and turn old; he saw his own raw skull again and groaned. Then another mask,

At Play in the Fields of the Lord

a new expression, hard and sly and cold. As he watched, it softened and turned young and wide-eyed, gentle; the muscles in his stomach eased, and he recognized the self of boyhood mornings. He was touched by this last face and grinned at it in embarrassment; but just as he grinned, self-consciousness returned to poison him, and the boyish face turned hard again and mean, and the lips drew back upon sharp teeth and the eyes glittered, and the whole body tensed with an anger of such murderous black violence that he recoiled from his own hate, falling back again across the bed.

A huge dead dog had its teeth locked in his throat, and the metal bar dragged at his chest again, and when he closed his eyes the Rage descended, a huge and multilimbed galoot in hobnailed boots and spurs, eyes bulging, teeth grinding, cigars exploding in its mouth and flames shooting from its ears, bearing a club spiked with rusty nails, wearing brass knuckles and outsize six guns; in its blind snot-flying rage, it blew its own head off by mistake. This thing came stomping down out of his mind, and he gasped, Look at *that* guy, that guy is so mad, he blew his own head off by mistake! His body relaxed and he howled with laughter, lying now with his back on the floor and his feet on the bed, and as he laughed, the gnawed and painful stake which had pierced his chest as long as he could remember cracked and opened like an ancient husk and turned to dust, and he could breathe again.

With the music rising in the summer breeze there came a gay preposterous parade along the highroad: calliope flutings and fanfare, with band wagons and floats and maelstroms of confetti, pouter pigeons and emerald parakeets, bursting drums and golden tubas, and gauzy fat-cheeked majorettes in crotch-tight sateen suits, chins bouncing on high squeaking breasts like taut balloons—*oompa, oompa, oompa, oompa*. And an immense blowzy one-man band of a hand-me-down Big Irma, beer-soaked and high-colored, all billowing bows and curlicues and furbelows of hue and texture

104

Look At Her Go, Hurrah Hurrah! all leer and wink,
hiking her skirts to turn the ankle, pretty still beneath
the mass of tired flesh, and trying in vain to shake a
ball of hair and dog turd from her heel, squinching and
squashing and squirting along like a banquet dumped
into a bag. She wore a gigantesque plumed hat which
she flew like a flag, and as the old tub pushed along,
batting her eyes and swinging her butt, she leaked
and sagged and oozed so woefully at the seams that
rats and crows fought for her leavings, while in the
front and alongside, as trumpets blew and pennants
flew and children snickered and horses nickered, stores
and provisions and water and fuel were crammed
aboard; varlets hurled up trays of tarts and heaved up
meats and slung up wine flagons and kegs of ale, while
others ran to pump in gasoline and air, barely able to
offset the waste and loss of the vast outpourings beneath—Big Irma meanwhile, nothing daunted, leering
and winking to beat hell, and curtseying prettily as the
bands played and hats were tossed and wild cheers
rent the air *hip hip hurroo* and winking her blinkers
and twinkling her pinkie and twirling a tiny parasol,
all giggling and goosed and poked, as if to say, Well,
sweet Christ knows I always done my damndest.

Once upon a time, at morning, a small blood-silver
river in the rising plains, the silver undersides of wind-
awakened leaves, the silver spider webs in dew. A small
boy hunting, poised, quick, listening, in a fine old-
smelling boat parting new reeds. Soft drops falling from
an oar, a newborn sun, far bugling . . . a swan. The
stalk, the shot, the yell of blackbirds, the white bird
turning a slow circle, head under water. Feathers floating and wild silence . . . That morning his skin tingled,
and he laughed aloud in that sky-high aloneness that
was not loneliness, the strength of a young animal
among animals in a soft summer sunrise . . .

horses,
rodeos, long murky bars and rotten sawdust smell in

high small sandy towns of the Great Basin, a coyote
trapped by hurtling cars where the road cut through
the rock, a lone whiskey bottle on the shoulder of the
road. Night voices, speed, a dirtied strength, a flight, a
maiming, a lost friend; women and bystanders overrun,
struck aside by wheels spun loose from flying axles,
flying hooves, by fenders: highways, sirens, howling
lights, a crash . . . dread silence . . .

                                                        smoke,
and twisted metal shards, flayed twisted limbs, a staring eye, and gasoline spreading like a stain of blood on
the stunned pavement: hiss of steam, oncoming sirens,
SIRENS, *I-A-R-R-A-O-W-A-O-A-O-W* . . .

                                                Meriwether
Lewis Moon, in ditch, head bleeding at the temple

> *Ever driven a convertible, Lew boy? Go ahead—
> try it.*
> *With the record you already made, Lew boy—
> Lewis.*
> *With the record you already made, Lewis, it won't
> hardly be no trouble, no trouble at all.*
> *Yeah, but Eddie, his grades are very good, he's
> got what you might call real native intelligence—*
> *Hell, just keep drinkin whiskies like you been doin
> right along, and then you parade that little Eastern gal
> of yours around the campus, you know, feelin her up
> and all, and throw a punch maybe if somebody gets
> smart—that ought to do it.*
> *All you boys want is a complete sellout of the
> Cheyennes in this state, and you'll give the dumb Injun
> three hundred brand-new all-American silver dollars,
> right?*
> *Well, there's no call to look at it that way . . .*
> *Make it two thousand, or this auto, and I'll be
> out of your miserable alma mater before daylight.*
> *Two thousand? Or this automobile? How in hell
> are you going to earn two thousand—scalp somebody?*

106

Hand it over and find out.

Look, Geronimo, we can get you framed for less than that!

Ah, come on, Eddie, they said they wanted it a nice clean job.

Well, there's the two, goddamit, Lewis—now when you going to earn it?

. . . eighteen, nineteen, two. Right now—you two fat turds get out and walk.

Hey, wait a minute, watcher language! No red nigger's gonna . . .

—Ow! Christ watchit!

In the mirror he saw one of them, face bloodied, help the other to his feet; they bawled for justice.

You mean that's their car you have downstairs? Oh, I can't bear it, you were almost graduated! Lew, listen to me, darling, this is no way to prove anything—

Lewis. I'm supposed to feel you up in public.

Oh, listen to you, sweetheart, look how drunk you are! If you really believe in what you're doing, why are you so drunk? Listen, it's not only a question of yourself—how about your people? How about the people who worked so hard to get you in here—

That's it, right there—I sold out when I first signed in as their pet Indian. And yours too, baby, yours. The only reason you're making it with me is because you don't come from around here. You goddamn liberals are all alike—all talk and no risk.

Don't be like that! How can we help you people if you won't help yourselves! Oh, can't you understand? I love you!

Love, love, lo-ove . . .

Down the road. The big two-tone auto stank of lotion and cigar butts, but it moved. It roared across the land like an apocalypse, almost to the state line, before the oil gauge flashed red; then he forced it harder still, grinding his teeth and driving the gas through it to burn it clean, until the tires reeked and the body shuddered, until the fat plastic dashboard bulged with warnings, until the whole fat contraption of church-going chromium and patriotic plush screeched and choked on its own heat and burst its block and screamed to a hissing locked fiery halt with eight million all-American motorcycles hard behind. *I-A-R-R-A-O-A-O-W.* A last swig and he broke the bottle, then toppled out, rolling and laughing, on the highway shoulder. Down he went through waving weeds into the swamp, hailing and cursing the cop silhouettes, with two thousand dollars and a hand cut by broken teeth, and nothing and nowhere, but free, by Christ, how free of their whole Indian game.

He headed eastward to New York. On a truck radio he heard the charges: grand larceny—an automobile and two thousand dollars—and felonious assault.

See, Lewis, it ain't gonna work. You find yourself another local.

I don't get it. You had a fight in here yourself only last week—you guys were drunk right on the job.

You don't fight the way we fight. We fight for fun, Lewis. Because we like it. Because we like it. We ain't tryin to prove nothin. So you just find yourself a nice white local where they fight the way you fight.

White local, huh? There's more Cheyenne in this blood coming out of my nose than there is Mohawk in all you bastards put together—

You got shit in your blood too. We never heard of Cheyennes, hardly, until you come along, and anyway, we ain't professional Indians like you. All we know about Indians, bub, is what we seen on television.

I-A-R-R-A-O-A-O-W . . .

Sirens, howling lights, another crash, another, still another: modern times. *CRASH, CRASH, CA-RASH*—that crazy kid is *CA-RAZY*—he began to laugh. The crashes became gimcrack destruction, a breaking and tinkling of deafening dimensions, a

108

mounting heap of slow jalopies hurling themselves together at a crossroads.

Port
scene with rum, tropical colors, high white birds, the lonely palms of dawn: a crazy-legged Negress dancing nude,

Wistaria,
her flesh . . .

Because the way things are goin they ain't no hope for none of us, lessen we don't get somethin learned here to us pretty quick . . .

Here was
Rage again, exploded now, hung-up like an old scarecrow, like a big broken toy with one loose eye and loose old parts and springs and stuffing every whichyway—all hung-up on itself, poor critter. Rage danced somewhat sheepishly to guitar and wind, as if to say: Well, just because I'm *angry* doesn't mean I don't enjoy a dance or two . . .

Lucidity. He sighed. He lay there all laughed out and loose, loose as a dead snake slung on a rail, lay there drunk with gentleness and pleasure. *Be a good boy, Lewis, do not hate so much.*

Oh good old Wolfie would die laughing. The thought of the Old Wolf laughing, *dying* of *laughing,* set him off again, but this time, even as he laughed, an apprehension came. He crawled to the corner of the room, where he crouched low, watching both door and window. The noises were surrounding him, there was something happening to him, something *happening,* and he felt too tired now to deal with it. If he could only stop this laughing, but he could not; his laughter grew louder and louder, and when he tried to stop he could not close his mouth. It stretched wider and wider, until he swallowed the ceiling light, the room, the window and the night; the world rushed down into the cavernous void inside him, leaving him alone in space, pinwheeling wildly like a jagged fragment spun out from a planet.

A terrific wind blew, and his ears rang with the bells of blue-black space; the wind sealed his throat, his flesh turned cold, his screams were but squeaks snapped out and away by the passage of night spheres. Nor could he hear, there was no one to hear, there was no one where he had gone—*what's happening, what-is-happening* . . .

He had flung himself away from life, from the very last realities, had strayed to the cold windy reaches of insanity. This perception was so clear and final that he moaned; he would not find his way back. You've gone too far this time, *you've gone too far* . . .

As he whirled into oblivion, his body cooled and became numb, inert, like a log seized up and borne out skyward by a cyclone; he struggled to reach out, catch hold, grasp, grip, hang on, but he could not. He could not, he was made of wood, and there was nothing to hang on to, not even his own thought—thought shredding, drifting out of reach, like blowing spider webs. He was gone, g-o-n-e, *gone,* G-O-N-E, gone—and around again. The howling was in his head, and all about lay depthless silence. His screaming was ripped away before it left his mouth, and the mouth itself was far away, a huge papered hoop blown through and tattered by the gales. The air rushed past, too fast to breathe; his lungs sucked tight, shriveled like prunes, collapsed. He died.

Death came as a huge bounteous quiet, in the bosom of a high white cloud. The wood of his body softened, the knots loosened; he opened up, lay back, exhausted, mouth slack, eyes wide like the bald eyes of a corpse. He glimpsed a hard light lucid region of his mind like a lone comet, wandering far out across the long night of the universe.

9

Toward dawn Lewis Moon came to the Quarriers' room. He entered without knocking. Quarrier awoke in time to find Moon going through the pockets of his pants hung on the chair. Moon met his gaze calmly, still going through the pockets, and a moment later held up the Niaruna dictionary in the dim light. Quarrier slipped quietly from his bed and trailed Moon into the corridor.

"What are you doing?" he whispered angrily. He was upset by his own nakedness.

"You haven't any clothes on," Moon remarked. "Is that a sin?" The pupils of his eyes were very large, and both his face and voice were gentle.

"Give me that dictionary!"

"No, not now." He was already moving off unsteadily; he disappeared into the stairwell. Quarrier ran back for his bathrobe, then went to fetch Wolfie. But Wolfie had found another place to sleep, for his bed was empty.

From the window Quarrier watched Moon drift down the center of the street to the edge of light and disappear into the darkness. Then he saw Andy running in the same direction. He started to call out to her, then stopped; he ran to the doorway, to the stairwell, then back to his room.

Quarrier was at his window when a climbing airplane roared over the hotel. In the jungle no one flew

111　　　　*At Play in the Fields of the Lord*

at night, and in the echoes of the plane's motor a tension swelled, a taut silence, cracked like glass by the sound of a first voice, which told him that the whole settlement had leaped awake. From across the town, a moment later, he heard Wolfie howling.

By sunrise all of Madre de Dios had convened to stare at the spot where the airplane had been. Guzmán himself came, in his private car, with driver. Everyone had an ear cocked for an engine, but everyone also seemed to know that Moon would not come back.

Nevertheless, Huben went over to the radio shack to try to contact Moon. Almost immediately the flyer's voice resounded, but Leslie was unable to tell how long Moon had been talking. Apparently the man had no audience in mind, for the monologue was in English. Who was he talking to, then? Leslie did not catch all of it, and in fact made no real contact; he was paid for his efforts in curses and strange maledictions.

It was now known that Moon was under the effects of *ayahuasca,* and the wonder was that on this rough mud strip, without lights of any kind, he had got into the air at all. Some of the wiser heads told one another that he had feigned the *ayahuasca,* that he had made off with the plane, leaving the Bearded One to fend for himself. Others stated flatly that under the spell of the Vine of Death, Moon had divined the location of Paititi, the legendary El Dorado, and had gone there, suicidally alone, to add his bones to those of all such jungle visionaries.

Wolfie, meanwhile, cornered Guzmán, and using Quarrier as his interpreter, demanded the use of the old army fighter as a search plane. Guzmán said that it did not work, and when Wolfie said that he would fix it, the Comandante shrugged. He jeered as Wolfie ran off with tools and gasoline toward the plane on the far side of the strip; it sat in growth up to its fuselage. But soon Wolfie was seen leaping up and down, cranking the prop by hand. The plane did not respond, and the squat figure scrambled back under the cowling and

112

dove down once again into the works. Everyone now dismissed the possibility that the Bearded One could start the plane, which had been famous for its treacherous and ugly disposition, and had not left the ground in more than a year. But an hour later the Bearded One was again swinging violently on the prop, and after a few dreadful coughs the airplane belched a cloud of smoke and came to life with a clatter of outraged metal. Wolfie ran back across the strip, shouting wildly through the black grease on his face. "Gas!" he bellowed at the Comandante. "Gimme some more gas!"

But Guzmán shook his head. *"Mecánico, sí,"* he grinned. *"Piloto, no."* He could scarcely turn over the property of his government to someone who owed him money.

"You got my passport, don't you? Look, I'll bomb them Indians myself!" Wolfie made war whoops by patting his open mouth, then made violent bombing motions.

The Comandante was amused. He laughed: "Ha, ha, ha, ha."

"I'm goin to kill this guy," Wolfie told Quarrier. "I shoulda done it the other night. You tell him to get that crate gassed up and oiled and do it quick, or I'm goin to knife him right here and now in front of all his friends." Speaking quietly, he kept his gaze on Guzmán's face, and El Comandante did not wait for the translation. "Pigs!" he shouted at his soldiers, who were standing there half dressed and unarmed, scratching at dirty undershirts. "You dare to come before me out of uniform! You will be punished!" He whirled in fury and signaled out his driver. "Mechanic!" He spat violently in contempt. "You saw? The gringo fixed a motor faster than you can wipe my windshield! Now prepare the plane for this true mechanic and do it quickly!" He turned again to Wolfie and bowed slightly from the waist.

Wolfie grinned into his face, disdainfully. "He's

chicken, ain't he?" he remarked to Quarrier. "He's chicken through and through." He watched as Guzmán's driver, shouting violent orders in his turn, directed the soldiers toward the drums of gasoline.

"Maybe he knows the plane isn't safe," Quarrier said.

"That's what he thinks, all right; look at that miserable face! But there ain't nothin wrong with that old heap except only maintenance. That's like what I hate about this lousy continent—no maintenance. Valves stuck, fouled plugs, and every other wire loose, but that's a good old swingin, practically brand-new American engine. And just as soon as I get rid of them bushmasters and tarantulas and all the other jungle crud which this is prolly layin around the cockpit, the Old Wolf is goin to be air-borne." He shook his head. "That crazy Moon. He's pulled plenty of cute tricks, but this one—" He threw his arms wide apart and staggered back, as if stunned by the walls of green. "Where does he want I should *start,* even, answer me that. And not a lousy chart, even, and somewhere out there on a sand bar on one of them miserable rivers, prolly layin on his ass eatin mangoes, this stupid drugged-up bastard is waitin for his buddy Wolf to come and rescue him. And I can't even land when I *do* find him—" He barked with exasperation, but the sound had a slight ring of despair. Wolfie blinked a little, shocked; his face turned red in consternation, as if he were facing the probability that his friend was dead.

"If I were you, I'd try the Niaruna country first," Quarrier said.

"Sure, sure. Like, where *is* it?"

"To the east. You were there yesterday."

Andy Huben was standing just behind them. "That's right," she said. "He was going eastward." She looked pale and tense.

"What is all this *eastward!*" Wolfie yelled. He threw his big hands up and out, summoning the half-breeds as his witnesses. "The marks all know exactly where he went, and his own pal Wolf didn't even know that he was *goin!*"

Huben hurried over. "Are you cursing at my wife?" he said.

"So who's cursin! What I'm tryna find out is how in sweet Christ does she know he headed *eastward!*"

Now all three stared at her.

"He told me."

"When did he tell you?" Huben said.

"Last night—I mean, this morning. Just before he left."

"Oy!" Wolfie cried, delighted. "Very good. I musta been sheltered as a yout' or somethin, I thought you people—" He jerked his thumb at Quarrier, then tossed his chin toward Andy. "First him and that Indian chick, and now it's her and Lewis—"

Andy slapped him hard across the face, and her husband came forward in a boxer's stance, fists up, bobbing and weaving. But the people, moaning, pressed so close that Leslie was restricted in his maneuvers and finally came to a halt. He was red to the point of bursting, and when he spoke, his voice was high with rage.

"You take that back!"

"Or else?" Grinning, a bad glint in his eye, Wolfie slowly withdrew his hand from inside his shirt; he raised the hand slowly and pinched at Huben's face. A moment later, when he withdrew it, there was blood between his thumb and forefinger. Huben paled, and the people gasped. "Big mos-*quito*," Wolfie enunciated. He grinned at Quarrier and winked. To Huben he said, "I was only foolin wit' you, Reverend. Like maybe you're kind of emotionally upset—I mean, you know, *neurotic possessiveness,* right, Reverend? Only don't come prancin around the Old Wolf again like that or you're liable to get fractured."

Andy said, "I heard him leave. You were asleep. I thought he was on his way to bomb and kill. I ran after him and begged him not to attack the Niaruna."

She turned toward her husband. "He promised he wouldn't."

"Promised!" Huben shook, in a fury of emotions. "What were you *wearing?*"

Quarrier said quickly, "Did he say anything else?"

"He said some other things. I'm not sure I understood them."

Her husband seized her by the arm. "Come on, Andy, we're going back to the hotel."

"Well, you accomplished what we couldn't," Quarrier called after her. Without turning, Andy raised her hand in a small fluttering wave, and both Quarrier and Wolfie laughed. "She's a swinger, ain't she?" Wolfie said. But Leslie took their laughter as directed at himself, and glared over his shoulder. At this, Wolfie snarled and cursed, but a moment later he had forgotten all about the Hubens and was worrying once more about his partner.

"Eastward, huh?" He rolled his eyes. "*East*ward, the man says." He waved his arm in a half-circle. "You can't miss it, right?" He slammed his big fist into his other hand. "Well, nuts to that. I'll get him out all right, one way or another—all I gotta do is *find* him. Lewis and me, we been in trouble worse than this, a lot worse."

Wolfie flew out an hour later, after going back to the hotel for his pistol, which he wore strapped to his hip. "So what's it *to* ya," he said to Huben, who, standing in the hotel doorway, had glanced at the weapon in disdain. "You think it's some kind of a *sex* symbol, or what? Maybe I wanna shoot myself a vulture."

The crowd at the airstrip cheered *El Lobo* as he tuned the motor—"*Ole! Muy macho, hombre!*"— saluting the beard and the gold earring, the mechanical genius and the revolver. It was commonly assumed, and confirmed by the infernal clatter of the engine, that *El Lobo* would disappear in the wake of Moon and die a hero's death before the sun had set.

116

"Introit et Kyrie . . ."

Quarrier turned. Here was the priest again; he had not even noticed him. Xantes was everywhere, hands folded behind his back, observing.

"So . . . the Requiem commences. Inevitable, eh? And I, for one, will miss him. Such a strange man, this Moon! A soldier of fortune, and of the classic type, and yet—how shall I say? There was something likable about the man, did you not find?"

"He's dead, you mean?"

"Do you not think so?" Xantes cocked his head. *"Y usted?* I understand that you are a student, like myself. You have read all the laws of this land, for example—?"

Quarrier laughed; they walked on a little way together. "Oh yes, I love to read. I wish I could read Spanish well enough to borrow—" He stopped short.

"By all means; one must do what one can to help dispel ignorance."

Quarrier knew that he was being jeered at, and he particularly disliked being jeered at in a kindly manner. But the priest was too adroit for him, and he exclaimed, "But why are *you* sympathetic to Moon! These men are mercenaries, very probably criminals . . ."

"How is it, then, that we pass so much of our time in talk of him? Do you deny it? If he is the ordinary bandit he appears to be, why can we not dismiss him? Surely you have noticed, Señor Quarrier, that the people we dismiss most vehemently are the very ones we find it necessary to dismiss most often? And let us be honest, it is not the banditry of the late Moon that so unsettles us. We all sit up, we call old names at him; we cannot be comfortable while he is there. Yet we circle in uneasily—what is his secret, what does this man wish to know that we do not?" He paused to cough. "And now, alas, he is gone away, and with him some sort of—*possibility?* For all of us." Xantes smiled, bowed, and set out toward the town.

"What is it you want with me?" Quarrier called, despairing, and the priest turned toward him, his brown cassock snapping in the dull wind of the airstrip.

"I would talk to you, Señor Quarrier, even if I had no better reason than the following: I have learned all of my English out of books, and I speak it very well, do you not think? But I have not many chances to practice it, and so I avail myself of every opportunity of . . . communication?" He smiled gaily and bowed again. "Good day, señor."

Wolfie was back while the sun was still high, careening down to a bad landing, out of gas; he took off a second time as soon as he had refueled. He left again at dawn the following morning and flew until dark, and he did this again on the following day, the same day that Hazel Quarrier, without warning or note, without even packing a bag, took Billy on the commercial flight and fled back across the mountains.

On the next flight, two days later, Quarrier flew out to fetch her. She and Billy were waiting for him on a bench at the main airport. Her plan, such as it was, had been to return to North Dakota, but she had neither luggage nor sufficient funds, nor had she applied to anyone for help. She had simply sat there in her foolish hat, as if awaiting divine intervention.

Billy, sensing something to be feared in her, sat at the far end of the bench. Quarrier picked up the silent child and touched Hazel's shoulder, saying, "Now come on, Mother, we're going back." She rose without a word and followed him. Later she said, "Well, I had a hot bath, Martin. Oh, I *needed* that bath so." In the plane he kept looking at her—had he ever really looked at her before this moment?

At the airstrip in Madre de Dios, Wolfie was preparing to fly out again for the second time that day. He looked tired and gaunt, and did not respond to Quarrier's nod. He seemed to feel that if he did not find his partner soon he would not find him at all. All his movements had grown stiff and hurried, and he kept dropping things. But to Hazel he muttered, "I'll tell ya somethin, lady—if *I* ever ex-cape from this Christly jungle the way you did, they won't get *me* back, *never*."

Hazel did not answer him. For the benefit of Huben, who had met them at the plane, she hung her head; at the same time she was smiling to herself, for she felt no shame at all. She was playing the game that they required of her—displaying a seemly penitence, yet dealing firmly with the little boy in proof of renewed stability. When the child shied from her, she seized his hand in warning. Only he, who had gone with her, knew her secret: she had not come back! She had found a glass sphere full of sun and flowers sailing high above the fair, and all this world beneath was a world of games.

The child watched her.

No, she thought, and she squeezed his hand so fervently that he squeaked in pain: I loved you in that other time, and I love you still. She peered close into his eyes and saw his tears; the sphere burst, the air rushed in, and a terrible mixed joy and sorrow overcame her. What would folks think! She pulled herself together and set off after Martin and Leslie, still squeezing Billy's hand. "Oh I'm so sorry," she implored Billy. "Oh don't look at me that way, I beg of you!"

She hurried onward, struggling to keep up. But she felt nagged and pulled by some outward force which kept her off balance and stumbling. Billy was yanking at her hand, desperate to free himself, and was filling the air with loud and nerve-shearing protests; now the random clatter of his words fell into place. For some time he had sought permission to walk along by himself, and had only cried out when, distracted and oppressed, she had squeezed his hand all the more fiercely. She was about to comfort him when Billy fetched her a kick in the shins. He had never done such a thing in all his life; and because the people behind her were sniggering, because Martin and

119   *At Play in the Fields of the Lord*

Leslie Huben were gazing back at her in perplexity—because, finally, she could not permit an eight-year-old this outrage even if he was in the right, she smacked him across the face.

In the silence that followed, while she gasped for breath, Billy stared at her, his eyes filling. It would have been better if he had cried, but he only shook his head back and forth in condemnation, saying, "Boy, Ma, that's not fair. Boy, Ma!" She slackened her grip, feeling very weak; coldly, he yanked his hand from hers and went forward to join his father. Over his shoulder he said, "You were hurting me. You hurt me."

Martin said to him, "If I ever see you do that to your mother again, you're going to get the hiding of a lifetime." But as he spoke he gazed reflectively at Hazel; when he turned around he placed his hand on his son's shoulder and they went on again as if she were not there. She fell far back, to make them feel bad—had they already forgotten that she was sick, that she needed love and care?

No, I can't bear it— She suppressed a scream. Folks always turned their backs to her, they always pretended she did not exist. *Wait for me,* she groaned, *oh for pity's sake wait.*

Alone! She was alone—they'd left a sick person to walk alone! Whimpering, she picked up her skirt as Momma used to, crossing the barnyard in the rain; she began to run, crying and laughing at her own fright, at the big frightened white knees pumping along. But there, the folks had stopped, and seeing their stern faces, she hastened to compose herself. "Goodness, wait for me!" she called out gaily, as if she were carrying the picnic basket. Their silence was awkward—did they think her too forward? She tried again, gasping in pain. "Goodness, I forgot about that *smell,*" she sighed, twirling a little. "This is surely the domain of Satan, Mr. Huben, I can smell sulphur in the very air!" Leslie cried out, "Why, that vomit smell, that's the sawmill, Hazel, you remember that! Why heck, you won't hardly call that a smell at all once you smell Remate de Males! 'Culmination of Evils'! How's *that* for the name of a town?"

Awaiting her reaction, young Mr. Huben glanced uneasily at Mr. Quarrier. Their uncertainty gave her a grip on herself—she would confound them. "I reckon it's as good a name as any," she said primly, "in *this* neck of the woods." Now Martin Quarrier laughed boisterously in relief, this coarse-looking fellow who imagined that he understood what he was pleased to call Miss Hazel's "quirky" sense of humor. But she had not fooled that child. He kept his distance, walking backward, as if skirting some ominous beast. They almost nodded at each other. I *know,* his face said. You have gone away again. You have forsaken us.

Yoyo had been sent to contact the Niaruna; he returned a week later with word that the plane had crashed and that Lewis Moon was dead. How had he died? Yoyo shrugged and smiled. He knew no more.

Wolfie, once he had understood—"What's he say-in, c'mon, what's he *sayin?"*—picked Yoyo off the ground and shook him like a rat. "Since when don't a bush pilot follow the rivers? Huh? And if he piled up along the rivers, I woulda found him—I seen every lousy river from here to Bolivia and halfway across Brazil. So where's the aircraft, huh? Where—is—the —aircraft?"

But Yoyo did not answer, not out of recalcitrance but because he spoke no English; instead he smiled enthusiastically. Though of neither an enthusiastic nor a smiling turn of mind, he had learned early in the game that gringos—and especially the *evangélicos*—respond-ed favorably to eagerness of any kind. When Wolfie's question was translated for him, he smiled again. It was true that he, Yoyo, had not seen the wreckage; it was far off—he pointed vaguely eastward. The plane, he said, had disappeared in the far country of the Yuri

121   *At Play in the Fields of the Lord*

Maha, the People to the East. The Yuri Maha, he explained, were of the same clans as the Niaruna, but now nobody went that way; the trails were lost.

Wolfie lowered him to the ground, but he kept his big hands clenched for a few moments on the front of the red shirt, glaring at Yoyo and breathing harshly, as if considering how best to dispose of him once and for all.

Leslie talked with Yoyo separately, but made no more headway than had Wolfie with this flexible personality; it seemed quite possible that Yoyo had gone no farther than the Tiro country and had concocted the whole story, making it as dramatic and final as he could in an attempt to please his listeners. Leslie did learn, however, that his own small band of Niaruna was most anxious that he return, as they were under constant threat of violence from their wild brethren and had been forced to take shelter in Remate de Males. A few days later the Hubens flew out to Remate, leaving the Quarriers to wait for the supplies.

10

At the end of his long night of uproar and hallucinations, Lewis Moon had a dream. He dreamed that he walked homeward up the bed of an empty river and out onto a blasted land of rusted earth and bones and blackened stumps and stunted metal, a countryside of war. In the sky of a far distance he saw a bird appear and vanish; but no matter how far he walked, the world was one mighty industrial ruin, a maze of gutted factories and poisoned ground under the gray sky. He came finally to a signpost, and the signpost had caught a fragile ray of rising sun. He ran toward it, stumbled, fell and ran again. The signpost pointed eastward, back toward the sun, and it read:

| NOWHERE |

Very tired, he turned back along his road, crossing the dead prairie. Though he had not noticed them on his outward journey, he now passed a series of signs all pointing eastward. Each was illuminated by a ray of sun, and each bore the same inscription:

| NOWHERE |

The terrible silence of the world made him move faster, and soon he saw, on the eastern horizon, the dark blur of a forest. He ran and trotted weakly, bewildered by the crashing of his feet upon the cinders. Another sign, and then another, pointed toward the wood.

As he drew near, the wood became a jungle, a maelstrom of pale boles and thickened fleshy leaves, shining and rubbery, of high dark passages and hanging forms, of parasites and strangler figs and obscene fruited shapes. But even here there was no sound, no sign of movement, not even a wind to stir the heavy leaves, sway the lianas; there was only the mighty hush of a dead universe.

He started forward, stopped, started again. Too frightened to go on, he turned around and saw what lay behind him; then he sat down on the road, and this time wept.

When at last he lifted his eyes, he saw a signpost at the jungle edge; it was obscured by weeds and leaves and the tentacle of a liana, and at first he thought that its inscription was identical to all the rest. But this sign did not point anywhere, and as he drew near and stared at it he saw that its inscription was quite different. It read:

NOW HERE

Astonished, he ventured on into the darkness of the jungle. Soon he came to a kind of clearing cut off from the sky by a canopy of trees, a soft round space like an amphitheater, diffused with sepia light. Everything was soft and brownish, and the ground itself quaked beneath his feet, giving off a smell of fungus and decay. In the center of the clearing he strayed into a quagmire; very quickly he sank, too tired to struggle. But as he passed into the earth and the warm smells of its darkness, he was still breathing without effort, and soon he dropped gently into a kind of earthen vault. Though closed off from the sky, this cave was suffused by the same soft brownish light as in the clearing far above. Here was a second sign, which read:

124

The passage through the soil had cleaned him of his clothes, and he was naked; as he stood there, small black spots appeared in pairs upon his skin. He pressed at them and discovered to his horror that the black spots were the tips of snail horns; at each touch a naked snail slid out through his skin and dropped to the cave floor. His hands flew wildly about his body, and the snails slid out and fell, until finally the earth at his bare feet was strewn with slimy writhings. Now, from the darkness near the wall, numbers of salamanders crept forward; each salamander grasped a snail behind its head and writhed in silent struggle with it, the soft bodies twitching back and forth in rhythm.

He backed toward one side of the room and fell into a tunnel. He ran along the tunnel, no longer afraid, for there was light ahead. He ran like a boy.

The tunnel emerged like a swallow's nest from the side of a high bank. Far below he saw a jungle clearing in a huge sunlight of the world's first morning, and in the clearing the Indians awaited him. Naked, he leaped into the radiant air, and fell toward them.

Moon awoke. He lay in a half-world between the dream and his narcosis, growing gradually aware of where he was. Though the room was dark, he could see the moth's white eyes above the door, and the glint of the bottle on the window sill. The man on the next bed was missing. In the background he heard singsong voices, a wailing and keening like a ringing in his ears.

The night air of Madre de Dios was fragmented by insect-singing and far barking, by the tocking of frogs in the puddles and ditches, the murmur of voices behind walls, by sounds of breaking. But the street below was rigid in its silence, and he wondered if he was not still in the dream. He rose slowly; though his head was light, he felt intensely strong and sure.

There was no question in his mind about what he

was going to do. He would not wait until it was light; he would go now. He lifted his watch to his ear; its tick was murderous. The numerals of the watch face, reading five-fifteen, glowed with chinks of light, as if time burning had been forced into the casing; its metal swelled and shimmered with constraint. At this, his chest began to tighten, and his breathing hurt the cold wound in his heart; he removed the watch, and holding it by one end of the strap, rapped it sharply on the sink until it broke. Then he dropped it out of the window.

He moved quickly without turning on the light. From his knapsack he took the last of the river diamonds, holding them a moment in his hands. He had found these on the upper Paragua, in Venezuela, bright alluvial diamonds, burnished clean by mountain torrents, green and blue and yellow and red. In the darkness, he could feel them burning, like fire and water of the universe, distilled.

He put one diamond in his pocket and slid the rest under Wolfie's pillow. His revolver, in its shoulder holster, he put on beneath his shirt. An instinct nagged at him to leave the gun behind, to go forth unarmed and clean; he slung it into a corner of the room. But after looking at it for a moment, his instinct weakened and he retrieved it.

He went out of his room and down the hall to where the missionaries slept; he opened the first door he came to, quietly but without hesitation. In the bed, his back to him, lay Leslie Huben. Beside Huben was the girl. He crossed the room and looked at her, the long hair on the pillow and soft mouth; he could smell the warmth of her. When he reached down and ran his fingertips from the corner of her eye along her temple, her eyes opened, widened. Slowly her hands reached for the sheet and drew it to her chin.

"Come with me," he told her, neither softly nor loudly.

She cried out faintly, like a child, which made him smile. She turned her head toward her husband, turned it back again.

126

"No," she whispered, "no, no, no."

He went out the door again and closed it. The next room was Martin Quarrier's, and he found what he was looking for in the hip pocket of the missionary's pants. Quarrier awoke and followed him out into the hall. The man talked on and on, and at the end he heard his own voice say, "No, not now."

He glanced back once as he turned down the stairs; the girl was watching through the door crack. When she closed the door, he kept on going.

He walked down the center of the empty street. On its last corner leaned a solitary man, a drunkard, attended by a dog. The drunkard was singing a sad slow mountain song, gasping for breath, lungs cracking. When Moon crossed his line of vision, he croaked, *"Dónde vas, amigo?"*

He kept on singing while Moon stopped, swaying, and regarded him. The drunkard's face waxed and waned, in caricature of idiocy, of rage and misery and innocence, of sensibility and soul. He sang softly out of his great mouth, his staring eyes and tear-eroded cheeks, his skull:

> *"Qué buen de bailar*
> *Qué buen de cantar."*

Was this man the solitary figure coming at him down the street? Moon said, *"Yo voy a otro mundo."*

"Sí." The man paused, contemplating Moon. *"Sí, claro."*

"Quieres venir?"

"No, gracias." And then the man said gently, *"Una copita, sí—ayahuasca, no. Buen viaje."*

Moon emptied his pockets of his change and gave it to the singer. The man demurred: it was not Moon but the *ayahuasca* that made the gift. Moon said, "No, I no longer have need of it." The man took it. "God will repay you," he said; he looked uncertain.

Sí, sí. Dios le pagará.

Moon walked on, his enlarged pupils drawing in

the faintest light; every sound and every smell enlivened him. In the nostrils of a lunatic, he thought, the night air is just as strong . . . In this moment he could scent, hunt out, run down and kill the swiftest creature on earth. Stalking the plane, he knew every sinew and muscle in his body, how each coiled and moved; in the darkness of the jungle night, he played cat, nerves taut, listening. He heard a small night animal and sprang for it, and was astonished when he missed it. An instant later he stopped breathing; something was hunting him in turn. He drew the revolver and ducked under the plane, rising silently behind the intruder.

The girl stood beside the wing. "Where are you going?" her voice said. "Are you going to bomb the Niaruna?"

"No."

"You must not."

"No." He laughed. He had not felt so happy since —since when?

"Are you sick? You look so strange! I suppose you're very drunk."

"No."

"What is it then? What are you doing out here in the middle of the night? Why did you break into our room?"

"To say good-bye."

"But we haven't even said hello yet!"

"Let's say it then: hello."

Look, look, she's smiling!

She said, "Your name is Lewis Moon."

"Yes. Your name is Andy. What were you christened?"

"Agnes. Agnes Carr."

"That's much better than Andy Huben."

"I tried for days to place your name; then I remembered." She had been running, and she paused for breath; gazing at him, her eyes filled with tears. "Your people, and the mission—they were all so *proud* of you!"

"Yes, they were."

128

"Yet you disgraced them!"

"That's what they said."

"May God forgive you!"

"Why should He, when I haven't forgiven Him?"
He laughed.

She looked disgusted. "You're not the least repentant, are you?"

"No. Suppose I told you that I didn't steal that money, that it was given to me."

"Why didn't you tell the truth, then?"

"Because the truth looked worse than what was being said. A thief is one thing, but a betrayer—do you always talk like this?"

"Like what, Mr. Moon?"

"Like a missionary's wife."

"I *am* a missionary's wife!"

"Then why did you follow me out here, with your hair still wild? Agnes Carr! Maybe you were never meant to be a missionary's wife."

"Mr. Moon, I came to beg you not to attack the Niaruna."

"All right."

"All right what?"

"All right, beg me."

"Oh please! You mustn't attack them—"

"I won't attack them; I'm just heading eastward."
And he told her eagerly about his dream, about how all the signs had pointed eastward; that Indians said the Source of Life, the Sun, lay in the East, and that in the West, where the Sun touched the Darkness, was the Land of the Dead.

She nodded: The Tiros believed that because the white man came to them from the far side of the Andes, he was the Spirit of the Dead. As she spoke she gazed at him, and her face changed. This made him happy; he awaited her, saying nothing. "How strange you look —your eyes, I mean! And your voice, when you talk about these things, it's so quiet, so gentle. I don't understand you! Why do you do . . . And just now, coming here, I saw you crouched on all fours, like an animal!

You looked like a cat! Really, you frightened me! What were you doing?"

He felt removed again and did not answer her.

She said, "You must listen to me. There's nothing east of here but jungle. For two thousand miles! You can't just *go* there!"

"That's the only way to do it—*go*. When there's a jungle waiting, you go through it and come out clean on the far side. Because if you struggle to back out, you get all snarled, and afterwards the jungle is still there, still waiting."

"I don't understand you." She looked annoyed; he was trying to see her body through her bathrobe. "You promise then?"

"I'll promise if you like."

She got down on her knees. "O Praise the Lord!" she said, and began to pray.

He too got down upon his knees, to see her face better. "What are you doing?" he inquired.

"Saying a prayer for you."

He took her hands and raised her to her feet. "Don't," he said. "Please don't do that. I knew yesterday that I would not attack them. Listen—I *know* something, Andy . . ." But he had forgotten what he wanted to say. He reached out to her and touched her face; her face implored him. "Agnes Carr," he murmured. He took from his pocket the wild diamond, the clear drop of river fire and mountain rain, and squeezed it hard into her hand. She ran. "Good-bye," he called.

Good-bye, good-bye.

It was still dark, dark and starless, when he turned the plane at the far end of the runway; he could scarcely make out the wall of trees at the far end or where earth merged with sky. His hands on the controls moved swiftly and precisely but he was breathing urgently, and he did not wait for break of day as he had planned. He roared away into the darkness, veering wildly from side to side; when he thought he was running out of ground he sighed, hauling back on the wheel, and the plane bounded aloft. The black wall was much too

130

close, and jumped at him; he rolled his wing to miss a treetop, hooting, and then he was high and clear. Already, off to the east, the horizon was fire-black against the glow of the morning sun rolling toward him across Amazonas. A lone black palm, bent sadly on the sky of dawn, sank away into the darkness as he rose.

He flew boldly, straight into the sun. He was sailing eastward into all the mornings of the world, as the cloud forest and dark mountain range, the night and the dank river mists fell far behind. There had never been a day so brilliant. The dawn light caused the swamps to glitter, and pierced the muddy floods with life. It sparkled on the canopy, and illumined from within the wings of birds; a flight of parakeets shimmered downriver like a windburst of bright petals, and an alabaster egret burned his eye. He laughed with joy and sang.

The cabin of the plane confined him; he would burst the plane apart. He was oriented to the sun, as if he had soared into its field of gravitation. He was the sun in the sun-flecked wings of a golden insect, crawling across the dome of sky inside his windshield; he was the sun in the white wings below, the sun in the huge voice of the bird morning. All air and light and sound poured through him, swelling the universe.

To meet the sun he had wandered from his course, and now he whirled off northward; today, without effort, he could feel his bearings like a bird. Remate was in the distance; he was headed straight for it, though he had not checked his compass. He *knew*. He could trust his eyes and hands to take him by dead reckoning.

At Remate the inhabitants rushed like chickens to the center of the clearing; he passed overhead, up the Espíritu. It was not until he crossed a Tiro village that he felt a first somber dread. Realizing where he was, not sure why he had come, his hands grew cold.

He checked his gauges. His journey to the sun had consumed much too much fuel; he must turn back now if he was to reach Madre de Dios. But Madre de Dios was the past, he had come across into the present, and in the next moment the dread left him and his mind soared once again. He switched on his radio set, wishing to sing something to the world; he sang "Shenandoah" and "Columbus Stockade" and "All My Trials," and the Portuguese words of "Jesus Wants Me For A Sunbeam":

"Brilhan-do, brilhan-do . . ."

He flew onward. Because he did not know as yet how he would do what he must do, he swung wide of the Niaruna village, circling at a distance, and all the while he talked and sang.

Another voice crackled thinly over the radio; it had been crackling for some time. He put the earphones on and listened.

"This is Les Huben at Madre de Dios. How do you read me? Over."

Moon pressed the button on his transmitter. "This is Jesus, up in Heaven," he said affably. "How do you read me? Over."

But Huben ranted on. Offers of help and prayers for Moon's safety were interspersed with flight talk: *"By my estimate,"* Huben's voice said, *"fuel-range ratio of your aircraft is very critical. Can I assist you? Over."*

"How about some last rites?" Moon responded. "Over." But he realized with annoyance that he had neglected to press his transmitter button.

Huben came back again: *"You are under the effects of a powerful drug; repeat, you are under the effects of a powerful drug. You must try to concentrate, you are in emergency; repeat, you are in emergency. May the Lord forgive you and keep you, Amen. Over."*

"Thus spake the Lord to Leslie Huben, His false witness: *I call heaven and earth to record this day against you, that I have set before you life and death, blessing and cursing.*" In the silence that followed he bellowed, "Deuteronomy, 30:16."

Huben's voice said, *"30:19. For the last time, fella, you are in emergency; repeat, you are in emergency.*

Where are you proceeding; repeat, where are you proceeding? Over."

Moon looked a last time at his gauges.

"*What is your exact location; repeat, what is your exact location? Over.*"

"I'm at play in the fields of the Lord," Moon said; he removed his earphones. "Repeat, at play in the fields of the Lord."

According to his own estimate, he would run out of fuel in a few more minutes. The girl had said that to these Indians the white man was a creature from the west; he circled wide and came in upon the Niaruna from the east, out of the sun. They spread like ants. A few stood still. They awaited him, just as they had awaited in his vision. But of course he could not land, not even a crash landing; flyers who pancaked their small planes onto the canopy had starved to death, for there was no means of descent from the monstrous trees. As for the river, it was too narrow and overgrown for an approach, and there were no sand bars.

In the vision he had leaped into the air, and he would do that here; there was no wind, and if he timed it right and used his shrouds, he might drop into the clearing. He reached back across the crate of bombs and dragged the parachute up front, then began his climb in a widening circle, higher and higher, with the sun, until the canopy stretched away so far on every side that the whole jungle lay beneath him.

The climb had burned up the last of his fuel. The gauge was lifeless, and he knew that he might stall at any time. His breath was short; the altimeter read 9600. He leveled off for his approach, so intent on his work that only when he braced the door open and the cold air seared his hand did his fear verge upon panic. But his breath came again, and with it a new exaltation; on such a morning, all light and purity and color, even death must be magnificent.

He tried to work himself into his parachute. But his vast solar energy was instantly exhausted; he sat there gasping. "Hoo, boy," he said, trying in vain to cheer himself. He bound his arm in the straps of the chute, and grasping the strut, inched out onto the wing; how cold it was, in this cold light of heaven! He was afraid again. He clutched the parachute to his chest, and with his other arm—the one run through the strap— he hugged the strut. Now he pulled the cord and the silk bulged at the crack.

Now you've done it. This time you've *really* done it.

The wind tore at his face, and his arms ached. Short of the clearing, a mile and a half above the trees, he kicked himself backward and away. Shoving his free arm among the straps, then clasping both arms tight to his chest, he closed his eyes against the gut-sucking suspense, and the blow of the silk snapped open; he fell the length of a long howl before the impact all but wrenched his arms out of their sockets. He blinked, in tears; he was alive again, laughing idiotically in the clean sunlight of the upper air, legs dangling and swaying like the legs of a rag doll, drifting, drifting down through the great morning, in a wild silence like the wake of bells.

11

The moon had turned, and a weak sun filtered through the heat from the sky somewhere above. The supplies had come on the DC-3 two days before, and now the Quarriers waited on the river bank for the mission seaplane that would fly them to Remate. Even Hazel, in her conviction that no other place on earth could be so awful, was glad to leave Madre de Dios, although she remained angry with her husband, refusing to understand why Padre Xantes and Wolfie should come down to see him off. Martin reminded her that in this place, where death from apathy was a constant threat, the most insignificant arrivals and departures were events that all attended, but she did not relent.

In recent days Wolfie had sought Quarrier's company, but he merely came and sat and fumed, and scarcely spoke. His beard had grown ragged, and there were small bits of tobacco in it. "You run inta Moon out there," he muttered now, averting his eyes, "you tell'm if he thinks Wolf's gonna hang around here forever he's off his nut, because I ain't." Quarrier advised him to give it up and go back home. "The Old Wolf can take care of himself, don't worry," Wolfie said.

Then Yoyo came, accompanied by the mother-and-daughter team which he had acquired from Huben's band of tame Niaruna, the same band that had given up two women to ransom the captive nuns. Les-

At Play in the Fields of the Lord

lie had seen to it that the union of Yoyo with the daughter was sanctified in the eyes of the Lord, but the mother had been angry at being excluded from the marriage, since in the eyes of the band she was Yoyo's first wife and her daughter little more than a courtesy to the new husband. But Leslie had placated her with beads and had thought of her subsequently, for religious purposes, as the mother-in-law.

Yoyo pretended not to hear Quarrier's greeting and peered about as if the missionary had addressed someone else. Finally Quarrier turned away and stared out at the jungle on the farther bank. Remembering the fate of Padre Fuentes, he was overcome by sudden dizziness; how had Leslie found the courage to establish a mission at the same location on the Río Espíritu? Or was it faith? It seemed to him that Huben's faith, to judge from the support it had had from the Almighty, must be far greater than his own.

Behind him, in elaborate insolence, Yoyo cleared his throat and spat. Quarrier glanced at Xantes, who raised his eyebrows and drew his cassock closer in a gesture of fastidiousness. So *that's* what you've taught him, the priest's expression seemed to say, and both men smiled.

Quarrier disliked the idea that the Niaruna mission had been set up through Yoyo, who with his wives, dog, shotgun, and trading goods went off every few weeks in Guzmán's canoe on a slaving journey up the inner rivers. In his red shirt with rockets on it, Yoyo crossed frontiers at will. He sat in councils, attended feasts, and everywhere was treated as a man of consequence. At the same time he was recognized by brown and white alike as a spy and a liar, an agent of Guzmán who was not trusted even by Guzmán himself. Yet many of El Comandante's operations, balanced intricately between the law, the practical realities of the jungle, and a nostalgia for the grand old days of the rubber boom when wild Indians were shot on sight, were based on the tribal information he obtained from Yoyo. Sooner or later the latter would reappear in Madre de

136

Dios, his canoe loaded with Indian artifacts, otter pelts and skins of caiman and boa. More often than not, he brought along one or more Indian children, purchased ordinarily from their parents, whom he sold to the plantation owners along the banks of the main rivers.

For reporting this situation Quarrier had got himself disliked by everyone in Madre de Dios—including, he suspected, Leslie Huben. Yoyo treated Quarrier with servile rudeness; like Guzmán, he had not forgiven the missionary for noticing the trade in slaves, and the hate in his moist yellow eyes was plain. Unlike Wolfie and Xantes, he did not wave good-bye to the Quarriers —the first time, Martin reflected, that Yoyo had ever declined an opportunity to imitate the white man. In the shadow of the warehouse, pistol on hip, the Comandante stood, thick and still in his white shirt and pants; he did not wave either.

On the bank at Remate that same afternoon, Huben stood, feet spread apart and fists on hips, considering the Lord's unconquered fields. Standing beside him, Quarrier felt rumpled and inept; his nerves, after the long wait in Madre de Dios, were frayed by doubt and fear, and he grappled constantly with an impulse to outrage Huben. Still, he had to admit that the man's confidence cheered them all, and he wondered if Leslie's true crime in his eyes was not simply the possession of Andy.

From where they stood, all of Remate could be seen; how dared they put it on the maps at all! Its dispirited clearing was surrounded on three sides by low thatched huts, like a debased caricature of a colonial plaza; the fourth side faced the Río Espíritu. In the mud of the clearing, thin dirty chickens picked and small hogs sighed.

To Quarrier, as to everyone who came there, the name "Culmination of Evils" caught the spirit of the place exactly. The clearing scarred a wall of jungle which could not be held in check; the green absorbed both fire and machete, flowing back across the tangle of ugly blackened stumps to close the wound. The huts fought off rank weeds and thick lianas which crept up from behind, and the interiors were infiltrated by pale tentacles, squalid liverwort and creeping fungi. The plaza itself, worn bare by feet and pigs, and beaten flat by heavy rains, had been a quagmire for half a century; its soil was a sterile orange-red, as slick as grease.

Through the prism of the mist, the heat of the low jungle sky seemed to focus on this wretched spot, where tarantulas and scorpions and stinging ants accompanied the mosquito and the biting fly into the huts, where the vampire bats, defecating even as they fed, would fasten on exposed toes at night, where one could never be certain that a bushmaster or fer-de-lance had not formed its cold coil in a dark corner. In the river, piranhas swam among the stingrays and candirus and the large crocodilians called lagartos; in adjacent swamps and forests lived the anaconda and the jaguar. But at Remate de Males such creatures were but irritants; the true enemies were the heat and the biting insects, the mud and the nagging fear, more like an ague, of the silent hostile people of the rain forest.

The inhabitants of Remate—ragged woodcutters for the most part, more Indian than not; a small detachment of Quechua soldiers on punishment duty; and the inevitable Syrian or Lebanese trader of the inner rivers who tended to these people's needs in the only shack in good enough repair to close and lock—all vied with one another to tell the Quarriers the latest news of the Niaruna. A party of warriors had appeared only the day before, in a large canoe. They had raised empty hands in sign of peace, then held up otter skins. The storekeeper had ordered the eight Quechuas to hold their fire, and the soldiers were still sullen about this.

"Why would you fire?" Huben said. "You've seen Niarunas here before." He was annoyed that he and Andy had been off downriver, testing the new outboard motor.

The storekeeper shook his head. Not those tame

Niaruna of the padre, he grunted, pointing disdainfully at a small knot of half-clothed Indians at the clearing edge. These had been *bravos* from the inner river.

Huben said, "We are not padres. We are not *católicos.*"

The storekeeper, a fat man of cold resilience, smiled briefly and shrugged his shoulders as if to say, It is all the same to us. He continued his account.

The Indians had been told to come to the bank and to keep their hands on their paddles; the Syrian had no confidence in the soldiers' aim, even on those rare occasions when they were sober. But the Indians would not come in until the soldiers had drawn back; the latter did so after shouting a little and shooting off their rifles into the air. For each otter skin, worth thirty pesos, the Syrian had given a machete worth four and a half; then the Indians withdrew. Out on the river they took up their bows and loosed arrows at the settlement, then slipped quickly to the far bank, paddling upriver in the shadow of the trees. The soldiers came running, firing as they ran, and in the battle a small child suffered a bullet wound in the leg. The Syrian reported to Madre de Dios a new attack by savages on the settlement of Remate de Males, and ordered large quantities of cane alcohol in anticipation of extra soldiers.

Seeing Billy's open-mouthed delight, Hazel shook her untidy head; she then looked bleakly at her husband. He suggested that she and Billy walk around while he and the Hubens saw to their lodgings. "Didn't I tell you?" Huben crowed. "Madre de Dios is like Omaha compared to this!"

Hazel and Billy had not been gone ten minutes when he heard her scream; she came rushing back to the Syrian's store, Billy in tow, her rough hair so disheveled that she looked mad. "This is no place for a child!" she gasped at him, as an admiring audience of halfbreeds fell into place behind her. "These people— why, they're monsters!" The monsters grinned shy monstrous grins, the cuffs of their pants slack in the mud.

One man had a small marmoset on his shoulder; its black head was pressed close to his own, like a demon whispering in his ear.

A drunken man in a canoe along the bank had called out to Billy, laughing evilly and pointing at the water; evidently he was suggesting that Billy would make a tasty meal for the piranhas. When she told the child to pay no attention to him, the man felt insulted. He shouted after them, and when they turned, seized a live chicken from the bottom of the canoe and tossed it into the water, causing his own wife to scream at him. Billy stared in fascination as the chicken, fluttering futilely, became soaked and began to drown. The piranhas did not appear, and the people on the bank laughed at the drunken man. Enraged, he jumped out of the canoe and grabbed a tame trumpeter bird which was picking along the water. Taking its legs, one in each hand, he ripped the flapping thing almost in half, then tossed it out after the chicken.

"Oh boy, Pa, you should've seen it!" Billy cried, unable to contain himself any longer. "Wow! The whole water kind of got all wrinkled and then there was this kind of little noise, you know, like *chopping,* and it got all red in the water and everything, and that old bird was gone and the chicken too—they went after the chicken too. And then—"

But here he stopped, for Hazel slapped him. "You see!" she cried. "You see what's happening to him! And now you want to take him even further into this awful jungle, to see still more dreadful things, more cruelty and filth! And you're risking his life—our lives!"

The Syrian, Señor Haddad, belched.

Quarrier took her by the shoulders. He had seen relish in Billy's face but he had also seen a kind of triumph in Hazel's eyes, the triumph of right, of the avenging angel. "You are free to go home," he said. "I won't hold it against you."

"Yes, that's it!" Hazel cried. "You want *me* to take the responsibility! Well, I won't do it!" She glanced at Andy Huben, who had come running at her scream and was now trying to slip away. "We are your family! We'll go where you lead us, Mister Quarrier!" She folded her big arms upon her chest, with an air that said that on the moral battlefield she was ready to take on all comers.

"I never doubted it," Quarrier said. When Andy had led Billy off to show him the tame Niaruna, he said to Hazel, "From now on, I'll also take the responsibility for disciplining Billy; I never did like to see a child slapped in the face."

Hazel startled him by cringing; she drew her arms up toward her face and moaned. He had never seen this gesture in all the ten years of their marriage; unable to look at it, he turned away. His eyes met the flat gaze of the merchant. Though the Syrian did not speak English, he had been interested in the exchange and had felt no inclination to avert his eye. Now he opened his bad mouth to smile, and shrugged his shoulders. Once this man had exclaimed to Huben that if the Niaruna could be given a taste for beads and liquor, their conversion would become a simple matter—why, look at the Tiro, he had said. But he had since become more philosophical about the stupidity of missionaries, and went on about his business without complaint. He had already amassed a considerable amount of money, in part through enterprise—his Tiro had shown him that the green pinfeathers of the common parrot would emerge yellow if dyed with toad-skin fluid, and he now sent quantities of rare yellow-headed parrots across the mountains—and in part because he preferred to live alone in squalor rather than spend his savings. The Syrian had no hope, no heirs, no joy, and yet he was content.

Señor Haddad, that same evening, sat with the missionaries around the crude table on the earthen floor of his store, gazing unhappily at his hissing lantern, which was consuming fuel. Because the community was lightless, its hours were the hours of day, but since he had sold them supplies and rented a shed to them which otherwise would have gone empty, he did not feel he could turn the lantern off under their noses. Quarrier was watching the avid face, flat and hollow like a soft balloon, when Huben pointed at the corner.

The tarantula did not make Hazel scream; she closed her eyes and shuddered, and Andy said, "Oh, goodness." Haddad picked up a flask of kerosene used for the lamp. Without leaving his seat, he jerked some liquid out toward the spider. When it was drenched, he flicked a match toward the spot where it backed around in a half-circle, all hair and knees, probing the spatter of kerosene with its bent legs. Hazel cried out at the same instant that the Syrian laughed, for the spider had ignited; the small flame ran a yard or more before exploding quietly, in a soft puff.

Quarrier did not know whether Hazel's cry was a delayed reaction to the spider or a reaction to the Syrian, or to the fact, suggested by the man's strange skill, that tarantulas were commonplace and that dealing with them in this manner was less hardihood than sport. It did not matter. Remate de Males might break her nerve entirely, and he dreaded the night, the hammock slung in the open shed, the night cries of unknown creatures, the brown water and the vile open latrine.

The four adults lay side by side, guts rumbling with fried manioc and beans, and listened to the drunken singing of sad mountain *huainus* by the soldiers across the clearing. The unseemliness of the sleeping arrangement had been outweighed, even for Hazel, by the lack of choice, and by the fact that the child, in all his innocence, was there to serve as a rein on lustful thoughts. They had searched the shed with a flashlight for night beasts and had fallen back, disheartened, before the swarms of giant roaches. Hazel had lain down to her rest without a murmur, but even in this blackest darkness Quarrier knew that she was rigid as a corpse, that one more provocation from the jungle would make her scream again and that one day she might not stop.

Yet he could scarcely keep his mind on her; it

turned insatiably to Andy Huben, who actually lay there in the same room with him, only a few feet away. He ached with a longing that was not lust and he ached with guilt; he could not sleep. Then he thought about what awaited them, and the fear grabbed his stomach and would not let go. He peered at his watch again: it was past midnight. Tomorrow had come, when they would go up the Espíritu. The small band of Niaruna led by Kori—the people related to Yoyo by marriage—would follow them upriver to the mission, and they would also take from the Remate garrison four Quechuas, known to the jungle tribes because of their uniforms as the "Green Indians."

Haddad's mosquito netting had a strange and acrid smell; just outside its close thick heat, the night insects whined. Quarrier slept fitfully. When daylight came, they rose exhausted in the cold jungle dawn, to a breakfast of watery *lima* fruit and a little farina meal mixed with hot water.

Four soldiers were hunted out and separated from their companions; if the four who were finally delivered in a mute and pitiable condition to the boats were not the same men assigned to the trip the day before, they were at least indistinguishable. They were Quechuas of the sierra, slack in the jaw and purple-skinned, with yellow eyes and stumpy mountain legs. The bleak gloom absorbed from their native tundra had been deepened by exposure to the jungle. All of them were full of drink, but the drunkenness only made them appear more brutish and unhappy. Quarrier nodded at them and smiled, and they retreated, bumping into one another like cattle; one of them crossed himself.

"They must think we're demons," Quarrier said sadly. "I wonder how the padre persuaded them to go." He thought with sympathy of Padre Xantes, who had had to countersign Guzmán's signature on the note to the corporal at Remate.

"They have no choice," Huben said. "The Quechuas have never had a choice about anything. The

Opposition has only used them, just as the Incas used them—they are a meek and stupid people."

"And shall they inherit the earth?" His own remark made Quarrier uncomfortable. Quickly he said, "Are they really stupid, do you think, or just resigned?"

"What's the difference?" Huben's ironic smile made Quarrier still more uncomfortable, and he turned away. He thought about his reservation Sioux, the terrible apathy of hopelessness that the white man preferred to call laziness and stupidity.

Billy was already in the bow of the canoe when Hazel came from the latrine; she was ashen. She would not tell Quarrier what the matter was; it was just too awful, too disgusting. But later she said that she had seen two giant frogs or toads squatting half buried in the fecal muck. Trapped in the water of the pit, they had grown fat on the swarming flies and were living out their lives buried in excrement.

"They live in it," Hazel choked. "They *live* in it. Why, no North Dakota frog could possibly—oh, this vile place!"

He tried to laugh, to tease her about clean-living North Dakota frogs, but she would not be comforted. She sat trembling in the morning chill, teeth chattering, all hunched in upon herself.

He wondered if Andy Huben had seen the frogs.

In the early mist the people stood in deferential rows, wide-eyed like children; their murmurings were as gentle and soft as water. Padre Xantes on his monthly visits had taught them that the *evangélicos* were evil; still, the people did not expect to see these *evangélicos* alive again, and one or two were moved to call *"Suerte!"*

"What are they saying?" Hazel demanded, glaring at them until they backed away.

"They are wishing us good luck," her husband said. He climbed clumsily into the second canoe, a long black craft hollowed out of a single trunk and powered by the ancient forerunner of Huben's new white outboard. The canoe already held Billy and

Hazel and supplies, in addition to two soldiers with their kits and carbines.

Huben had a similar load, but with its new out-board, his boat would be faster. This was the motor sent with the blessing of Leslie's sponsors in Wisconsin; before departing the United States, it had had its photograph in *Mission Fields*. Now that he had his outboard, Leslie prayed almost daily for barbed wire to fence the mission hut so that the Indians, with their lice and smoky smell and dirty fingers, would give them a little privacy.

Leslie wore black basketball sneakers, a red baseball cap on his taffy hair, and a T-shirt tucked into lastex bathing tights pulled up above his waist, so that, with his short torso and long legs, he looked like a high-hipped boy; the golden hair and soft tan of those legs—Hazel said that they reminded her of a pullet—caught the dull light reflected from the river. On the lap of his wife, seated facing him, was his new short-wave radio, which invoked for its proud owner friendly voices from all corners of the globe. This morning he had summoned up American music from Panama, popular tunes to which he crooned accompaniment. The music wandered on the river in the thick cotton mists of dawn; it rose, fragmented, through the roar as he cranked his motor.

Now Leslie stood up in the stern, and spreading his arms far and wide, cried, "Praise the Lord!"

"Praise the Lord," said Hazel, chin out, dogged-ly. She sat opposite her husband, facing the motor.

Maneuvering his boat into Huben's wake, Quarrier waved to the people on the bank; they did not wave back. He was depressed by the settlement Indians, by the filthy pants, the rotting undershirts of their deliverance. The weakest and most opportunistic people in a wild tribe were those who prospered under the white man—a fact no less true because Lewis Moon, in their conversation that night in Madre de Dios, had made this point. He was glad to leave Remate, as he had been glad to leave Madre de Dios.

There were chambers of cold air upon the river. He was tired and nervous and cold, and shook so violently that he could scarcely steer. When the canoes had rounded the first bend and Remate had disappeared from view, he nodded to Hazel and they prayed. One hand on the outboard tiller, the other to his forehead, he prayed that the Lord would bless them and keep them, that His work might be done, Amen. She prayed dutifully for the health and safety of His servants, Leslie and Andy, that they too might work for the Glory of the Lord, Amen. He watched her as she prayed. How grotesque and right it was that at this moment, stubbornly erect, borne against her will into the hated jungle, she should be facing *backward*—this poor great mule of a woman, he thought, with the last grace kicked out of her.

He said, "Almighty God, we pray for Lewis Moon—"

"No!"

"—that he be still alive, and that he may walk safely from the wilderness, to seek his own salvation in Thine eyes, Amen."

She spoke in hate: "I'd pray for Guzmán first!"

From the river rose sad supplicating limbs of submerged trees, writhing and shivering in the current; on a sand bar at the bend ahead a pale caiman five feet long lay with its jaws agape, straining to swallow a sword of light which pierced the green escarpments. At the approach of Huben's motor it rose on its short legs and ran, carrying its body clear of the ground, like two men borne forward by a heavy log which they are about to drop; headlong and obscene, it plunged into the current. A thrash of its armored tail and it was gone, leaving a soft spreading welt on the slow water.

At Billy's shout she had turned her head in time to see the reptile, and was gagging.

"They're harmless, Hazel. They say only the black crocodiles are dangerous."

"The crocodiles," she muttered. "The *black* ones.

146

Where are *they?*" She fixed her eyes on the big red hands folded tightly on her lap. He did not want those hands to touch him, ever again.

A scent of the jungle caught him unaware; he stared at the engulfing trees. Perhaps the canoes were being watched, had been watched since they left Remate. But this was Tiro country, after all, and the Tiro had been tame for many years; like the Quechua, they had made their peace with exploitation. At the same time one never knew what impulse might seize this people, whose resilience must have its snapping point, and for whom, unlike the Niaruna, stealth and treachery ranked high among the virtues; on this narrow river it would be the work of moments to fill the chests of the Lord's ambassadors with arrows. Having hidden any food and valuables, the Tiro could then paddle downriver to Remate with the news of another Niaruna massacre.

Quarrier stared at Billy's small eager body pressed into the bow. Perhaps the only thing staying the Tiro hand was that the idea had not occurred to them. He shuddered violently with cold. A need for peace came over him; he had an impulse to cut the motor of the boat and drift silently backward into green oblivion, letting his hand trail in the cool water.

Along the river banks where sun had touched the earth, wild walls of flowering trees and shrubs sprang up on every side: pea vines with yellow flowers, stilt-root garcinias and spiny palms, myrtles, cecropias and acacias, pineapple, and plantains with their scarlet blossoms. Hazel pointed at the pea vines, wondering if the fruit in the pods tasted anything like the garden pea. She also recognized deer callaloo, with its edible greens, but when Quarrier angled over to the banks to let her pick some, she held them in her hands suspiciously, then dropped them into the water. "It's some foreign kind of pokeberry, like we have home, but different," she muttered. "I don't trust it." And she relapsed into her dejection, though Billy sought frantically to bring her back, pointing out bright barbets, jacamars and tanagers which crossed back and forth in front of them; he shouted as a stream of parakeets spun around a treetop, and a small, somehow familiar emerald bird bounded from limb to limb ahead. "A kingfisher!" Billy called. "Lookit that funny kingfisher!" They saw huge ant nests high up on the trunks, and the hanging nests of the caciques and oro-péndolas: "Lookit the giant orioles!" But Billy's voice was deadened by the motors, and as the sun rose higher the birds and colors vanished, like the mist. Hazel had long since turned to stone, and the child stopped calling.

They went on into the growing day, up the brown river, the green canyons. The dry season had already begun; the river was shoal in places, with sand bars lengthening at the bends, and sunken trees emerging like great black feeding reptiles of another age.

A spotted sandpiper bobbed and teetered; when it flitted off—*peet-weet*—Hazel cried out in recognition of this gentle bird from home and burst into tears. The Quechuas swung slowly around to grunt and peer and gape. When Quarrier smiled at him, Billy glanced at his mother, shrugged in an effort to look unconcerned, and turned away again.

The wan glaze of the strip of sky over their heads had clouded to vapor above the trees, and the fierce greens had softened, thickened, closing off all sound; the motor's roar rebounded from the green, defeated by the weight of stillness. In this world gone dead Quarrier saw a sloth, pressed to a high trunk for camouflage. Eyes fixed on the tree, he reached out to touch his wife, then turned when he did not find her; his hand was wavering near her breast and she watched it without expression. The boat jumped a sunken tree and yawed around, sluicing a spray of water across their legs; it plowed into a canebrake at the bank, and the motor stalled.

Over Hazel's shoulder, in the sudden silence, he met the gaze of the Green Indians. He grinned. *"Muy estúpido,"* he said. They did not smile back. Nor did Hazel; her face was straining, but she could not help him. Billy's careless whistling, well meant, was thin and airy, and pained Quarrier worst of all.

"There was a sloth," he said, "up in that tree." He pointed.

She nodded, brushing aimlessly at her wet skirt.

"I wanted you and Billy to see it."

She nodded again, and he dropped his eyes in fear of the smile that she would force. Now the river silence he had longed for was unbearable; he yanked violently at the cranking rope, twice, three times, four, rocking the boat with the misspent strength of his own clumsiness.

They reached the abandoned settlement at Esperanza as the sun, shrouded by the pall, slid across the narrow avenue of sky between the treetops. In 1912 the Niaruna, enraged by the brutality of the white man, had put aside their inter-village quarrels and banded together to destroy this place; there had been three survivors. The old rubber camp had lain at a confluence of streams, and the last trace of it was a banana grove gone wild; after the massacre a metal cross had been erected on the bank. The memorial was ten feet high, on a concrete base, and for a time it had apparently been tended. But now the vines were so thick upon it that only one arm protruded through the green; it had lost its form and soon would be difficult to find. Quarrier yelled at Huben, "Shall we stop and clean that cross?" but Huben said, "That papist cross?" and shook his head.

The Niaruna station was a two-hour journey above the Esperanza ruin. Perched on a bank of rufous clay above a river bend, the mission shed was visible a quarter-mile downstream. Both Tiro and Niaruna recognized the place as a frontier, which the Niaruna, but not the Tiro, crossed at will.

Now the clearing came into view. On both sides

were plantations of manioc; well, Quarrier thought, Padre Fuentes was here long enough to plant. Then he stared at the mission bank in disbelief.

"Hey, Pa!" Billy turned around, mouth open, frightened. "Pa!"

Now Huben saw what they had seen; he slowed his motor, then circled back and came up alongside the second boat.

"This could be very good," he said, "or very, very bad."

Quarrier was glad of Huben's coolness. In plain view on the bank stood a party of Niaruna, fourteen men, each with his black bow of chonta palm and long cane arrows. The bright black hair on the brown shoulders was arrayed in fur and feathers, and the faces and chests were streaked in bold patterns of red-orange dye. Another band of red wound up each muscled leg—the serpent. Except for a fiber band which held the penis of each man pressed to his belly, the savages were naked; but at the end of the line, also in face paint and carrying bow and arrows, was a barefoot Indian dressed in shirt and pants too big for him, and wearing on his head the dark blue neckerchief which the missionaries recognized as that of Lewis Moon.

The boats slid forward, slow against the current; the Green Indians cocked their rifles. Hazel Quarrier leaned forward and dragged Billy back across the seats into the stern. "May the Lord forgive him," she said. "May he rest in peace."

"Amen," Huben said. "He who lives by the sword, right?"

"Oh Leslie," Andy cried. "You needn't gloat!"

"Suppose they try to drive us off," Quarrier said irritably. "Are you going to shoot?" One of the two soldiers in his canoe, still half drunk, leveled his rifle, and Quarrier shouted at him; gazing back at the missionary with yellowed eyes, the soldier opened his mouth wide and probed the front side of his lower teeth with a slow tongue.

"We will shoot into the air," said Huben. "Let us pray . . .

> *. . . Thou shalt not be afraid for*
> *the terror by night; nor for the*
> *arrow that flieth by day;*
> *"Nor for the pestilence that*
> *walketh in darkness; nor for the*
> *destruction that wasteth at noonday. . . ."*

The Indians stood rigid as the boats approached. Their naked silence was so close, so overpowering that the women turned their heads away. All prayed. The Indians had raised their bows when the soldier raised his rifle; they were still tense. Then the warrior in Moon's shirt and pants loosed an arrow which dropped neatly between the boats, causing them to circle once before proceeding.

"Satan is surely among them!" Huben cried. "Even the serpents on their legs—!"

He called out to them in greeting, and the man in the blue neckerchief snapped his head sideways in a gesture of contempt; now he drove two more arrows into the ground, so that they formed an X, facing the missionaries. He then stalked toward the trees.

"Friends!" Huben shouted after them. "We are your friends!" He waved a gift ax that he had grabbed from a pack, but they were gone.

"How did they know we were coming?" Andy spoke to Hazel, trying to smile. "Isn't it strange?"

Hazel did not answer: she held Billy to her breast, muttering fiercely. The boy tried discreetly to work free; he glanced unhappily at his father.

Quarrier said, "Well, what did you think of those wild Indians, son?" His own voice sounded froggish to him; he longed to turn and go, and keep on going.

They stepped gingerly onto the bank, leaving the motors running. But even after they had shut the outboards off and begun the process of unloading, Hazel Quarrier sat stolidly in her seat. When her husband

151   *At Play in the Fields of the Lord*

came and laid his hand upon her shoulder, she raised her eyes and stared about her.

"The *black* ones," Hazel murmured. "Where are *they?*"

12

The feathers of the crossed arrows, trembling in the light air, were all that stirred in the quiet of the clearing. A feathered club leaned like a token barrier in the doorway of the main shelter, a dolefully sagging structure of bamboo and palm fronds. These were bad signs, even to Huben, who liked to dismiss such heathen doings as inconsequential. When Quarrier took the club and stuck it up under the thatching of the roof, Huben demanded, "What are you saving that for?"

"Because it interests me. These warning signs invoke some kind of evil spirits."

"Evil spirits!" Huben exclaimed scornfully. He began a loud casual humming, accompanying his faithful radio which blared away on the far side of the clearing. Quarrier marveled at this man, who was convinced that Moon and Wolfie were possessed by demons, yet could dismiss the Indian equivalents with such conviction. *"Bye, bye, love,"* sang Leslie Huben. The blare of the music was unbearable in the tense silence of the jungle; Quarrier crossed the clearing and snapped off the radio.

"Relax, fella," Huben called.

For a long time after those painted shapes had vanished back into the forest, the missionaries saw no sign of a wild Indian. In the first week they set about clearing the vines, repairing the thatch roofs, weeding the low undergrowth from the yard and freeing the roof cross from the strangler fig that was dragging it to earth.

The plantation of maize and manioc had been looted, and many half-ripe vegetables left to rot. The Indians had taken everything of value except the short-wave radio, which they had hurled into the river; Huben found it in a muddy pool below the bank, the silt swirling past its metal face. They assumed that this pillage had been done by the wild Niaruna, but Quarrier became less certain of this when, three days after their own arrival, Kori's band of outcast Niaruna from Remate appeared in their canoes; too innocent as yet to lie adroitly, they brought suspicion on themselves by the vehemence with which they condemned their brethren. "The people of Boronai," they yelled. "They are still savages! They are not like us!" Kori insisted that Boronai and his savages had been the culprits in the looting, and to prove this he burst into tears right on the spot, out of pure shame that such Niaruna could exist. Huben was annoyed when Quarrier laughed.

Kori's people had been harried toward extinction by stronger clans of their own tribe. Each time they took refuge at Remate they invited the contempt not only of their wild tribesmen but of the Tiro and Mintipo half breeds, who saw their own position threatened; the latter now had rags to wear and bits of broken glass and ribbons, and were only too glad of the opportunity to despise a people they had always feared. They persecuted and harassed Kori's poor hunters, sluttish wives and malcontents, who rapidly lost all confidence and sought to adapt their ways to any group that would tolerate them; self-devouring, they smiled gratefully and indiscriminately from dawn to dark. Kori himself smiled so constantly that Leslie wished to change his name to "Happy," but neither Andy nor the Quarriers shared his confidence in Kori's beatitude, and the christening was given up.

Quarrier was sorry that soldiers had been used to establish the mission, though it was true that the death of Fuentes made a strong case for this precaution;

Padre Fuentes had erected shelters on Tiro ground, imagining that he and the sisters would not be molested so long as they remained outside the Niaruna forest. Huben did not hesitate to claim the place a few months later, and established Kori there almost immediately. It was through Uyuyu, whom Padre Xantes had designated as their shepherd at Remate before leaving for Madre de Dios, that Huben had persuaded Kori and his band to accompany him: how could the padre be angry, Uyuyu said, so long as they wore clothes and thanked the mighty spirit named God-Jesu for their food? He promised them that they would be well fed and safe, and they believed him, having already recognized that Uyuyu was more intelligent than themselves and that he understood much better how things worked. Padre Xantes had given Uyuyu a bright silver cross on a neck chain and trained him as a teacher, and Huben had given Yoyo a bright red gringo shirt with bright blue gringo penises on it. At first Yoyo wore the crucifix outside his shirt, but after Huben told him to throw the crucifix away, he wore it inside.

From the beginning Huben had received support from Guzmán. "The local Comandante is a fair and broad-minded man; the Lord put those entreaties in my mouth which would open his heart to our work here with the Niaruna." These joyful words had appeared in Huben's first letter from the Niaruna, the one read by the Quarriers in *Mission Fields*. And indeed, things had gone very well. Though the wild bands refused to come out of the jungle, they had at least come close enough to steal from the Lord's gardens and they had not attacked. When Huben had gone out to meet the Quarriers a few weeks later, he took the soldiers back with him to Remate, leaving Kori and his band at the new station.

So far as Kori was concerned, the withdrawal of the soldiery had been a bad mistake. Although he agreed heartily with Huben that the mission was perfectly safe—he had learned from Yoyo's prosperous example to agree heartily with the missionary about

155   *At Play in the Fields of the Lord*

everything—he had fled the place a day or two after Huben's departure, taking with him his eight machetes and his silver crucifix, awarded him by his former spiritual adviser, Padre Xantes, in compensation for the two women of his band delivered to the savages as ransom for the nuns. In Remate, throwing the last of his prestige to the winds, Kori had claimed that they were driven out after a furious battle with these savages; but on Huben's return, smiling expansively, he had agreed with Leslie that this impression had been mistaken. He promised to return immediately to the mission on the Espíritu. His people were glad to leave a place where their nakedness had been laughed at and where they had been treated with contempt, not only as savages but as *protestantes.* The charge had only bewildered them, since they had no idea what the word meant.

The first long days were days of hope. Because Quarrier admired Leslie's supreme faith and self-confidence, they worked together very well, hunting food, clearing and planting the mission garden, and teaching the Indians what they could. Leslie was a hard worker and an effective one, far more skillful than Quarrier with tools and plants and shotguns. And Leslie liked work for its own sake, taking strength from it; when his hands were in use, his whole face eased and softened, and a tentative humor would replace his tiresome sense of moral right. With the vanity evaporated, with sweat on his dirty face and his hip-pocket comb forgotten, the face took on a true handsomeness of strength.

They worked on the language late into the evening, and coaxed the Indians toward prayer. The crude chapel they had built—crotched saplings supported its eave pole, the bamboo sides were walled with mud, and the roof bamboos were overlaid with palm fronds—seemed to Quarrier the loveliest building he had ever seen. They restored a small shelter for the Quechuas—Kori and his band had moved back into their own communal *maloca,* a rectangular palm house which, in their spiritual decrepitude, they scarcely bothered to clean out—and they put up a lean-to cookhouse shed; they partitioned the main shed and constructed a stove of baked mud brick that would burn wood. They replanted the manioc and planted papaya and bananas, and every day they went out to the clearing edge and checked the presents for the savages that they had placed on racks raised above ground. The gift racks were set on five-foot poles, not only as a protection against ground insects and animals, but so as to be readily seen; one had been erected on each of the three edges of the clearing, and a fourth a short distance into the jungle, on a faint trail leading eastward.

A time came when the gift racks were emptied each night for a fortnight; they prayed earnestly. Then Billy found his friend Mutu playing with one of the Lord's machetes, and Kori's people were told to return the gifts. Both Huben and Kori were enraged. "Are we not Niaruna too?" Kori howled. "Does God not love us?" When Leslie answered this with a stern lecture about stealing, Kori responded with a violent lecture of his own: Did not his people share with the gringos everything they had? Did not Mutu teach Billy everything he knew? Then why did the gringos lock up their food and knives and tools, and share with the Indians only when they wished the Indians to work or pray? His people had taken the articles from the racks to punish the gringos for their bad manners.

The soldiers were furious that Kori's band might have got away with something, and offered to shoot the entire lot for theft; once again, they muttered, as it had been since the days of the Inca, the faithful Quechuas had been foully used. The Quechua *católicos* and Niaruna *protestantes* stamped and ranted, mutually unintelligible, and by no means clear as to why they had been dragged out to this pesthole in the first place.

Huben planned to return to Madre de Dios after the rainy season, leaving Quarrier in charge at the new station. The prospect made Quarrier uneasy, no less so because Hazel was most anxious that the soldiers stay. Her fear and dislike of the jungle had not overcome her loyalty, if not to her husband, at least to their marriage vows; nevertheless she made it clear that she thought his attitude irresponsible and pig-headed and one which placed the child in danger. Shortly after their arrival at the station on the Espíritu, she had retreated into a vast and unforgiving silence, against the day when disaster would prove her right.

Quarrier told her, in effect: If we sincerely believe that we are here in Jesus' name, then our son must share our responsibility and our risk; if you do not agree, then you must go home with him to North Dakota. Hazel turned on him, started to cry out, raised her fists, dropped them, groaned, blinked, burst into tears and turned away, martyred again. "Is that what you want?" she sobbed. "That's probably exactly what you want! Well, we're not going!"

Hazel was disgusted by Kori and his people, who were constantly underfoot, or rummaging among her things; once when she was trying to sew, Kori's old brother squatted before her, and placing his hands upon her knees, gazed up earnestly into her nostrils, as if to see what made her tick. The next day, having established himself as harmless, he lowered his head to peer beneath her dress, persisting in this until she jabbed him smartly with her needle.

The Indians' nakedness she could accept so long as it seemed innocent; she eventually became resigned to the custom among young mothers of giving suck to dogs, and to loud, public, devil-may-care flatulence. But she decried the wholesale preparation and consumption of their masato beer, to which they devoted nearly half their manioc crop; she tried with no success to teach them that all excess manioc should be reduced to farina meal, which could be bartered in Remate for printed gingham and cotton shorts.

Hazel became obsessed with shorts and dresses, once she perceived how sensual these Indians were.

158

Though they went off into the bushes to make love, they indulged publicly and with much laughter and enthusiasm in erotic games. The girls stroked one another's breasts; the women grabbed the hands of men and clapped them, giggling, to their crotches; casually, young boys masturbated one another. Quarrier himself was shocked. Yet everything was done in great warmth and good spirits. The Indians of all ages touched one another constantly, consolingly, as if to affirm and reaffirm the solidarity of the clan against the night, wild creatures, storm, against dread spirits. He tried hard to convey this idea to Hazel, for he saw that her rigidity confused them and would do harm. On one occasion Hazel struck away the hand of a young woman who was stroking the genitals of her little boy. Seated on the ground, the mother stared at the white woman, astonished.

"But I gave him pleasure!"

With her Indian sensitivity to disapproval, this woman became more and more angry, and her sulking infected the whole band; the Indians grew moody and depressed. Finally the woman and her husband had to be taken downriver to Remate, and Quarrier said to Hazel, "The next time you strike an Indian for any reason, it is you who will be sent away; they do not understand it and it could be very dangerous for us all."

She said, "And Billy? Do you want him watching these filthy tricks? Is that what you want?"

"Unless you tell him they are filthy, it will not occur to him; it will all seem very natural."

"Natural! And if one of those nasty little monkeys puts his hands on him?"

"He might enjoy it," Quarrier said harshly.

Hazel did not know that her son, at eight, was a seasoned voyeur, having accompanied his friend Mutu on innumerable expeditions into the bushes to watch their elders puff and groan and thrash about with one another in the dirt. Billy had not yet connected this engrossing spectacle with the phenomenon of birth, much less suspected that he himself was the product of a similar compulsion on the part of his parents. After his first experience, in fact, he ran to report a wild and fascinating Indian custom to his father—"Boy, Pa, what savages they are!"—describing it as a kind of death struggle between man and woman. "What good does it do them?" he demanded of his father, a little embarrassed now by the details he had suppressed not only because they upset him but because a description of acts so outlandish would never be believed. "You should've seen it! And afterwards they just kind of lay there in the dirt! Grown-up Indians, just laying there looking up at the sky. Like they were trying to remember something. It made me feel so funny." The child's voice grew thick and halting. "Real grownups, the way they *looked*. I felt sorry for them, Pa. I felt so *sorry* for them!" When Quarrier took Billy in his arms, the child burst into tears. "You should've seen it," Billy blubbered. "It was awful."

Quarrier failed to comfort him with the concepts of God and love, the creation of children, human birth. As he began, the little boy was staring at him, innocent, but as the implications gathered, as the realization came that this man beside him had grappled with his own mother in that desperate manner and that, still worse, he himself was the consequence and living proof of such activity, he gradually turned his head away. The nape of his thin neck was fiery with astonishment and shock; Quarrier did not dare touch him. For a long time, father and son sat there together, digesting the ways of the world.

Billy whispered, "You mean, in your *birthday* suits?" He did not turn to see his father nod.

"And Mrs. Huben—she does that with *Mr.* Huben?"

Now Quarrier grew very red himself, and was glad that Billy did not turn around on this occasion either.

"You mean . . ." Billy exclaimed at last, "you mean . . ."—his voice rose high and clear—"you mean. . ."—and he jumped to his feet, and standing there under the giant trees, pointed at himself, a small outraged boy named William Martin Quarrier, aged eight: "You mean I just came crashing down into Ma's *under*pants?"

One day Andy saw a face among the leaves. Catching her breath, she leaned minutely to one side, to be quite certain; the brown face, like a leaf shadow, leaned with her. When she straightened again, it straightened; when she leaned far sideways, it leaned far sideways. She smiled; it did not smile. When she called quietly to Leslie, it disappeared. After that she saw fleeting shadows several times, but they would never answer.

Not understanding about shoes, the savages buried bamboo slivers in the pathway to the gift racks, to pierce the white men's feet; the racks themselves were left untouched. The whites had to assume that wherever they went, whatever they did, eyes watched them; they felt permanently self-conscious and afraid. All they could do was wait, and the wait was endless. Only Billy Quarrier, who played with Mutu and had his own small bow and arrows, welcomed the shadow faces in the trees; the child's bottomless joy in his new life gave strength to all of them, even Hazel, who rarely left the cook shed. There she took solace in the sight of household articles, and hoarded the last of the cheerfully packaged foods from home.

Hazel never tried to penetrate the jungle wall, even to inspect a gift rack, and she had avoided the wall itself since the afternoon when, resting in its shade, she was spied out from directly overhead by monkeys; these animals, after their habit in the presence of invaders, lavishly befouled her, and this so suddenly that it seemed to Hazel that the heavens had opened up and voided on her. She burst into tears when the others laughed.

In a dream that night Hazel stood in a church with a clean simple country altar and stone bowls, and the cold clean light of a late North Dakota autumn

161   *At Play in the Fields of the Lord*

streaming through the glass, and a choir singing. She was lost in the beauty of this experience, and stared enchanted at the choir. But the choir lacked red cheeks and seraphic faces, and its members were not innocent; even as their voices soared they sniggered and itched and hitched soiled cassocks to scratch white hairy legs, and some broke wind. Their faces were loutish and their mouths pimply, and they were passing things around. The flaunting of their frailty in such a place disgusted her and pained her heart, and this pain in her heart was like a wound, and the wound transcended her, forming again as a round opening in the clean granite ceiling of the church, like the base of a chandelier. She gazed up at the vaults of stone to ease her pain, and then the hole opened and spewed slime, which dripped on the stone and glass and silver of the church, and down the singing faces of the choir. But the psalm still swelled throughout the church, and the voices remained brave and pure, and a light shone everywhere, inextinguishable, illuminating the slime itself, transfiguring it, infusing the very stink of it with eternal life.

Hazel was so frightened by this dream that she woke Martin. Oh, how disgusting! My mind—what is happening to me in this place! That hole—do *you* ever dream such sickening things? Does everybody, or is it only me? It was like those monkeys—those creatures with men's faces in the trees . . . Oh Martin, help me, that hole was the hole of God—! She shook her head behind her hands.

But the end of the dream is beautiful, Quarrier said. She was stricken and would not be comforted; he knew that she hated him for having listened, for failing to take her in his arms.

Billy could not find his mother any more; the distance grew between them. He turned more and more to Andy, who loved to play with him. The sight of them, heads together, inspecting odd flowers or small creatures of the jungle, gave Quarrier such pleasure that he scarcely noticed that Hazel watched them too. One day after breakfast, when Andy and Billy were crouched in the dooryard on their knees and elbows, exclaiming at how the sunlight caught the blue of a pet morpho butterfly, Hazel came forth and said to them in a monotone, "That lovely color isn't real. It isn't real." She reached down and pinched off its wing and ground it between her fingertips, then held out her fingertips and muttered, "See, it turns to gray. It's nothing but gray dust. Dust unto dust." In tears, she started back toward the hut as the butterfly flopped along the ground in a crippled circle.

"Now Hazel, honey . . ." Martin started, much upset.

"Well, that was silly of you, Hazel, I must say!" Andy jumped up, shaking off Martin's hand. But if Hazel had heard she gave no sign, going on into the hut. "It doesn't help her to indulge her, Martin," Andy said coldly. Seeing the child's face, she groaned with exasperation, and sank to her knees and hugged him. "If we start giving way to our nerves like that, we're all going to be in trouble," she warned Quarrier over the child's shoulder. "If there's a way to reach her, you'd better find it."

"If you'll excuse me, you seem a bit on edge yourself."

"That's right! We're *all* on edge! And small wonder—we're not idiots! But even a slap across the face can be more help and comfort sometimes than 'Now Hazel, honey'; it can bring you back among the living." Her voice trailed off; Billy was watching them.

"She's gone *crazy!*" Billy muttered tearfully. "I hate her!" Andy managed a little laugh and whirled the boy off the ground, and his father said, "Don't blame your mother, Bill. She's feeling kind of peaked in this heat."

He had never called him Bill before, intending it now as an appeal and compliment, and Billy nodded. "Sure," he said, "it's kind of hot, all right." Self-conscious in this mature role, he twisted rudely from Andy's embrace and snatched up the butterfly, handling it roughly.

"Where are you going?" Andy said.

"Give this stupid old butterfly to Mutu. The Indians will know what to do." He ran off toward the shelters, where the crippled butterfly would be replaced by one of a litter of wild pets. The Indians could tame practically everything but Jaguar and Scorpion and Sloth, who was always climbing. Sloth's wits were too slow, the Indians said, for it to realize that it could not climb to heaven.

"He's had to grow up a little, poor old Billy," Martin said, and was startled by the sharp look that Andy gave him; she had changed since they came here, too.

"Who hasn't?" she said. She followed Hazel into the Quarriers' quarters.

Though he dreaded her departure, Martin knew he would be happier with Andy gone. Her presence was not worth the distraction she brought him. Or rather, it *was* worth it, and this made him feel guilty. He watched her constantly, observed her smallest way and habit, and could not give up his vice even when he realized that Hazel knew. How could he explain to Hazel that he loved Andy as anyone might love a pretty child, as unattainable as an angel? True, he had once imagined himself in love with Andy, but surely that was only an evasion of unhappiness; the girl was a kind of lovely wraith that he had shaped to fit his need.

And he and Leslie, though much closer than before, would never work well together among Indians. When the wild bands were contacted, Leslie intended to infect them with a need for cloth and beads, mirrors and ax heads. Once this need was established, their exposure to the Gospel would be assured, and conversion would simply be a matter of time. It was a basic method, used by missionaries across the world, but to Quarrier it reeked of coercion. How did it differ,

164

he asked Leslie, from the alcohol tactic suggested by the Syrian at Remate, which Huben had disdained? Call it economic pressure or call it bribery—would Jesus have approved it? Look at the people of Remate; was *that* what Salvation meant?

Victims of the Opposition, Huben said.

Well, how about Kori? So far as Quarrier could see, the Niaruna of Kori had no real idea of God, either Catholic or Protestant; they mouthed the few religious terms they knew in return for food and care. Leslie had weaned Kori from his extravagant adoration of the Catholic Blessed Virgin, replacing Her in the old man's imagination with the concept of a good old-fashioned Hell, and these days Kori, without provocation, would smile beatifically and say, "Fire Place no go, all time, all time stay good, Amen." Kori was a tall lean-faced old man with a gratifying dignity of feature, and his photograph was to accompany Leslie's next letter to *Mission Fields*.

Quarrier intended to start clean, having inherited from his father, an old-time missionary in China, a mistrust of the "rice Christian," lured to the faith by food. The one lasting method of conversion, he felt certain, was to lead them out of the darkness by Christian example—the food and medicine and time should be given freely. He would not bribe the Indians to love Jesus, nor force them into Christian marriage. One night, excited, he declaimed at supper that marriage might be *bad* for jungle Indians, since their chronic malaria was thought to reduce fertility; the more various the pairings, the less chance of extinction. Hazel sent Billy out-of-doors; to judge from her expression, extinction was a far, far better state than sin.

Finally, Quarrier disliked the presence in the camp of four Quechua soldiers, with their dim notions of Catholicism—not that the Quechuas and Kori's Niaruna mixed, for the soldiers, given their heads, would have shot down their compatriots at a moment's notice. But he felt certain that the wild bands would not come in so long as the soldiers were in camp;

he asked Leslie to take the Quechuas away. He felt perfectly safe without the soldiers, he said; if the mission had not been attacked in the first month, the chances were that it would not be attacked at all. Kori, when asked by Huben if he agreed, nodded vigorously, for it was his principle to agree with everything the gringo said and with nothing said by his own people, of whom he was deeply ashamed.

Quarrier felt well-nigh omnipotent at the prospect of his own calling. Even the jungle excited him, especially in those mysteries of early day, with the huge trees shifting in the sun and vapors like tattered masts, the dense smell of flowers from the river walls, the cool clear bells of the forest voices and the thunder of red howler monkeys, like oncoming storm. Hunting along the river, he and Leslie and Billy had started wild pig and capybara from the banks and sand bars, and had glimpsed an ocelot and a shy tapir. The birds like jewels, the kaleidoscopic butterflies, the banks of pink mimosa and purple tonka bean astonished him; the jungle seemed a kind of Eden. Billy was so excited that his happy voice seemed part of the clear forest triumph, absorbed and refracted, echoing back.

Then the rains came crashing down, and in the humid spells between, Quarrier knew what Hazel dreaded: the oppression of the jungle, the poisonous green flesh and weight of it. Its latent violence crawled on his skin like fever, causing him to shake and sweat.

The rains had scarcely ceased when the Hubens left, taking the soldiers with them. In his doubts about this day, Quarrier had all but put it from his mind, and he found himself unprepared to see them off. He still had need of Huben's experience and assistance, and most of all of Huben's faith. Staring down into Andy's wistful face as she smiled up at him from the canoe, he knew that she was going off with part of him attached to her, as if his body would be subtly torn, as if he would now slowly bleed to death. To hide his agony from his wife, he played the fool, taking the risk that Hazel would interpret his noisy cheer as last-minute

166

doubt about the advisability of sending back the soldiers. The Quechuas yawned at him from the canoe,
unmoved by his wave of parting.

Leslie cried, "God bless the Mart Quarrier Family!
You have the Almighty command to *go!*" Andy Huben
called, "God bless you." Her face was still misted by
her parting with Billy, who was so hurt and disap-
pointed by her desertion that he had spoken rudely and
was now throwing mud balls out into the river, close
to her canoe.

Quarrier knew what his son was feeling; he felt
like throwing mud balls of his own. Himself in need, he
could not help his wife, whose emotion was causing
her to pant. Red hands clasped white, she stood flat-
footed in her best black shoes and dress of hearts and
roses, staring at all of them as if they were a pack of
hostile strangers. What's happening? her wild eyes
seemed to cry.

Leslie gunned his motor, and the overloaded dugout turned downstream. Even after the Hubens had disappeared, the river was watched by the Mart Quarrier
Family. Standing there as the silence grew, they could
not look at one another, and hardly spoke for the re-
mainder of that day.

The jungle walls had crowded in much closer.
Kori looked furtive; the mission might be under
scrutiny at this very moment. The wild men were right
there behind the trees, doubtless plotting an attack
now that the soldiers had departed. For the first time
in days Quarrier remembered the fate of poor Fuentes,
in this very place. So nervous was he that he had to
force himself to check the gift racks, and he felt exhausted by his effort to show calm for Hazel's benefit.
But his wife's morale had risen with the departure of
the Hubens; she worked busily, almost cheerfully. And
while he was grateful for this change, he found it
strange—was this the cheerfulness, he wondered, of
the Christian martyrs? Watching Billy, he was racked
with doubt about his decision to dismiss the soldiers,
and prayed twice during the day for Divine counsel.

167   *At Play in the Fields of the Lord*

He was awakened a few days later by a high whining angry singsong from the clearing. Kori, facing the jungle wall, was speaking too rapidly for Martin to follow. When the old man finished, a voice came back out of the jungle, also in rapid singsong and also angry; this voice was not whining. Dressing clumsily, in haste, Quarrier came out into the clearing, holding his hands clear of his sides to show that he was unarmed.

A naked man stepped forth out of the shadows. He was a strong, stolid Indian of middle age, in a crown of monkey fur and toucan feathers, arm bands of fiber and hide ankle thongs, with a necklace of two jaguar incisors set back to back, tips to each side, and a fiber band strapping his penis upright to his belly. His rectangular face was streaked with red *achote,* and twin serpents were painted on his legs. He was followed a moment later by two younger men. The savages carried short lances and bows and arrows, and all three gazed unrelentingly at Quarrier as he walked forward.

In a thick voice he called out, "Welcome! Welcome to the Niaruna people! Welcome, friends!" He had rehearsed this greeting many times, but now it resounded in his ears as false and frightened. Kori gesticulated angrily, then folded his arms on his chest; his people chattered nervously among themselves. In the half-dressed state imposed upon them by the missionaries, Kori's people lacked any dignity: the eight men in ragged trousers fell back before the three wild Niaruna from the jungle, who showed their contempt by disregarding them. The savages did not respond to Quarrier's greeting, but neither did they retreat as he walked toward them.

Over his shoulder Quarrier called to Billy to bring three machetes and a mirror; the boy came flying, barefoot and unbuttoned. When Quarrier took the gifts from him, the man in the monkey crown grunted and snapped his head, chattering rapidly at Kori; Kori yelled out in his dreadful Spanish that Boronai wished

168

to receive the gifts from the child. Billy retrieved the three machetes, which he carried against his chest like logs of wood, and his father laid the mirror on top of them, instructing him to give the mirror to the man wearing the crown. In this instant the vulnerability and beauty of his little boy, mouth wide, eyes shining with good will and expectation, took Quarrier's breath away; he wished to say something to his son, but there was nothing to be said.

Billy ran forward, and unable to see the ground, sprawled on his face; the Indians in both groups laughed. But when Quarrier approached to make sure that Billy had not cut himself, the naked men raised their bows. Quarrier stopped. Then, ignoring a shout from Kori, he moved forward again, holding his arms wide, and helped Billy to his feet; the latter, unhurt, had gathered the gifts while still on his knees, but could not rise under the load.

The Indians lowered their bows. When the mirror and machetes were delivered, the man removed the monkey crown from his own head and placed it on the head of Billy. The child fled back toward his father, leaping like a goat. But Boronai stopped smiling when the white man extended his hand toward the Indians; again Kori called, *"Gringo, no vengas."*

Hazel came out with a large bowl of rice. She walked without a tremor, and Quarrier smiled at her in a flood of gratitude and admiration. She did not flinch when one of the younger savages pointed at her and then at Quarrier, and resting his weapons on his shoulder, jammed one forefinger back and forth through the fingers of his other hand, nudging his companion as he did so. She placed the bowl upon the ground, between her husband and the Indians, then retired out of sight.

Quarrier sat down before the bowl, his son beside him. Pointing at it, he made an eating motion with his fingertips. The three savages came forward and squatted on their haunches; one shifted sideways to keep an eye on Kori's men. When Kori himself approached the feast, this young warrior raised his lance as to a dog. Kori yelled at him, but came no farther.

Quarrier was dry-mouthed with excitement, and a vast relief poured through his body. Exultantly he said to Billy, "The Lord be praised, Bill—oh, the Lord be praised!" Billy whispered, "These are real ones, you found the *real* ones—that's more than Mr. Huben did!" The child's words made him laugh aloud; he recognized the happiest moment of his life.

Then the hard-faced young Indian who had driven Kori from the feast reached forward with his new machete and jabbed Quarrier sharply in the chest; Boronai and the other man, who had stopped eating, grunted in angry approval. For in his excitement, in his conviction that the Lord had blessed his decision to dismiss the soldiers, that for the first time in his ten years of mission work he had actually accomplished something in Jesus' name, Quarrier had so forgotten his own knowledge of Indian ways as to reach into the bowl of rice; he had had some vague idea of demonstrating that the food was not poisoned. When the Indian jabbed the steel into his chest, he dropped the rice slowly back into the bowl and despite his pain tried to smile; at the same time he grasped Billy's arm, for the child had reached to stop the blade.

The Indian's face was taut with a hostility beyond anything that Quarrier had ever seen—a flat hard squint between the fierce bands of charcoal and livid paint that made the wild eyes vibrate. The gaze horrified Quarrier; he sat there, faint and stupid in the sunlight, feeling the warm blood trickle down his chest.

13

He drifted down a vast blue sky toward the morning.

The empty plane slid peacefully away, back toward the west. He mourned it: a derelict ship could be commandeered, but a derelict plane was irredeemable, droning blindly toward oblivion. It was as if such a machine would never strike the ground, but must vanish soundlessly in some far corner of the heavens, in a burst of sun. He was still a mile above the ground when the engine sputtered, coughed, sputtered again and failed, and in the enormous silence of the sky he watched his plane fall off the edge of life into its final glide. The spectacle gave him a turn of vague uneasiness; the machine had only come alive as it was about to die.

The rush of silence in the wake of the dead engine left him face to face with his own apprehension; his remarkable plight startled him so that he cleared his throat to assure himself of his reality. A few hours before, he could not have distinguished reality from hallucination, and the one thing that persuaded him that he could do so now was his awareness that were he not still under the effects of *ayahuasca,* his lack of regret at this very moment could only be insane. For here he was, on this fine morning, coming down from the sky in a parachute into which he was not even strapped, with a mile to go on the strength of arms already in such pain that they felt broken; unless he

At Play in the Fields of the Lord

bound them more securely in the back harness, he was not sure they would hold out, and if he did bind them, he would be unable to work the shrouds to steer the parachute and would lose his chance, already remote, of landing in the Niaruna clearing.

High in the sun-white and whirling blue, he struggled to work a loop of harness over his shoulders and up under his arms. A twisted shroud bound the revolver tight against his ribs, and the metal hurt him; he wished he had thrown it away. Spurts of fear robbed him of strength. He rested a moment, then brought his knees up to his chin and got one leg through a second loop, an arrangement which turned him on his side, like a trussed chicken. This freed his arms to seize the shrouds; he was now able to haul himself upward to a better angle. In this way, tied in knots, he continued his descent.

The airplane, still visible, was dropping as lightly as a leaf; it would disappear into the forest without a sound.

He hauled mightily on the shrouds nearest the clearing. The day was windless, but there had been currents in the upper air that he had not gauged; he would fall short. He slacked off on the near shrouds and hauled hard on the back ones, for if he had to fall short, he had better fall far enough away to give himself a little time; dangling from trees at the clearing edge while the Niaruna shot arrows at him was only the most unpleasant of the variations on his own death which now confronted him.

This much was in his favor: the Niaruna were in awe of the plane and therefore of the man who came to them out of the sky; if this coming were accompanied by the explosion of the plane, by the only loud sound they could ever have heard on a clear day, so much the better. And the mere sight of the parachute's great white canopy should insure a respectful welcome; if he comported himself properly, they would have to accept him as some sort of deity.

At the same time, his safety now or later was so

uncertain that the calm he felt must spring from another source. Was it the *ayahuasca* then? He did not
think so, for the shock of the jump, with the struggles
of the descent, had sobered him to the bone.

Swaying down out of the sun, with the calls of
strange birds and the faint shreds of savage voices rising to meet him, he watched the plane crash as he had
prophesied, in silence, in the distance, leaving the
canopy through which it plunged all but unscarred, as
if it had dived beneath the sea. There was only a thin
plume of smoke, invisible to the Indians, for with the
wing tanks empty, the explosives had survived the
crash. And this was bad luck, for the plane had banked
in its descent and had come down no more than a mile
beyond the village.

By rough estimate he would strike perhaps a quarter-mile short of the clearing, near the river; there was
a pocket in the trees on his line of drift, and he steered
for that. The Indians were still in view, running and
howling like goblins; two men started across the clearing in his direction, then ran back again.

First the river, then the clearing disappeared. He
saw the far wall of the clearing, then the rolling greens,
still sparkling with dew—green leaves, blue sky, a
bright red bird. He worked his leg out of the strap before the trees rushed up to seize him; he dropped
through the canopy into the shadows. His knees were
bent for the roll and tumble when the chute caught
on the middle tiers and stopped him short; stunned by
the jolt, he swung helplessly in the forest gloom, some
thirty feet above the ground.

In the seconds that he hung there, straining to
hear if the shrieking and jabbering were coming closer,
the explosives in the airplane ignited. Though the roar
was muted by the weight of vegetation, a thunder rum-
bled through the forest, stirring the leaves and echoing
dully in the naves and somber avenues. When it had
passed, there came a silence so complete that a faint
rain of twig fragments on leaves a hundred feet above
his head was clearly audible.

He was delighted, like a little boy astonished that his plan has worked; high in the air he cheered. But a moment later he was shocked by the irrelevance of his own voice in this huge and awesome silence. A wood moth with large eyes on its wings danced past his face as if he did not exist, and down the forest came the *tee-tee-too* of a cotinga; its live green flicked between dark trunks and was swallowed up again.

He worked quickly to free himself. Then he was hanging from the harness by his hands. He raised his knees in order to strike the ground with his legs bent, winced in advance, and dropped. He hit and rolled in the soft humus of the forest floor, clambering to his feet in the same instant and pitching toward a shelter of high buttressed roots. He crouched there, his heart pounding, the revolver in his hand.

In the first awareness of the object in his hand, he came close to panic. Far from reassuring him, the revolver reminded him of his helplessness; its cold touch had broken through some vague protective spell. He pressed back against the roots. Alone in this darkness, with nowhere to hide, nowhere to flee, he felt like a creature fallen down a well; his fear would strangle him or stop his heart. Even now the Niaruna, bows taut, on quick silent feet, were circling in upon him, and though he raged at himself that the Indians must not find him helpless, he could not move.

Be frightened then, but keep your mouth shut. Sinking back, he let his limbs splay drunkenly. In a few minutes the terror subsided and he was able to breathe freely and stand up.

He peeped over the root walls; for all he knew, a Niaruna warrior might be crouched on the far side of his own tree. Then he straightened and shoved the revolver back into his belt. He must not crouch or peep again, but must brazen it out like an immortal.

Except in rain, the great force in this nether world was silence; his first footsteps did not make a sound. The forest was still as quiet as it had been since the

174

explosion. There was no air to stir the leaves, and no bird called. Filtered through the tiers of branches and the white silk of the parachute above, the morning light was vague and luminous, sepulchral, like the light in a dark cathedral; the brown-greeniness of the atmosphere was so tactile that he could rub it between his fingertips. The forest life went on far overhead, in the green galleries; it was only in the sun space cleared by death and fall that new life could rise out of the forest floor. Beneath his feet the ground was not ground at all, but a dark compost of slow seepings and rotted leaves which, starved of sun, reared nothing but low fungi; it gave off a thick, bitter smell of acid.

He sensed that he was still alone, but this feeling he did not trust, nor did he cling to it as a good omen. Possibly the explosion had put the Indians to flight, but he could not count on this. Any movement he made might be provocative and therefore dangerous, but he had the initiative and he must keep it. He started toward the village.

Ahead of him a dog was barking; there was no sound of human voice. He moved slowly, picking his way around the monstrous root masses of fallen trees, climbing over the dead trunks. Far over his head, at the edge of light, loomed strange parasitic ropes and shapes, and hanging air plants and lianas, red bromelia, huge ant nests like excrescences on the high columns. The enormous tree trunks, smooth and pale, disappeared into this riotous world, supporting it.

The bark of the dog, tentative at first, was now turned toward him, and was steady. He was filled with rage against this dog, whose outcry tore his nerves; no matter how he chose to meet the Indians, its mindless yapping might weaken the aura of the supernatural that could save his life. Perhaps he should signal his arrival by shooting it down with the revolver, but this thought was scarcely concluded when its barking rose to a high fit of shrieks and then subsided. The silence sifted down again, like shifting vapor.

He was too tense now to reflect on this event, which only reminded him of human presence; at least one Indian had not run off in panic. His hand strayed wistfully toward the revolver. But except as a last resort, this was not his weapon: he had already gauged his arsenal, which consisted of—in order of importance—the Descent from the Sky, the Explosion and the Initiative. The first two were already spent, and the last was risky.

The quality of light had changed, and lianas entwined the lower trunks, and undergrowth, a wall of leaves—the jungle edge. He was right on top of the Niaruna village. He dropped to his hands and knees, then slid forward and a little to the right; he moved by inches, careful not to commit his hands without checking first for biting ants or worse. There was a passage through the leaves, and a broken glimpse of the Indian clearing. Through the coarse odors of the foliage, he caught faint smells of human excrement and wood smoke. He wriggled forward, stretched close to the ground; a hunting wasp, night-blue in color, flicked back and forth before his face, then fretted, hard wings clicking, on a leaf.

A high-peaked maloca, perhaps eighty feet by twenty, occupied the back of the clearing, parallel to the river, with several round huts placed at random on the two remaining sides; the round huts were dilapidated, their doorways rank with weeds. All of these structures were thatched with palm fronds, and camouflaged by ground and forest, like huge oven nests of birds. Each had a single entry facing eastward. The clearing itself was a bare ground littered with small fires and half-burned logs, rotting palm-leaf baskets, old torn matting, broken clay pots, wood mortars and pestles, an old dugout canoe used as a trough, a half-completed dugout, and near one of the fires, some coils of fresh clay for new pottery. A vegetable patch half overgrown with passion-flower vines was visible behind the maloca, and behind this patch the manioc plantations, rude broken clearings of burned tree trunks and piled undergrowth, stretched inland from the river.

At the near edge of the clearing, not ten yards from his face, an orange dog lay in the sunlight, flanks twitching and dirt clotted on its tongue. A long cane arrow with bright blue-and-yellow feathering protruded from its body just behind the upper forelegs.

To the left of the dog, on a stump beside a hut, sat a blue-and-yellow macaw; the bird's wings and tail were virtually denuded. Its head was cocked, and it rolled its white eyelid up and down in a slow heavy blinking that was almost audible, as if to bring its bald eye into better focus; it shifted white fleshy feet upon the stump, but did not cry out. In the silence the bird uttered one soft gargle of apprehension and was still.

The macaw saw him. Because this was so, the savages across the clearing, though they could not see him through his screen of leaves, knew exactly where he was. There were three of them in view. The nearest, a powerful Indian with broad heavy features, was older than the other two. All three were staring at the point of his concealment, and all three were on their knees, unarmed. All three—there was no mistake about it—had their palms pressed together at their chins as if in prayer, though one man kept dropping his left hand to scratch uneasily at his groin.

He blinked and stared again, so powerfully did this scene affect him: the passion flowers and the bird, the green walls climbing to bright sky, the painted men, the ringing silence of the morning, strangely intensified by fear, by sun and death. The same light that spun from the live feathers of the bird caught its dead feathers on the arrow. Except for the execution of the dog, this tableau must have been intact for the near hour since he dropped out of the sky.

The Indians awaited him. He backed up slowly, inch by inch, to a point where he could stand.

So elated was he, so sure once more of the inevitability of his coming, that he had to caution himself against some idiotic act of glee. He felt omnipotent, as if by stepping forth into this sunlight he might transcend the past, and future too. Wasn't that the talent of a god?

But in the daylight, gods were mortal and took mortal forms. He stripped himself of all his clothes, all but his belt, which he used to strap himself in the manner of the Indians. With his right hand he held the revolver and with his left clutched the wadded clothes behind his back. He filled the air with loud strange whistlings that savages might associate with the supernatural; then he stamped forward, hurting his bare feet, and crashed out of the darkness into the light.

The macaw shrieked. One Indian threw himself backward and ran for the cover of the forest, but the other two held their ground. The older man seemed to shrink into himself, prepared for death, but the young warrior thrust out his jaw, face muscles quivering.

Moon stood there rigid beneath the sun, like something sprung out of the earth. The terror of the Indians was so vibrant that he felt foolish standing over them. He decided to sit down, not only because his penis band was slipping, but because, since his legs would no longer support him, it was the most sensible thing to do. In an effort to look godlike, or at least ritualistic, he sat down cross-legged, one arm akimbo.

The man who had fled at his approach scrambled back out of the jungle and took his place with the others; he moved bent over, almost on all fours, to indicate that he had not really abandoned his position, had perhaps never been absent at all. The feathers in this man's headband were askew, and his wide mangy belt of monkey fur made him look shorter than he was. His face was live and ugly, and he muttered over his shoulder at someone in the bushes; Moon heard the giggle of a girl. The other two frowned, but they did not take their eyes off Moon; the younger one looked restless, on the point of action, as if at any moment he might take Moon's initiative away from him. Moon raised his fingers to his mouth, then dropped his hand, raised it again and dropped it, after which he rubbed his stomach. He then looked pointedly at the oldest of the three men. This man had long hair to his shoulders and a broad face with lines as deep as scars; he wore a simple headband without feathers and the curved incisors of a jaguar in a pendant on his chest. Except for a thin bellyband, he was naked. He rose slowly and came toward Moon, his face a mask of pride and terror; he stopped a few feet away. The other two rose also, but remained in place. Their gaze was so rigid that Moon could not support it; he fell once more to rubbing his stomach and putting his fingers to his lips.

The headman turned and called out to the jungle, and a girl came forward. Though uneasy, she did not seem afraid; she moved with a kind of saunter. Her wide smile, because it eased his tension, seemed to him beautiful. The girl continued to smile even when the headman spoke to her angrily; she raised both hands to her mouth and peeked at Moon around the Indian's shoulder.

The headman took her by the arm. He pointed at the girl, then with both hands made a motion away from his own chest toward Moon and said, *"Pindi tai' nunu kisu."* Moon guessed that the girl had been placed at his disposal; if so, for the moment he was safe. The girl went off toward the fires and came back in a little while with cakes of manioc and a calabash of masato. Behind the headman, for Moon's benefit, she pantomimed drinking the masato; she staggered, rolled her eyes, and touched her throat, as if about to vomit.

Encouraged by her boldness, the rest of the band came slowly from the forest; small children ran forward, slowing suddenly as they neared. They edged in, one by one, dragging one leg around the other. There were forty or more people now in view, of which sixteen—he counted them—were men; there were few old people, and few children. All, from a distance, watched him eat and drink.

The sun was higher now and the birds silent; the sound of his feeding was the only sound in all the world. He did not want to look the Indians in the face lest they perceive his utter helplessness; around him the brown legs moved closer. He felt pale and foolish and hemmed in, like a nude in a thorn bush, and the warm grassy smell of their crowding bodies brought on another fit of fear. He wished that he had not removed his clothes, he wished that he had brought presents for the tribe, he wished that he was in Barbados. He was exhausted from lack of sleep, from nerves, from the withdrawal of the *ayahuasca*. His mouth was so dry that the rancid manioc turned to chalk; yet he could not spit it out, for fear of giving insult. The suspense among the savages was so intense that he felt claustrophobic; they awaited him. He had come to them out of the sky, a god, a spirit, and now he sat here, weak and naked, head bowed. They moved closer.

On impulse he threw his arms out wide and scowled vilely at the sun. Like deer surprised, the Indians froze for a moment where they stood, and a low gasp and exclamation—*h-chuh!*—was lost in a dismal moan of fright as they broke and fled. In a matter of seconds he was alone in the jungle clearing. He held his pose for a few moments to let them feast their eyes upon him from the bushes. Then he took up Quarrier's notebook and found the words for "come" and "friend." Huben had discovered that a makeshift verb without tense or declension could be formed simply by adding *wuta* to a noun; a note in the margin said, "*Wuta:* cannot really be spelled phonetically, sounds like spitting out grapeskins, *thspoota.*" Another note read, "Yoyo says the headman to the east is called Boronai." He put the notebook away and called out, "*Marai-wuta,*" but his voice cracked so badly that he had to start all over again.

"*Marai-wuta!*" He beat himself upon the chest. "*Mori! Mori!*"

Behind him he heard a speculative grunt, and whirled to face the young warrior who had awaited him in the clearing; this man stood at the jungle edge behind him. In the anger of surprise Moon waved him

180

forward to join the others; though the man obeyed him, he did so casually. The band convened behind him. For a Niaruna, this warrior was tall—his slim body and small shoulders made him appear as tall as Moon himself—and like the headman, he wore his hair long. The mouth in a lean jutting face was held perpetually half open, as if about to lick its chops, and the nostrils, too, were ravenous. The hair was held back by two long feathered wooden needles which pierced his ears, and his face was framed by two broad lines of black which, starting from the point of a large V between his eyes, zigzagged around his eye sockets and down the sides of his face. The bright eyes and bold clear structure of his face, with the black marks like side-burns, gave him the fierce aspect of a falcon.

This man had stalked him successfully from behind, and he himself had demonstrated anger; some sort of confrontation must take place. Moon tapped his own chest and repeated his name, then reached across —and now the Indian flinched—and tapped the other. The Indian, if he understood, affected not to, and was silent. After several failures, Moon knew that he had lost face. He pointed suddenly at the headman. "Boronai," he said aloud, and the Indians sighed in astonishment. Boronai himself looked surprised and angry at hearing his name pronounced, but he said nothing.

The young Indian now tapped himself slowly. "Aeore," he said, pronouncing it syllable by syllable, *AY-o-ray,* and the other Indians giggled covertly. Then he pointed at the heavy-set warrior in the monkey-fur belt: "Tukanu," he said, and the Indians laughed again, all but Tukanu. Aeore pointed at Moon. "Moon," Moon said encouragingly.

"Kisu." In an odd flat accusatory tone, a tone mixed with fear and suspicion, Aeore contradicted him.

Moon nodded vigorously. Pointing at each of the three men who had awaited him in the clearing, he said, "Boronai. Aeore. Tukanu." Then he tapped himself. "Kisu-Moon," he said: it seemed best to retain his name, having already stated it. "Kisu-Moon. *Mori. Mori.*"

"Kisu-Mu," Aeore said, unsmiling.

This is him, Moon thought, this hungry one. This is the man who shot the arrow at the sky.

14

In his first days, the dread in his lungs lay heavy as cold mud; he was never certain when he went to sleep that he would awake at all, and often, awaking, he would try to pretend, by keeping his eyes shut and backing into sleep again, that he was elsewhere. But now he had lost track of the days and could rest peacefully, and he slept a great deal, as if years of fatigue had overtaken him.

He was at a beginning and at an end. He had thrown away his bearings, like a man who treks at night into a wilderness and hurls his map into the wind and drops his compass to the bottom of an unknown river.

Though the air was hot, his body had turned cold in the gloom of the maloca; he drew his knees up to his chest and clutched them to him, then opened one eye, like a peephole. To judge from the light it was midafternoon. About him, the hammocks were empty, but he sensed a presence and turned his head to see the smooth, dusty back of the girl Pindi. She was squatting by the embers of the fire, threading black polished nuts and bits of river mussel on fine strings of silk grass, her breasts with their large dark nipples swaying, her cropped hair touching the bold bones of her face. She wore a loincloth woven from soft fibers of wild bark, a bracelet of armadillo shell, and a beetle-wing necklace, iridescent. Now and then she paused to spin the bast upon her thigh.

Moon studied her with pleasure: the wide young mouth hung open in absorption, the swelling of her thighs and hips which rested on her heels, the dusty skin which merged with the soft earth, the sun-born colors of her ornaments. Beyond her, their heads silhouetted by the hard glare of the clearing, a row of children peered in at him from outside, and beyond them some figures passed, truncated by the hairy fringe of thatch. A soft clamor of activity drifted from the far side of the clearing; there the men, laughing and hooting, were working on a new dugout.

The enthusiasm of these people for their new friend knew no bounds. Even on that first morning they had smiled more widely than he had thought men could smile. The Niaruna were still touched by sun.

The women had stood behind their men, arms around their waists, and the girl had laughed aloud. *"Kisu-Mu mori Pindi,"* she had said, giggling so violently, both hands to her face, that finally, unnerved by her own boldness, she had hid behind some of the other women. Boronai had dragged her back to Kisu-Mu. *"Boronai puwa Pindi,"* he said, using both hands to indicate his own forceful techniques of copulation. *"Naki Kisu-Mu puwa Pindi."*

"Kin-wee," Moon said: Good. He tried smiling at Boronai, and Boronai smiled back.

"Wai'lua." Boronai placed both hands gently on the ground and gazed about his clearing. *"Wai'lua."*

My earth, my earth—could that be it?

"Wai'lua Niaruna," Moon hazarded; there was a certain risk in this, since the white man's name for a savage tribe was often a derogatory one provided by its enemies. But at his words the People smiled—all but Aeore of the falcon face, who yelled contemptuously. At this, the warrior named Tukanu stepped away from Aeore and pointed at him. "Yuri Maha!" Tukanu exclaimed, as if thereby distinguishing Aeore from the rest of them, for now all the people near this Indian

184

moved back a little. Aeore gazed at Moon without expression.

Boronai went to the maloca, his people trailing behind him, and stopped before he entered. He turned politely to face Kisu-Mu and recited a singsong speech of welcome, then turned back again and preceded him inside.

The interior of the maloca was fully used, with hammocks strung in tiers from all the posts, and gourds and packets, palm-leaf baskets, arrow bundles, flutes, feather crowns, monkey-skin drums, drying vines, tobacco leaves and other articles suspended from the rafters. Earthen pots, mortars and pestles, manioc sieves of wickerwork and thorn-board graters lined the walls. There was an ancient rhythm to the chaos of the place, a genial ungeometric order, and even the dirt floor was smooth and clean; as they stood there, an old woman with a feather broom swept the ground beneath a set of hammocks at the center. Moon supposed that these hammocks were occupied by Boronai, but he did not protest; he accepted the hammock as he had accepted Pindi, to avoid the discourtesy of refusal.

He approached the lowest hammock, but stopped when the Indians laughed; jabbering, they pointed at the blackened hearth beside the tier, then at the girl Pindi, then at the hammock. It was Pindi who slept there so that she might tend the fire in the night. The girl placed her hand on the middle hammock, and he managed to slide into it without dumping himself in un-godly fashion onto the ground.

He arranged himself on the hard cords of mesh, stained red from painted bodies, and inhaled the Indian smell, the strange sour grassy smell; it was not unpleasant but it startled him, and feeling trapped, he lurched wildly in the hammock before easing down again. He was dimly aware that the Indians were still standing there, contemplating the spectacle that he presented, not out of bad manners but because privacy and quiet were not conditions of their sleep. Giggling, they pushed at Pindi, anxious that she get into the hammock with him. The girl was frightened, and refused.

When he awoke some hours later, he was given to eat what must have been, to judge from the Indians' delight on his behalf, the finest cut of the dead orange dog.

In the daytime he went naked; at night he wore his shirt and pants against the humid cold. The savages did not consider this a weakness, but a proof of his superiority. He was already used to the night cold, the biting insects, the mild chronic malaria; though the food—mostly half-cooked fish and manioc—had given him dysentery, Boronai had cured him quickly with some seeds from the greenheart tree. The insects were no problem except at twilight and at night, when they were checked by the smudge fires under the hammocks; the smoke, in fact, brought him more discomfort than the mosquitoes, for he soon learned to slap the insects as automatically and unthinkingly as the Indians. Meanwhile, his body had hardened, even his feet, which still fettered him to the ways of his past life. His fears for them—ants and infections, bone bruises, scorpions, tarantulas and snakes—obsessed him, and yet his most pernicious foe was the common chigger flea. Every few days Pindi dug at his poor feet with a bone needle, popping into her mouth each small fat mite that she extracted.

It seemed a good sign that a wife of Boronai had been lent to him, though he was not sure how the Indians reconciled his need for women with his spiritual estate. Observing Pindi, Moon thought out carefully his whole situation, returning over and over to the same question that the Niaruna must have asked themselves: who was he?

As Kisu-Mu, he had been identified with Kisu, the Great Spirit of the Rain; when his sneakers wore out, as they soon would, the Great Spirit would be an invalid. He struggled to toughen his feet, running barefoot in the village yard and stamping up and down on logs along the river; he hoped the Niaruna would regard his behavior as strange and godlike rather than pathetic. As soon as he could make himself understood, he asked Boronai for bits of the tough tapir skin so that he could make moccasins. Since he knew no better than they how to cure and sew hides—and for this he cursed Alvin Moon "Joe Redcloud" and the whole degraded Indian nation—the moccasins emerged as twists of wood. By now his feet had toughened, but they still got cut too easily; in the jungle climate, without disinfectant, any cut might be his last. And in the forest he did not know where to step; not only did he not recognize the shapes and colors that the Indians avoided, but his feet were not as sure as theirs, nor his eyes as sharp. He spent his whole time staring at the ground.

In those first days he had gone with Tukanu to Huben's mission, hoping to find a pair of sneakers. His quest had put him in bad humor—not least of all because he felt grotesque wearing shoes while otherwise naked—and his humor worsened when he did not find the sneakers that he did not wish to wear. He and Tukanu found nothing useful. Boronai had told him that his people had taken nothing, and Moon himself had seen no article of civilization in the Niaruna village. Boronai could only suppose that Huben's *manso* Niarunas, the people of Yoyo and Kori, had looted the House of God; that, fearing attack, they must have fled to Remate almost as soon as Huben had gone away. When Boronai had led his people there, planning to kill Kori and his worthless men and to adopt the women and children before some other band took advantage of them, they found the mission ransacked.

On his trip to the mission Moon had asked about the radio set lying in the shallows; Tukanu acknowledged that Boronai's men had done this. Tukanu himself had been poking at the radio, hoping to find food in it, when suddenly the spirits of the box had snapped and whined at him. As far as Moon could piece the strange story together, poor Tukanu, yanking crazily at the controls, had tried to keep the spirits in their box; instead he turned the volume up to a loud blare, at which the whole war party fled into the jungle. Then Boronai had rallied them, saying that these were demons of the white man, that if the box was destroyed, the demons would have no home in Niaruna land. Boronai led the bravest men toward the shed, and from a distance the warriors shot arrows and hurled clubs and lances through the doors and windows. After a terrific struggle the voices of the demons died, but they kept on snarling and coughing for a long time, until at last Boronai himself rushed in with a club and beat the box to the floor. Then the box was seized and hurled into the river, but not before biting and cutting two of the warriors who grabbed it.

Tukanu had likened the white man's Demon House to Kaiwena, the piranha fish, which snapped at fingers even after it was speared and dying. After the battle with the demons, the Indians were leery of the mission, imagining that it swarmed with vengeful spirits. They left a feathered club of warning and went away.

Tukanu had fiddled with the radio in the first place because, of all the band, he was the one most informed about the mission; during the period of Huben's first appearance he had spied on it for some weeks as scout for Boronai. It was Tukanu, in fact, who had proposed the massacre of Kori's people. During the period of his surveillance he had fallen in love with an old woman named Taweeda, whose husband was Kori's brother. He had met with her often in the forest, and she encouraged him to come back with her to the mission, saying that if he got down on his knees and spoke to Huben as she instructed him, he would be given food and presents and could wear the same bandages in his sores that had attracted him to her own person. Tukanu was enthusiastic about this idea and took several praying lessons from Taweeda, but his conversion was thwarted when Boronai forbade him to show himself. As an alternative to salvation, Tukanu had hit upon a massacre, from which his friend Taweeda would be spared.

At one time or another Tukanu had wished to marry every woman in his own village, and he had actually contrived to marry Pindi. First, he had gone around for many moons chanting incantations and clutching aphrodisiac charms and talismans of love, all to no avail. Second, he had killed a tapir and dumped the entire animal at Pindi's feet. Finally he had seized her up and bore her off into the weeds to work his way with her, whereupon, out of indifference, she permitted him to marry her.

In the few months of their marriage Pindi was so unfaithful that Tukanu replaced his talismans of love with fetishes to control her lust. Moreover, she refused to work for him no matter how often he beat her; her failure to do her share in the communal work caused dissension throughout the village, until the whole band became ill and began to waste away. Finally Boronai invited Pindi into his own household in the role of wife. She came gladly, and henceforth did her share, and Boronai made no objection when she slept sometimes with Aeore. Tukanu let her go without rancor, declaiming loudly that gay and pretty girls made the worst wives, and that a woman of wide back and sour mien would suit his purposes far better. But in the village there was no one of this description who had not already refused him, which accounted for the joy he felt when, one day in the forest by the mission, he surprised the surly, broad-backed old Taweeda and mounted her forthwith, without resistance.

All this Moon understood later from Boronai and Pindi, but that day, standing in the mission clearing listening to Tukanu, he could not make head or tail of the Indian's story. When he finally understood, he had the explanation for the Indian genuflection he had glimpsed on the flight with Wolfie and on the day of his arrival. During his praying lessons Tukanu had gathered from Taweeda that the white man's god was Kisu, the Great Spirit of the Rain. Taweeda said that the white man's Kisu invited the spirits of good Indians to drink masato with him in his Sky House, and sent the spirits of bad Indians to live down in the mud like frogs. Huben had told Taweeda—who told Tukanu—that Kisu was angry with those Indians who paid no attention to his anger, and although Tukanu found this idea of an almighty power rather foolish, the first appearance of the great bird in the sky had lent support to Taweeda's silly story. For want of a better course he gave his people praying lessons then and there. The day of Kisu-Mu's descent, they decided to pray again, but the trouble was that he had not remembered anything about the prayer except the physical position, and so they had remained silent.

"We wished to pray," Tukanu said piously, "but we did not know what to say."

On the third morning after Moon's arrival, another airplane had appeared out of the heavens. At the distant sound, Aeore ran from the maloca and sprang in a bound to the center of the clearing; body tense, his bow and arrows in his hand, he knelt, pressed his ear to the earth, frowned, leaped up again and whooped shrilly in alarm.

Shouting and jabbering, the Niaruna in the village gathered at the edge of the clearing. At a command from Boronai, a silence fell. The sound of the airplane was unmistakable, and an uproar started; the women seized the smallest children and moved toward the shelter of the forest. But Aeore, and then Boronai and Tukanu, had turned to gaze at Moon, who rose slowly and walked toward them. He wondered if the plane was searching for him or whether it had been sent by Guzmán to attack; he could take no chances.

Pointing and gesturing, he had told Boronai that a great bird was coming to their village, that they must put out all fires and take their dogs and hide from sight. Boronai shouted at his people, who scattered off

190

into the jungle. Moon himself hid at the jungle edge, and Aeore crouched just behind him, like a warder.

The plane was circling off to the west; the pilot was reconnoitering the mission station. Then it came on again, passing to the north of where he stood. In a moment it might spot the point where his own plane had plunged into the sea of leaves. But the drone was steady, changing only as the plane came around in a wide arc; on this course it would pass eastward of the village.

Then the plane had turned. When it came in, high over the trees, Moon recognized the Mustang fighter from the airstrip at Madre de Dios. When the machine went into a sudden sideslip, losing altitude quickly, in a dangerous and peculiar "falling leaf" maneuver, like a wounded goose, Moon grinned; Old Wolf, he thought—I'll miss that sonofabitch.

The plane flew briefly out of sight beyond the wall of trees. Then it came on again, and he crouched down. Crossing the village, very low, it seemed to fill the entire sky; its passage shook the treetops of the canopy, and nuts and twigs and bits of leaf rained earthward in its wake. It came in with its left wing pointed to the ground, and Moon caught the blur of the pale bearded face. While the Mustang was gaining altitude for its turn, he pointed at Aeore's bow and arrows, then at himself, and made a shooting motion at the sky. With a rude grunt, Aeore shoved the weapons at him.

Naked and painted, Moon stepped out to face the plane, and shot an arrow at his old friend Wolf. The arrow arched weakly and harmlessly, but it was greeted with machine-gun fire. The bullets tore into the canopy beyond the clearing. Then the plane faded, strained, and circled round again to come in from the same direction; he made for the nearest tree trunk, waving at Aeore to follow him.

Wolfie came in this time on a low power-dive, preceded by a stream of bullets that whiplashed the thatched roof of the hut, danced in puffs of earth across the yard, and chopped to shreds the wooded edge where

191   *At Play in the Fields of the Lord*

Moon had been standing. The plane did not return again; it wandered far off to the west, quartering back and forth, then dying out.

Aeore fingered the shattered twigs, yelling and spitting, Kisu-Mu's fear of the bullets had not been lost on him, and from this time forward, he made no attempt to hide his suspicion of the Great Spirit of the Rain. Moon had wondered first if Aeore's hostility might have to do with Pindi, but now he was sure this wasn't so.

The girl rose and came to his hammock. She flinched when he put his hand on her shoulder; at the same time she watched him boldly and possessively. Running his fingertips along her temple and down across her small neat ear, he marveled at the cool rubber quality of her flesh; there was real spring in it. She giggled and laid her head on his chest, then placed her fingers gently on his lower belly, inspecting the coarse hair.

"*Tsindu*," she muttered fondly, and wrinkled her nose. The Niaruna were all but innocent of body hair, which they regarded as a sure sign of promiscuity. Since they associated hairiness with the *guhu'mi*, the forest demons, he had thought at first that this feature might enhance his aura of the supernatural, but their line between the sacred and the profane was an obscure one. They now took a more familiar tone with Kisu-Mu, and teased him not only about his pubic hair but about his tender feet, his terrible aim and his inability to eat lice. From the start they had been much more curious about the revolver, the gleam and weight of it, than they had ever been about airplane or parachute, which were beyond all comprehension.

He led Pindi out the side door of the maloca and off among the trees, where he made love to her. The children came along to view the spectacle; though he drove them off, a few slipped back to cheer the couple on. There was no solution short of infanticide, since

192

Pindi refused to lie with him after dark. In daylight Kisu-Mu was harmless and could be dealt with as a man, but in the night, when the jaguar and fer-de-lance, the vampire bat and *guhu'mi* were abroad, it was dangerous to sleep with spirits. Nightfall and the moon were sacred. For all Pindi knew, Kisu-Mu might turn himself into Anaconda-Person, and she would give birth to snakes.

They rolled apart and lay there on their backs, enjoying the sun on their bare skin and the languor in their legs. Then Pindi followed him to the river, called Tuaremi, and the other Niaruna abandoned the dugout they had been working on and followed them. She came into the water with him, and the children ran in too, and they all splashed one another. The people on the bank took great delight in everything Kisu-Mu and Pindi did, and clearly wished they would do more; one old woman, cackling maniacally, made sexual pantomimes with her hands, causing one of the younger men to lie down on his back and kick his legs up in the air for joy.

When Moon came out of the water, he found Boronai awaiting him. The headman held a bamboo tube of the red achote paste; with a thin spatula he drew on the legs of Kisu-Mu the twin serpents of the Niaruna, to protect him from the bite of snakes. From his pouch he took some waxy black genipa berries, grinding them on his palms and spitting on the paste, which he then mixed with tapir grease; with his fingertips he drew a short black bar on Kisu-Mu's cheekbone and a harsh black line under his mouth, while the others laughed and whooped in admiration.

"Kin-wee, kin-wee!" they called out. Good, good!

Then Boronai addressed the river Tuaremi, angrily at first, then in placating tones, invoking its spiritual indulgence. The Tuaremi brought the People food and carried them on their journeys, and when the day came it would carry them eastward in the death canoe, into the Morning Sun. The People lived on the rivers, in the avenues of light; of the dark forest they were much afraid. Yet the only sky that most had ever seen was the narrow strip of sky over the torrent.

They led Kisu-Mu back to the clearing. His feet were sore and he slipped and stumbled, glancing at Aeore as he retrieved himself; the man was forever catching him off guard. They crossed the clearing to the maloca, where the women remained outside; in the cool shadows, Boronai sat down upon the ground, motioning to Kisu-Mu that he sit opposite. When the men had gathered, Boronai began speaking in a strange new voice, a kind of singsong, violent and shrill by turns, breaking off now and then to place his hands upon Kisu-Mu's shoulders and stare fixedly past his head. He spoke of the great days of his clan, of how they controlled the hunting and the fishing rights far down into the country of the Sloth People, the Tiro, and from there across to the Tuaremi, and far to the east, toward the Sea of Life; all that land was of his clan. But now the clan had been forced westward by the Yuri Maha, their own kinsmen to the east—here Tukanu pointed at Aeore, for Kisu-Mu's benefit— and they had been threatened from the west by the Green Indians and the Tiro. The Ancestors were very angry. He, Boronai, was very angry, and all of his people were very angry.

To prove this, Boronai shouted at Kisu-Mu in terrific anger, and his men shouted angrily at one another, especially Tukanu, who was so angry that he jumped around in a circle, farting like a tapir. But the only one truly angry said nothing and sat quietly, gazing at Kisu-Mu. And now, as Boronai spoke softly once again, Moon realized what was happening—that Boronai and Tukanu were inducting the Great Spirit of the Rain into their clan.

Moon could never be sure of his own status, especially in the hostile eyes of Aeore, whom he saw as the greatest threat to his security. In the long fear of the early days he had considered provoking an incident, then bringing forth the revolver like a wand of Kisu and striking Aeore down. It was only a matter of time before some episode would bring Aeore's suspicions out into the open. Yet to kill the man who had shot the arrow—well, why not? What difference did that arrow make? His own superstition annoyed him.

Once Aeore asked where he had found his white man's clothes. How did such things go from Remate, where all white men lived, to Kisu-Mu up in the sky? Because this was the first time he ever saw Aeore smile disarmingly, Moon had answered warily, in a manner which pleased neither of them.

Kisu-Mu was also the white man's god, according to Tukanu, who had learned this from his woman at the mission. It seemed logical to the Niaruna that Kisu-Mu should be an Indian spirit in the daytime and a spirit of the white man at night; spirits, unlike ghosts, took the form of Man. Most spirits, said Tukanu, were very hairy or had two heads; at the very least, their legs did not bend at the knees. Yet Tukanu seemed willing to accept Kisu-Mu's unspiritual appearance, while Aeore was not.

Aeore seemed to know that Kisu-Mu was not Tukanu's Kisu, but an agent of Kisu with strong shamanistic powers and therefore a rival of himself. Unlike Boronai, who was a great headman and who possessed certain skills of curing and divination, Aeore was training to become one of the rare jaguar-shamans. The year before, the young warrior had killed a jaguar single-handed with a lance, and while he did not wear its teeth upon his chest, out of respect for Boronai, he could now, under the effects of nipi, assume the form of Jaguar and consort with other jaguars in the night forest. Meanwhile, to enhance his reputation, Aeore became more and more ferocious, and submitted himself to prolonged tests of abstinence and endurance. In recent months, Tukanu told Moon, Aeore would have usurped Boronai's shamanistic role—though not the role of headman, which was related to one's status in the clan—had it not been for Kisu-Mu's induction into the clan by Boronai.

"If Kisu-Mu was an ordinary man," Tukanu said cheerfully, "Aeore would kill you."

The same evening that Boronai took Kisu-Mu into the clan, Aeore waylaid him at the forest edge. Silent, he made Moon sit down, and squatted opposite him; with rough strokes of his thumb he wiped away Boronai's markings. Then he painted on Moon's face the black lightning across the cheekbones that he wore himself, and the same narrow band of red beneath. Then he followed Moon to the maloca.

Tukanu saw by firelight what Aeore had done, and started shouting. Aeore caught Moon's gaze and held it. When Tukanu raised his hand to smear Aeore's work, Kisu-Mu frowned; the hand paused and then Tukanu spun in a half-circle and stamped his foot down on the earth. Boronai watched them, silent as stone. Moon tried to placate Tukanu, but he painted himself thereafter in the manner of Aeore. Sometimes he went down to the river and gazed with pride at the wild new face reflected there—how near and distant were the morning days when, as a child, he had seen his face in the spring rivers of the northern prairie.

Another moon had come and gone and would soon come again. His skin was darkened by the sun, he wore red serpents on his legs, and Pindi had cropped his head in the round style of the Niaruna, with short bangs in front. He wore thin fiber bands above his biceps and below his knees, a plaited bellyband, and a crown of monkey fur and yellow toucan feathers, and he carried a black hunting lance made from the iron heart of chonta palm.

Standing there naked in the open air as the dugouts of the missionaries circled, then came on again, he wanted to whoop like a small boy in a game. Tukanu was infected by his mirth; his broad cheeks puffed out like the cheeks of a ground squirrel, then deflated in noisy giggles. The other warriors, until now nervous and surly at remaining in plain sight, began to giggle too; the tittering swept up and down the line.

Only Aeore was unsmiling. Sensing that Moon watched him, he turned his head slowly like a predator; above the fierce band on his cheek, his eyes glinted impassively at Moon before fastening again on Quarrier and Huben, on the four Quechuas. His hand whitened on his bow. Aeore would take no chances with the intruders; at the first sign of threat he would loose an arrow at the canoes and disappear, for he was wary as a fish.

That day, when they had first heard the distant motors, the other Indians ran about like birds, but Aeore gazed steadfastly at Moon, as if to fathom him. Though the boats were less than three miles away, straight across the forest, they were still several hours from the mission, for the Espíritu in its upper reaches wound back and forth upon itself like a fat brown snake.

Aeore was anxious to ambush the invaders at a sharp bend in the river below the mission. Boronai was against this idea; he said that the missionaries might go away and leave the Niaruna in peace once they found the place abandoned. Aeore, backed by his own group of younger warriors, spoke violently to the older man. He said that the People must attack their enemies as fast as they appeared, or the enemies would soon control their forest as they controlled the forest of the Tiro; if necessary, the People could seek help from the Yuri Maha, the People to the East.

When it seemed that Aeore would prevail, Moon supported Boronai. Aeore, said Kisu-Mu, should lead the young warriors to the mission. They would stand on the bank in war paint and Aeore would shoot an arrow near the boat in warning. Then the Indians would vanish, and soon the white man would go away. To signify his leadership, Aeore would wear the clothes brought by Kisu-Mu.

It was important to Moon that the missionaries think him dead, but with this gesture he had again aroused Aeore's suspicions. The Indian was interested not only in the fact of things but in how they worked;

in this sense he was less primitive than any of his tribe. Kisu-Mu's possession of white man's clothing was much more significant to him than airplanes and parachutes, which could be readily dismissed as magic. He greeted Moon's suggestion with surly silence and might have refused it but for the envy he saw in the face of Tukanu.

While Aeore arrayed himself in khaki, the other warriors renewed their paint. Moon could not resist an impulse to go along; he smeared himself heavily with red achote and blurred his features as best he could with the black genipa. Then the band ran swiftly through the forest, crossing the low ridge which separated their own stream from the watershed of the Espíritu, and came out at last in the mission clearing. At the edge of the clearing Moon stopped and removed his sneakers.

Both boats had soldiers in their bows. When they circled at the sight of the Niaruna and Moon laughed aloud, the Indians, infected, giggled with him, especially Tukanu, who made little sounds like small explosions fore and aft; it was this talent that had given him his public name, for Tukanu meant "Farter." But Aeore stamped his foot in rage and fitted an arrow to his bow.

The lead boat circled back; then both came on again, very slowly. Aeore whooped a violent string of words that Moon could not understand, and a second later loosed an arrow. It struck the water right between the boats, and the Niaruna howled in triumph.

As the white men drew closer, the Indians grew restless; Aeore stepped forward and raised his bow a second time and drove his arrow at an angle into the ground; he strode past it, whirled, and shot another. The arrows formed an X upon the bank, facing the missionaries, who were now so near that Moon could see the strain on the white faces.

Now Aeore grunted something and moved toward the jungle. The others followed. In the shadows of the trees, lined up on a great log, his companions watched while the Great Spirit Kisu-Mu tied old scraps of canvas to his strange soft feet.

Not since infancy, Moon thought, had he been in a situation in which he was the slowest, blindest, clumsiest and most inept member of a group; it was like being born all over again. This idea restored his spirits somewhat, and perversely he winked at Aeore. The warrior responded by turning on his heel and moving north into the forest. The motors of the boats had stopped, and already through the foliage they could hear the excited voices of the missionaries.

The band moved eastward toward the Tuaremi.

Though he moved much faster and more quietly than in the early days, he had to struggle to keep up with the Niaruna. He had never envied anything so much as the identity of these people with their surroundings, nor realized quite so painfully how displaced he had always been. He simply did not belong, not here, not anywhere. His trip to the mission had been a bad mistake; he would not return there. Seeing a savage in blue neckerchief and khakis, the missionaries would be certain that Lewis Moon was dead. And so he was.

The Indians moved like shadows of an owl, flowing in silence across fallen trees and skirting evil pools in a pigeon-toed, shuffle-step trot that looked awkward but was not, while he, stepping more surely than ever before, seemed by comparison to flounder along like something wounded. Yet as the mission fell behind, he moved more eagerly, and an ease returned to him, filling his body like warm sunlight.

15

Days opened out, and furled again at night, like jungle flowers. Another moon turned in the sky and then another; in the full moon he thought sometimes of the moths flying between planets. He was content.

The Indians ate their main meal of the day at sunset; the men ate first, and the women and children took what was left. Usually there was fish and manioc, and sometimes a stew pot of meat bits and capsicum peppers. In the Time of Waters, meat was very scarce and fish were few, though the men went out every day. One evening there were only two small sabalo for the whole village. Boronai made a joke of this, saying that these monsters had broken three of his best spears; he pretended to hand out giant portions that he could scarcely carry. Covertly, he broke his own humble piece and slipped some over his shoulder to his eldest wife, whom he called the Ugly One. The name was not derogatory, nor did she take it in that way; old age was ugly and youth beautiful. Once Moon had surprised the headman on the path from the plantation; Boronai was trailed by the Ugly One, who had been sick, and he was carrying her heavy net of manioc tubers. The Indian, who had been laughing gently with his wife, became intensely mortified and angry at the sight of Kisu-Mu; he dropped the net as if he had picked it up by mistake, and shouted at the Ugly One to get it down to the maloca as fast as her short legs would carry her. For some days after this, he glowered indiscriminately at one and all, to show his people the tyrannical person with whom they had to deal.

Nevertheless, Boronai was very gentle with the Ugly One, who was treated better than most women; the men hooted at him amiably for giving her the fish, and Boronai shouted angrily in embarrassment. In the up-roar, a child ran against the palm basket of hot manioc, sending the food flying into the dirt; the Indians laughed more loudly still at this new joke on themselves, though the accident had spoiled all the dull work of many hours and would cause them to go hungry. Even the child joined in the laughter.

Now Aeore came in. He carried a large pirarucu, the largest fish the Indians had seen in weeks, and a sigh of admiration rose around him. But Aeore did not share it in the open way that the two small fish had been divided; he stared at the people with his own curious mixture of shyness and contempt, as if he did not intend to share with them at all. Then he broke off a large piece for himself and slung the rest down carelessly before them. The Indians turned their heads away out of embarrassment, ignoring Aeore's bad manners in the hope that the bad feeling he had brought would fade away.

The fish feast was already as depressed and sullen as the poor meal of moments before had been hilarious. Aeore sat to one side, eating alone, and no one spoke. Finally Tukanu, staring straight ahead at nothing, spoke his thoughts, his angry voice blurred by the last shreds of Aeore's fish still in his mouth: "The one who does not like us—why does he eat with us? Why does he live with us in our maloca? Why does he not go away to his own people?"

Aeore tossed his last piece of fish onto the ground in front of Tukanu, as to a dog, and stalked out of the maloca; Boronai seized the arm of Tukanu, who was thrashing to his feet. Had Boronai not publicly re-strained him to save his face, he would have been forced to attack a man of whose night powers he was much afraid.

Boronai's intuition and decisiveness made him the natural leader of the village. He ignored the episode of the fish. But afterward he talked casually to Moon, arriving eventually at an oblique defense of Aeore. Though Boronai rarely agreed with Aeore about anything, he saw something fateful in the coming of the young Yuri Maha; the future of his band must lie with one who had come to them mysteriously out of the Sun forest to the East.

"He is still too young to lead us; we must wait." Boronai contemplated Moon as he said this, and his eyes were without savagery; unlike the others, his eyes were never flat and blank, reflecting nothing. Boronai, his people said, had the gentle soul of Tukituk, the forest tanager.

More and more Moon was drawn toward the mission, to test his disguise again, just for the fun of it. Boronai watched him. Yet he knew that to visit the mission was to dissipate a mystery, to break a spell, before he had penetrated to the heart of it and made it part of him.

The time had come when Moon could move barefoot through the forest. He trailed the fishers who damned the streams and poisoned the fish pools with barbasco; he spent days wandering with the young boys, who taught him how to fold a green-leaf cup to drink the clear water of a creek—his hand-and-slurp technique, roiling the bottom even slightly, they thought extremely rude—and which berries and nuts and insects and mushrooms could be eaten. He learned the names of plants and creatures, and which were valuable and which useless, and which were inhabited by spirits; some of these the Indians would not look at, and some they pointed at without speaking. He learned to find an occasional mark with bow and arrow, to make a fire with a hand drill, to move without sound, to sing.

He was now accepted so completely that he doubted if the Niaruna wondered any more, or even cared, whether or not he was man or spirit; their line between the sacred and profane was serpentine. He was part of their life, and they cared for him and fed him as they would a dog, a macaw or a child, since he could not—or *would* not, as the Indians saw it, not comprehending helplessness in a grown male—take care of himself. His efforts with spear and bow and arrow were more amusing than helpful to them; they only grew angry once, when in the early days, drawn to the manioc plantations out of curiosity, he had caused a great disturbance among the women. Both Tukanu and Boronai informed him sternly that the plantations were notorious places for liaisons, and that a man's presence there would lead to discords which the band could not afford. The women had jeered in cheerful disbelief at Kisu-Mu's interest in their work; one had lain down flat on her back, her hands behind her head, writhing provocatively, until Pindi came and beat her with a stick.

He was already fluent in the language, fluent enough to know that Leslie Huben's notebook contained serious mistakes of definition and interpretation. "These primitive souls have a legend of the Deluge!" Huben had scrawled ecstatically in one margin. "Isn't this a sign of the Lord's blessing?" But many peoples, Moon reflected, had a legend of a deluge, since in the ice ages the seas had risen all around the world. Under "Our Savior," Huben had noted, "I figured out from Yoyo that the Niaruna have some kind of a heathen Sky God. So temporarily I have settled on this name, pronounced Kee-soo, for our own God Almighty, to make His work go faster here."

But the Niaruna Creator was Witu'mai, an Ancient of Heaven who also ruled over the Sky of the Dead; He was revered with neither fear nor ceremony, for He lived far off in the sky. It would be foolish, Tukanu told Moon, to waste much breath on spirits so remote; far better to placate the malevolent spirits who circled the village at night, like Tutki, the bald, hairy, huge-eared, one-eyed dwarf with blue-green teeth, feet faced backward, a gigantic penis and an appetite for little children, or like 'Hanga, the nightmare incubus who made strange whistling sounds to lure men to their doom, and told the shamans where to seek wild honey.

"Listen!" Boronai said. "We have our river and our forest, we have fish and birds and animals to eat, and Witu'mai has taught us to grow manioc! Surely we are living in a golden time!"

This speech so tickled Moon that he laughed aloud, sharing Boronai's happiness; he laughed at the extraordinary experience which had befallen him—the *perceiving,* through the Indians, of a wilderness which heretofore had seemed to him a malevolent nether world, poisonous and stagnated, miasmal. But when he asked what Boronai would do if the white man came, the headman said that he had inherited a potent fetish which would make even the angriest man laugh. "The white man will laugh so hard," Boronai exclaimed, "that he will no longer wish us harm, and will go away! Look, you shall see!" He took out his fetish, made from the dried skull of a witty bird; he invoked it strenuously, eyes glittering. When Moon only sat quietly, expressionless, Boronai faltered, then stopped entirely. Without a word he laid the famous fetish carefully away.

Moon had meant to warn him that the white man was not so lightly turned away; now he felt ashamed. He said, "Perhaps the white man will not know how to laugh." Boronai did not answer; when he spoke again, it was of other things.

He bathed his senses in the river, drifting downstream and stroking back again, downstream and back again, in the cold water of the sky. The flood water was roiled and gritty, but the river was bright with a wild sun of the rainy season. Upstream, a canoe danced on the afternoon reflections and came sailing down upon him, swirling past his head. A lean black dugout like the rest, it was better shaped and better made, with symbols carved on the gunwale's inner rim, and because it rode so light upon the current it was recognizable at any distance. It was the one canoe in all the village in which he had not been welcomed.

He swam ashore. "No fish," he said.

"No fish," Aeore said. He watched Kisu-Mu expectantly as if to say, If you are the Great Spirit of the Rain, why don't you stop the rise of waters? He jerked his canoe onto its side to bail it. In pride, unsmiling, he held it there after the water was all gone, so that Moon might marvel at the carved gunwales. When Moon asked about the carving, Aeore looked surly again and let the canoe fall back so that it grazed Moon's feet.

But the next day at dawn Moon rose and followed when Aeore left the maloca. The warrior said nothing. They went down to the river and slid the canoe into the Tuaremi.

The high ground on which the village lay was now almost an island, for the river had jumped its banks and rolled drunkenly across the forest, swirling around the buttressed roots of the great trees. The people were frightened of the flooded forest, which they thought an unnatural place aswarm with ghosts and spirits; because Kisu had brought about the flood, they sulked openly when Kisu-Mu, ignoring the prayers made in his hearing, failed to intervene in their behalf.

Since Aeore, the most hostile of the Niaruna, was also the most shy and deferential, they went along in silence. Tukanu and all the rest, when not actually stalking game, made a great commotion on the water, banging the canoe sides with their paddles, imitating and conversing with the passing creatures—Ho, Otter, will you bring us a fine fish?—singing, laughing, telling dirty jokes and creating a general racket of good feeling. Toucan! Toucan! Take me with you! But Aeore moved silently, bending his body to the canoe so that his craft flicked through the rapids like a fish. When Moon turned, impressed, to watch him, Aeore burst into a smile, then hid his pride by whistling clear imitations of the sunrise voices and grunting fiercely at a young caiman on a floating tree. He huffed, hissed, and flapped his elbows in imitation of the primitive hoatzins in the low branches; he fluttered like a hoatzin in the water, then became a piranha, whirling away from the hoatzin in distaste—all of this to the rhythm of his paddle.

But in a moment, as a cat tucks up its tail behind, Aeore stopped smiling, and his eyes withdrew into his painted mask; driving his paddle down against the current, he spun the canoe toward the bank with a twist so savage that water splashed across them. Moon was nearly thrown out wide into the torrent. Then the canoe escaped the flood, passing through a crack in the green wall into the jungle.

Like forest birds crossing the river, they had passed from light into darkness; the air in his lungs turned cold. The Indian observed him, eyes in shadow; the canoe slipped silently through the gleam. He faced ahead again, taking a paddle. In the light filtering down through the high galleries, the ghostly tree boles loomed and turned and fell back into ranks. The one sound was a hollow *toonk* as his paddle tip probed a sunken root or timber; they glanced about them lest they wake the giants. Farther from the river, the water changed from muddy brown to a clear black, no more than a foot in depth, from which pale faces of dead leaves peered up like supplicants. They scraped aground. Aeore backed off soundlessly and they moved on again, winding down the high dark avenues, silent as water snakes.

Far overhead, in a torn place where the light had pierced, birds clicked and fretted at a monkey; the capuchin, clutching its squashed fruit, peered down aghast at the canoe, like a mad subhuman visage in the high window of a tower. The troupials screeched and scattered, and the monkey leaped, too late: a harpy eagle, crest erect, flopped and swayed on the thin branches where the monkey had been foraging. It too peered down at the canoe with a wild mask of rage, oblivious of the weak squirming in its talons. Aeore, shipping his paddle, addressed the eagle reverently in low orisons, while the monkey stared downward sadly, as if reproaching them for the moment of inattention that would cost its life. It still clung to its fig, and even as the eagle cocked an eye to peer at it, raised the fruit vaguely toward its mouth.

Aeore moved on, in awe. He pointed with his paddle at stray shadows, shapes, but often Moon could only guess what he was pointing at; his own eye could not pierce the creature's camouflage. They saw agoutis and opossum and a small jaguarundi cat, all perched in fungus gardens of fallen trees; on a massive trunk in a small glade, three peccary raised their bristles and backed into a circle. Aeore did not seize his bow, though in this season meat was scarce. The Indian only nodded at the peccary, murmuring something that Moon could not catch; the pigs left off clicking their tusks and resumed their rooting in the decayed wood.

Helicon butterflies on black narrow wings crisscrossed the silences, and far away a bellbird tolled. Parrots fled, and an iguana, and a small swimming viper; the loop of a large boa constrictor hung suspended from a branch. Aeore urged all of these to go their way. The flooded forest, combining unnaturally the forces of earth and water, was a common ground where all creatures moved in quiet, with respect.

The bellbird clanged again, remote, unearthly; coiled in the stern, head sunk between his shoulders, Aeore looked trapped. The white bellbird Ulua was the spirit of a girl killed in the act of incest; if heard too close, Ulua's call would lead its victim to the spirit world, there to keep her company forever.

S-ss-tchuh! The Indian swung his paddle tip to fend off something in the water; he backwatered. Snout pressed to a submerged root, tail swaying sinuously in the silence of the pool, a huge salamander lay in wait; in the tannin blackness its red blotches glowed. This salamander, drawn from its subterraneum by high water, was out of place, and thus a sign of evil; they fled back toward the river. The bellbird trailed them, still invisible: the bellbird's call was urgent, as if it flew in search of them. When it did not cease, but came still nearer, the Indian paddled without grace, in open flight.

Moon wondered if Aeore had not taken him along as some sort of spiritual protection, like a live talisman; when he asked the panting Indian if he had ever before visited the forest in time of flood, he got no answer.

They struck the river at a point upstream from the place where they had entered, whirling out beneath the trunk of a fallen tree. Here in the world of time and weather, the light seemed bright, though it was raining. He was cold to the bone, and paddled violently to keep warm, in hopes that his ineptness with the paddle would console the man burning behind him. To mollify Aeore further, he inquired once again about the carved symbols on the gunwale. At first Aeore affected not to understand him; when Moon put his finger on one of the carvings, the warrior snapped, *"Tarai,"* which signified both jaguar and shaman, leaving Moon no wiser than before. But when Moon touched another figure, then another, Aeore said churlishly that the symbols told the story of Tepan and Amanaitu, and the destruction they had brought upon the world.

In the days of the Ancestors, Boronai said, there was no death among mankind. There were no old people and no floods, no scorpions and no mosquitoes, no famine and no pain; nor did the vipers possess venom. Jaguar was a friend to Man and hunted with him, and both were creatures of darkness, for there was no light: the Sun lived on the far side of the World.

Boronai . . . Boronai's eyes were deep and soft,

*as if he knew something that the others did not know,
longed for something that he could not know himself.
Here in the forest, unable to express himself except in
legend, Boronai was condemned to silence. Look at the
others, the firelight in their eyes, the eyes of cats; they
are savages, and they are ugly, even Pindi. Even Pindi.*

Among mankind was Tepan, who lived with his
mother in the night forest of the World and kept a
fishing weir along the wide black river. But Tepan's
weir was torn and the fish taken, and he set a macaw
there as sentinel. Soon the macaw called out, *a-ra-ra,*
but Tepan was asleep and did not hear.

"Like Tukanu," his nephew said. *"Be still,"* said
Tukanu, "and listen."

Then Tepan set a dove on guard, and when the
dove cried, *hoo, hoo,* he ran to the river and with his
arrow shot a large caiman straight between the eyes.

"The caiman," Pindi said, *"sank with a sound
like this"*—*she blinked her eyes at Moon*—*"glou,
glou!"*

Then the dove called again . . .

"Glou, glou," Pindi repeated, pleased that Moon
had laughed.

"No, no," a child cried angrily. *"Hoo, hoo!"*

. . . and Tepan saw, on the far bank, a beautiful
maiden.

"Her name was Pindi," Pindi said. *"Glou, glou!"*
*All the men frowned at Pindi, and the women hushed
her, and she sulked.*

When Tepan asked the maiden who she was, she
burst into tears, saying, "No! You must not ask!"

"My name is Pindi."

At first the maiden, whose name was Amanaitu,
would not wed Tepan; when at last she agreed, she
warned him that he must not try to seek her parents'
consent. But Tepan objected, and finally she led him
far away, to her own village.

Now, the father of Amanaitu was Jaguar, and
Jaguar was furious that his daughter had married Man,

and would not recognize the union. Jaguar said, "Henceforward, Man and Jaguar shall no more hunt together, nor shall they be friends."

"Now it grows bad," said Tukanu to Moon; like the children, he looked frightened. Only the old women, poking and cackling, seemed more entertained than awed. "How did bad happen?" Tukanu demanded. "How did bad happen?"

And the day came when an owl appeared to Tepan's mother to say that Jaguar had killed Tepan.

"Aow! S-ss-tchuh!" Tukanu blubbered, glaring accusingly at Moon. "Didn't I say it? And now it grows still worse!"

The mother of Tepan followed the owl to the village of Jaguar. She recovered her son's body and returned. At the funeral ceremony, nipi was drunk, and two kinsmen of Tepan volunteered to avenge him. They traveled to Jaguar's village, where a feast was under way, and there slew both Jaguar and his wife.

Now his listeners all cried out, but Boronai watched Moon. Moon thought: How calm he is! How well he speaks! And he is telling his story to me, to me. And why?

The kinsmen were caught, but the people of Jaguar, frightened by so many deaths, forgave them and set them free, calling after them that there should be no more death, that all must live in peace.

But Amanaitu left Jaguar's village and went to the village of Tepan, where she slew the men who had killed Jaguar. Then she cried out, *"Now there shall be no death!"*

Boronai . . . He sees me nod—look, he is almost smiling! And how Aeore frowns! Is Aeore the least innocent or the most?

But a terrible voice rolled from the Heavens: *Death!* And there was flood and earthquake, wind and fire, and fish swam out on land and crawled, and animals who had lived in peace attacked one another, and most of the Earth's living things died in the deluge.

Pindi said, "Glou, glou"; but Moon refused to catch her eye.

Now the People cried out to the Great Ancestor Witu'mai, "It was not our fault! If Tepan had not killed Caiman, if Jaguar had not killed Tepan—! Is it not the fault of Witu'mai that bad people appear on Earth?"

Tukanu was furious, pounding his fist upon the ground. "It was not our fault—!"

Then the People congratulated themselves that an explanation had been found, and that all was well again. But the Ancestor sent a Messenger in the form of Man, saying, "Before this time you lived in eternal darkness and eternal life. Now you must choose, forever. You may have eternal darkness with eternal life, or you may have light and death. If you choose the first, and then take a life among you, you shall thereafter have the second."

The People cried, "But why do you make us choose, when we will only quarrel? We were happier before!"

And they glared at one another, and harangued and fought. Some said that they had had enough of darkness, and others said that they did not wish to die, and others reviled the Messenger for giving them their choice, and slew him. Then the People stopped fighting, and gazed at the Heavens in dismay.

And the terrible voice came from the Heavens: "You have chosen. You shall have light and death."

And the Heavens cleared, and the World was quiet once again. The Sun appeared, and a warm light bathed the World.

But even as they praised the Sun, an old man died.

Tukanu was incensed by the visit to the flooded forest, swearing loudly that Aeore's irresponsible behavior would bring the *guhu'mi* down upon their heads; in his excitement he also swore that he would take Kisu-Mu there himself and bring back a canoe bursting with game. To prove this, he shot arrows high into the air in demonstration of his prowess. But until the Falling River Time, when the Tuaremi was sucked back into its channel, Tukanu did not go near the deluged regions, nor did any of the others. Pindi told Moon that night spirits roamed the flooded forest even in daylight, and that the giant anacondas came up out of their swamps and swam among the trees. Aeore believed this too, yet he had dared to penetrate the unknown, for he would become a jaguar-shaman, a wanderer of night worlds.

Aeore was proud of their adventure, and when the rivers fell again he often took Moon in his canoe. They hunted tapir at the salt licks and speared huge pirarucu in the Creek of the Agoutis; they gathered resin for glue and canoe-caulking from the balata trees, and strychnos vines to make curare poison for their arrows. Once, on a journey of several days, they probed the still creeks to the north, and poled across huge viscous swamps where slept the Mother of Anacondas. They cut wild cane to make new shafts, and wandered among sites of ancient villages now overgrown in purple-flowered tonka bean. They studied strange carvings made by the Ancestors on the river rocks, from which Aeore had copied those in his canoe, and they portaged the Monkey Rapids from which the People sprang.

Rarely did Aeore express himself; their communion was a silent one. He seemed intent on revealing to Kisu-Mu an inner mystery, for what purpose Moon never knew; this mystery became the more obscure the more he tried to solve it. Aeore gave the Great Spirit of the Rain no credit for omniscience, assuming from his ignorance of Niaruna ways that Kisu-Mu had much to learn. Yet he did not permit himself the liberties that Tukanu took with Kisu-Mu; nor would he, Moon thought, until he had resolved a point not even suspected by the others—that Kisu-Mu

212

was not a god at all, but a common trickster, like the trickster turtle.

One evening in this period the young warriors who had served that day as scouts returned from the mission with the new machetes and packets of salt put out on the gift racks. The village split immediately into hostile groups. One of these, led by Aeore and composed largely of those who would not share in the booty, ranted furiously that the white man had come to stay, that he had come as an enemy—had he not brought in Green Indians with their guns?—and that he must be driven out or killed; his group then broke into factions of its own, disputing ownership of the four guns that would be captured in the victory.

A second group was led by Tukanu, who had acquired one of the machetes, and who—though he had never seen a gun actually fired—asserted forcefully that the Green Indians could kill ten Niaruna with each shot, and that any survivors would be deaf as stones. This estimate of the power of guns had been passed down to Tukanu from those forebears who had participated in the great massacre at the rubber camp, long, long ago.

The two groups faced each other in the center of the clearing. The men were stiff as stalking dogs, exchanging insults in a vibrant whining singsong and fingering their weapons; much of the abuse was ritualized, one side looking past the other as it spoke, while the recipients of the abuse politely awaited their turn. Then a remark was made which caused both sides to shout at once; Aeore called out that one of Tukanu's allies had long wished to kill Aeore himself. Since Aeore had ambitions as a shaman, he was simply making a discreet threat on the accused's life. The threat, with its overtone of sorcery, frightened all the men on both sides, and Boronai, seeing the village on the point of self-destruction, commanded the scouts to return all presents to the racks by sunrise, in the exact position they had found them. The scouts agreed to this more readily than Moon expected, though not before a last sulky exchange which nearly upset the compromise. But once it was seen that nobody would get the presents and that the band would revert to its usual custom of sharing food, feather headdresses, canoes and, under certain circumstances, dogs and wives—everything, in fact, according to the need, except for bows and cooking pots—the hostility vanished quickly, and by the next day all was as gay and amicable as before. After this episode, nevertheless, the factions led by Aeore and Tukanu remained intact.

So far, Moon had forestalled Aeore's demand that Boronai attack and kill the missionaries. Guzmán must not be given his excuse to wipe out the Niaruna. He tried to persuade Aeore that if the Niaruna took no notice of the mission, the white men would soon go away; if they did not, the mission gardens could be destroyed and the white men threatened. But Aeore insisted that the white men wished to make slaves of the Niaruna, as the Niaruna once made slaves of the filthy Tiro; that the white men were teaching evil—*emita*—to Kori's band, and would do as much for them. Moon tried to understand the latter point, which had something to do with Kisu; but when pressed for an explanation, Aeore only spoke more angrily and incoherently. Boronai and Tukanu, as well, were extremely uneasy on this subject, and refused to talk to him at all.

The scouts continued to watch the mission, and the day came toward the end of the rainy season when the Hubens and the Green Indians went away downriver, leaving the Quarriers alone. Meanwhile, Tukanu had been seized once more with love for his Taweeda. He wished to abduct her from the mission, and would have done so had not Taweeda herself refused to go along. Taweeda had now become addicted to beads and bandages, and could not understand why Tukanu did not present himself to the missionaries and avail himself of the same supply. At a loss, Tukanu decided to comply. As the band suffered from a shortage of adult women, and since Tukanu seemed convinced that Taweeda would come away with him sooner or later and perhaps bring her husband with her, Boronai gave the love-struck man his blessing.

Aeore, having first denounced Tukanu, then proclaimed that he too would go along, to make certain that the Farter spoke the truth. Moon persuaded Boronai to go with Aeore, lest Aeore provoke some lethal incident. The headman agreed to this on the condition that he be accompanied by his young wife Pindi, who had come originally from Kori's band in exchange for the captive nuns, and wished to see her people. For a moment it seemed that the entire group, which a few days before had shouted fiercely for the slaughter of the Quarriers, now meant to go there and befriend them; Moon only suppressed a mass evacuation with the greatest difficulty.

As she left, Moon studied Pindi's gait, knees close together and feet out to the side, hips shifting prettily despite her noticeable pregnancy; he was not consoled by Tukanu's last-minute offer of an old woman to tide him over during Pindi's absence.

In the days that followed, Aeore and Boronai stayed at the mission; they could not persuade the stubborn Tukanu to come back home with them. Not that any of the three were happy there; unlike Pindi, who was much amused by mission life, the three men were soon dispirited by evidence of their own inferiority. The white man, it seemed to them, had everything, and the Niaruna nothing. This idea was encouraged by the people of Kori, with their beads and mirrors and machetes, their bright blue shorts and their familiarity with the white man's ways; Kori did not waste an opportunity to treat Boronai and his men like savages. For psalm-singing, translating, and doing women's work which the three refused to do, these cowards were well paid in gifts, and the discrepancy increased.

Tukanu told Moon later that for his part, he would have sung psalms willingly for a knife, but that Kori had told Quarrier that Boronai's men were dangerous and lazy, and Boronai himself, offended that no deference had been shown him, had forbidden Tukanu to save his soul, much less wear blue shorts. Boronai remained at the mission only because Tukanu's woman would not leave with them; he feared the loss of one of his best men. Taweeda had a bright red dress to wear, and had been promised giant beads when she found Kisu; she had found Kisu instantly, experiencing a miracle right on the spot, but Quarrier was not generous like the other white man. He had not accepted her conversion, and she would not leave the mission without her beads.

Quarrier's woman had learned all about Tukanu and had told Taweeda that she was bad, bad, bad, but as Taweeda's husband knew all about Tukanu also, and accepted his lot with the serenity of the wise coward, Taweeda did not understand what all the trouble was about. On the other hand, she needed giant beads more than she needed Tukanu, and as Tukanu himself thought this logical and fair, he was content to wait.

With his companions gone, Moon quickly became restless; even the fishing and hunting began to bore him as he became expert, and like the Niaruna, took his expertness for granted. He began to think again, and the more he thought, the more an ambition hardened. What had not occurred to him in the beginning was how he might help the Niaruna; nor had it occurred to him soon after his arrival in the forest, so intent had he been upon survival. But now he saw that he could help protect these rivers from the white man; with any sort of leadership, the Indians could rule their wilderness indefinitely.

Aeore's ambition was an alliance with his own People to the East. Why not? Boronai said that before the rubber slavers had scattered them, the Niaruna and the Yuri Maha had been a single people, and that the clans had banded together to destroy the rubber camp in the year that he was born; why wouldn't they do it in a new emergency? From the Niaruna world, the jungle spread eastward, all but unbroken, for two thousand miles—a new Indian nation, the greatest of all time, greater even than the Iroquois!

When the resolve burst upon him, filling him with energy, he was lying in the midday dust of the maloca doorway, his head nestled on the Ugly One's old yellow dog. Excited, he jumped to his feet, sat down, jumped up again. In his impatience, he got the revolver out and cleaned it. He had not looked at the gun in months, and after rubbing it bright, he turned it in the sun and marveled at it; the gun was the one piece of metal in the village.

16

The Río Espíritu, on which the mission station was located, was a small tributary of a river system which flowed northward, draining the Andes, before turning east into the Amazon; the upper Espíritu was separated by a few miles of high ground from a nameless stream which, flowing directly eastward, joined the system of the river Purus. Both systems carried swiftly in the rainy season to the Amazon, but they traveled through different countries, losing themselves in ever greater rivers which in turn lost themselves, at points a thousand miles apart, in the great Río Mar.

Months had passed, and a second coming of the rains, and Billy Quarrier's world of birds and light, glades, rivers and bright-feathered arrows had again shrunk to a dungeon of rain-beaten huts, cut off by dark high dripping walls and a mud river. For some days the boy had lain in bed, limp from malarial delirium; quinine had not helped him, and Hazel had refused to give him a potion brought in a wooden bowl by the Niaruna. Because of bad weather it had not been possible to fly him out from Remate de Males.

Then one morning came a forecast of clear weather. As he spoke on the radio beside the cot, Quarrier watched a dark stain spread slowly on Billy's sheet. He had just arranged with Far Tribes Headquarters for a pontoon plane which would meet them the next day at Remate, but now he removed his earphones.

He could not speak. He stared at the sheet, then drew it back and lifted the child out of the cot and stood him on the floor before his pot. Billy was half asleep and weak and had to be supported; his skin felt hot and damp, and for the first time since his birth Quarrier was conscious of the odor of his breath.

"Billy, honey," he said, "you were wetting your bed."

"Oh," the child said, opening his eyes, "I didn't mean to, Pa."

"No. What I mean is, I want you to do a little more, into the pot. Can you do it?"

"Yes." But the child began to urinate with his arms and hands limp at his sides, and Quarrier reached down and took the small thing between his fingers, turning it toward the pot. The sensation was vaguely disagreeable. This strange tiny scrap of flesh was part of his own son, and his own son, by the next morning, would be dead.

For the urine was dark and discolored; in the pot it looked vile black.

From the doorway Hazel said, "Is it all right then? Are they going to meet us?"

"Billy has wet his bed."

At his tone, she darted forward. "For goodness' sake, what do you expect? Poor baby!" Worried and irritable, Hazel forsook the Indian child whose infection she had been bandaging; expressionless, the little girl watched the bandage unravel and drop onto the mud earth of the shed. After a time the child rose and came over and looked at the dark stain on the sheet, then at Quarrier and then at Hazel; she ran out of the hut.

Hazel stood there, gazing at the stain. In an odd voice, the more grotesque in this large woman who had never used baby talk in all her life, she said, "Now Billy-Willums, you're much too big a boy to wet your bed." She crashed down on her knees and grabbed the child's body in her arms. The act stirred him awake, and his arm rose slowly and wrapped itself around her neck. Over her shoulder his eyes widened, then focused vaguely on his father.

"Papa," he said. "Pa, I'm thirsty."

Hazel's face came around, glaring fiercely at Quarrier. "You see? The Lord has heard our prayers! He's better! We'll take him out of this dreadful place—is it all arranged? The Lord willing, we'll take him out this very day. Now get him water, do you hear me? Get him water!"

At Quarrier's elbow the receiver said, *"Niaruna Station, Niaruna Station. I repeat—is anything the matter? Over."* A moment later it said, *"We assume your transmitter is out of order, Martin. Les Huben called in this morning and is on his way to you—look for him on your way downriver. The aircraft will come to Remate de Males tomorrow at 1700 as arranged. If you do not make contact, we will try to get help in to you. The Lord's will be done. Amen. Over and out."*

Quarrier put on the earphones and took up the mouthpiece. "This is Niaruna Station. Do you read me? Over."

"Come back, Martin. What happened to you, fella? Over."

"Billy Quarrier has blackwater fever," Quarrier said. "We will stay here. We are not coming out. In the name of the Lord. Amen. Over and out." Once again he removed the earphones. He got down on his knees and put his arms around Hazel and his son. Like his wife, he was dry-eyed. *"Our Father which art in heaven,"* he began, *"Hallowed be thy name . . ."*

She wrenched away with a little grunt of pain. "You're insane," she said. Billy, hearing her tone, opened his eyes again. She laid him back on the bed, then lumbered to her feet and hurried toward the door. When Martin caught her in the yard, she struggled with him. "I'm going to fetch water," she said. "You're insane. Have you ever seen blackwater fever? No! It's just malaria, no more, no less, a bad case of malaria!" Hazel's face was stern and brisk, but her voice was rising to a scream. Out of green and brown walls at a little distance the Indians materialized. "I told you this was no place for a child! I told you, Martin, as the Lord is my witness!" And there sprang from her throat a terrible sound, quite unlike anything he had ever heard, and she sat clumsily and hard on the mud ground, as if struck backward. He hauled her to her feet again and tried to take her in his arms, but she broke free and pitched away toward the river bank. She was crying now, little shuddering cries of pain. "We are leaving this den of Satan!" she screeched at him over her shoulder. "Get them on the radio, do you hear! Do you hear me, Mr. Quarrier?"

He went back into the hut.

"... *lost contact temporarily with Niaruna Station ... blackwater fever ... repeat, all stations, all stations ... pray much for the salvation of Billy Quarrier who, though only nine years in this life on earth, is a fine ambassador of God among the savage Niaruna ... for Martin and Hazel Quarrier, that the good Lord may assist them in this time of need ... now Praise the Lord ..."*

Into the mouthpiece Quarrier said, "Now Praise the Lord." He turned off the machine, then went outside and switched off the small generator. Billy's friend Mutu slipped past him into the hut, and when Quarrier returned, was crouched by the bed talking rapidly to Billy. The sick boy's face was staring through the mist of fever, and his hand was clenched on his friend's wrist. When Quarrier tried to lead the Indian boy away, Billy cried out weakly, "No!" And Mutu, his face urgent and frightened, repeated a question several times, tugging each time at the sheet. Quarrier did not understand the question, but it was clear that Billy did; his son had long since spoken the language better than himself, and this awareness reminded him that sometime before morning came again this child before him whose name was Billy Quarrier—Billy Quarrier, he thought, Billy Quarrier; what did such words *mean*—and who had not lived long enough to commit a sin, would die. When he realized that Billy was watching him, he turned away and wiped the tears from his cheeks with both hands.

"Billy, what is he asking you?" he mumbled. Good Lord, I am talking to him, and he is going to die!

"He wants me to name my enemy," the boy said in a strange voice.

Going to die, going to die, going to die . . . "You have no enemy," Quarrier said. "My Lord!" He turned around. The Indian boy was speaking rapidly again, in the thick breathless speech of the Niaruna.

"He says the tribe will kill my enemy," Billy said. When his father took his face between his hands and kissed his forehead, the child began to cry, but while he cried he kept on talking peacefully. "He says that Boronai will find out who my enemy is, because if I die it means I have an enemy." He yawned through his tears and closed his eyes, smiling forgetfully, then opened them, afraid.

To the Indian boy Quarrier said, "He has no enemy. He is very sick. He was made sick by the mosquito. His only enemy is the mosquito. Tell Boronai that no one must be killed." The child stared at him, not understanding, then turned to Billy once again and repeated the question. Billy told him slowly what his father had already said, but his voice was vague, as if he did not understand it either. To his father he said, "The Indians say I am going to die, but here I am, alive."

"Yes," Quarrier said. He forced himself to meet the boy's gaze. Before he could stop her, Hazel came in and took Mutu by the ear and hauled him toward the door of the hut; the boy cringed from her and ran.

"Pa!" Billy yawned again, eyes closed. "It's kinda scary," he murmured. "Am I really going to die? I mean, *really?*" He began to cry again.

Quarrier took him in his arms. Turning to face Hazel, he said, "Yes, honey. You are going to die."

The water in her cup slopped onto the floor. "Curse you," her mouth said silently. She stopped crying; later it occurred to him that she never cried again. "May the Lord curse you." To Billy she said aloud, "Of course not, honey. Of course not. Papa is only fooling. Why, you'll be up and around in no time, and this afternoon we're going down the river, and you'll have a nice ride on the airplane, you—"

While Hazel spoke she made tentative movements toward Billy, but her husband, sitting on the cot edge with his son in his arms, made no gesture of relinquishment. They watched each other.

"Did you arrange about the plane?"

"We're going to stay here. Our work is here, and this is Billy's home."

She whirled and went outside, where she awaited him.

"You're a devil!" she said. "A devil! How dare you!" Her voice rose. "All your life you've been a stupid, stubborn man, and all your life you have been wrong." Her voice rose. "We won't talk now about the cruel and sinful thing you told that child. But how dare you claim to know this is blackwater fever—or even if it is, that he is dying!"

"Even the Indians know, Hazel. Please don't do this."

"How do they know?" She took him by the shirt and shook him. "The chances are they've never seen blackwater fever in their lives!"

"They may not know blackwater fever. They know when somebody is dying."

"How? I asked you, how? You'll drive me mad!"

"I don't know," he said. "But they always do." He turned and gazed into the shed where his son lay on his side, eyes wide, observing them. Then he seized Hazel by the arm. "Hazel, listen. This thing runs its course in twenty-four hours. We can't get him to a hospital before that, and even if we could, it would be too late." Still gripping her arm, he said, "Billy is dying. You know it as well as I do. We must help each other."

She tried to speak, but she could not. He left her standing there. From behind her, across the compound, the voice of an old woman had commenced a funeral wail.

In the shed the boy said weakly, "Pa?"

Quarrier took him in his arms again and squeezed him, and stared down into the small, scared face.

"Are you crying, Pa?"

"Yes, Bill, I am."

"I've never seen you cry."

"No."

A little later he said, "Pa."

"Billy, honey . . ."

"Why did God . . . You won't get mad at me?"

"No, Bill, I won't get mad at you."

"Then why did God have to go and make mosquitoes?"

"I don't know," Quarrier said. "I surely wish I knew."

Toward twilight Leslie Huben came, alone in his long canoe. Quarrier was grateful that Huben had come, but he was not glad of it, for he did not feel up to the effort of conversation, and he had reason to think that Huben's was less an errand of mercy than an inspection trip. In the eyes of the new Regional Supervisor of the Far Tribes Mission, Leslie Huben, Martin Quarrier was doubtless doing badly. As he walked down toward the river he saw that Huben, already on the bank, had assumed that arms-akimbo stance of his as he looked about him. But the smile on his face was not a bold, swashbuckling smile; it could scarcely be called a smile at all.

Boronai and his men appeared out of the jungle from downriver; they had been stalking Huben. The Indian women gathered on the bank. Though Kori's Indians knew Huben, they made no move to go to him and take his hand, nor did they answer his hearty call of greeting. Huben's expression changed rapidly from puzzlement to annoyance.

"You were foolish to come alone," Quarrier said, and frowned; he had meant to greet Huben with something more hospitable.

"I see I was," Huben snapped, his tone accusing. "What's turned them against me?"

"Indians aren't sentimental, Leslie."

"I know that, Martin, I know that. I've lived with these people too, remember?" He smiled suddenly and vigorously. "Well, how are you?" He sprang forward up the bank. "Greetings in the name of the Lord!"

When Quarrier took his hand, an old woman shuffled forward, giggling, and also shoved her palm at Huben; though Leslie knew that she was begging, he chose to misunderstand this and took the hand in his own. With his other hand he roughed her head affectionately, much as he might have greeted an old teammate.

"What's this one's name?" he said. "I can't remember."

"That's old Taweeda."

"But why is she naked?" He looked annoyed again. "You certainly haven't done much, Martin, to loosen Satan's hold. They all had Christian clothes when I left here, and now they're just as savage as when I started."

"I kind of discouraged their use of clothes," Quarrier said. "They didn't have any others to change into. They wore them even when they were wet, and I lost one old fellow to pneumonia."

"You mean you encourage them to go naked?"

"I don't think nakedness is a sin."

"I see." Huben smiled doggedly. "Well, Martin, we can discuss your progress later. Now tell me, how is Hazel? And how is the little patient?" They walked slowly toward the shelters.

Leslie agreed with Hazel that Billy should be taken out; weren't there other diseases that discolored urine? Did Quarrier have faith in the heathen instincts of these savages—and if so, Huben's tone implied, how did he reconcile that faith with his faith in the Lord God Almighty?

"This has been Billy's home," Quarrier said coldly. "It is the only home he knows. He will die among people who love him in their way, and he will die in truth, without hypocrisy, in the name of our Lord Jesus Christ." He stared pointedly at Huben. "Amen," he said.

Huben looked discomfited and vexed. "Home!" he said, glancing around the muddy yard. "My goodness!"

Hazel said to her husband, "Leslie has had the kindness and courage to come to us in our time of need, and all alone, and you are rude to him. You are a stubborn and willful man and you have taken upon yourself the sin of pride. May the Lord have mercy on your soul!"

"Amen," Quarrier said. "I don't mean to be rude," he said to Huben. "I'm only trying to think clearly."

"This is a terrible time of trial for you both," Leslie said, trying to mend things. "Now let us pray."

While Billy lived, the Indians came to him one by one, paying no attention to his parents; they did not speak to Billy but simply laid a hand on him, in parting, and went away again, expressionless. Only the old women, chanting their singsong in the huts across the clearing, gave any evidence of grief. The silent procession filled Hazel with horror; Martin had to restrain her from seizing her broom and driving the naked mourners from the shed. "They are paying respect," he said to her, over and over. "It is their way." During the visits, Billy smiled a little in a sleepy way, as if remembering something.

By nightfall Billy was unconscious; he did not wake again. Hazel and Leslie sat with him throughout the night, but Martin lay down on his bed and stared straight at the ceiling. He rose only when his son's breathing broke and faltered; then he hurried to the bedside. When Billy breathed peacefully again, he turned away. "Perhaps you would like to watch over your own son," Hazel whispered, "and give poor Leslie a rest."

"Watching won't help him," Martin said harshly. "Leslie can sleep whenever he likes."

Even now, he thought, she's scoring points in her private war; she can't restrain herself. And he thought bitterly about Hazel's love for Billy, a love that was most lavish and emotional at those times when she felt sorriest for herself. It was not Billy she embraced but the child Hazel; not Billy whom she cherished but the Hazel who, at Billy's age, had felt unloved, and whose injury was recalled to her by the smallest rejection or rebuke. A quarrel sent her running to her child in an excess of crooning love which had nothing to do with the real love she actually felt; it sickened Quarrier, not because it was insincere but because the true object of it went unrecognized. He had known his wife to rout their child out of his sleep to bathe them both in her own emotion; the snuffling and wallowing was at times more than he could bear. Even when still very young, Billy had sniffed out the strangeness of this behavior, and with a vague, dignified expression had searched his father's face for some sort of explanation. Once he had tried to question his father, but Quarrier had only hushed him: "Another time," he said.

Another time, another time. Ah Christ, who would have thought that time would have run out so very suddenly? The time to convey his love for his own son before he died, was that so much to ask—this love choked him now for want of a way to shout it out. But wasn't this the charge that he had made against his wife? Martin Quarrier, are you not sorry for yourself? I am; before God I am. I am heartily sorry. Perhaps Hazel knew, perhaps she *knew* . . . something I did not know. The doom and bafflement that came in time to every face—perhaps she had glimpsed this even in Billy's shining eyes, had anticipated all the wounds to come, and rushed to cover him. He stared at Hazel's back, at her bent neck; he felt sick to the heart.

Ah, Hazel, poor dumb suffering brute . . .

That huge bafflement was the inescapable affliction; he had seen it on every face he knew. The startled look on Andy's face when, once or twice, he had seen her lift her head from knitting to stare at Huben: *Who is this man? Why am I with him?* Or Leslie himself, under God's new outboard power, roaring up triumphantly to greet his flock, only to be met with a sullenness close to hostility: *But I've given you love; why is it you dislike me?* Or that man Wolfie, stunned by the curtness of his partner so soon after he had saved Moon's life: *How do ya like that? Well, how do ya like that?* At moments, stunned and groggy at the hands of life, even the hardest face looked innocent: *Where has life gone? What will become of me?*

Another time, another time.

Billy had dignity, all right; he had *integrity.* He had never noticed such integrity in a child, though perhaps all children started with it. One day he had beaten Billy for disobeying Hazel, not because Billy had been bad—since the morning she had hurt the butterfly he had lost his last confidence in his mother and instinctively resisted her—but out of his own frustration with his wife. Billy had not given way to rage or tears but had remained dry-eyed and silent, craning his head back to stare straight into his father's eyes, and regarding him in this thoughtful way for some time afterward—not in anger or contempt (he had actually taken his father's hand after a minute, and had sat with him quietly by the river), but with that same questioning expression, making his father feel inept, unwise.

Later he saw Billy walking alone across the clearing, trying to work everything out. The little boy was talking to himself; he stopped and raised his arms and let them fall again, walking onward.

Toward dawn, Billy opened his eyes, strained forward, then fell back from life with a look of wonderment, staring ahead of him as at something astonishing, his small face wide-eyed, the clean mouth slightly parted, as if he were about to say, "Hey, Pa! C'mere, Pa! Lookit!"

Hazel stiffened like an animal pierced through the spine. She made a tiny peeping sound, like a baby chick (now how in the world does she make a sound like that?) and Leslie wept, simply and quietly (well, Leslie, please forgive me). It was Leslie who closed the wide blue eyes (now why is he doing that to Bill?). Martin got down upon his knees and opened up the eyes again with a gasp of love and stared deep into them, but they were glazing so rapidly that all he could see was a mirror of his own disbelief. He took the dead boy in his arms. Billy's body was so warm, and he still had that soft powdery smell that he had had as a small baby. "Good-bye, Bill!" he cried out, clutching him tight. "Oh Bill, oh Billy, listen—!" When Leslie touched his shoulder, he eased the body down again. Leslie closed the eyes a second time, and all three prayed.

"As it is written, For thy sake we are killed all the day long; we are accounted as sheep for the slaughter. Nay, in all these things we are more than conquerors through him that loved us. . . ."

In the morning, on the highest ground, Martin and Leslie dug a grave. Martin made a heavy red cross of mahogany; this was planted as a headstone. The Indians watched him, but made no effort to assist. Death was not inevitable; death was unnatural; the failure to name an enemy they saw as cowardice, and the rapidity of the funeral, with the imprisonment of Billy's spirit in the dark cold earth, was an insult to the dead.

Nevertheless, Kori's men remained that morning in the village, and so did the wild Niaruna, and though Quarrier spoke the funeral service in English, every Indian was present in a sullen circle, and every one of them stared angrily at Hazel's stony grief, offended that she did not wail and tear her hair.

"Verily I say unto you, Except ye be converted, and become as little children, ye shall not enter into the kingdom of heaven. Whosoever therefore shall humble himself as this little child, the same is greatest in the kingdom of heaven. . . ."

But when Hazel sank onto her knees and held up her hands in prayer, the naked people imitated her so readily that afterward Huben exclaimed, "Yet you say you have no converts here! Not a single believer in all this time!"

"You knew that, Leslie."

"Not even that old woman wailing, the one who greeted me yesterday? Surely Taweeda wishes to believe!" Huben grasped Quarrier in a rough embrace and smiled at him, tears in his eyes. "The Lord is here with us this morning, Martin Quarrier! I can feel it in my heart—these lost souls are ready for the Lord! Did you see them on their knees? And perhaps the Lord, in all His wisdom, has seen fit to take Billy Quarrier to His great fold in order that these poor souls might see the light and know His Son Jesus Christ at last!" Huben gazed skyward. "Let us lift up our voices!

> "Waft, waft ye winds His store-ry
> And ye, ye waters roll
> Till like a sea of glore-ry
> It spreads from pole to pole. . . ."

Quarrier, gone pale, waited for Huben to stop singing. Hazel, who was struggling to sing also, began to falter. "Martin—" she said, for her husband wore such a look of rage and grief that it seemed to her he might go mad.

"The Lord," Quarrier said in a strange voice, "did not take my son. Death took my son. But if He had, the Lord would not be welcome to my son. Do you understand that? *He is not welcome to my son!*"

230

The Indians watched, and the warriors beside the headman, Boronai, pointed at Huben, grumbling. Boronai observed the white man without expression.

"May the Lord forgive you," Huben said.

"You were kind to come here," Quarrier said. "It took courage. But I must ask you to leave me alone; I will try to make my own peace with the Lord, and if I cannot—why, I cannot."

17

Preparations had been under way since the moment that the Indians knew the child would die. The women had gone out to the plantations along the jungle edge and had brought back large bundles of manioc to make masato. Now the men were using the utensils of the women, and the women and children were nowhere to be seen.

A rude tray was taken from the women's cooking fires, and onto this tray was scraped the bark layers of a woody vine. A mortar was brought, and the reddish shreds of bark were ground up in water in the mortar. Leaves of another plant were added, and the resulting infusion placed in a clay pot. The men squatted in a stolid circle and watched it boil.

Quarrier approached the fire. Intent upon the flame, the Indians took little notice of him. He picked up a flowering length of the vine, with its neat leaves and small clusters of flowers, saying to one of Boronai's men, "Why do you make nipi?"

"Boronai will drink nipi," the one called Tukanu said. "Then he will speak to Kisu."

"No," Quarrier said, "no, he will not speak to Kisu. A man cannot speak to Kisu except through prayer."

"Boronai will speak to Kisu," the one called Aeore said; it was this man who had once stabbed Quarrier in the chest. For Quarrier's benefit he spoke slowly, as to a child, and his contempt was open; with Billy the Indians had spoken naturally. "He will speak to Kisu, and Kisu will tell him the name of Billy's enemy. We will revenge the death of Billy." Aeore's face grew sullen; he blew air suddenly from his mouth to indicate impatience, and would not speak further. He was a hawk-faced Indian whose muttering ways recalled to Quarrier the Sioux troublemakers in his former mission. Aeore was the worst sort of savage, lazy and arrogant, vain, volatile and treacherous.

To Tukanu, Quarrier said, "Billy's enemy was the mosquito. You must not kill any man."

Tukanu, a short heavy man with a stupid face, said something rapidly and angrily, then heaved around on his buttocks so that his back faced Quarrier. But Quarrier understood. Tukanu had said, "The enemy sent the mosquito."

Kori's men imitated Tukanu and Aeore and turned their backs to him, though Boronai still watched him from the head of the oval circle. Gazing down at the impassive backs, Quarrier felt a wild impulse to kick them. After all his work with the Niaruna, this sullen resistance was the only thing he could count on. To Boronai he said, "You must not try to speak with Kisu. You must not kill."

Boronai watched him without expression. Then he said, "We do not ask you to obey the Kisu of the Niaruna. Why do you ask us to obey the Kisu of the white man?"

Over his shoulder, Kori said to Quarrier, "The people are angry with you. Billy lived like a Niaruna, and yet you did not treat his spirit as a Niaruna spirit must be treated. The spirit of Billy will be angry and will bring us harm. Now Boronai will drink nipi. He will listen to Kisu. Then he will find the enemy of Billy and kill him; then the spirit of Billy will go far away and sleep." Since Boronai had settled at the mission, Kori and his tame Indians had discarded all pretense of Christianity and were waiting to be bribed anew. As for Boronai, he refused to listen to Christian

At Play in the Fields of the Lord

teachings or even accept gifts, and his intransigence had infected all the rest.

In the afternoon the men of the village covered themselves from head to foot with the red achote, and a few smeared it in their hair. By the sinking fire Boronai sat alone, staring fixedly at the pot.

"What are they doing?" Huben inquired; he had joined Quarrier in the doorway of the shed.

"They are making nipi."

"From a vine bark? A vine with small white flowers?"

"Yes."

"It is evil, Martin. It's *ayahuasca,* the same stuff that fellow Moon—"

Quarrier shrugged. "Sometimes it's used medicinally. An emetic. I haven't discovered all its uses, but I am keeping notes. Also it's used for religious purposes—prophecy, divination, things like that."

"What are you saying, Martin?"

"Ours isn't the only religion in the world," Quarrier said. "If it was, we wouldn't be here."

"Do you know that this nipi of yours is a dangerous narcotic, that it turns men into maniacs, that life is often taken as a result of it? Look what happened to that man Moon!"

Quarrier watched a bird fly across the river, black as a spirit of the dark to come against the last sharp silver light; the swiftness of the jungle night impressed him strangely every time he saw it. He tried to concentrate on Huben, who looked offended that his outburst had gone unanswered.

"They will take a life this time too," Quarrier said.

"And you're not going to stop them?"

"I know I must try, but I also know I cannot stop them."

"You admit that?"

"I don't *admit* it, Leslie. It's a statement."

"And what if I stepped over to that fire and dumped that cursed brew of Satan upon the ground?"

"I think Boronai's men would kill you, because that stuff is sacramental. They might let me get away with it because of Billy, but I'm not even confident of that."

Huben shook his head. "I'm beginning to believe you," he said slowly. "Not one soul in this whole wilderness realizes that God loves them! These people are as savage as they were when I first made contact with them!"

Quarrier nodded. "I have four wild Niaruna here, including the girl. They haven't killed us, they were fond of Billy and they have a word for our Lord Jesus Christ. I can't claim more than that."

"But why? What have you left undone?"

"You mean, I suppose, *What have you done wrong?* And I don't know." Quarrier turned to go into the shed. "I've prayed and prayed and I've racked my brain and I don't know. They don't like me, and they don't like what I teach. If it hadn't been for Billy, they would have killed us or driven us out long, long ago."

Hidden in the darkness of their shed, they watched the savages. Hazel watched with them, but she did not speak and did not really see. She gazed steadfastly at the cross on Billy's grave, which wavered in the shadows of the flames.

In the firelight, his warriors brought a feather crown to Boronai and fixed it on his head. His arms and shoulders were painted bright rusty-red, and his face was smeared with whitish clay. On this mask were drawn sharp lines of black, two beneath the eyes and two passing from the ears, skirting the corners of his mouth and forming a small cross at the chin. Boronai maintained, as he had for hours, his squatting position by the fire and a fixed, unblinking stare.

Finally he stood, and a calabash of the manioc beer was brought to him. He raised it ceremonially, the light flickering on the broad muscles of his arms and legs; he returned it untouched to Aeore. The calabash was passed from hand to hand, and the red

235   *At Play in the Fields of the Lord*

figures drank it off, refilled the calabash and drank it off again. Standing there, they began a slow shuffling stamp while Tukanu filled the calabash another time. Meanwhile Aeore took up the smaller pot that had been cooling near the fire and presented it to Boronai.

Now Boronai began to chant, more and more loudly, his mouth splitting the white mask; while his men stamped violently in rhythm he spread his legs wide, threw his head back and drank the nipi at a gulp. He straightened again, breathing hoarsely, then turned slowly in a circle, arms extended toward the jungle night, which surrounded the clearing like a high black wall.

"Kisu!" he shouted. *"Kisu, ne binde nipi. Boronai u tima!"*

" 'Kisu,' " Quarrier whispered to Huben. " 'I have drunk nipi, that I may go to you!' "

"Are you sure of all this?"

"I've questioned them. Billy spoke their tongue so well that I could use him as interpreter, and I deduced what I could." He pointed at a large packing box beneath his cot. "Those are all notes on the Niaruna."

"You're not here as a sociologist, Martin." Huben was fretful and snappish; he was glaring at the Indians, who had commenced a monotonous grunting stamp, up and down, up and down, chanting in time to the slap of their bare feet upon the mud, and passing the calabash back and forth. Each time it was emptied, a man fell out of line and filled it up again. Stamp, scrape—*eugh! aagh!* Stamp, scrape—*eugh! aagh!* Before long, a man leaned out and vomited a gutful of the masato, forcefully and neatly, without losing step; when the calabash next came around to him he drank heavily again.

Stamp, scrape—*eugh! aagh!* Stamp, scrape—*eugh! aagh!*

"All these tribes drink masato," Huben persisted when Quarrier said nothing, "and most of them use nipi, and they all get drunk and disgusting like this,

236

and fight and fornicate and kill! That's why we're here, Martin, can't you see? Perhaps if you had spent less time taking notes . . ."

"Well, they never drink the way our Christian Indians do—just to get drunk." He tried once more to put his arm around his wife's shoulder, to comfort her, but she was stiff as chalk. When Billy died Hazel had said, "Suppose he hadn't died in twenty-four hours? Suppose he hadn't? Suppose, through blind stupidity and pride, you caused his death? I know you think that because you were right, I should forgive you, but I don't. And I never will."

Boronai was bellowing incoherently; he had taken a second draught of nipi. His warriors kept a close eye on him and speeded the tempo of their dancing; the red bodies gleamed like salamanders in the firelight, coiling and sweating, and strange whooping calls were interspersed with heavy grunts and breathings. When Boronai, with a sudden screech, ran for his bow and arrows, the others scattered to the edges of the compound, trying to avoid him, but still they danced and grunted, jerking eerily in the far shadows of the firelight. In the center, all alone, the headman stood, enormous in his crown, the mouth hole in the ghastly mask twisted by a sound wrenched from his body; he fitted an arrow to his bow, and the head of the arrow moved in a slow circle, like the head of a snake. Then he circled, stalking the red figures in the background. Nearing the shed, his black silhouette sprang suddenly into its entrance; he jabbed the arrow toward the four corners, ignoring the white people drawn back into the shadows.

Huben murmured, "What is he doing? I don't like this."

At the sound of Huben's voice, Boronai leaped back into the firelight and drove the arrow violently into the earth, then another, then another, so that all the arrows quivered in the same spot. He raised a final arrow and brandished it, then fell upon his knees and stared at the sky, bringing his hands up slowly before his face and clasping them, as if in imitation of Hazel at Billy's funeral.

The red bodies danced toward Boronai from the shadows and, grouped around him in a circle, imitated him. They maintained the *eugh! aagh! eugh! aagh!* of their grunting, and one man, then another, sat back upon his heels to belch out the yellow fluid of his masato.

"It's disgusting," said Huben angrily, "disgusting, sinful drunkenness. To think they could pray and vomit drunkenly at the same time!"

Quarrier said, "The vomiting is a purge. To clean their souls." The expression that came to Huben's face did him more good than anything in days.

Hazel said, "You are insane. Even if what you say is true, you are insane."

A bat swirled in the golden smoke over the fire. Still on his knees, Boronai straightened and stiffened; muscles rigid, soundless, he fell forward across the fire logs. Aeore and Tukanu dragged him out and laid him down, brushing the cinders from his chest, while Kori's men fetched a new calabash of masato. Drinking, they squatted by the fallen headman.

At dawn Boronai was still in trance, stretched out on the ground beside the fire. Around him the men curled, lying almost in the embers, for the dawn was dank and cold, and the early sun was sealed off by the green walls, the shrouds of mist. The forest macaws remained oddly silent; high off in the world of green they were content to ruffle their wet feathers, blinking slow reptilian lids and shifting big pale feet.

As Quarrier and Huben came out of the shed, Tukanu rose unsteadily and grunted at the others. The cracked red of his face paint in the morning light gave him a swollen look; his eyes were red and there was dirt in the black disheveled hair cropped close around the ears.

"The noble savage!" Huben said. "My goodness!"

Tukanu turned his gaze from Quarrier, whose greetings he had ignored, to Leslie Huben. The others rose behind him, all but Boronai, who lay as still as death. In the silent clearing the women of Kori's band materialized. With them was Pindi, Boronai's young wife, who sauntered forward with a saucy swing of her big pregnant belly; she grazed Tukanu with her bare hip and confronted Huben. Taking hold of his shirt by the upper sleeve, she tugged at it, then pointed at herself: *"Cushma le mato Pindi."*

When the wild Niaruna had first come, Boronai offered to share this girl with Quarrier, not because he wished to—the idea plainly displeased him—but because, sensing the void between Quarrier and his woman, he saw the offer as an obligation to his host. Quarrier's refusal had so astonished and insulted him that he threatened the white man with his lance. Quarrier called out to Hazel, and together they acted out a macabre charade of bliss, which sorely offended the headman's idea of good taste. Under her breath as she stroked her husband's head, Hazel said sarcastically, "You might have made the sacrifice, to spare our lives."

And Quarrier said brutally, "I didn't refuse because I didn't want her. I refused because I wanted her. If I hadn't wanted her, God might have accepted such an act as sacrifice."

Later he had begged Hazel's forgiveness, but Hazel had been cheerful. "At least you said something I could get mad at!" She laughed wildly. "Imagine being condemned to live with Jesus Christ!"

"Do you know what you're saying?"

"Yes, I do."

Cushma le mato Pindi. But Pindi's smile was less cajoling than contemptuous; when Leslie did nothing, she tugged his shirt again, then yanked at its throat, tearing a button. When he reached down to pick it up, she stooped and snatched the button from beneath his hand, then sashayed fat-bellied around him, laughing at him.

The Indians had picked up their bows and arrows and were forming a loose circle around the missionaries; they clearly expected Huben to be named as Billy's enemy.

Quarrier said, "I think you'd better go."

Huben said, "I think so too, but will they let me?" He cleared his throat. "I don't like the look of this. Maybe you and Hazel had better come out with me."

Hazel, who had been watching from the doorway, came toward the fire with a big pot of rice and water. The fire was centered between the tips of three large logs, which were inched forward as they burned; an old woman came forward and moved one of the logs, and Hazel set the pot over the flame. This was their fire, and the food was meant for them; the Indians put down their bows, yawning and stretching. But Tukanu shot an arrow straight up into the sky, so skillfully that it thudded down again but a few yards away. He did this several times, bending his bow farther and farther, and each time stared at Leslie in triumphant malice. The Indians sighed restlessly at every shot, for it meant that they had to keep an eye out for the arrow; whether Tukanu took this as a sign of recognition or whether he was caught, like a small child, in the snare of his own bravado, he kept at his solitary game, the more intensely as his audience lost interest, until finally his bow snapped. The other Indians laughed at him, and though Leslie did not laugh, the furious Tukanu singled him out anyway and shouted at him, waving an arrow.

Seeking to deflect Tukanu's outrage, Leslie turned his back on him. At the fire, Hazel had uncovered the pot of rice, and the Indians, no longer concerned about Tukanu's arrows, were squatting around it, dipping their fingers and yanking them out again, getting as much rice as they could without being burned. Huben had brought a big grin to his face, but Tukanu spun him around and shouted at him contemptuously; when Huben did nothing, Tukanu jabbed him in the chest with the point of his arrow, harder and harder, until he

240

drew blood. Huben put his hands up to protect himself, and Tukanu jabbed him in the hands until they bled. The other warriors leveled arrows at the white men.

Huben held his ground, but over his shoulder he said to Quarrier, "Can't you control this? You had better control this."

Quarrier stepped forward and laid one hand on Tukanu's shoulder; pointing the other straight at the sky, he shouted, "Kisu!"

Tukanu shrank back, and all but one warrior lowered their bows; this one, Aeore, released his arrow at Huben, but caught it in the fingers of his bow hand as it left the cord. The warriors grumbled in excitement.

"We're going," Huben said, "this very minute."

"All right." Quarrier felt weak with fear. "Take Hazel to the boat. I'll speak to them." To Hazel he said, "Never mind your things." She followed Huben, who had assumed an angry expression and had marched straight at the largest group of Indians, and through them, toward the river. Neither he nor Hazel turned to look back. The big sweat-streaked back of Hazel's dress, the baffled gait—Quarrier came to his senses, raising his hands high above his head.

"You are bad people!" he shouted. "We have come as friends. We have brought presents, and now—" he could not find the Niaruna words. On impulse, he seized the arrow from the hand of Tukanu, who grunted in surprise. Around the circle the bows came up again. Quarrier pointed the arrow after Huben, then at his own chest, in imitation of what Tukanu had done. "You are bad people!" he shouted again.

He intended to break Tukanu's arrow, to hurl the pieces to the ground, but he caught himself in time. Tukanu stepped forward, his broad face thickening with anger. Quarrier handed him the arrow before he could demand it, then turned his back on the Indian and raised both arms into the air. "We are your friends," he bellowed. "In the name of Kisu!"

Behind him Tukanu grunted once again; whether

or not the Indian had raised the arrow, Quarrier never knew.

The Indians followed him to the river bank. They talked rapidly among themselves, pointing and spitting. Huben was adrift in his own boat, though well in range; the river here was scarcely twenty yards across. In the Quarriers' boat Hazel awaited him; as he cast off he said to her, "Don't look frightened, Hazel. Look angry if you can." Hazel looked neither frightened nor angry. Later he wondered if it had not been the spectacle of this woman, so clearly undismayed by—scarcely interested in—anything they might do to her, which had impressed the savages and stayed their hand.

The Indians were yipping and gesticulating, at a loss; seeking leadership, they clustered around Boronai, but he was still deep in his nipi. When Quarrier shouted, "Kisu!" Boronai had blinked and risen to his feet. Tottering, he had followed the procession to the bank. But now he only gazed at Quarrier, impassive. Then Aeore sprang free of the group and loosed a high arrow after Huben, but the gesture was tentative and the arrow struck harmlessly in the far bank beyond Huben's boat, where it could be retrieved. Nevertheless, it served as an incitement; the savages ran down along the bank, fitting their arrows.

Quarrier surged to his feet, nearly capsizing his boat. "Kisu!" he bawled. "Kisu is angry with you!"

Again the Niaruna stopped and stared.

A rage of pure despair came over him: so many long months of hard work, the loss of Billy, and for what? He circled the canoe and ran it full speed toward the Indians, ramming it high upon the bank. They scattered, grunting.

"I am staying here," he said to Hazel. "You can go out with Leslie." He waved at Huben, who was already circling back.

"I shall stay with you," Hazel muttered, "until death do us part."

"What are you doing?" Huben called. "Come on!"

Quarrier waved him off the bank. "We're staying,"

he yelled. "But you must go!" He felt certain that with Leslie gone, the Indians would calm down.

"God bless you then," yelled Leslie Huben. "Praise the Lord!"

18

While Leslie was absent from Madre de Dios, Yoyo came to notify Andy Huben that a large consignment of barbed wire had arrived on the plane from the coast and been dumped at the airstrip; Andy must come immediately and sign for it. This was quite unnecessary, since the local agent could just as well have brought the slip into the town, but the opportunity for a small ceremony was not permitted to go to waste. The citizens had assembled to view the epochal cargo, the like of which had never been seen in Oriente State, and the bolder among them were fingering the bales, which were lined up like soldiers for Andy's inspection. *Just as I thought,* their judicious expressions said, *the finest quality.* Yoyo rushed forward, and with cries and kicks drove off a dog that had ventured to lift its leg upon the wire; as its official guardian, the Indian was extremely jealous of the wire, the transfer of which to the river front, the river barge, and Remate de Males promised no end of opportunities for self-assertion and abusive shouting.

In the dull soft airs the wire gleamed; the sheer bulk of it broke down the stoicism with which Andy had received, that morning, the news of Billy's death. When suddenly she wept, the airline agent was already launched on an official sort of speech. The onlookers nodded wisely. Such cargoes did not arrive in Madre de Dios every day, and with the *emoción* of the *evangél-*

ica, the success of the presentation ceremonies had been assured.

Andy's *simpático* performance at the airstrip was so well received that her return to the Gran Hotel was attended by throngs of admirers; the soft-voiced men speculated loudly on the uses of barbed wire, hoping to be corrected and enlightened. Since the truth sounded so foolish—*my husband prayed for this barbed wire to insure his privacy at the mission*—she pretended not to hear, and the natives were much too timid and polite to question her directly. How hopeful they were, she thought, in the total hopelessness of their existence! If she was not careful, their childlike shyness would start her crying all over again. Overwhelmed, she turned in the hotel doorway to smile at them, tears in her eyes, and the small men, in consternation at this sign of favor, tossed bright bouquets of compliments and smiles, and nudged, wrestled and congratulated one another, disregarding the jeers of fat Mercedes in the window.

Oh Billy—she lay down on her bed and laid her pillow on her breast and hugged it. And Hazel, and Martin, that poor dogged Martin—what kept people going? The image of Martin Quarrier's coarse red bewildered face brought on her tears again. Getting down on her knees beside the bed, she prayed for him, but in the middle of the prayer she caught a self-conscious note in her voice and stopped. On the bed again, she drew her legs up and wrapped her arms around her knees and tried to squeeze the last tears from her heart.

But her heart refilled, and filled again; she cried for everyone. Everyone seemed to her as innocent as Billy, an innocent encrusted over; even Guzmán, even that terrible rude fat Mercedes in Guzmán's kitchen, even Lewis Moon, that night he was last seen on earth: *Listen! I* know *something, Andy* . . . And Yoyo. Running to fetch her, Yoyo had allowed his crucifix to slip outside the bright red rocket shirt given to him by Leslie, and in his haste to stuff it back in hiding, had dropped something from his breast pocket, where he

kept old pencil stubs and scraps of wastepaper; she
had picked up this paper scrap just now and looked at
it. On the back of a leaflet advertising *Rayo Blanco
Aguardiente* was pasted a picture-book Baby-Jesus-in-
the-manger, so large and vigorous that his birth would
have killed the Virgin outright; beside the picture was
an inscription in crude Spanish:

JISU LOVES UYUYU

JISU LOVES UYUYU

JISU LOVES UYUYU TODAY

UYUYU DREAMS IN HEAVEN

"Why, it's like a fetish!" Leslie exclaimed when he
saw it two days later. "Just like his crucifix!"

She wished she had not shown the paper to her
husband but had found a discreet way to get it back to
Yoyo. "I suppose 'Jisu' means 'Jesu,' " she remarked.
"It shows more trust or faith or something than I
gave him credit for."

Leslie's sudden return had taken her aback; she
needed more time to grieve and to compose herself.
She had not been able to hide from him—or from herself, which depressed her even more—the disappointment she had felt at seeing him; in trying to redeem
herself by fussing over his wounded hands, she had
only increased her feeling of discontent.

Perhaps Lewis Moon had been right, perhaps she
was never meant to be a missionary's wife; she was of
old missionary stock like both the Quarriers, but she
had never gotten a real "call," as Leslie had. In fact,
she had seen in Leslie an escape from the soul-crippling
religious strictures of her father's house; attended as she
was by mild young men in rimless glasses, the handsome and adventurous Leslie, with his worldly past and
his longing for foreign lands, had seemed an ideal combination of Christian decency and warm-blooded man-

246

liness, and she had been proud to walk out into the modern world upon his arm.

Not that she did not love him still—and she *had* been frightened, goodness knows, by the tale of his near martyrdom—but in the end those hands in their clean bandages annoyed her. She wanted to feel as proud of Leslie as he wanted her to feel, but she did not.

Leslie had scarcely returned to Madre de Dios when the news came of a Niaruna raid against Remate. One savage had been killed—the only casualty on either side—but in their retreat the raiders had revenged themselves by murdering a Tiro family caught on the river. This news was gratifying to El Comandante, who immediately applied for government sanction of a campaign against the Niaruna.

On the radio that morning Quarrier had said that he and Hazel were willing and able to continue at the mission without help. But in the turmoil of their grief, the Quarriers were hardly in a state to judge things fairly; the Niaruna raid, which Leslie had not mentioned to the Quarriers for fear of alarming them, was evidence enough that the mission was still in danger. When Andy said mildly, "I suppose we'll be going right back in, to lend a hand," Leslie had reared back, angry and defensive, waving his bandaged hands like a praying mantis.

"You're not going! It's too dangerous!"

"I'd be ashamed to stay here; I'm going with you, Leslie."

"All right then! All right then! But in that case, I'm going to ask Guzmán to give us soldiers!"

She began immediately to pack her things. It was clear that Leslie had been badly frightened, which was natural enough, but since he could not bring himself to admit this, there was no way she could reach out and help him. He sat there glaring while she packed. When she paid no attention to his mood, he reminded her that he had still said nothing about the date of their return to the Espíritu, at which she straightened up and gazed at him and said, "I should think you'd prefer that I give you the benefit of the doubt."

The unfairness of this remark infuriated him— what had gotten into her? It was not until suppertime that he trusted himself to answer her with composure. Sitting at the table, he regarded her sternly for a while, to impress her with his seriousness even before he spoke: There had never been any question of not going back; he had simply expressed disappointment that once again the Tiro and Mintipo believers would be left defenseless against the evil influences of the Opposition; he had simply been annoyed at her presumption, at her entire *attitude*, in fact, since his return from his dangerous journey to attend poor Billy's funeral in the wilderness.

"You didn't go there for the funeral," she reminded him. "You went there to tell Martin that his work was unsatisfactory; Billy died while you were there."

Leslie struggled to maintain composure, but his voice cracked under the magnitude of his grievance. "Now wait, now see here, honey, you've been acting out of sorts ever since that night you went and followed that outlaw out there to the airport—the fact is, you never *did* give me any kind of decent explanation of how you came to do a thing like that! Good Christian women have no business—"

"Why were you so afraid of that man Moon?" she said. The question was put calmly, as if his fear of Moon was a fact well known to both of them, and it took him entirely off guard: it had never occurred to him that she might think that her husband was afraid of *anything!* He sat there aghast, all the more upset because Xantes had entered the salon and taken a table near by, so that he could not reprove her. Had Xantes heard? Leslie's passion was such that he must tear his hair or beat his breast or bang his head against the wall, but because of the bandages on his hands he could not even clench his fists, much less crack his knuckles under the table.

Moon! Would that man never cease to plague them? Well, darn it all, he hadn't been *afraid* of Moon exactly, what was there to be *afraid* of, he just knew right from the start that a man like that meant trouble. Two or three times before in life he had seen a man with Moon's expression—a hitchhiker once, and another time a man standing on a street corner—and they always made him feel exposed and wretched. Until Moon came everything was perfect, what with the Niaruna station just opened up and the defeat of Fuentes; far be it from him to wish any man's death, but the Lord had surely intervened against the Opposition at a key moment, and the proof was when He sent the Quarriers to help out in His work while those Romans were short-handed. Before that man's arrival he had felt triumphant in the Lord, and brave, and Andy was proud of him. But the very first time he had seen Moon, right here in this hotel, and Moon had looked him over with that funny flat expression of his, he had gotten a kind of nervous feeling, kind of silly or *unmasculine* or something, and here he was, bigger than Moon and an ex-athlete, and morally in the right!

When he got his breath, he spoke to Andy from behind his water glass so that Xantes wouldn't hear. "How about 'love, honor, and cherish'?" he said. Maybe a rebuke like that was a little hard on her, because probably she felt bad already about what she had said to him. Still, this was no time for her to be disloyal! Recalling the Espíritu and his own escape, his mouth went dry and he put his fork down, food untasted. She hadn't even been there, she hadn't *seen* those wild ones! The image of Tukanu's brutal attack constricted his whole chest: what had led the Lord to forsake him at a time like that? He had kept his head, but he couldn't go through such an experience again; and it stood to reason that if the Lord could forsake him once, He could do it twice.

If only Martin hadn't done so poorly, everything

249   *At Play in the Fields of the Lord*

would be just fine. There would be an established Niaruna contact, and he could stay right here in Madre de Dios and set up his regional headquarters and win through to victory over those Romans, the way he was supposed to. Perhaps staying here was his foremost sacred duty—he pressed his glass of ice water to his forehead and prayed for Divine guidance. He *was* a little shaken up, who wouldn't be, and there was no one but the Lord to turn to. Under his breath he tried to pray, but his mind raced on ahead of him. He couldn't confide in Andy. Why, Andy and the Quarriers, they had always been frail reeds, dependent on him; if they thought Les Huben was afraid, what would they do?

He and Andy were still tense and silent when Moon's partner approached their table. The bearded brigand of the year before was now merely unshaven, the sanguine cheek olive and thin, the flashing teeth tobacco-broken and protruding. He looked at his feet as if unable to meet Leslie's hostile glare. "I was very sorry to hear about the decease," he mumbled. "This was a very nice kid." Wolfie's cigar was gone, and the gold earring and beret, though he still wore his huge dark glasses.

"We'll tell the Quarriers you sent them your condolences." Leslie spoke in a military tone, then resumed eating.

"Yeah. Condolences." Wolfie glanced at Andy, placing his hand tentatively on the back of a third chair. "I was thinkin maybe I could sit down a minute; you know, get the news and all. It ain't often I get a chance—"

"Please do—" Andy began.

"If you don't *mind,* Andy," Leslie interrupted. To Wolfie he said, "I've been away. We were looking forward to a family dinner by ourselves."

"Sure! Yeah, sure! Pardon me, I'm sure." Wolfie was already retreating. "Like I said, I just wanted to send, like you know, my condolences."

"Thanks very much," Andy smiled after him. "We'll be sure to tell them." Still smiling, she turned to

Leslie. He frowned quizzically, a leaf of lettuce poised before his mouth; from her expression he knew that something unbearable was about to happen, and it did. "Do you know something, Leslie?" she said quietly. "You've shrunk."

"Ah!" cried Padre Xantes, observing Wolfie's dismissal from the Hubens' table. "The excellent *Lobo!* Will you join me?"

The gesture spared Wolfie an ignominious retreat across the whole salon; he sat down, shrugging, nonchalant, his back to the Hubens. "Thanks," he said. "So how you doin, Padre?" But Xantes scarcely glanced at him, so intent was he on the table of the missionaries.

"And what is your opinion of all that wonderful American wire?" the priest inquired loudly. "Imagine the cost of shipping it down here—why, the shipping expense alone would support my mission for six months!" He smiled ingenuously, hands folded before him on the table. "Imagine! And will it be used to hold the heathen *in,* do you suppose, or keep him *out?*" He gave Wolfie a roguish smile, at which Wolfie, disconcerted, cleared his throat and spat forcefully out the window.

"Maybe they wanna raise crocodiles," Wolfie said. He was wondering why he had not taken Leslie Huben and picked him up out of his chair and slapped him silly. What's got *inta* me! he mourned. What's got *inta* me! But the missionary's rudeness had taken him by surprise—after all, you go up to people to hand out *condolences,* man, you don't expect a kick in the face! —and he hadn't had time to think. If he had had time to think he could have yelled, *Well, you take your family dinner, you schmuck, and shove it up your ass,* somethin salty like that to let 'em know what was what, only maybe change "ass" to "anus" on account of the girl.

"Imagine!" Xantes exclaimed again; he shook his head. "Our friends—I could not help but overhear them—are still discussing your remarkable associate,

Señor Moon. Isn't it amazing how that fellow caught our imagination? I have a theory—I have still not got quite to the bottom of it—but I have a theory, I have a theory."

"You got a theory, am I right?" Wolfie gazed balefully at the priest, perplexed by the volume of the other's voice.

"Yes indeed!" the priest insisted, pausing to insure the attention of the Hubens. *"Despite* the opinion of our evangelical friends, I did not have the impression that Moon was . . . godless? *At play in the fields of the Lord!* Eh? These final words of Moon, the evangelicals found them sacrilegious, no? But might not they have been just the reverse? St. Thomas Aquinas, a Dominican"—and Xantes modestly inclined his head—"St. Thomas spoke highly of 'playing in the world—' "

"Well, saint or no saint, he stole that from *Proverbs!*" Huben called, provoked beyond endurance.

Slumped in his chair, hands in his pockets, Wolfie grunted disagreeably. "Look, I ain't deaf, Padre." He got to his feet. "You wanna make a speech to them people," he said, "you better go sit at their table."

He went outside and around past the kitchen to the servant's room where he had lived since El Comandante had put him to work with mop and rag at cleaning the hotel. The spectacle of the bearded knife fighter scouring his latrine had been a comfort to El Comandante in his hour of disappointment over the failure of his Niaruna program; he passed his days in supervision of his new servant, carrying a small chair about with him to ease these duties.

In his dark corner Wolfie lay down, thinking, If I spend any more time on this pad, I am liable to get bedsores, if first I am not gassed to death by the stink of garbage. How in the name of Christ did he get trapped in a jungle sink like this—he drove his fist against the wall so hard that he shook the whole hotel. It was too *much!* When he got so desperate for company that he went and let the marks *insult* him, it was time to make a break. He socked the wall again, and from somewhere in his rotten hotel big Guzmán bellowed.

Moon wasn't coming back, and that was that. The diamonds would take him home. But first maybe he would write Azusa and find out where home was these days. *Right now,* Wolfie said fiercely, and he sprang up and ran out to find paper, feeling decisive for the first time in months.

DEAR AZUSA—

This is me. Did you think I was dead? Ha, ha. Where are you living at. I am writing care of your mother, tell the old fart Hello (like hell). Zoose, I miss you and Dick, I am awful lonely, and if you will just let me know where are you living at I will come on home and settle down a while, all right? Don't be sore at me, bygones are bygones, baby, right? I am kind of tired and lonely, like I said. Remember that time in the art movie I fooled you with that popcorn? Ha, ha. Well, baby, keep it hot for me, you always were a swinger, Zoose. Like maybe you been doing a few tricks on the side since I was gone—well, that's okay, I mean, who *hasn't,* right? Forgive and forget, okay, Zoose?

So how is Dick? He ain't no infint anymore, I bet. Since I last seen him, I been shot at in the Congo, Cuba—all over—and I'm just as broke and stupid as I ever was! Well we had some laughs, though, wait til I get home and tell you, you will break up. Only now my partner got hung up on some local kind of junk and went and got killed on me and crashed our aircraft along with it, and without him it ain't a funny scene no more. Because before this happened, him and me made a lot of very comical scenes which I

At Play in the Fields of the Lord

will save them to tell you when I get home.
Write quick to the address below and let me
know where are you at.

Your wandering Jewish boy and common-law husband,

WOLFIE

He put his letter down, sighing with love. Dick!
Imagine! He was going to see his very own flesh-and-
blood! And good old Zoose—the memory of her big
warm breasts made him twitch all over. Hastily he
licked the envelope and pounded it shut, then yelled
for fat Mercedes, who occupied the adjoining cell. Due
to proximity or love of him—he had forgotten which
came first—Mercedes washed his clothes and ran his
errands and received him frequently and without
charge into her flawed person; at his call, she came
banging into his room. In the poor light, he decided,
the moles, soiled teeth and stove-steamed hair could be
forgiven, but a cooking odor of cheap olive oil per-
vaded her, and the lumpy form beneath the coarse
black dress looked dirty even after she had taken her
weekly bath. At seventeen, devoid of grace, Mercedes
was long since disillusioned, and it was her chief aim
in life to take offense. The permanent furrow on her
brow stemmed not from despair but from an anger at
the world that had doubtless commenced at birth; she
grabbed at sex and food and drink as temporary and
barely adequate consolations against the day of her de-
mise and heavenly ascent, when she would be recom-
pensed for the ultimate outrage of having been put on
earth at all. Even now, she gazed suspiciously at
Wolfie's letter.

"*Aeropuerto!*" Wolfie ordered. "Go and mail it."

"*Quién es?*" she growled, snatching it up.

"My *mujer!*" Wolfie cried, ecstatic. "My *niño!* Me
fly away to *Estados Unidos!*" He jumped around her,
making wild flapping motions like a bird.

"*No!*" She threatened to tear the letter up, and

254

might have done so had not her beloved clapped his hand upon her crotch and in this wise propelled her backward toward his bed. For a Catholic, in his opinion, her morals were deplorable—not because she went to bed with him but because she felt none of the guilt, the mortal terror of damnation, that might have lent romance to her company. Mercedes had made some low bargain with her God, and she stuck to it.

"Let go of that!" He knocked her hand away. "You catch me in that zipper, Shorty, you're goin to be piss out of luck." He turned his back on her, to finish taking off his pants in peace. Padre Xantes, at confession, must be derelict in his duty. These Christers—! Her avidity aroused him; standing there naked in his shoes, he saw the rampant profile of his trunk in the low mirror by the sink, and the hunched figure on the cot, intent on it. Human beings! He shook his head. Lookit the poor human beings!

Mercedes, happening to see the mirror, caught Wolfie smiling at her attentions. *"Qué quieres?"* she challenged him, rearing back. He turned around and pulled her face against him, but in his mirth, his belly made her head bounce. When she caught him peeping once again, she spat on him: *"Sin vergüenza!"* Clearly she was in no mood for tenderness, so without further ado he jumped on her, and away they went, smackety-smack. She came immediately—*"SANta María!"*—and, hell-bent on seconds, kept on going. In his mind's eye he could see their struggle as the next act of the tableau glimpsed in the mirror, and he gave a great cough of laughter. At this she flung her lover out and cursed him vilely, then snatched the letter to Azusa and scuttled to the door, where, in a crouched position, she began jumping up and down like a tarantula.

"Lobo! Mercedes love *Lobo, entiendes? No irás a los Estados Unidos!"*

"Gimme that letter!" Wolfie roared, still throbbing. "That's to Azusa and my infint, Dick!" Like a satyr he danced after her, for she had dragged the letter between her legs, then spat on it, and was now tearing it in half; it was in quarters by the time he knocked her sprawling.

Clutching the remains, he tottered backward and sat on the bed. His head still spun with ruptured bliss, his missive of love had been destroyed, and El Comandante, pounding at the door, was threatening him with extradition and certain death for introducing immoral persons into the Gran Hotel. Wolfie hobbled to the door and opened it a crack and peered with despair at a brutish face mad with the scent of lust. "This is a human being?" he inquired rhetorically, over the wild rattling of the chain. To Guzmán he said, "I arr es-spik you In-gliss, Jack—you wan fock woo-mans?"

"Ch-jack!" El Comandante said. "Ha, ha, ha, ha." He came into the room. "You go, I stay," he said. But when he saw that the prize was kitchen Mercedes, bloody-nosed and stinking in the corner, he lost his temper once again and called Wolfie a pig and seducer of children. He grabbed the girl by the hair and yanked her forward on her knees and kicked her buttocks with the instep of his boot; the quaking flesh produced a dandy jiggle and an intriguing sort of hollow *thock*, like a slab of meat slapped down on a marble counter, and he fetched her a second kick and then a third, each one more satisfactory than the last, upon which, after a moment's reflection, he cleared his throat and ordered Wolfie out of his own room. "We arr es-spik In-gliss," he told Wolfie. "Gurl mus be ponished!"

Wolfie got dressed and went into the salon, where he ordered eight drinks set up in a row and drank them down as rapidly as possible, listening to Fausto whine for payment. When he had swallowed down the last, he gasped, grinned broadly and charged the drinks to El Comandante.

"I es-spik you!" Fausto cried. "He be vair ongry!"

When he went back to the room, Guzmán was gone. Mercedes, looking murderous, was splayed out on the bed like someone crucified. "Move over," Wolfie said.

"Maricón," Mercedes said.

256

"Piss on you."

"I pees on *tú mismo!*" Mecedes said, and burst into tears.

Wolfie undressed and lay down naked on top of the sheet, extremely drunk, and went straight off to sleep. Toward dawn he was awakened by a drone of flies, a headache, a charged bladder and a bad smell. He reached out with his hand; the girl was gone. In Madre de Dios, he thought disgustedly, the fresh food smells like garbage, and the garbage smells like . . . Oy! He leaped up out of bed.

He cursed the girl but felt no rage against her; on the contrary, he marveled at a revenge so implacable and to the point and at the same time so unspeakable. Human beings! And recalling the mirror image of the night before, he tried to laugh.

If only Moon was here to see how his old pal Wolf was making out in life! What I mean is, Lewis, he would say, this is one hell of a way to wake up in the morning, Lewis! When they take a guy and actually come and hunch over him like *frogs,* man, when they come in the night and piss on you, man, as a token of their esteem, man, it is time to take a hint, it is time to go and seek your fortune, you know? Like *else*where!

He stood barefoot on the gritty floor, stained, naked and in tears, waving his hands at the angry flies for want of a solution. He peered about him at his sallow cell, his funky cot, the depressed kitchen court outside his window. One thing, he thought, when you hit bottom, you sure as hell don't mistake it for no place else. He took a deep breath, trying to smile.

Well, between you and me, Lewis, this ain't too much to show for forty years; this ain't no place for no Talmudic *scholar.* And at this he began whimpering with mirth, *snee, snee, snee, snee.* Hey Lewis, lemme ask you, are we ever goin to *amount* to anythin, you and me?

On a low rise above the slow brown river stood the Iglesia de la Virgen. Andy faltered in the road and stopped. The old church burst with chords. Its door was open, and she crept in out of the brightness of the day.

The interior was damp and deep dark-brown, and smelled of atrophy. A lone old woman crossed herself at the sight of the *evangélica,* and fled through a side door; the door resounded. A gasping human voice rose with the organ, and small candles flickered on pale gilt and silver at the altar.

> *"In Paradisum*
> *Deducant te Angeli . . ."*

She had never dared enter a Catholic church, and was astonished at the panoply of this small chapel of the backlands. In place of a communion table was a great stone altar and sepulchrum, with linen cloths, red candle glasses, and the vessels of the Eucharist; there was a canopy over the altar, and everywhere a wealth of silver plate. Two small windows of stained glass threw a theatrical and ruby-tinted light upon the altarpiece, and the whole was given benediction by a statue of the Virgin in a dark niche.

In this magnificence, as if enthroned, sat Padre Xantes, head bent to the organ; his head rolled joyfully as he sang, and his eyes were sealed by ecstasy. He had not seen her. She was moved by his unequal struggle with the mighty instrument, by his poor straining voice. Now he held a note, mouth open wide in song, as if drinking holy raindrops from the Heavens.

> *"Domine . . ."*

The voice cracked on a note, coughed in vexation, and took up a soft rapid incantation:

> *"Inclina, Domine, aurem tuam ad preces nostras,*
> *quibus misericordiam tuam supplices deprecamur:*
> *ut animam famuli tui WILLIAM QUARRIER,*
> *quam de*

258

hoc saeculo migrare jussisti, in pacis ac
lucis . . ."

Had she heard Billy's name? How queer she felt! Though she knew no Latin, the priest's ritual voice in the unearthly light evoked half-memories of illuminated manuscripts, of fat abbeys and round-pated monks, fair countrysides and far cathedrals against towering windy skies crossed by dark birds. Music and voice and soft dim light consoled her; she peered about her like a child.

"Requiem aeternam dona eis, Domine . . ."

Above the organ was a dark oil painting of a black Christ *in extremis;* a white Jesus in the altarpiece hung in life-size terracotta crucifixion. In this cruel work the wounds were lovingly incised, like bleeding mouths in the soiled shiny skin. Christ's eyes rolled heavenward beneath a crown of thorns like spikes; his hair was matted and his face shrunken, his body was twisted and meager, and in his agony he wore a bright green loincloth, like the shiny dress material for a doll. His indignity was unbearable, and she turned away.

"Libera me, Domine, de morte aeterna
 In die illa tremenda
 Quando coeli movendi sunt et terra . . ."

"We are a cru-el race, we Span-i-aards," sang the tenor voice; Padre Xantes, still humming a little, drifted forward from behind the organ. He moved into the candlelight as if he had awaited her. "A cruel race, for we humiliate Him still, with our poor vulgar worship." He gestured at the littered altarpiece. "It is scarcely a Fra Angelico, this relic of the noble *conquistadores*. But the black Christ of the painting was done by an Uyuyu of an earlier time, a convert more mystical, it would seem, than his religious teachers . . ." He gestured at the

259   *At Play in the Fields of the Lord*

dreadful crucifixion. "As for that holy garment, it was blessed somewhere and sent along to me; a bird had snatched its predecessor for its nest." When she did not smile with him, he nodded vaguely, sighing. "And do you like our church? I fear I am not in voice. Perhaps I am coming down with . . . influence? *Influencia?* Have you not caught it yet? The influence is everywhere in Madre de Dios. I fear for the poor Indians."

"Influenza." She shook her head. "I mustn't interrupt your service."

"But you are welcome here. It is only a rehearsal of the liturgy, the so-called Office for the Dead. And the service itself will be informal, a simple gesture to please myself; it is a sort of memorial service for two people who were not members of the Church."

"Oh, I see! Well . . . but I must be going!"

His voice was soothing but insistent. "The service is for the innocent child, your countryman, and also for Señor Moon. The child's death recalled to me the death of Señor Moon—is it not possible that this Moon also occupied some special place under the eye of God? Fools and children, no? And so a service for the two seemed quite appropriate."

"But we . . . there was already a service for Billy!"

"And Moon?" Padre Xantes smiled. "In any case, I doubt if my little service will do the child much harm. The music is a Requiem used also, I believe, in certain Protestant churches."

She nodded, doubtful. "Yes. I know the music."

"The Requiem will be performed on the organ by myself, and sung in all its parts—baritone, soprano and choir—by the tenor voice of the same personage. Unless *you* would sing the soprano in my place." He raised his hand. "You may do it in good conscience; there is no Roman Mystery being performed here."

"But Moon was hostile to the church—your church as well as ours! Why are you doing this?"

"Why *not?*" He gazed at her; she could not answer. "Do not be unquiet, my child. Let us say that I was drawn to Señor Moon, who was plagued by my own troublesome search for knowledge, and that—while he was certainly very hostile to the Church—I did not feel that he was an unreligious man. Will that not satisfy your doubts?" He smiled. "I could inquire, after all, why you have come into this church. But I will not, because I see that you do not know."

"I heard music . . ."

"Yes. The music is very beautiful. When one considers the soaring monument of art and toil and tears and song and love built up across the centuries in hope of God, one feels . . . what does one feel?" He shrugged helplessly.

She nodded. Suddenly she said, "Father, do you still believe that his death was inevitable?"

"I *prefer* to believe so." The priest winced before he smiled. "The fall of Icarus—does it not affirm us? Otherwise, our own careful solutions appear . . . vain? *In* vain? Or even worse."

"But suppose he *didn't* fall."

"If he did not fall, then he may put us in the un-Christian position of wishing secretly that he had."

From where they stood, in the flickering mystery of the altar, the rectangle of sun which was the door to the day outside seemed hopelessly remote. She gasped for breath. "Padre Xantes? Please—forgive me, Padre —do *you* truly believe?"

He took both her hands in his. "My child, is that a question or a confession?" He bent his head when her tears came. "I do." He lifted his surplice with his fingertips, as if in proof, then dropped it again, shutting his eyes on the glisten of his tears. "I love the Church," he whispered. "And . . . a man like myself . . . I need it, you see . . . I *need* it."

He turned his back on her and moved behind the organ. "Shall we sing?" He struck a chord. "The soprano solo of the *Pie Jesu,* perhaps—*Pie Jesu, Domine, dona eis requiem*—and then the *In Paradisum,* no?" He gazed at her. "Grant them rest," he instructed her enigmatically, his face gone old. "God grant them rest."

19

After the death of Billy the wild Niaruna disappeared, taking with them the boy Mutu; they did not come back. Kori and his band avoided Quarrier. They put on their pants and shirts again, despite his protests, and one night, after stealing what they could, they fled the mission.

Now there was a mission station and no Indians. Quarrier sent word by radio that all was quiet, but Leslie returned with Andy a week later, bringing with him four new Quechuas and news of the murder of some Tiros.

On their way upriver, the Hubens had found Kori and his people in Remate. Kori would scarcely listen to Huben, having pledged fervent allegiance to Padre Xantes and the Church of Rome. Huben told Kori that he should be very ashamed of the great wickedness of this sin, and Kori said earnestly that he knew he *should* be very ashamed but that he wasn't.

Leslie gave full credit to the Lord for their safe deliverance from the episode with Tukanu, alluding several times to his own agonies during his ordeal; he wore the wounds upon his hands as if they were stigmata, and spoke over and over of the arrow shot at him by Aeore. Quarrier did not bother to point out that Aeore rarely missed except intentionally. He was happy to see Andy, to watch her smile, and he did not hear Huben when the latter, as if conscious that his voice had lost its audience, addressed him.

"What?" he said. "I'm sorry, Leslie, I didn't—"

"I said, what was the word you shouted at them?"

"Kisu. Isn't that how it's pronounced? It was in that dictionary that Moon took, the one you made up with Yoyo. It's the Niaruna word for our Lord Jesus." Martin frowned. "Leslie, are you sure . . . I mean, you saw how frightened they were when I yelled out that name . . ."

"Well, I don't really remember this 'Kisu' of yours," Leslie said shortly, getting to his feet. "But I'll give you credit, fella—it works!"

"I mean, why are they so *frightened* of us? You'd certainly think, after all this time—"

"Well, it's very strange, I must say," Leslie interrupted, as if unable to imagine why Quarrier would want to frighten Indians. He seemed nervous and distracted; he glanced at each of them, one by one, frowned, muttered, shrugged, and went outside.

> *"In Paradisum*
> *Deducant te Angeli . . ."*

"What are you singing, for goodness' sake! Isn't that some kind of *Latin?"*

Huben bang-banged his heels upon the floor; he was checking his shoes for scorpions. His voice was clear through the partition, on the other side of which the Quarriers lived in silence. Once they had heard the Hubens making love, and were goaded into making love themselves; Quarrier thought of this as the most sordid act of all his life.

"In Paradisum: it's the last part of the Requiem."

"Well, I don't get it. My goodness, Andy, this is no time for Opposition songs!"

"A sunbeam, a sunbeam, Jesus wants me for a SUNbeam . . ."

263   *At Play in the Fields of the Lord*

Quarrier smiled.

"What has *she* got to sing about," Hazel was muttering. Her big back to her husband, she had been speaking to the mosquito netting inside which she lay, but now she rolled over on the bed like something struggling in its cocoon.

"Heh, heh," she sneered, through the pale netting; of late she had affected the evil laugh of oldtime movie villains. "The sociologist! Researching with Indian harlots, in the Sodom called Mother of God!"

At other times, for days and days, she did not speak. She passed most of the hours of light in sleep, and at night sat in the open doorway, slapping vaguely and rhythmically at the *pium* gnats. Quarrier would lie awake and watch her. He could not reach her any more, and did not try. Daily his wife bore the cross of her own grief, and the red bites which covered her were marks of penance.

Oh God, she called out to the heavens, where are the seasons in this place? Are there no seasons but rain and rain and rain? Is every day the same terrible twelve hours, no more and no less, forever and ever? Answer me! Are we in hell and do not even know it?

Declaiming, she paced up and down and up and down, at bay before the dripping walls; yet she was conscious of her husband's eyes, and made a sport of her own suffering. She pointed to the jungle. "Look at it! Look at it stare back at me! No privacy, no privacy! If I could only fly over those trees, get up, get *out*—aagh!" She clawed at the big body that she hated, and clawing, found a tick. "Ticks! Redbugs! Sweat bees! Spiders big as frogs! Oh God!" She gasped for breath and began weeping, and then, with a sly glance, she raised her eyes heavenward, hands clasped piously beneath her chin.

> "I am re*deemed,* but not with sil-ver
> I am re*deemed,* but not with gold
> Bought with a price, the Love of *Jee*sus
> Precious price of Love Untold!"

When her hymn was finished, she said to him almost inaudibly, "Why don't you help me?"

"What?"

"Help me," she murmured, smiling sadly. "All you do is *look* at me. Do you think I can't see what you are thinking? Do you take notes on your disgusting wife, the way you take notes on the savages?"

He rose and went to her.

"Stay away from me," Hazel said. "I cannot bear your comforting—you are only comforting yourself." She gazed at him. "Help me," she said.

He stood there, helpless.

"*Do* something," she said. "Do *anything*. Shout at me, hit me, but for pity's sake let me know that I'm alive!" Her voice was rising. "It's all the things you judge and understand! It's your awful *compassion* that is so unbearable, it's your Christian *mercy!*"

There was silence on the far side of the partition.

"You're a regular little four-eyed Jesus!" Hazel cried.

He gazed at her without expression. "I can't talk to you when you're like this," he said, and walked outside.

"*Oh God, don't turn your back on me again!*"

He whirled to answer her; the Hubens drew back from their doorway. "Mind your own business!" he shouted at them.

Andy had started forward, but now turned to Hazel, who was in hysterics. Leslie came tentatively toward Martin, who had sunk to his knees. "I guess Hazel's still kind of upset," he said.

"I haven't helped her, not one bit—I've failed her!" Quarrier shuddered. "And maybe I failed Billy too—perhaps she's right. My God, what kind of man am I, that I ruin everything I touch!" He pounded both fists on the ground, face streaming. "I had four wild souls right here for months, and not one of them was saved—they hated me!"

"Now Martin! Martin, you mustn't lose your head like this, this isn't like you—" In desperation, Leslie spoke of the trials given by the Lord to all His servants, at which Quarrier immediately stopped weeping and stamped off rudely to check the gift racks.

Despite the fact that they had lost contact with the Niaruna, that even Kori had backslid all the way to Rome, Leslie clung to his idea that Billy's death had been the means of a Niaruna conversion. Quarrier's outburst only affirmed his conviction that Quarrier must be at fault, not only for his failure to see and utilize the workings of the Lord, but for the anguish of his wife. Leslie's attitude toward Hazel seemed to be that if no notice was taken of her, she would come around again, or perhaps go away.

But Andy was glad that the problem of Hazel had been brought into the open, and later she said to Quarrier, "You mustn't mind if Leslie doesn't seem to realize how serious the situation is. Leslie's such an optimist, you know; he can't bear to look at anything but the bright side of things."

Quarrier nodded; Leslie had even convinced himself that they were under no danger of attack, that the Niaruna would soon return despite the presence of the soldiers. "Perhaps you could talk to her, Andy," he said. "She will not talk to me. She blames me for Billy's death, you see, and . . . well, for other things . . ."

"I've tried," Andy told him, "over and over. But she always says *you*'ve put me up to being nice to her. She always says . . . she . . ."

"What? She always says what?"

"She speaks so strangely, Martin. She talks about how big and ugly she is—why, she isn't at all!" Andy interrupted herself to dab her eyes. "She has such dignity and style sometimes, she's very *handsome*, Martin!"

Her tone seemed to suggest that if Hazel had any such idea, Quarrier must have put it in her head. Well, Hazel had thought she was big and ugly long before he met her; he hadn't given her the idea. On the other hand, how much had he done to rid her of it? Perhaps his love, in those days when he had loved her, had not been enough. He remained silent.

"I may as well tell you, Martin—Hazel is a very sick person." Andy's fierceness touched him. "She . . . one minute it's all fire and brimstone, and the next . . . she blasphemes . . . I mean, *awful* things . . . I can't even repeat . . ."

"I know," he said. "She thinks . . . I think it's the jungle. The jungle is evil to her in some way, she isn't herself here."

"That must be it," Andy said. After a pause she said, "She even accuses you . . ."

"I know," he said. "About Billy."

"Martin, if I had been Hazel, I would have wanted Billy to be flown out too." When he nodded, she reached over and took his hand. "But I was thinking of other things . . ."

"My Indian harlot? I don't excuse myself. In my heart I had sinned . . ."

She took away her hand. "Martin, she says that you love *me*, not her—oh, not *love* exactly!" She clenched her fists in embarrassment and vexation. "I mean, that you *lust* after me, that's her expression. How can I talk to her when she thinks that? Oh, the poor thing, how lonely she must be!" Andy was crying again. "It's so absurd and sad!"

"Yes," he said after a moment.

"Yes what?"

"Yes, it's absurd and sad." He was flushing so violently that when she stood up he felt she must have seen through to his heart, and had recoiled from him. But when she spoke her tone was level, and she looked him straight in the face; she was giving him the benefit of the doubt.

"Martin, I don't mean I've given up. I'll try again, and again and again, if necessary. But you must try, too; you must show her how much you love her, these days especially. And one day, you'll see, you'll both be so happy again."

Though he nodded, his heart sank at her words.

In this moment he scarcely cared about Hazel and her great unwieldy problems, or about the Niaruna, or even about Billy, or their God; he cared only about this childlike girl in a pale blue dress. His rough face had never concealed a thing, and he turned away.

When he groaned aloud, she kissed him clumsily on the cheek. "Martin, please don't despair. Really, you're such a *good* person, and I'm so glad to have you as my friend in Christ. I mean, I can *talk* to you, really *talk* to you, you're so darned honest!"

She continued in confusion, almost angrily, "Oh, we all get a little lonely sometimes, all of us. You and Hazel aren't the only ones." Her hands worked feverishly at her dress. It had begun to rain, but she did not seem to notice it. The words rushed out. "Leslie's a wonderful person, you know that . . . why, he was such an athlete, you know, in school, and he's so handsome and brave . . . well, you know all that. And as I told you, he's so cheerful and good-hearted, he's such an optimist . . . Only sometimes . . . some things he doesn't care to look at . . . There's an awful lot of things he thinks are dirty, that he can't even talk about, things he can't *eat,* you know . . . I mean, you've noticed . . . Well, I mean, he's *fastidious.* My goodness, I'm not *complaining,* you know. I'm just so glad to talk a little." Andy stood there looking past his shoulder, the rain pouring down across her face. "Sometimes—I don't mean *really* but—you know, he even finds *me* a little dirty!" She opened her mouth and gave a peal of surprised laughter. She laughed a little loudly and too long; in the rain her tears were indistinct.

Over her shoulder, in the doorway, he saw his wife observing them. She was nodding sardonically, with a terrific leer; she waved at him. "Yoo hoo, lover!" Hazel cried.

They went in to the makeshift table. Leslie said grace: "We thank Thee humbly today, O Lord, for this nice lunch of canned beans, sent in to us by kindly friends at home, to nourish and sustain us in Thy work. We thank Thee too, O Lord, that despite our trials, we remain healthy in Thy sight and that her grief has not prevented Your faithful servant Hazel Quarrier from carrying on her work in the fields of the Lord, nor his intestinal afflictions the work of Martin Quarrier. For God is the Kingdom and the Power and the Glory, forever and ever. Amen."

Hazel guffawed in a short loud burst, spitting across the table the baked beans she had sneaked into her mouth. "Intestinal af*flic*tions," she muttered. *"I'll* say! Why, Job himself—I've never seen anything to beat it!" And she jerked her head contemptuously at her husband, at the same time hunching low toward her plate to fill her mouth with beans. When she came up again she smiled at Andy, nodding craftily. "Heh, heh," she said. She maintained her good spirits throughout the meal, exclaiming loudly at every subject that came up, and especially at Leslie's account of some fornication he had ferreted out among the outcast Niaruna at Remate the year before.

"Don't worry," Leslie told them. "The Lord saw fit to put His words in my mouth, and I scared the daylights out of them. Really, it was disgusting! I had warned Kori earlier in the day that he must not touch that child, that he was a sinner in the eyes of the Lord, and five minutes later I caught them in the bushes, laughing and holding hands and touching. Well, you can just bet I told *them* about the wrath of God! So that night I slipped around the shelters—you know, turning on my flashlight—and sure enough!"

"You mean Kori?" Hazel Quarrier said, holding her fork poised at her mouth. "Wow! Getting set to know her *carnally,* I'll bet!"

"Well, not exactly. Kori was asleep. But he sure sat up quickly when the beam of that flashlight hit him. He'd learned his lesson, I'll tell you that!"

"Wow! May God forgive him for his lust," Hazel Quarrier said, and stared straight at her husband. "Heh, heh," she said. She peered slyly at each of them. "Eh?" she said. "Well, say, it's great to be in the thick of the old fight, getting the old Devil's blows right in the

At Play in the Fields of the Lord

breadbasket, eh, friends? Satan doesn't waste his ammo on a half-hearted bunch! Nosir, he hits his hardest when a fellow is hitting him, and *hurting* him, right?" She sat back in her seat and belched. "I read that message right in *Mission Fields,* in one of Leslie's letters."

"Hazel—"

" 'Some work in sultry forests,' " Hazel bawled, starting to laugh, " 'Where apes swing to and fro. Some fish in mighty rivers, Some hunt across the snow . . .' " She stood up and bellowed down at them with all her might: " 'REMEMBER ALL GOD'S CHILDREN WHO YET HAVE NEVER HEARD, THE TRUTH THAT COMES FROM JESUS, THE GLORY OF HIS WORD!' "

Martin walked outside again into the yard. He stopped short, standing in the rain; there was no place to go.

The world one day was blue and green, and the child by the river had stood still a minute, listening. His hair shone white in the bright hard noon, and behind him at the jungle wall burned purple cassia and yellow-flowered pea. On a near bush sat a white bellbird; it turned its flat head sideways, then snapped it to the front again as its voice tolled.

The little boy danced toward the brazen bird. The child's voice was as pure as the bird's call, a sweet fleeting sound lost in the sun and trees. The white bellbird blinked slowly, snapped its head and clanged again, a vibrating metallic ring so mighty that Billy would not believe a thing so delicate had made it. He went still closer, then knelt, observing it. The white bird's fearlessness made Quarrier uneasy, and he threw sticks at it, to scare it off into the forest.

How often he had watched his child fly out across the clearing, his arms like wings and his mouth open to drink the wind. On Billy's belt was an empty holster with a special thong which, strapping the holster tip to the thigh, permitted a faster draw. The holster was designed for older boys and was much too big for Billy, and its thong was fastened to his bare leg at a point somewhat below his dirty knee. The gun itself had been lost months before, and the weapon protruding from the holster was a crooked twig.

In Billy's last days his appearance had been shocking. The head on the pillow was huge on his scrawny neck, and his huge eyes were red, and his smile, distorted by his slackening grasp, looked insidious and sly; he lay on his bed, staring for hours at a time at the only two pets small enough to keep at his side—a caterpillar named Little Imsquint and a brook salamander he called Pipflow. And though his parents loved him all the more, could scarcely bear to look at him without rushing to hug him, at one point they gazed at each other, their eyes inches apart as they tucked him in, and saw the fear in each other's stare.

"Here I go! Listen to me, Pa! Listen!"
Listen, listen.

> "Elemeno P. Q-R-S, T-U-V,
> Dull Byou X, Y and Z.
> Now you've hurt my ABC.
> Tell me what you think of—
>
> *ME.*"

The tropic rain had ceased, and shafts of light broke through the swirling gray; the weak sun glittered in fat puddles in the yard. He stood there staring in apathy, feet rooted to the mud. He blinked, as if just awakened: how unreal everything seemed! How easily, in the absence of children, the whole experience of life became abstracted, a pattern of words and daydreams. Because the life in Billy was so fresh and immediate, he had served as a reminder of reality.

When he raised his eyes again, he was looking straight at a still face almost hidden in the green of the lianas, ten yards off. His heart pounding, he let his gaze slide past it, though he kept the brown blur in the corner of his eye; the face stayed where it was.

Very quietly he turned back again, holding wide both open hands. Smiling, he said quietly in Niaruna, "Welcome. We are friends."

The face remained immobile. In those early months, in the nervous time before Boronai's band appeared, he had been fooled by leaf shadows and shapes, by sun-browned fruit, by the black-and-brown feathers of a hoatzin on the far bank. But this was a living presence; he could feel the dark eyes burn him. Probably there were other eyes; he let his eye travel the green wall.

Because of the anger of the Niaruna the day the contact had been broken, he had agreed that at the first appearance of wild Indians the soldiers should be alerted. But the four Quechuas were bored and tense; he could see them now, squatting in the shadows of their hut, observing the gringo who stood out in the rain and talked to himself.

The savage was still in view. Quarrier did not signal the soldiers. They would only scurry for their rifles, and this first new contact would be broken.

He spoke again. "Welcome! We are friends!" He pointed at the mission shed and made an eating motion with his hand. When the face remained stolid, he said, "Tell Boronai that Martin is his friend. Tell Boronai to come here to see Martin."

Now the Quechuas leaned out of their hut, staring stupidly at the jungle, their faces curling in the surliness of ignorance. The savage ducked from view, or rather, vanished, for Quarrier was not aware of any motion, nor had a leaf been turned. "We are your friends! We are your friends!" he called. But there was only airlessness and the dripping of dead rain, and silence.

Huben was standing in the doorway, his radio in his hand like a small suitcase.

"They're back." Quarrier was grinning happily, the first time he had grinned since Billy's death.

Huben wanted to post sentries. "These people have already killed Moon and that priest, and they

272

tried to kill us too. Listen, fella, we're dealing with the most dangerous tribe in the eastern jungles!"

"If we post sentries against them, Leslie, we might as well go home. And if they want to attack us they'll kill the sentry first, and we'll be one man less. Anyway, those four soldiers couldn't stop them. They can get us from the jungle, one by one."

"You're very casual about it, I must say!"

"No. I'm frightened. But I have faith that they will not attack so long as we let them come to us and do not go to them." Then he said sincerely, "Perhaps you'd prefer to take Andy and Hazel back to Madre de Dios."

Leslie went red in the face. "Are you suggesting that I don't have the courage to stay here?"

"No."

"You're taking on a lot of responsibility, Martin Quarrier! You took responsibility for Billy too, remember?"

"What are you trying to say?" After a cold pause he said, "If we tell the soldiers, they'll be firing those guns of theirs at shadows. In my opinion they have no business here at all. They are Catholics and we are Protestants. It isn't fair to them and it isn't fair to us, and anyhow, they are a hindrance to us."

"Guzmán ordered us to bring them in."

"He didn't order us to keep them. If the Niaruna wished to kill us, they would have done so long ago, soldiers or no soldiers."

Huben said, "Well, I happen to agree that it's an offense to the Almighty to harbor four papists in our very midst."

Quarrier glanced at the papists, who were squatting like toads under the large silk-cotton tree by the river. "The poor devils," he said. "They'd be glad to get back to Remate."

"In that pit of Satan they'll be drunk day and night, cursing and blaspheming; that's the Opposition for you!" Leslie smote his fist into his palm. "All right," he said, "I'll take them back tomorrow. But from now on, Martin, try to remember which of us is Regional Director."

Quarrier nodded. "With your permission, "I'll check the gift racks."

"Go ahead," said Leslie Huben, patting him on the shoulder.

Each of the racks held a new machete, a steel ax head and a jar of salt. At first Quarrier had checked them every morning, noon and twilight, but after a time he visited the racks only once a day, for fear that he might be scaring off the Indians. He would move slowly from one rack to the next, saving until last the one on the jungle trail; this one would give him the first clue of Indian presence. He could not get over a painful dread that his first clue might be a silent arrow, tipped with poison.

Andy saw the second Indian, and the third and fourth. One man appeared out of the forest by the river, standing clear of the tangle in plain view, only a few yards from her. The Indian watched her calmly until, gathering up her wash, she got up off her knees; then he turned and disappeared. The next day she saw another one, and perhaps two, a mere shifting of shadows in the trees. Her husband attributed this latter sighting to her nerves, but Quarrier said that he had heard the Indians whistle, a sound like a cricket that they made with a small signal flute hung from the neck. After that, although all three searched the jungle wall from dawn to dusk—the soldiers had been returned to Remate, and Hazel was oblivious—the Indians did not show themselves again for several days, nor were the gift racks touched.

The missionaries' tension grew like fever. Their suspense and fear were made still worse by Hazel, who spoke wildly of the jungle and could talk of nothing else, describing obscenely the obscenity of the flowering and rot, the pale phallic trunks and dark soft caverns, the rampant hair, the slime and infestations. Once she ran naked from the hut at noon to sprawl and roll in the center of the clearing, writhing and howling, her arms extended to the forest, shivering as in a fit. "He is here," she cried, "Satan is in this place, and He will take me!" Quarrier reached her first and took off his shirt to cover her; she was sweating so in the terrible humidity that she was covered with dirt and bits of leaf and humus.

Huben came forth and preached to them of demons. His rantings penetrated Hazel's shock; she cried out, *"Eloi, Eloi, lama sabach-thani!"* and her eyes rolled in her head. When he realized that she was saying what Christ Himself was said to have uttered *in extremis,* he castigated her the more, until Quarrier gave Hazel to Andy to lead away, and went to Huben and shook him violently, saying, "Stop that, stop it, do you hear! She cannot help it!"

Their faces were inches apart.

"She has a demon," Huben muttered. "The demon must be exorcised!"

"My wife is sick. I am going to send her home."

"You can't do that! You can't leave us here alone! My wife should leave here too! We'll all go!" When Quarrier said nothing, Huben said, "It's very obvious that the Lord has not worked things out to open His doors to this tribe. He is warning us of our peril, Martin. We must go."

"I'm not going. If you are taking Andy out, I'll send Hazel with you. Otherwise I'll radio and have her picked up at Remate."

"You mean to say you wouldn't accompany your wife, in her condition? Don't you recall your marriage vows—in sickness and in health? I won't permit it. We're *all* going."

Quarrier wished to see to Hazel, but he turned back. "There's nothing I can do for her, and you know it; I only make her worse. Leslie, I'm not leaving, no matter what you say. My work is here."

"I tell you, I won't leave you here alone!"

At dinner nobody but Hazel spoke; she was cheerful, and ate her canned tuna fish with appetite. Quarrier had told her she was going home, and like a child, wide-eyed and excited, she told them all about the farm in North Dakota; the silos and corncribs, the grain elevators shining in the distance, the blue sky and the golden plain without a tree.

In the morning there was a broken arrow on each of the three racks around the clearing, with the presents still untouched; on the rack in the forest the presents were also untouched, and coiled on top of them was a fer-de-lance. It was a big one, at least six feet long, its head crooked neatly on the blotchy pattern of the topmost coil; it seemed to stir. Quarrier was close enough when he first saw it to find himself transfixed by its flat eye, and for a moment he did not realize it was dead. A file of huge black ants moved up and down the pole, and others swarmed upon the snake; in the dim light it shivered as they devoured it. Peering closer, he could smell the jungle flesh, sense the snip and clicking of a million pincers, the red-toothed struggle for food and space and light, the strangler figs and probing root, the silent hunters and devourers, the broadcasting of cells and seeds and energy in mindless waste. And he saw for a moment what his deranged wife had seen in her agony of the day before, that in this place they were forsaken; then there swept over him the significance of the snake, and he groaned aloud and sank to his knees and prayed.

"Almighty God," he began in a half-whisper, "show us the true way to these people, for I have failed to find the path—" He rose suddenly with a cry of pain and jumped about, slapping at his pants and kicking, for the ants on the ground underneath the pole had rushed to the attack. Once again he thought, Can God be laughing at us?

From the edge of the forest he could just make out the weak glint of the machete, overflowing with cold scaly coils. Already the machete blade was coarse with rust, and before long the termites would eat away the wooden haft and the cross carved upon it.

276

On this same day, in the late afternoon, Andy sought him out. She was very upset. At first he thought that she was still shaken by Hazel's breakdown, by the growing dread, the stifled panic, which had infected all of them. She did not have to say that she could not entrust what had just happened to her husband's nerves.

Upstream from the camp, cut off by a thick underbrush, there was an oxbow where the river bent around an island of massed driftwood, and here Andy had gone to bathe alone. All had agreed that they would bathe out of pails of water, less because of caimans or piranhas—the caimans this far upstream were very small, and the piranhas, so long as one had no open wounds, were harmless—than because both the whereabouts and attitude of the savages were still uncertain. But the longing to feel clean and private, if only for a few minutes, had eroded Andy's morale, and finally she had disobeyed the rule. Taking a cake of soap, she had slipped away behind the huts and made her way to the deep pool. She was nervous about the creatures of the river, but after peering into the water for a long time, she had taken off everything but her sneakers, and slipped in.

After her bath, having no towel, she sat down on a log to dry herself in the pale sun. In her private world of leaves and warm wood and clear water, she felt happy and relieved for the first time in weeks. Sabalo trout were drifting in the shallows, and she could see bright shells of the fresh-water mussel. A sandpiper came and teetered cheerfully along the margin, and a tiny emerald hummingbird perched near her head.

But while she sat there, absolutely still, the birds took wing; when she turned her head, she saw a Niaruna. He was standing in the opening at the jungle edge, a tall warrior with a crown of fur and bright red feathers, and two red snakes curling around his legs. His arms above the biceps were bound in strips of bark; his face was masked in black and crimson streaks.

She tried to scream, but she could not. He put down his bow and arrows and came toward her.

"Why didn't you scream?" Quarrier demanded, more resentful than horrified.

"I don't know," she said. "I was too afraid. I just don't know. I started toward my clothes, but then . . . he . . . he stopped me. He put his hands on me."

"And you were both . . . You didn't have any clothes on!"

"No, you *know* that," she cried out. "What are you trying to do to me?" Until now she had not faced him, but had stared nervously at the ground. When she raised her head, her cheeks looked feverish. "No, I didn't scream! After that first second I wasn't afraid; I knew he wouldn't hurt me!"

"But you were naked!"

"Oh, you're just like Leslie! That's why I didn't tell Leslie, because he'd be so angry, just like you are!" When Quarrier only grunted miserably and dropped his eyes, she said bitterly, "I'll tell you something else. I *was* naked, and I wasn't ashamed. Am I a sinner, Martin? Am I a *sinner* then?" More quietly she said, "Maybe it was because he was naked too, because he belonged there where he was, with the fish and leaves and sun, with that emerald bird. For the first time the jungle seemed like paradise, bugs, heat, mud, and all, and he was part of the jungle, he was beautiful. And *I* was beautiful." She looked away, bewildered. "What have we done to ourselves, Martin? Oh, I saw something right then—"

Before he could ask her what she meant, she smiled in an exultant way that frightened him. "He wanted me"—her mouth hardened—"really *wanted* me."

"You mean you—"

"No, I didn't."

When she spoke again, her voice was strange. "Don't you think that religion comes less naturally to women?" She shrugged. "Women like me who don't have children—we probably have too much time to think. Lately I've been thinking quite a lot." She paused for a deep breath. "I think women get more religious as they get older, or when they begin to fear life, or suppress it in themselves. Or in great disappointment. Especially then."

Rudely, Quarrier cried out, *"What?"* He knew that his feelings were totally unreasonable, yet he felt that she had been unfaithful to him, had betrayed him.

"Especially in disappointment," Andy said, staring at nothing. "Then they think, *There must be something else.* And the church holds out the only hope."

He burst out, "You said he . . . he stopped you!"

"Yes. He put his hands on me, he touched me, very gently. As if he were blind."

"I'm astonished he didn't—you know, *assault* you. I mean, an *Indian!* They aren't romantic. And you say he wanted you! You *know* he wanted you!"

"Why do you question me—oh, don't be such a child!" She moved away from him, angry again. Her voice was hoarse. "You might as well know this, Martin, because it's true: I wanted *him.* When he touched me, I almost burst. I wish he *had* assaulted me, how do you like that?" Her eyes were too bright and she was jeering "How do you like *that,* Martin? I've never wanted anything so badly in all my life. But you, you're such a *good* man, you'll say I'm possessed—"

"No, Andy. Please."

"But I pushed him away. And then he went. And my immortal soul was saved." She coughed repeatedly.

They sat in silence for a time, watching the twilight birds; a woodpecker tocked on hollow wood, far back in the forest.

Quarrier said, "You look kind of feverish. Do you feel all right?"

"No, I don't. I think I'm coming down with flu."

"Why, that's very serious! The Indians have no resistance—"

Andy said, "I think it was Lewis Moon."

20

Boronai and his people had come back to their village angry and upset. The white man had disdained the medicine that the People had prepared for Billy, and the funeral had seemed to them an insult to the dead. Not only had the white people not howled loudly enough, but their funeral ended while the Niaruna were still waiting for it to begin.

Then the white man laid the child deep in a hole, threw mud on him, and trapped his spirit in the dirt forever with a heavy piece of wood instead of sending it eastward in a death canoe, to be gathered in by the Morning Sun and led up to the sky. The white man insulted the Niaruna by not joining in the Indians' night of mourning, and they tried to forbid revenge. Worst of all, they called out in praise of Kisu, instead of commending the boy's soul to Witu'mai the Ancestor—but here the Indians stopped talking, gazing uneasily at Kisu-Mu.

Once again, due to his link with Kisu, Moon could get no explanation from the Indians, only ill-mannered silence. Aeore, who had been squatting upon his haunches and spitting excitedly on the ground, now snapped his head in calculated rudeness, then rose and stalked off.

Tukanu had returned from the mission in an especially ugly mood because Taweeda, tired of the mess that the *evangélicos* had made of things, had fled downriver with Kori to become *católica* again. Boronai too was angry. In his night of nipi, he had seen that the enemy of Billy was none other than his own worst enemy, Kori, who had fled to Remate before he could be put to death. When Aeore announced in a loud voice that he would lead a party to Remate to kill Kori, Boronai grunted in approval; he glanced at Kisu-Mu suspiciously, to see if the Great Spirit of the Rain had any objection.

Moon knew that his protest would no longer prevail; he remained silent. Four young warriors went off with Aeore, carrying a small canoe across the watershed to the Espíritu. Three days later the party returned, minus one warrior who had been killed by the Green Indians at Remate. The execution of Kori had been a failure, but on their return they had attacked and killed a family of Tiro caught fishing on the river. The tall missionary and his woman, they reported, had rejoined the Quarriers at the station on the Espíritu.

The raid upon Remate and the murder of the Tiros meant that time was running out; now Aeore, with the full support of all the band, would go the next day and kill the missionaries, who had not left as Kisu-Mu had prophesied.

Moon took Aeore aside and explained his plan to him. When Aeore understood that Kisu-Mu would support him as the jaguar-shaman of the whole federation, he nodded his head in approval; he even agreed, after a brief dispute, that his leadership should be established slowly, that Boronai need not be challenged and put to death. The headmen of the People to the East must be gathered at a drinking party, and their support for the federation enlisted with due ceremony.

Aeore saw that if he himself proposed the plan at the council, his leadership would be all but established in advance, without unnecessary acrimony. He responded quietly and intelligently to every proposition, studying Moon's eyes; he even accepted Moon's demand that the missionaries not be killed—or not, at least, until the federation had been established.

Moon said that in event of battle they must keep their losses at a minimum, and Aeore looked incredulous: to accept in advance the sacrifice for tactical gain of even one of their own warriors was offensive to him. Aeore was sensitive on this point; because of the death of one of his warriors at Remate, he felt he had lost face. Yet his reaction, which would have been typical of a Cheyenne, was a rebuke to Moon, reminding him as it did how far his long experience as a white man, as a white soldier, had removed him from the Old Ways.

In this period Pindi had her child, of which Aeore was said to be the father. But Pindi and Aeore had not been together often, and Moon guessed that the child was his own. The Indians preferred to believe that the father was Aeore, for might not the offspring of a spirit be a monster? Pindi herself referred to Aeore as the father of the New Person being made inside of her.

Pindi had little use for the New Person, and had told Moon that Boronai would give her herbs to rid her of it. Moon had immediately gone to Boronai and told him that abortions must be forbidden. Boronai looked at him carefully. "It is very common," he said. "It is her right." Moon asked him how he reconciled abortion with the knowledge that his band had grown small and weak; why had they made such efforts to procure Taweeda? Why had they taken the boy Mutu? Boronai nodded sadly. "One day we will vanish from the earth," he said. It no more occurred to them, Moon thought angrily, to provide against this future than it occurred to them not to kill, in time of plenty, more wild pig and fish than they could eat; they gorged on life as fast as it appeared, and were saddened afterward by their wastefulness.

Boronai did not really see the sense of preserving a child its mother did not want, even to avoid extinction, but he had helped Moon persuade Pindi that she should have the New Person. The idea made Pindi apprehensive. From the way she looked at him, Moon supposed that she feared the child was his, though she said nothing.

In the weeks before the birth, Aeore was to share Pindi's seclusion. "It is *I*, after all," he said meaningfully to Moon, in a manner intended to deny Moon's parentage, "who must give New Person breath. It is *I* who must form New Person's soul. The woman makes only the body of this New Person."

But because his role in the pregnancy meant passing long days in his hammock, eating nothing but manioc lest New Person choke on fish bones, Aeore decided that the former husband Tukanu, who had a taste for indolence, might as well be father. This was agreeable to all parties, and Tukanu set about his parental duties that very day. He went groaning to his hammock, and there racked his poor brain and smote his brow, that his own wisdom and attainments might be infused in New Person. His labor, when it came, brought him far more suffering than his ex-wife underwent; he howled so in psychic agony that the whole village quaked with the uproar and took fright, astonished by this pain that could not be endured in silence. Tukanu lay exhausted for three days afterward, while his people came to his hammock, one by one, to marvel at him.

Pindi, on the other hand, was delivered by herself, out in the manioc plantation. There were twins. After resting a little, Pindi dug a hole in the ground and placed the girl twin in it and covered her with dirt; the boy she brought back to the village. She cauterized the umbilicus with an ember, washed him quickly, and took him to Boronai, who painted the red serpents of the Niaruna on his legs, placed a string of red seeds around his neck and tied soft fibers to his arms. Moon asked if it might be better to feed the child first and get him warm—the day was wet and cold—but the Indians only stared at him, surprised that he took notice. "Until it is painted," Boronai said, "it is not a Person. It is nothing." He lifted New Person above his head and presented him to the attention of the four winds, that they might aid the child on his life journey. Then he went down to the Tuaremi and blew tobacco smoke, and spoke an incantation to the Mother of Anacondas.

It was the Ugly One who learned from Pindi of the twin. When she mentioned it to Moon he ran to the plantation, and the Indians ran gaily after him. The baby was half uncovered, and its mouth was full of dirt; he knelt beside it.

"Kin-wee?" the Indians said. *"Kin-wee?"* Good? Good?

He snarled at them to drive them back. Their eyes were flat with the intensity of their pack intuition; they were insulted by his horror, and his anger threatened them.

Well, the little girl was dead—what would he have done had she been living? And perhaps she was better off. He crouched there in the rain. Was this his child? Then he deepened her grave and placed the muddy blue scrap of flesh that was not a New Person back into it; covertly he kissed his fingertips and touched her forehead. He could not get over the idea that she had never felt the sun. He covered her, and stood. "You do not give such a child a funeral then?" he said.

A funeral! The Indians giggled in relief that he had joked and was no longer angry with them.

It is not a New Person! It is nothing!

Moon returned to the maloca and stared at the one on whom had been thrust life. He had never had a child, and he did not quite know how he felt about this one, with its tiny twitching fingers and its wrinkled blindness and the tiny organ which had saved its life; in a way, it was a murderer already.

Pindi had heard from the others that Kisu-Mu was angry.

"Only animals drop more than one," she said. "I was ashamed."

Since Kisu-Mu's arrival in the tribe, the Indians had feasted in honor of the palm-nut harvest, of the

284

small Fish People who lived in the Tuaremi, of the Mother of Manioc, of the Morning Star and of the Moon; the brave Moon, Boronai said, had wished to be the bride of Sun until, learning that the People of the Tuaremi would be destroyed by the collision of Sun fire and Moon tears, she had chosen to go her separate way around the far side of the Earth.

Now the Pleiades had risen in the heavens, and the rains relented. The beasts drifted out of the dying forest to drink once more along the rivers, and fish collected in the deeper pools, and a new feast was held. This "Feast of the Falling River Time" marked the beginning of the Indian year, and the new plantings.

Aeore took advantage of this feast to summon all the villages along the Tuaremi. Boronai himself, not suspecting that the feast was meant to lay a base for a great federation, issued the invitations in person, going away with Aeore downriver. The headman hoped to heal the feuds between the clans, some of which were so serious that had Kisu-Mu not been in Boronai's village as an attraction, most of the People to the East would have spoiled the party by disdaining to appear. Aeore felt insulted in advance, so nervous was he; he was still angry that his village had not been invited to a drinking party given downriver on the moon previous, a party he had counted on refusing.

For several days wild-shouting fishermen speared fish in the dammed and poisoned pools. Moon yelled at Boronai from the bank that they must use barbasco sparingly, or the fish in the whole Tuaremi system would be wiped out and the Niaruna threatened. Boronai said mildly that the pools where most Fish People lived were too large to poison; when the river was high, the fish would replenish the small pools which had been poisoned in the Falling River Time. "This is our way," he cautioned Moon; with a deft thrust, he pierced a dying sabalo on his trident spear and tossed it, sparkling, into the shallows.

The fishermen brought in large pirarucu, matamata turtles, some small caimans and a whole dugout

At Play in the Fields of the Lord

of bright small fishes; the hunters returned with guans and tinamous, red howlers and black spider monkeys, a few peccaries, four capybara, and many pacas and agoutis. The young boys ranged the river banks and forest for palm and cashew nuts, for berries and rose apples and guavas, for palm heart from the terminal shoots of the young trees, and for palm fruits for the masato; they brought large leaves full of white palm weevils taken from dead trunks.

The women smoked the fish, and dug and hauled and cleaned the bulky manioc, grating it to shreds on scraping boards inset with teeth of the piranha, then wringing the poisonous fluids from the mass by twisting it in a mesh bag hung from a tree. Some of the manioc was baked into flat cakes, which would be dipped into a common pepper pot. The rest was masticated by the girls and women, then spat out into wooden troughs where, mixed with water and palm fruit, the paste fermented; by the day of the feast it was strong and thick and sweet.

Off in the forest the men fashioned giant masks of bark and palm fiber. The place was kept secret from the women, who were forbidden to suspect that the legs protruding from the Mask were human; the woman who saw a Mask before the dancing, Tukanu said, was subject to mass rape.

Meanwhile the maloca had been repaired and cleaned, though not so scrupulously as to make it appear that Boronai was giving himself airs. The guests would already be offended that Boronai's village claimed the presence of Kisu-Mu; they would be on the lookout for an excuse to show disgust for the whole boastful performance and go away.

Finally the men painted their faces and bodies with the greatest pains, as if one false line would undo the whole effect. They were less careful in their decorations, choosing impulsively from the shells, trinkets, feathers and fur strips at hand; monkey-fur bands and caps of egret feathers were favored, but no two chose alike, there was no pattern. Often the head decoration was capricious: an old animal tail, bird claws, a plume of river reed, pink petals of mimosa. If one wanted an ornament belonging to another, the object was admired lavishly; its owner, failing to convince the admirer that the object was ugly and worthless, was obliged by courtesy to give it up and make himself another.

Only Aeore never asked for anything, nor was he asked. His paint and dress were constant as the plumage of a bird, as if he knew exactly who he was, had always been and always would be. His lean canoe, his falcon face bands and his bold crown of jaguar fur and yellow toucan feathers all singled him out as the man apart that he meant to be.

Moon asked the People why they were so careful to go painted. Tukanu said, "It protects me from the heat and Insect People." And Pindi said, "I wear it so that I may know Pindi in the river's face." But Aeore said passionately, "We are naked and have nothing! Therefore we must decorate ourselves, for if we did not, how are we to be told from animals?"

There it was. The unbearable thing was not the fear that the Great Spirit had forsaken man, nor even that in granting awareness of death, He had made man's hope ridiculous, but that from the beginning He had made no real distinction between the mindless animals and mankind.

One midafternoon the canoes of the Yuri Maha came into view, in single file under the banks; against the current they moved slowly. They approached in silence and drew up at the landing. Astern, the headmen of the clans steered the canoes; they stared straight ahead as their people debarked, as if struck dumb by the poor appearance of Boronai's village, while for their part, the people of Boronai took not the slightest notice of them.

In the shallows the strangers washed themselves. They adjusted fur-and-feather headdresses, seed necklaces and anklets, and bellybands of warm sun-reds and orange. Their face paint, which they freshened and greased, was a dead white, encircling the cheek-bone. The men were fully armed with bows and arrows and short lances, and they carried these with them when leaving their canoes.

The procession of grim painted men moved up the bank toward the maloca; their women and children were received with merriment at a rear door. The boy Mutu had learned the names of every headman and recited them in awe to a younger child: "The Ocelot! This one is the fierce Ocelot!"

While waiting to be invited in, the strangers inspected Kisu-Mu, though no man stared at him—whether from politeness, pride or fear he could not tell. Only the one known as the Ocelot, who had stepped aside to speak with Aeore, looked at him pointedly. He was a tall Indian with a narrow restless head low on his shoulders, and he glared from beneath his crown of feathers like an animal about to come out snapping. His whole manner was a taunt: you may have fooled these upstream simpletons, but you are not fooling the great Ocelot of the River Tuaremi. Yet when Moon acknowledged the taunt by stepping forward, the Ocelot turned away.

Now Boronai appeared in full array, wearing a sun crown of white egret plumes; on his chest hung his jaguar incisors and a strange cylindrical ornament of greenish stone. The stone had been drilled from one end to the other, and the drilling had been done with bamboo points. When Moon had doubted this, Boronai explained that the task had occupied two lifetimes. Moon asked where it came from, and Boronai pointed north and east. "Long, long ago," he said, "in the time of the Ancestors." The trails there were now lost.

Boronai ignored his guests until they presented themselves formally at the maloca entrance. Here the greetings exchanged took the form of speeches, shrill and ritualized, without warmth, as if host and guest were both prepared for insult. The guests were on no better terms among themselves and were careful not to jostle one another; the feather crowns fairly shook with indignation.

This great silent procession of savages, canoe after canoe, drawn out of the vast forest to the east, stirred Moon to the heart; it filled him unaccountably with sadness. The meager bands and the small stature of these more primitive and horseless Indians did not detract from the true dignity of the Old Ways—ways he had heard about but never seen in the poor shanties of the North American reservations—and now they were meeting in council as had their northern brethren nearly a century before. He felt himself one of them, and proud. This jungle would absorb big Guzmán like a sponge; here, he thought, exulting in the angry, proud, suspicious faces, the Indian can resist indefinitely.

The Yuri Maha gazed at him briefly and impassively, and passed one by one into the maloca.

At twilight the clans sat face to face, exchanging greetings, histories, and insults in the form of compliments. They argued obliquely about fishing rights, disputing the placement of fish dams and weirs and the length of time a dam could be maintained without causing hardship to the clan farther below. Boronai's clan, as the one farthest upriver, was repeatedly accused of selfishness, although the wording was kept circumspect out of courtesy to the host. "We do not say that you keep weirs across the river pools to steal our fish. We only say, Perhaps your fishers have forgotten. We only say, The clans of Boronai have always been forgetful clans. We only say, There may be a bad feeling."

Aeore's willingness to accommodate every grievance perplexed and irritated Boronai; it was only when the young warrior proposed his idea for the federation, and declaimed loudly that his leadership had the support of Kisu-Mu, that Boronai began to understand what was afoot. He gazed at Moon with a wide depthless stare. Moon had not thought that Aeore would mention him, and wished that he had taken pains to consult Boronai in advance. But he had waited too long, and now Boronai felt himself betrayed.

The women kept off by themselves near the rear door of the maloca. They were bored by the slow and solemn rituals, and fretted impatiently for the moment when the men's drinking would break the feast wide open, when they could hoot and screech and pretend terror of the Masks, when they could dance and sing and flaunt themselves, when they could be fought over, and fornicate. Meanwhile they pushed and giggled, and they screamed with dismay when a huge bark-cloth phallus, part of the dwarf Tutki, blundered into their area and tripped and fell. The phallus lay bewildered on the ground. This Mask had been entrusted to little Mutu, whose head fit so far inside it that he breathed out of the eyeholes; in his blindness the boy had become separated from the Tutki Mask, who was supposed to guide him from behind.

The feast began with violent gorging. The masato was served up by calabash from the huge trough, and Moon drank enough of it to become dizzy. The Indians gulped it in such quantity that every so often each man would vomit to make room for more. They drank and sighed. The anger and lust and vomiting, the intense, excessive feelings were only expressions of life, of *being,* too great to be contained; this purge was a sacred purpose of the feast. Yet a part of Moon was disgusted, and his disgust kept him outside of things; he felt self-conscious and impatient. He ate crocodile and monkey, but his share of fat weevils he presented to Pindi, who received them gladly as a sign of love; for the rest of the evening, flirtatiously, she threw manioc paste into his face.

Under the moon, dancing had started, and the lines of men stamped up and down, faster and faster, slow steps, then quick ones, to the whistle and discordant rhythms of crude flutes and drums of monkey skins.

290

Some of the Masks sang as they danced. *I wander, forever wander,* Turtle sang, *and when I get where I yearn to go, I wander once again.*

In the middle of the night the women joined the dance; in separate lines, giggling wildly, they pranced up and down, up and down. They paid small attention to drum or flute, and as the evening lengthened the instruments paid no attention to one another, as if the point were not rhythm but pure din. Past, present and proposed liaisons were now under dispute, and Tukanu's uncle pummeled one rival even as his wife crept off into the darkness with another.

The Yuri Maha also fought among themselves, and finally the discord became general; the fire shuddered and the black walls swelled with voices. Moon, not sober himself, cursed the sprawled leadership of his federation; it did not seem possible that harmony could be drawn out of this ruin. The Yuri Maha were doing all they could to insult their hosts, and finally a drunken headman accosted Boronai himself. It was the Ocelot. He fingered the strange green cylinder of stone hung on Boronai's chest, exclaiming loudly, "What a beautiful thing! How I wish that I could wear it!" As the stone was unique in the region, and the greatest possession of the village, the man's behavior was an extreme provocation, forcing Boronai to be inhospitable. In the ritual way, Boronai cried out, "No, no, it is old and useless, you would shame yourself by wearing it!" But the Ocelot exclaimed again over its beauty, and again Boronai exclaimed over its ugliness. In the firelight they faced each other, chest to chest, red and feathered like two giant birds. The exchange was repeated over and over, with small variations, until the tension grew too much for the Yuri Maha; he snatched unsuccessfully at the stone.

The Indians sighed and crowded closer. As loudly as possible without shouting, Boronai said, "My brother wishes this poor stone of my clan, although he knows that it came from the north rivers long ago, and that we have no other, and that for all other clans it has no meaning. Therefore I ask my brother not to desire something which is of no use to him."

But the Ocelot, very drunk, was not skillful enough to back off without loss of face; he glared about him, trapped. He would have to shout something unforgivable about Boronai's hospitality, and Boronai, anticipating this, cried quickly, "Here! Wear it as you wish, so that you will know that it is worthless and of no use to you. Then you may leave it here with us!" Boldly, he placed the stone around the other's neck.

Boronai's people moaned, for the Yuri Maha postured foolishly, vaunting his moment, and did not return the stone. But his companions had recognized Boronai's wisdom and his efforts to save the drunkard's face; they groaned loudly in disapproval, and the Ocelot removed the stone and draped its string roughly around Boronai's neck. As he did so, Boronai glanced at Aeore, who had run to the maloca for his weapons. Then he gazed at Moon. Unable to bear the headman's contemplation, Moon retreated outside the circle of the fire.

In his great drunkenness Tukanu sat himself down beside the Great Spirit of the Rain and laughed jovially into the Great Spirit's face. In the firelight his eyes flickered with grotesque humors. He told of a "thing" he had once wounded, a "thing" Moon was unable to identify because of the extreme thickness of Tukanu's speech. Imitating the strange creature, Tukanu crawled dazedly through the shadows, dragging one leg and braying. Then he imitated the brave Tukanu, hauling sternly on his mighty bow—*thicnk, thicnk,* said Tukanu, to show how solidly his final arrows had punctured the wounded flesh. On his knees he played the thing again, bringing his forefeet up under his chin into a position like prayer and rolling his eyes heavenward, all the while emitting hollow braying groans of fear and agony.

By the time Tukanu pitched forward on his face,

Moon realized that what he saw being enacted were the last moments of Padre Fuentes. Acting both roles, the Indian scrambled around like a dog after its tail; he succeeded at last in wrenching a machete from his own corpse and beheading himself with loud coughing grunts accompanying each chop.

Tukanu held up the dripping head. *"Kin-wee?"* he said, out of breath. *"Kin-wee?"* In an access of joy and pride he wrapped his arm around the Great Spirit's neck, embracing him, then tightened his arm and cut off the Great Spirit's wind; when Moon elbowed him sharply in the ribs he sat back, laughing feverishly, then reached over suddenly and yanked out a twist of the Great Spirit's hair. On their knees they faced each other, the one in cold tears of pain and fury, the other howling in triumphant glee. Between them fell a sudden and total silence; to Moon, in this moment, the void between himself and the world of Tukanu seemed infinite, beyond all hope of traverse. Tukanu was leering senselessly, conspiratorially; he inched forward. Breath harsh as the scrape of rocks, he stared into the eyes of Moon, who inhaled his savagery like a violent odor: the yellowed eyes, the choked nostrils, the drunken vomit smell, the pores. Now the Indian twisted him by the chin, forcing him to stare into Tukanu's black pupils, inches away, pupils like pure black holes into the savage brain. Moon swayed in vertigo; through those black holes he was drawn far back to the beginning of the age . . . The Indian brought him up short by licking his face as a dog licks, and squealing again with laughter.

Tukanu did a somersault, then sprang up to join the dancing, dragging at the Great Spirit of the Rain with a violence not quite playful; Moon yanked free but was seized immediately by other Indians. They meant to include him in their dance, and they laughed and howled encouragement. He stamped up and down, up and down, holding two painted figures by the hands, and grunting and shuddering with the best of them. The Indians sang:

"If we were great beings
If we were not so weak and small
If just once we could dance long and hard with
   our souls clean
Then we would dance out of our skins like
   Parami the Butterfly
Then we would fly to that faraway land where
   there is no flood no pain no death
Then we would fly away into the sky."

Back, back, *back*—stamp. Forward, forward, *for-ward*—stamp. The exertion had his head spinning; when he raised his eyes to the black fringes of the jungle night, the brilliant stars, he swayed and nearly fell. The man behind him yanked him upright. Peering closely at this face, a violent crisscrossing of red and black, he saw that it was Aeore. "You have painted a new face," he said. *"Tarai,"* the Indian said; as of this night, Aeore considered himself a jaguar-shaman, and his jaguar teeth gleamed upon his chest. Moon glanced around for Boronai but did not see him.

Then Aeore went off with Pindi into the bushes; the other Indians laughed and pointed and a few went along to observe the spectacle.

Moon's humor worsened with each drink. He had watched Pindi as she danced, provoked by her bold smile and tossing hair, the soft skin of her face, the childlike habit of sucking her lower lip inside her teeth, the bold striping of her thighs and hips. She actually reminded him of Andy Huben, and he tried to imagine how Andy would look with curlicues on her behind. Very well indeed, he decided. And he was considering how best to lure Pindi to his side when Aeore, who had been petting her unmercifully, rose and took her by the wrist and led her away from the circle by the fire.

Moon felt annoyance that the Niaruna, drunk or sober, should treat his spiritual presence so casually; it was plain that they were more afraid of Aeore than of Kisu-Mu. Even the faithful Tukanu soon lost interest in him. With the departure of his faithless Taweeda, he

294

had taken up with an old woman; when this salacious elder, her mouth ringed with yellow foam from the masato, came to him and placed her hand upon his groin, he sprang up instantly and was led off into the bushes.

Pindi returned and entered the maloca. Afraid of his own anger, Moon did not call out to her. He weaved stupidly through the ruins of the feast, staring down into the faces of his federation; those Indians who were not off in the undergrowth lay heaped around the fire in a torpor, arms flung about one another like huge children. The slack, broad-featured faces, livid with paint and tapir grease and sweat, stared up at him like so many demonic masks. In the shuddering light, in the groan and fume and pant of breath of sprawled brown bodies, he smelled something infernal, like the stench of dying moths lying burned at the base of a lantern. But the smell was no smell of evil but only of mortal exhaustion, of the renewed and endless and irremediable failure of the Niaruna to escape their doomed flesh, as their legend promised, and dance away into the sky. It was only he who had drunk idly, merely to get drunk. He pitied their innocence with all his heart; yet, gazing at human beings so reduced, he could not restrain disgust and fear.

From the shadows at the corner of the maloca, Aeore was observing him; the Indian did not trouble to conceal himself. They gazed at each other across the flame, in the whisper of night insects. Moon crossed over to him. "Tell me your name," he ordered, though he had not known that he would say this. Aeore was startled; scowling, he backed into the shadows. Moon sprang at him and bore him to the ground and grasped his wrists. "Tell me your name," he said. The Indian went wild with fright, rolling and kicking in Moon's grasp; for once he seemed convinced that Kisu-Mu was a spirit. Moon struggled to hold him, wary of so much fear; the Indian bit him, frenzied. They thrashed and rolled in the fire shadows until Moon's greater weight exhausted Aeore, who lay back, panting,

At Play in the Fields of the Lord

teeth bared, burning. He had not once cried out. "Tell me your name," Moon gasped again, but this time he knew that he had lost. He winced angrily and stood up, releasing Aeore, who sprang sideways on all fours before he rose and backed away. In Aeore's face, emotions fought; if that man could be sure, Moon thought, for just one second, that I am not a spirit, he would kill me on the spot.

In the morning the yard stank with vomit and was aswarm with flies. Moon had a headache, his stomach was sour with masato, and the sourness seeped all through him. He felt poisoned. For the first time since he had joined the tribe he spoke angrily to Pindi. He told her that she took poor care of New Person, that she had not observed the period of quiet that was necessary for the safety of the infant soul, that—he was disgusted with himself as soon as he had said it—she must choose between Aeore and himself, or there would be *emita*—evil.

The girl crouched on the ground in terror. She begged him to tell her what she must do. And because he did not really care enough about her to command her to leave Aeore, he stood frustrated a moment before he said, "I wish that you take better care of New Person. I wish to know Aeore's clan name. Then there will be no *emita*."

Pindi cried out that Aeore had no clan name. It was said among the Yuri Maha that he had no father, that his mother had copulated with a spirit in the forest. After the birth she had run away in shame to join her spirit-lover. Each newborn child had been a star whose light thereafter would be missing from the heavens; since the orphan's parentage was so obscure, he was called Child-Star, which signified that he was nameless.

Moon told her that he must gain power over Aeore in order to control him, for the good of the whole Niaruna federation. This meant nothing to Pindi; she pleaded wildly. To speak Aeore's name would surely attract harm to him; he might die!

He awaited her in silence. More and more stricken, glancing fearfully about, she said finally, "I will whisper the name." He bent, and she whispered, "Riri'an," and then she began to cry.

21

The canoes of the Yuri Maha had slid away down-river, but a few of the strangers, the Ocelot among them, lingered in the village to help their new allies drink the last masato. The feast that Moon had thought a shambles had been judged a great success: all agreed that the Niaruna were a mighty nation, that the clans must side against the white man and the Green Indians, that peace must be made with all the tribes east to the Morning Sun. Aeore was acknowledged a jaguar-shaman, and now the Ocelot was trying to reclaim him, as if Aeore had never left the forests of the Yuri Maha.

Aeore had become ever more arrogant; he now spoke openly to the Ocelot of his suspicion of the Great Spirit of the Rains. And it was too late to reverse the course of things.

One morning Mutu found and killed a large fer-de-lance. A ceremonial was called by Boronai, from which the women were excluded—"O Taka 'tdi, we did not wish to do you harm, but only to set you against the enemies of the Forest People"—and the next day Aeore carried the dead snake to the mission and arranged it upon the gift rack in the forest; then he placed a broken arrow on each of the other three racks. He too spoke an incantation, as if Boronai's speech had been of little consequence; he now wore his new face paint and his jaguar incisors at all times.

Moon accompanied Aeore to the mission. He crept up to the clearing edge and was straining for a look at Andy Huben when Quarrier, who was alone in the clearing, turned and caught him off guard. Moon froze where he stood, and for a second the missionary's gaze swung past. But then Quarrier was speaking to him, and he stood there at a loss, considering what he must do. He had only to duck backward to disappear behind the vines, but he had an impulse to try out his disguise—more as a game than for good purpose— and so he stared back fiercely. His game was spoiled by the hope in Quarrier's face; Boronai had shamed him with that same innocence the day he had shown Moon the fetish that would bring laughter to the angriest man on earth.

The next day the mission was scouted again, and again Moon in his restlessness went with the party. He strayed off from the others, circling around behind the mission sheds, until he found Andy sewing in her dooryard. From the forest came Tukanu's cricket whistle, but he did not answer. He watched her for a long time, and when she slipped off toward the river, he followed.

He crept down along the bank. Like a child, the girl was dogpaddling, kicking her sneakered feet in the shallow water, her hair in her face, her solid back and bold white hips awash. Every few moments she stopped to listen. When she came out of the water and sat gingerly on a log, he wanted to turn away, but he could not. He was aroused, and his bellyband hurt him; he fumbled to ease it. Because he could neither avert his eyes nor suffer the covert, peeping role in which he found himself, he stepped out into plain view. But her back was to him, and he had moved quietly out of habit, and he stood there for a maddening long time before her head turned slowly and she stared at him. Her lips parted in fright and her arms crossed on her breasts as she rose and turned away from him; she had gasped, but she did not scream. There were drops of water on her back, and red marks and bits of bark on her white hips.

He moved forward. In Niaruna, she was saying "No," over and over. He placed his hands gently on her shoulders, then drew her body back against his own, feeling her flinch and shiver as he touched her. The sweet smell of her body filled him, the air and sun danced on his skin; and he swayed in a torrent of sensation. He slid his hands onto her breasts. Her taut buttocks relaxed and opened out against his belly, her profile turned toward him, toward his mouth, her body turned . . . Later he imagined he must have kissed her, but perhaps he hadn't, for just then she sucked up a short desperate breath and held it. Her body tightened; she was going to scream. He stepped away from her. She faced him.

Though he had never taken his eyes from her, he could not recall an hour later what her body looked like, remembering only the arms, simple at her sides, the wide stricken eyes and the pounding wonder in his head.

Then she was gone. From the direction of the mission he heard her coughing.

That evening, for the first time, Kisu-Mu persuaded Pindi to sleep with the Rain Spirit after dark; they went down to the river bank near the canoes. He had grown used to the Indian way of love; in this world where the plants writhed, where seeding and flowering, life and death, were all entwined, one could copulate as naturally as one would sleep. Yet he still disliked making love before an audience, and was enraged when Pindi's laugh revealed what Kisu-Mu was up to, and brought the Indians flying from their hammocks. Pindi called greetings as round heads appeared over the bank, and jokes and speculation flew. Moon clutched her brutally in frustration. His skin was quickened by the cold and by the rough ground, he wished to shake and crush her, strangle her, devour her. In a fever he searched the girl's hard rubbery body, the

300

strange cool skin, the unnamable strong odors which goaded him. His whole body was like iron.

Sensing this, Pindi stopped laughing and struggled wildly to receive him; she yipped in pain as he forced himself inside her. A minute later, splayed out on the dirt among the weeds and insects, his head spinning, he stared up at the black leaves of night where the hunting lizard, throat vibrating, tuned its senses to the shrieks of laughter. The only unhappy thing about it was that before the Indians had come to watch, before he lost himself and screwed the world, he had pretended that he held not rank brown Pindi, but the white clean pious flesh of Andy Huben.

"Kisu-Mu! Kisu-Mu! Kin-wee? Kin-wee? Ho, Kisu-Mu?"

How strange it was that a creature he had held so often in his arms, who had laughed and moaned with life only days before, should now be dying. He did not want to go to her. He had taken the small Indian girl so much for granted, like the food; it sickened him to realize that he had waited until she was dying to become aware that she was more than a smiling toy to him, that he was fond of her. As for Pindi, she had seemed to love him, though he could not be sure of this: love was a land he had not learned much about. In any case, he could not weep if his life depended on it, as it occurred to him that it well might.

Pindi had caught his own bad cold—where had he got it? She had mounted a wild fever, then sunk into a coma; it looked like influenza. It had scarcely occurred to him to seize medicine from the mission, when he heard the ululating whoop of an old woman, followed by a groan and stir, as if a wind had passed across the village.

Boronai was giving up his leadership; while Pindi lived, the cures were performed by Aeore. For three days, and throughout her final night, Aeore danced and chanted. Brandishing a gourd rattle full of spirit

voices, he sucked demons from her body and blew tobacco smoke upon her, but Pindi did not rise out of
her fever; she only moaned, and gazed expectantly at
Moon. Aeore too awaited him: if Kisu-Mu was content
that Pindi die, then all his cures would be in vain. But
when she died, at the end of a violent fit of coughing
brought on by the tobacco smoke, Aeore yelped in
surprise and grief. When Moon came into the maloca,
the Indian was shouting in heretic rage at the "Old
Murderer in the Sky." Then he rushed outside and
went howling off into the jungle.

No nipi would be drunk to determine Pindi's
enemy. The men glanced at him furtively; the old
women muttered openly with old women's cynical fearlessness, nodding their heads: she who had dared sleep
with a spirit in the night had brought a god's infection
on herself. They could scarcely revenge themselves on
the Spirit of the Rain, and as for him, he could not
proclaim that Kisu-Mu was innocent, not only because
they might kill someone more innocent still but because their instinct had been right: an infection had
been brought by Kisu-Mu.

Too much was happening at once. The strength
he needed was displaced by listlessness; he felt constricted, short of breath. In the afternoon, along the
river, his feet went out from under him, and he slid
clumsily down the bank. The frailty of his body had
returned, and the need to take care where he placed
his feet. He felt abandoned by the wind and sun.

Four more Indians had flu and lay weakly in
their hammocks, coughing; the strange epidemic frightened them. But New Person, whom Pindi had given to
the Ugly One's daughter to suck and rear, had so far
escaped. Moon told the Ugly One's daughter that she
must keep the child away from all the sick people.

New Person was healthy, full of push and noises.
He spent his days in a cane-splint basket, on a bed of
silk cotton from the lupuna tree; in fair weather he was
taken out to the plantation in a hip sling. Moon liked to
watch him; Look at him kick, he thought, look at him

kick! In other days he had picked him up and smelled him, and felt him gently to see how he was made, but now he was frightened of infecting him, and kept his distance.

When the people at the mission showed no signs of leaving, but on the contrary made new plantings in their garden, Aeore led three men to the mission garden and destroyed it. Because he suspected that Moon would be angry, he returned to the village in an anticipatory rage and yelled out that the following day an attack on the mission would be made. The white men meant to stay, he said to Boronai, and there was no excuse for further delay.

Since Pindi's death Aeore had been in a state of grief the more fanatic for being inadmissible; he had painted his whole body black with genipa as a protection against ghosts, for he saw evil omens everywhere. The other members of the tribe, infected by his rantings, were surly and volatile as well.

Moon cautioned Aeore obliquely, addressing his remarks to Boronai. It would be foolish, he said, to kill the missionaries, for many more soldiers would return to take revenge on the Niaruna. Therefore a war party must go to the mission and tell the white men that they must leave Niaruna land, that if they were not gone by the next moon—about eight days away—the Niaruna would attack them.

Seated on the ground, Boronai nodded uncertainly. He could no longer control Aeore, and he knew it, and he knew that the tribe knew it, and he had enough sense not to put old leadership to the test. Since the missionaries had first appeared, since Kisu-Mu had come and the ways of the People had been disrupted by fear and greediness and strife, Boronai had grown old. His shrewd bright eye had dimmed, like the eye of a shedding snake, and in the way that the snake casts its skin he was preparing to recede stoically from his days, to die in the way the Indians so often died, by releasing his hold on life without a struggle. Boronai's people seemed to know this, for they spoke of him indulgently, and began to neglect him as an old man would be neglected. He was not old in years, but in the swift rhythms of the jungle he had been defeated and replaced. The life he knew was coming to an end, and he would go.

So now, for a long time, the headman was silent. Then he spoke in the silence of the clearing, recounting his life and the old history of the tribe: how they had arrived out of the sky, how they had come to these rivers from far off to the East where the Sun was born, how the white man had come to them out of the West, where the Sun died. The Indian was the Spirit of all Life—was he not born, and born again, in everything upon the Earth?—and the white man was the Spirit of the Dead. But now the white man was among them, and must be driven out.

Boronai spoke sadly, in simplicity. It was this enviable simplicity which in those bright green early days he had thought within his grasp that Moon felt himself on the point of losing. Even the sense of the universe he had glimpsed under *ayahuasca* had slipped away from him; was that because he had not really earned it? He was sick to death of thinking, of *words*. One knew the jungle best when one no longer struggled, when one flowed with its rains and wind, breathed with its creatures, drank from its rivers out of green-leaf cups, took shelter from it in the common warmth of the night fires.

The headman was silent again. Moon watched a huge blue butterfly bounce across the sunlit clearing; it lit on a passion flower at the jungle wall, then closed its wings and disappeared.

The spirit in the white man was evil, and his teachings were evil, but these white men had not yet done the Niaruna harm. Therefore, like the bushmaster and fer-de-lance, the great anaconda of the backwaters and deep swamps, the missionaries must be approached politely. They must be told that there was no home for them in Niaruna land, that they must return to their kingdom to the West, that if they did not do so their house here would be destroyed, that the Niaruna were a brave people and would kill them with their arrows.

Boronai raised his hand. To his people he said, "Aeore will lead you, and Aeore will speak for you."

There was a murmur of approval. Aeore gazed at Tukanu to see if he would make objection. Tukanu was silent.

Moon agreed that the missionaries must be driven out; this first step would activate the federation. The headmen of the Yuri Maha were coming to the village frequently and were clamoring for massacre; nevertheless, with his reverence for protocol, Aeore would obey Boronai's last command. After that, the missionaries would be in danger, for the new headman had lost all awe of Moon and scarcely listened to him.

That night Boronai's wives lay with other men. Even the Ugly One was taken by a virgin boy. When Aeore left for the mission the next day, Boronai did not ask to come, and was not asked. He lay in silence in his hammock, his eyes closed, expressionless, while the women barged past him and chattered loudly across his body, as if he were invisible. With his heavy somber dignity, his lined heavy face, his heavy stillness, he reminded Moon of the monolithic old men of his boyhood.

Moon accompanied the twelve warriors who arrived at the mission a short while after daybreak, when the river mist still strayed in whorls among the stumps and skeletons of the felled trees. When one of the white men came into the yard, they stepped out of the jungle in a file. They were in full paint and feathers, and each held a long black chonta bow and long cane arrows. Aeore took his place at the end of the line, where the Niaruna leader always stood, with open space on his right hand, his arrow hand.

Leslie Huben had a white face towel across his shoulders and both hands full of toilet articles. He stared at the savages, at Aeore's blackened body, and made obscure small sounds; he spread his hands and

305   *At Play in the Fields of the Lord*

dropped his things to show that he was unarmed. Then he said in English, very loudly, "Praise the Lord!"

At the edge of the forest, the Indians remained motionless; they muttered excitedly about Leslie's pretty toothpaste tube. Huben called out again, over his shoulder, "Praise the Lord!" and came toward the Niaruna, his arms wide. He wore a flesh-colored bathing suit with rust spots on it, and a two-day beard.

"Niaruna! Welcome to the House of Kisu!"

The Indians glanced at Moon and grunted, all but Tukanu, who sniggered without smiling, and Aeore, who raised his bow in a careless way, as if he were stretching, and drove an arrow into the ground a few yards in front of Huben.

The missionary halted. "Niaruna! We are your friends! We have presents for you! We will eat with you!" He held out his arms imploringly, still smiling, and Moon shifted in discomfort. He recognized Huben's courage at the same time that he despised him.

Now Quarrier appeared, and behind Quarrier came Andy Huben.

"*S-ss-tchuh!* There he is," the Indians murmured fearfully. "The Hairy One." Tukanu, who had seen Quarrier's naked chest, had told them that this missionary was the white man's *guhu'mi*, that he taught evil, that his penis was so gigantic that he wore those long cloths on his legs to hide it, that his glasses, which served as mirrors, enabled him to gaze for hours into his own head.

Andy came forward firmly and took her husband's arm. "Welcome, friends," she said. She looked them all straight in the face until she came to Moon; she started, but did not avert her gaze. And because she was not ashamed, he suddenly felt foolish in his nakedness.

Quarrier's face was set and angry. He had halted beside Huben, glaring at the arrow. Then he searched the faces. "Welcome, Aeore," he said. "Tukanu, you are welcome here." He smiled briefly at the Indians he did not know. "We are happy you have come," he

306

said. While saying this, he stared straight at Moon; then he moved forward, past Aeore's arrow. A second arrow thumped into the earth, so close to his shoes that dirt flecked at his khakis; when he moved past it as well, all the bows came up.

"Martin!" Huben said.

Moon murmured to the Indians that they must not harm him. Quarrier, who had halted, came forward once more until he was opposite Moon. To the Indians he said, "Where is my friend Boronai? Tell him he is welcome here. Tell him we have planted a new garden."

Aeore raised his arm and pointed at the river. His voice mounted angrily as he spoke. With his finger, in eight sweeping arcs, he traced the sun's course across the sky. When the moon was old again, he shouted, the white man must be gone.

"I wish to speak to my friend Boronai," Quarrier said.

"This is what Boronai has said!" Aeore banged himself upon the chest with the heel of his hand. "This is what Aeore has said!" He stalked away into the forest, and the others followed.

Moon was at the end of the file, and as he turned to go, the missionary said softly, "Moon." He was not looking at Moon, but at Leslie Huben, who had rushed to the jungle wall and was pleading loudly with the invisible savages in Jesus' name. Quarrier said quietly, "You are a madman. This is your doing, isn't it?"

"Paleface speak with fork-ed tongue," Moon said, and grinned. He was surprised that Quarrier had recognized him; he felt naked and absurd. And the sound of his own name pronounced aloud had startled him; with the use of it, a spell had been rudely broken.

In his realization that Moon's presence had made the whole episode a farce, the blood rushed into Quarrier's face, and his big hands rose in fists. "Curse you!" he grated. "May the Lord curse you!" He grasped Moon roughly by the upper arm. "This is your doing,

At Play in the Fields of the Lord

isn't it? Now answer me! And you made them destroy our garden!"

"This is *your* doing, Quarrier." Moon pried the man's fingers from his arm. Over Quarrier's shoulder he saw Andy gazing at her husband, apprehensive; Leslie was still exhorting the vanishing Niaruna at the top of his lungs. "Does she know, too?" Moon said.

"You are a monster!" Quarrier exclaimed. "Just look at yourself! A painted demon! How can you stand before her in your nakedness—" He stopped short. "How dare you?" he muttered. "How did you dare?"

Moon said, "You people better get out of here." He started away again, but now Leslie Huben was coming at him, the terrible smile still fixed upon his face. "Welcome! You are—we are your friends in Christ! Eat! Eat! *Kin-wee? Kin-wee?*" Huben made eating motions. "*Kin-wee? Kin-wee?*" In English he cried, "Help me, Martin!"

"You've undone all my work," Quarrier muttered. He held Moon by the shoulders and was shaking him rhythmically. He spoke dully, thickly, surprising Moon by the strength in his grip. "All that hard work," he said, "which cost me my son and now my wife."

"Martin, you know better than to touch an Indian!" Huben snapped. "And you're speaking in English!" When Quarrier let go, Huben whirled once more on Moon. "*Kin-wee? Kin-wee?* Niaruna *mori* Quarrier, *mori* Huben, *mori* Kisu? Eat? Presents? *Kin-wee?*"

"Leslie! Stop it!"

Andy held a handkerchief to her face, and as she came close Moon could see that she was feverish. Her skin was soft and flushed, and her eyes blurred, and she was not steady on her feet; nevertheless, she was looking him straight in the face.

"Andy, keep away! Go back to bed!" Huben exclaimed. "Do you want to give them flu?"

Moon said, "So you're sure it's flu?" Quarrier nodded.

308

"Eat? *Kin-wee?* Presents?"

"Leslie, don't! It's Lewis Moon."

A cricket whistled. Turning his back on them, Moon went off into the forest.

22

On the evening of her encounter at the river, Andy had spoken to Quarrier in the same flat voice: "I think it was Lewis Moon."

Quarrier had jumped to his feet. "Why, that's impossible," he said. He picked up a stone and hurled it at a silk-cotton tree; insanely, it bounced straight back at him, making him skip clumsily out of the way. "No! Why, even Moon wouldn't run around naked like that, barefoot." He trembled with outrage. "And anyway, Moon is dead!"

And now Andy said, "It's Lewis Moon," in that same odd noncommittal voice. And Moon went off into the trees without a word, before Huben could react.

"How? . . . What do you . . . How? In the name of Christ—" Huben's passion, when it came, astonished Quarrier—"how could you let me make a fool of myself, talking to Satan in Jesus' name . . . How *could* you?" And to Andy: "You were looking at his nakedness, and you knew he was a white man!" He whirled around again, but Moon was gone, and this set him howling at the looming faceless wall of the still jungle. "How dare you! How dare you stand there and flaunt your filthy sinful nakedness in front of Christian women!" He rushed at the forest in a frenzy, became entangled in the vines and fell. "Moon!" he screeched. "You're leading these people to damnation! You will suffer, Lewis Moon! The torments of the damned!"

"Hee, hee! You hear that, Moon?" Hazel, laughing in the doorway, shook her fist at the jungle wall, then collapsed backward to a clatter of fallen pots.

At Quarrier's glance, Andy said, "No, I didn't tell him." She went to her husband, who scrambled to his feet; he shook her so violently that when he released her suddenly, she crumpled to the ground.

"How could you!" he gasped. "How could you look—" He stared at both of them in hatred, then turned his stricken face at the mute forest. "We've lost them," he muttered. "We've . . ."

"Leslie—"

"We've *lost* them! Don't you understand that, Quarrier, you stupid oaf!"

Andy said, "Why is a white man's nakedness too filthy and sinful to look upon, when a red man's nakedness is not?" She was still seated on the ground.

"Go back to your bed!" Huben shouted. "It's the intent! His intent was sinful, it was mocking, he made fools of us!"

"Make a fool of us, will you!" Hazel shrilled. "Take *that!*" She smote the open air with her prized fly swatter. "And that! And that!"

"It's more serious than that," Quarrier said. "He's leading the tribe against us."

"He wouldn't let them kill us!" Huben sneered. He glanced uneasily at his wife but did not help her to her feet, as if this would acknowledge that he had laid violent hands upon her. He was beside himself; in another moment, Quarrier thought, he is going to weep or wring his hands. "But . . . a devil like that!" Huben burst out again. "I'm not going to take any chances, I'll notify Guzmán! Wait till he hears about this outlaw threatening us! Why, he'll have soldiers here so fast—" He broke off and trotted toward the radio shed.

"Leslie, listen, you can't do that!"

But Huben only raved and choked and raved again. He insisted that the Lord's work would never be done among the Niaruna as long as Satan had his demon there corrupting them. Quarrier shouted angrily

311   *At Play in the Fields of the Lord*

that neither could the Lord's work be done if the Niaruna were all dead.

"Better dead than to live in sin!" cried Huben, livid. The words hung in the air between them.

There, thought Quarrier, it's out.

Huben was fiddling feverishly with the radio set, his muddy toothbrush stuck behind his ear. Startled himself by what he had said, he added quickly, "What's the alternative? Do we run away with our tails between our legs? You ought to know Leslie Huben better than that!"

As Huben's voice railed at the transmitter, Quarrier turned away and went back into the yard. "How do you feel?" he said to Andy, helping her up.

"I don't feel," Andy smiled. "I'm not feeling these days."

"So you didn't tell Leslie about the business at the river?"

Andy glanced at him as if his question were insane; she did not answer. Instead she said, "You weren't very happy about his nakedness either, Martin. You were accusing, too. And Leslie has more cause to be upset than you have." She eyed him carefully. "After all, he is my husband." His face reddened; he was shocked by a new hardness in her, he felt betrayed by her hostility. "I talked to you because I thought you were a man," she said. "Leslie is a boy."

Because her bathrobe was drawn tight, he stared at the firm shifting of her hips as she walked back to the hut; he despaired of his peeping, but he no longer struggled to control himself. Since knowing that Moon had seen her naked—oh Lord, *touched* her—he himself could scarcely think of her any other way. His spiritual love had been ousted unceremoniously by a lust so brutal that he despised himself, despised his thick red body and its thick red needs; he thought with envy of the self-flagellation said to be practiced by the Opposition. He could taste Andy Huben, he could smell her—her mere proximity made him twitch. He was enslaved by the pretty body in boy's blue jeans, knew every crease and swelling of it when it moved or bent. Once, squeezing past her at the stove, he had scarcely restrained his fingertips from brushing across her hips. Hastening off, hand tingling, he was grateful to the Lord for the strength that had restrained him; yet he did not dare to glance back, for fear that the radiation of his hateful lust had given him away. The whole situation was ludicrous, but every time he tried to laugh he would weep and tear his hair.

Huben's message was transmitted to Guzmán, and the next morning word came back: El Comandante would be delayed for a few days, but would arrive on the Espíritu with a punitive expedition before the moon was new.

Leslie was chastened by Guzmán's phrase, but he could not bring himself to consult with Quarrier about what to do. On the third day he radioed Madre de Dios that the mission could handle the situation and that no expedition would be necessary. This decision restored to him his brisk bearing and the bold crooked smile of the buccaneer. "We're going to *fight* Moon, mister!" he declared. "We're going to win this big one for the Lord!" And he laughed a two-note laugh of triumph, big and booming—"Huh-*ho,* boy!"—and shook his handsome head; this challenge was just his meat.

Leslie's idea was that they would take the women out to Remate and come back with four more soldiers. Even Moon, he said, would not be so coldblooded as to risk his Niaruna against firearms. But the next day Guzmán's answer, mentioning both the savage raid on Remate de Males and the bloodthirsty murder of the Tiro family on the river, advised them that El Comandante could no longer sit idle while his people were being slaughtered by savages under the influence of international adventurers; the expedition would arrive in a few days.

At night they listened to the insects, the moths and lantern flies and locusts which clacked and fluttered at the light. The insects nagged at Quarrier's nerves—what drove them to seek the light like that, what made them flail themselves to death in pointless struggle and bewilderment and pain? One kind of locust made hideous small sounds when its wings burned, then fell to earth and crawled in circles around the lantern.

Quarrier was desperate to warn Moon of what was coming, but there had been no sign of Indians since their last appearance, and he had no idea how to reach their village. The atmosphere at the mission—even Hazel was aware of the hopelessness of their alternatives—was silent and hostile, with discord seeping in all directions. Hazel was the only one who spoke at all, offering dark little fragments from the bitter tumult of her mind.

"The Ambassadors of the Lord," she snorted. Or, *"He that loseth his life for my sake shall find it.* Matthew 10:39." Or, "We are enjoying the profits of a business deal we entered into with the Lord. We have thrilled to see our new brown friends grow so rapidly in Jesus . . ."

"Please, Hazel," Quarrier said. "You must help us pray for guidance."

"Let not your heart be troubled!" Hazel shouted. She added quietly and sadly, *"Neither let it be afraid."*

"That's it, Hazel," Leslie said. "Let us speak the Holy Scriptures with respect."

"John 14:27," Hazel said. "Please pass the Ajax Flavor-Sealed Canned Tuna that He hath sent us in His wisdom and His mercy."

On the third day they heard a motor on the river; Guzmán's invasion had begun. Toward noon a flatboat came, with eight armed men; they did not put their carbines down until they collided with the bank, and they held the flatboat hard aground by running their pandemoniacal old motor full speed ahead, the thick mud churning.

All eight shouted tempestuously above the smoke

and din. "Hah, *evangélicos!* Where are the *salvajes?* We saw no sign!"

They were not soldiers but rivermen, delivering the shipment of barbed wire. They were barefoot and mustachioed, lean grinning brigands; they shared a mangy wild-eyed boldness, like a dog pack, and a furtive wild-eyed fear, not only of the savages but of these *protestantes*. Fortified by cane alcohol and by the news of the Tiro massacre, they were anxious to shoot Niaruna and take women.

"Hah, *evangélicos!* You do not have the women here? Where are the women? Let us speak with them! See! We have presents!" The halfbreeds held up beads and liquor, like pilgrims bearing alms.

But when they saw that there would be no sport, they jeered and cursed among themselves, pricking their hands as they dumped their cargo on the bank. One, grinning, held up his twin bleeding palms: *"Estigma!"* Departing, they shouted innocent obscenities to console one another, and fired their carbines at the descending sky.

That afternoon, unable to sit still, Quarrier took one of the boats upriver; it relieved him so to break out of their dungeon that at first he felt unafraid. But the small river soon became a creek, dark and tangled where the jungle swarmed across it; the outboard went aground on shoals of mud. Sure suddenly that he was being watched, he crouched there in a bursting silence, half blinded by his sweat, then fought the boat into the clear and fled downriver. The next day he set out on foot, seeking the Niaruna trail; a few yards past the gift rack, where the remnants of the dead snake oozed and stank, all signs of man gave out entirely. He pushed farther, unwilling to go back and at the same time wondering what he would do if he actually found a trail.

His mind refused to concentrate; though he was no more than a quarter-mile from the station, he was soon lost. He touched a tree, dismayed anew by these dark twisted amphitheaters, the hanging ropes, the quaking rot beneath his feet that breathed its reek with every step. He was a hundred feet below the leaves and flowers, a soft blind denizen of caves. He stumbled around in small half-circles. A strange explosive *pop* made him lunge with fright; it was only a small manakin snapping its wings. The bird sat perched in silhouette, in a long lonely shaft of sallow light.

In the dark tunnels of the rain forest the dim light was greenish. Strange shapes caught at his feet, and creepers scraped him; putrescent smells choked his nostrils with the density of sprayed liquid. He fell to his knees on the rank ground and began to pray, but instantly jumped up again. He had wandered into a cathedral of Satan where all prayer was abomination, a place without a sky, a stench of death, vast somber naves and clerestories, the lost cries of savage birds—he whooped and called, but no voice answered.

The jungle pinned him in. Hadn't he heard that even an Indian careless enough not to mark his departure from a trail might lose himself forever in this forest? It was growing dark. His best course was to remain where he was until the others missed him, and came out and called. But he was not a woodsman, and he was terrified of the jungle creatures; standing there, he turned his head every few seconds in response to sounds—the chewing of insects, a twig fallen from above, the mindless peep of distant tree frogs. He was so taut that at a small noise behind him he jumped sideways and backward, tripped and fell. Expecting the leap of a jaguar or the big probing head of an anaconda, he was astonished to see two Indians, one on each side of a huge pale tree. In the dim light, they were little more than shadows. They seemed to wait for him; he was surrounded.

"Welcome," he begged; he could not rise. "Welcome!"

Fear shook him without mercy. He tried to pray, but no prayer came.

316

One Indian raised his hand, palm outward. "Redskins all day all day be good. Fire Place no go."

"I was lost," Quarrier said. "I came out to look for you."

"How much medicine can you spare? My people are sick." Moon came closer. He was wearing ragged pants. "I gave them flu." He glanced at his companion, who looked astonished at Kisu-Mu's conversation with the white man. He shrugged and continued, "They're very sick. The girl Pindi, and now Boronai, and some of the children; they're all going to get it."

"Flu!" Quarrier said. "She didn't come that close to you!"

With his spear Moon pierced a leaf. "So how much medicine do you have?"

"Enough. I'll have to ask Huben."

"Very good. Let's do it." Moon started away, followed by the Indian; they headed in the last direction Quarrier would have thought to go.

He plunged along behind them. "Listen," he called. "Huben's pretty upset."

"I know," Moon said.

"I don't blame him." Quarrier was rushing to keep up; he felt irritable and out of breath. "I'd be upset too. You have no business—"

"I didn't think you'd recognize me, Quarrier."

"I don't mean that time. Andy told me about what you did, down by the river."

Moon stopped short. "She spotted me too, then?" He laughed angrily, shaking his head. "Some Indian!"

"She said you didn't molest her."

"No," Moon snapped. "I didn't *molest* her. I came just close enough to get her goddamn flu from her. You had no business letting her walk around—"

"We didn't know," Quarrier said. "She brought it back from Madre de Dios."

When they reached the clearing, Quarrier told Moon to wait where he was. "If Huben sees you," he said, "he might get upset again."

Moon said, "I'm wearing pants—what more does he want?"

Huben was sitting at the table in the cooking shed, staring at his radio. The instrument stared back at him, like a boxed oracle. More and more these days, Leslie lost himself in world news and the latest tunes. *"I have a special message,"* the radio addressed Leslie, *"for all you friends out there—"* But when Leslie heard what Quarrier had to say, he turned it off. "So he's come to us on his knees, has he? I knew it!" He slapped his hands down on his thighs and rose. "All right, where is he?"

"He's not on his knees, Leslie."

"Where is he?" Huben said. They went outside.

At the clearing edge the missionary confronted Moon. Hands in the hip pockets of his shorts, he rocked back and forth on his heels.

"Big Chief Crazy Horse," Huben said at last. "Now tell us exactly what you want."

"You know what I want."

"First you come here and tell us we have eight days to get out, and now you have the nerve to come back here and ask us for our medicine." Huben laughed aloud while the others watched him. Moon said nothing. Finally Huben stopped his laughter, sighing a little, as if it was all too much for him. "And what do we get in return?" he said.

"You brought that medicine for the Indians, right? Well, now they need it."

"How badly?" Huben said. "Badly enough so that unless they get it, they'll be too weak to drive us out? Do you really expect us to help you undo the Lord's work with this tribe, to aid and abet the work of Satan?" He shook his head. "My goodness!"

"In other words," Moon said calmly, "you're willing to let the whole tribe die. In Jesus' name, of course."

Huben yelped in disbelief. "In Jesus' name! How filthy those words are in the foul mouth of the blasphemer!" The missionary's teeth were bared, and he was panting. "A devil! An obscene drunkard and forni-

cator, a sinner too shameless to cover up his shame"—
he glanced with hatred at Moon's body—"who would
come here naked before the eyes of good Christian
women! And now you have the nerve to tell me that it
is the servants of the Lord Almighty who are willing
to let these people die!"

Moon was gazing at the huge rolls of barbed wire.
"That's right," he said. "Let's have that medicine."

"I will not!" Huben shouted. "As God is my witness, I will not! *Be ye not unequally yoked together
with unbelievers: for what fellowship hath righteousness
with unrighteousness? and what communion hath
light with darkness?*"

Moon turned to Quarrier. "You go along with
that?"

"Yes."

"I don't mean the Scriptures," Moon said irritably. "I mean about the medicine."

Quarrier said, "Leslie, we cannot save these souls
for Christ if they are dead."

"I tell you, I will not put into the hands of this
painted demon the healing provided in all His mercy
by our Lord! Can't you see that? Are you too stupid
even to see *that?*" Huben shook both fists in Quarrier's
face.

"What he wishes to do now is a Christian act."

"It is a *selfish* act! For his own demonic purposes! To lead those people into darkness and corruption!"

Moon said, "You're saying it again: if these people don't play it your way, you'd just as soon see them
dead."

Huben glared at Moon. "You're with *them,* aren't
you? The men in black! The Opposition!"

Moon said to Quarrier, "What's all *that* about?"

"Don't try to slip around me," Huben said, nodding his head. "I saw you plotting with that priest in
Madre de Dios."

"Listen," Moon said to Huben, "you're a very
stupid man, believe me. Go in and lie down. Take a

319   *At Play in the Fields of the Lord*

vacation, maybe." He looked thin and tired; he was in a hurry. "Now look," he said to Quarrier, "you people make up your minds."

"He can't have it!" Huben shouted. "I'm your superior, Martin Quarrier, and don't you forget it!"

"Please be quiet," Quarrier said. "This is my mission, Leslie. You said so yourself." When Moon nodded at him in approval, he took a deep breath, saying harshly, "I am not on your side, Moon. I agree with everything that Leslie here has said about you. You are committing a terrible sin among these people. And you're not going to get this medicine for nothing."

"Oh, shit," Moon said, losing his temper. "Your hypocrisy stinks worse than his, and you haven't got the excuse of being stupid! At least he admits it's not the Indians' lives he cares about, only their souls." He pointed at his Indian companion, who was urinating. "Do you love *him?*" He spat angrily on the ground. "The hell you do! Beneath all this phony love you people preach, you have no respect for Indian ways. You tell him his superstitions are ridiculous, and when he has nothing left, you ask him to believe instead that Jesus walked on water. You buy his dignity with beads. You—ah, Christ, just hand over that medicine!"

"You are going to send the sick ones here," Quarrier said, "and we will treat them ourselves."

Moon nodded his head, while Huben folded his arms upon his chest and cackled triumphantly, as if it were he, not Quarrier, who had dealt Moon the coup de grâce.

"Yes, you are," Huben cried, "unless you're willing to admit that it is you, not us, who don't care about the Indians' lives, who are more concerned with personal ambitions." He laughed ferociously. "And when we tell the Niaruna that you are a white man, and how you have misled them, you'll be very glad of our protection, Mr. Lewis Moon."

"Very good," Moon said, "very good." He bowed abruptly to Quarrier. "I underestimated you." He said something in Niaruna that Quarrier did not catch, and

320

the Indian stepped forward. The savage had watched the whole performance without uttering a sound, or rather, had watched Moon, frowning; Moon must be desperate, Quarrier thought, to expose himself this way. Moon said to Quarrier, "Pindi is already dead. Boronai may die. He is too sick to come here to be treated."

"The Indians can bring him in," Huben said.

Moon swung his arm back, slamming Huben in the stomach; as the man sank, Moon grasped him by the shirt front and twisted the collar tight upon his throat. Quarrier started forward as Leslie fought for air, but the Niaruna stepped in front of him, drawing an arrow.

"Would you really go that far?" Quarrier said quietly. "Would you kill your own kind to get your way?"

"You'll have the answer in a minute," Moon remarked as clinically as if he were taking Huben's pulse.

Huben, the breath knocked out of him, was turning a bad color. When Quarrier ran off toward the shed, Moon dropped the man, and Leslie crouched there on hands and knees, his head down, coughing. The Niaruna turned his bow and aimed his arrow at the missionary's neck. When Quarrier returned with the medicine box, Leslie got to his feet and pitched away across the yard, in tears. Andy, who had followed Quarrier, met her husband halfway across the yard and took him in her arms. Over his shoulder the girl looked at Moon so coldly that he could not face her, and turned away.

Quarrier did not want to look at Moon; he busied himself with the medicine chest. That open mouth, that mouth forced open by bewilderment and need— on this face, among all the faces he had ever known, he had never thought to see it. Both glad and saddened, he said quietly, "You didn't have to hit him."

"No." Moon raised his head. "I hope you'll get her out of here."

"Otherwise you'll be forced to kill her too?"

"If Aeore had his way," Moon said, "you'd be

dead long ago." His voice was cold again, and he took the sulfa drugs from Quarrier without thanks, giving them to the Niaruna, who placed them in a fiber bag slung over his shoulder.

When Quarrier had instructed him in the dosage, they stood a moment, regarding each other. Then Moon said, "So long, Preacher. Don't hang around here after the new moon." He started away.

Quarrier called, "What can you hope to gain by this? Do you imagine you're helping these people?" He had followed Moon into the trees, and as they went, the eastward trail materialized. What had always seemed a hopeless tangle was now pierced by a vague but definite path leading away from the Espíritu. "The Niaruna are still considered animals—why, even if you signed some sort of treaty, it would be broken!" When Moon kept moving, Quarrier yelled, "As a Plains Indian, you should *know* that!" This time Moon stopped and turned to face him. Quarrier paused, taken aback by the ferocity of his expression; then he said, "You're not a savage, Moon, and you never were, and you never will be."

"Well, why are *you* here, you holy bastard? Do *you* really know?"

"I think I was searching for something more important than my own life. That's what we're all after, isn't it?"

Moon contemplated him. "I don't follow you," he said. He went on into the forest. "Get her out of here," his voice came back. "I'm warning you."

"I'm not leaving!"

"You're going to get killed then. Like Fuentes."

"God's will be done!"

As Quarrier retreated toward the mission, Moon's voice trailed after him: "It will be. In four days."

23

When the canoe rounded the last bend toward dusk, two silhouettes appeared in the western light. The man at the motor was the Indian Yoyo, and his passenger was Padre Xantes.

"Good evening," the priest said when the canoe touched the bank. The missionaries on the bank said nothing. Quarrier went down the bank and helped the little man ashore, but Huben stood high above, arms folded on his chest, expression thunderous, a Jehovah in high sneakers. "You are not welcome here," he called.

"Nevertheless," the padre smiled, "here I am, and here I shall remain until I have said what I have come to say." He took Quarrier's hand and was hoisted up the slippery bank, at the top of which he shook his cassock out and lifted his straw hat long enough to mop his brow. Now he looked at Quarrier and nodded. "Good evening, my son," he said. He gazed benignly at Huben's long bare legs. "Am I in time for the sporting event?" He smiled broadly, glancing about the clearing. Seeing the barbed-wire rolls, he raised his eyebrows: *"Ein' feste Burg,* eh? What a strange idea!"

"What is it you want here, Father?" Quarrier said. He flushed a little; could his use of the term "Father" be taken as recognition of the unrecognizable? He set his jaw. "You cannot start back tonight, as you must know."

"I planned my journey in this way," the priest confessed. "I wished to make certain of a hearing. But I am not here on a social visit. I have my own provisions, and I will sleep cheerfully in our friend's canoe." He nodded at Yoyo, who was fiddling uneasily with his motor.

"That won't be necessary," Quarrier said. "You will be our guest."

"Yoyo!" Huben said. The Indian looked up, smiling indiscriminately at all and none; when Huben planted his fists on his hips, the Tiro slipped forward along the canoe and came up on the bank. As he did so, the crucifix around his neck slipped out of his red shirt and dangled for a moment; he snatched at it as at a gnat and stuffed it back in hiding.

Hands folded on his stomach, Padre Xantes smiled. He continued to smile as Huben berated the Indian for consorting with the priest, and for bringing him to the mission on the Espíritu. Yoyo jabbered frantically that he was hired, that his was the only boat available, that Padre Xantes had not attempted to corrupt his mind. When he was finished, Huben reached into the bright shirt and seized the crucifix; he held it in his hand contemptuously, then bounced it back on Yoyo's chest.

The priest stopped smiling. "You are not respectful to the symbol of our Lord," he said.

"Well, what do you want with us?" Huben said.

Yoyo, smiling once again, slid away from Huben and disappeared behind the shed.

The priest sighed. "I am here to join with you against a common enemy, to help you—or at least to warn you."

"What is it you wish to say, Father?" Quarrier asked. He felt a quickening impatience with both Leslie and the Dominican. Huben was the aggressor, but the priest enjoyed confounding him, tasting his own words with relish as he might taste food, the pale hands folded primly on his belly, the little black shoes, incongruous in the mud, peeping innocently from beneath his cassock.

"It concerns our gallant Comandante," the priest said. "The Comandante has convinced himself through radio contact with Señor Huben that the missing American, Señor Moon, is alive—is, in fact, with the Niaruna at this very moment. Señor Moon, it seems, is leading the Niaruna on raids against the Tiro, in which Tiro have been killed."

"He's lying! I never said that on the radio!"

Disregarding this, Padre Xantes said, "Is it true that Moon is still alive? Amazing! Do you know, I was certain that this man must die even before he disappeared"—he puckered his thin mouth, musing—"because he makes bold to fly into the sun, into the face of God, one might almost say! What a fellow!" He laughed with admiration. "His friend, the magnificent Wolf, assures me that this Moon is indestructible, eh? We shall see!"

Quarrier said impatiently, "Mr. Huben is telling the truth."

"I didn't even speak to Guzmán!" Huben cried. "I sent him a message through the airline agent at the radio shack!"

"I am sure you are quite innocent," Padre Xantes remarked, not without contempt. "But the Comandante has a way of hearing things as he wishes to hear them —the mark of the good politician, would you not say, even in your own progressive land?" He shrugged his shoulders. "It does not matter. What matters is this: Guzmán has reported to the Minister of the Interior that the Niaruna have been in—infected?—by criminal elements, apparently from across the border; that they have made not one but a series of murderous raids on the peace-loving Tiro; and that they threaten not only the mission of the Americans upon the Espíritu but the settlement at Remate de Males. As you know," he said, "our government treasures the lives of you Americans. All that splendid money . . ."

When the missionaries only stared at him, he added, "Alas, our Comandante has received permission to subdue the Niaruna by any means at his disposal. And he is a man who takes great satisfaction in his work."

Night had come as the priest spoke, and the air thickened with mosquitoes. Huben made no objection when Quarrier said, "Please come inside, Father, and share our supper with us."

Andy joined them, and treated Padre Xantes with civility, but much to Quarrier's relief, Hazel could not be prevailed upon to break her bread with him. Huben praised the Lord for sending them nice corned beef hash, at which the priest said disingenuously, "How kind of Him! We too believe in the universal causality of God." When Quarrier gave the blessing, the simplest one he knew, Padre Xantes crossed himself as if in defense against prayers so barbarous, then murmured his own. When he raised his head again, he smiled thinly at the company and said, "This is perhaps the first time that a Dominican has supped in a Protestant mission. In my small way I have made history."

Quarrier said, "I am still not certain about why you have come."

"Have I not told you, Señor Quarrier? The Comandante wishes to exterminate the Niaruna."

"Wouldn't that be a defeat for the Protestants?" Huben demanded. "Isn't that exactly what you want?"

"The defeat of the Protestants would be very gratifying, Mr. Huben," the priest said, "but not at the expense of an entire tribe."

"Well, I for one don't trust you," Huben exclaimed, pounding his fist upon the table. "You are still angry because I took the Niaruna away from you, and you think that somehow you are going to steal them back, isn't that right?"

"It is true," the priest said, "that you *evangélicos* will fail here; you have failed already. And when you abandon your efforts, it is true that I will renew my own on behalf of the true Church. But I cannot hope to do this if there is no tribe to teach. Therefore I am proposing that Protestant and Catholic join forces to save the Indians; this is the most important thing, wouldn't you say so, Señor Huben?" He regarded the missionary coldly.

When Huben only jammed his fork into his food, the priest said quietly, "As to the anger you attribute to me, there is little to be angry about. I am aware, Señor Huben, that you have received much credit for having contacted the fierce Niaruna. But the truth is that you only contacted the estimable Uyuyu, who, despite what he has told you, is not a Niaruna but a Tiro, and whose relatives-by-marriage are no more than a weak band of Niaruna outcasts who have loitered about my mission house at Remate de Males for more than a year. In other words, neither Catholic nor Protestant has made real contact with the Niaruna; you imagine that you have taken from me something which, in fact, I have never had."

"You're lying! We *are* in contact with wild Niaruna! We had four of them right here for months! And Yoyo was the key to the whole tribe! You know very well how much he meant to you, so just never mind pretending that you weren't angry when you lost him!"

While Huben spoke, Padre Xantes gave attention to his food. He provided himself with a large mouthful, which he chewed slowly; when he had finished, he wiped his mouth, turning to Quarrier. "I never *had* him," he said. "Do you people sincerely imagine that you have him now?"

Quarrier said nothing.

"Mr. Quarrier, at least, has doubts. The Indian is not equipped—or not as yet—to make the fine distinctions in his manner of worship that our two faiths permit themselves. In this fearful world of jungle, of darkness and flood and dangerous beasts, he cannot be expected to grasp the eternal significance of the apostolic succession, much less our dispute over the relative significance of the Virgin Mary. Eh? While Uyuyu may actually believe in Jesus Christ, he cannot imagine that the difference between the Protestant and the Catholic Jesu is as real as we pretend. Also, one must keep in mind that Christianity has been good business for him; quite naturally he will lean toward that faith which pays him best." The priest closed his eyes for a moment, smiling, and Quarrier smiled also. "Uyuyu, of course, would cheerfully support *both* churches, but we are too petty to permit this, and so he does it anyway, but furtively, which is to say that he actually supports neither."

The priest paused, grinning toothily. "You gentlemen may know that the Inca and Maya, the Chibcha and Nahua, and many other groups, had the concept of a humanlike god. This god, called variously Viracocha, Quetzalcoatl, and so forth, is characterized by facial hair, a large white body and a brief stay on earth. While these were also attributes of Jesus Christ, I fear that El Comandante comes much closer to Uyuyu's conception of the Godhead than anything the poor fellow has learned from us."

"Now listen here—"

The padre, enjoying himself, lifted his palm in interruption. "Permit me"—and he inclined politely toward Leslie—"permit me to recite a hymn of the heathen Inca:

"Creator of the World
    Maker of all men
    Lord of all Lords
    I am blind with the longing to see Thee
    To know Thee
    Might I behold Thee
    Might I know Thee
    Might I ponder Thee and understand Thee
    Oh gaze down upon me, Lord
    For Thou perceivest me
    The sun and moon
    The day and night
    The spring and winter

328

Cannot have been created without sight
By Thee, O Viracocha!

"Eh?" Padre Xantes basked in their surprise. "Does it not sound oddly like St. Augustine? Once I instructed my flock that our Creator was not to be confused with their own. But one man said, 'How do you know?' and I could not answer."

Leslie jumped to his feet. "These are words of Satan! This man is cynical and corrupted, and yet we let him sit there, eating the food of the Lord and laughing at us!"

"Well, I must say it's very good, whosoever food it is," the priest remarked; he passed his plate to Andy for a second helping. "Thank you so much, señora." They watched him fill his mouth again—he ate methodically, moving from one item to another, like a man packing a bag—and after a time, when no one spoke, he said, "As to the matter of cynicism, Señor Huben, would you not agree that it is cynical to bribe a simple Indian from a rival faith?"

"I did not—"

"To suggest to him that his fidelity would be rewarded by permission to . . . sell slaves, for example?" The priest set down his knife and fork. "If I recall my history correctly, one reason behind the Protestant revolt and the Reformation was the practice among the clergy of selling indulgences."

"You are making a very serious charge," Quarrier said, raising his hand to forestall Huben's outburst.

"I make it in all seriousness," the priest said.

"I'm sure Mr. Huben would deny it just as seriously," Quarrier said coldly. "And needless to say, I would believe him."

He spoke with more conviction than he felt. He had the unhappy feeling that he agreed with every point the little man had made; at the same time he was ever more irritated by Xantes' smug urbanity, by his smiling assumption that his serenity in the face of

Huben's boorishness had won the latter's companions to his side. It annoyed him that in his accented, elaborate way the Spaniard used their own language more skillfully than they did; he was even annoyed by the priest's ability to eat so heartily and calmly on the enemy's own ground, whereas the enemy itself was so upset that it could scarcely eat at all. And while he did not question Padre Xantes' motive in coming here, he wondered if this opportunity to debate, to subtly deride their efforts, was not more important to him than his concern for the Niaruna. So now he said, "And anyway, it seems a strange matter to bring up when you have come here to co-operate with us in trying to spare the Niaruna."

"*Sí, claro.*" Xantes, frowning, put down his fork with a neat click. "I have abused your hospitality disgracefully." He made a short bow to Huben. "My apologies, señor. Our differences of opinion have no importance here this evening."

Even to Huben, the priest's skilled candor was disarming. He grunted doubtfully.

"And you believe," Quarrier asked, "that your church would support you in co-operating with us?"

"I did not ask their permission lest they refuse me. Seven centuries ago Pope Innocent III instructed our Dominican Order 'to extirpate heresy'; as you people are heretics, I have no business among you." He smiled. "I am quite a renegade, you see. I am perhaps the only Spaniard on this continent who supports the idea of a single Christian Church, a reuniting of Catholic and Protestant."

"We do not support that idea here. In fact," Quarrier said, and this time he smiled himself, "we are tempted to believe in some past union of the Catholic Church and Satan."

The priest laughed heartily. "So I gather, so I gather," he said, delighted, and helped himself to pickles. "And the two have met from time to time. They have been seen in company, I assure you. The Inquisition—why, I doubt if even your fundamentalist

Lord of hellfire and damnation would have approved the Inquisition!" He crunched loudly on his pickle. "Our Christian—that is, *Western*—outlook is rather lugubrious, do you not think? We have persuaded ourselves that abnegation"—and he touched his cassock, not without irony—"and self-sacrifice are superior to joyous self-expression, to the emotions—to simple *being*? Now . . . if we could just take time from our teaching of our poor Indians, we might *learn* something from them. After all, the Indians come out of Asia, theirs is essentially an Eastern culture; they do not seek for meaning: they *are*. They are not *heavy* the way we are, they are light as the air; their being is a mere particle of the universe, like a leaf or wing of dragonfly or wisp of cloud. Unlike ourselves, they are eternal."

"This conversation is all very sophisticated, I'm sure, but aren't we forgetting something, Martin?" Leslie stared in an accusing way at all the others, one by one, mouth open in self-righteous injury. With his long blond hair and callow face, his sport shirt and shorts, he looked like a young boy who, confronted with injustice, takes himself too seriously. Andy watched him; when she caught Quarrier regarding her, she turned away.

"Yes, Leslie's right," Quarrier said. "We must decide about the Niaruna."

There was little to decide. Yoyo, who could follow a trail, would lead Quarrier to the Niaruna the next morning, for time was running out; Guzmán and his soldiers might appear at any time. According to the priest, El Comandante had arranged with Moon's partner, El Lobo, to bomb and strafe Boronai's village; they were only awaiting a shipment of small bombs.

Without Moon's leadership, Xantes said, Wolfie had gradually come apart; drunken and lonely, he had now been threatened with extradition by the playful Comandante unless he made an honest woman of fat Mercedes, who was with child. On the other hand, if he bombed as he was told, he would be given his passport and airplane passage west, across the mountains.

"To the Land of the Dead," Andy murmured. She looked down at her hands when the men gazed at her. These were her only words during the meal, for she merely shrugged when her husband requested an explanation.

Padre Xantes did not want Yoyo to return with him, for fear that Guzmán might learn too soon that the Niaruna had been warned. He had already told Guzmán of his feelings about the massacre, which El Comandante—not having to pay them heed—had accepted in good grace. On the other hand, once Guzmán learned that his plan had been betrayed, the padre's future would be uncertain. He shrugged philosophically. "It appears I must defend myself with blackmail," he remarked. "After all, it can be proven that Guzmán knew that there was but one raid on the Tiro and that the Niaruna are not—in*fected?*—with foreign criminal elements as he claimed in his report, but only by a pilot he had sent in, without authority, to kill them." He shrugged again. "It is all so sordid, no?" he said, with an odd kind of satisfaction.

Huben stared at the little priest with open loathing. While Quarrier sat in morose silence, the two soon fell to bickering again. Intent on what Xantes had called the "fine distinctions," Huben derided the Catholic exaltation of the Virgin Mary, while the padre, less angry than amused, called all Protestant teachers "outlaw priests," since they had not been ordained by the true clergy—those on whose shoulders had been laid, across the centuries, the hands of the apostles. Huben referred him to Acts 8, in the first verse of which the Christians *were all scattered abroad throughout the regions of Judaea and Samaria, except the apostles.* The fourth verse read, *Therefore they that were scattered abroad went every where preaching the word.*

332

"Those were *not* apostles," Huben crowed. "They were simple Christians!"

Xantes sat forward, not quite smiling. He was less discomfited than gratified that Huben was putting up some sort of fight. They passed on to a dispute over the Eucharist. So it went, back and forth, back and forth, more and more petty, more ludicrous. Should there be water in the wine? Should the service be in Latin?

Thus you would haggle and nag each other, Quarrier thought, until Heaven crashed about your ears. He got up, unnoticed, and retired to his room.

On his knees, he prayed for the soul of Billy Quarrier, dead at nine of blackwater fever in the uttermost part of the earth—and now Hazel sat up and stared at him. The hanks of stiff black hair had fallen forward past her eyes like horse blinders, so that her ears stuck out. Her gray-green eyes were bright, her mouth was big and her nose and teeth were small; he glimpsed a savage animal, mad with the suffering twisted and crammed into her big racked body. At one moment he saw the apparition of a girl once lovely to him, and in the next all human ugliness, red-eyed and cornered and swollen, although her outward face was set, her green eyes dry as pebbles in a desert river.

He had scarcely talked with Hazel since the death of Billy; they could no longer communicate, and preferred not to talk at all. Quite apart from her grief, Hazel was torn in half by loyalty to her marriage vows on the one hand, and by a vengeful resentment, a lack of respect for him, on the other; she would leave him if she had the courage, if she didn't feel that search for happiness on earth must be immoral. He would leave her too, as perhaps Andy might leave Leslie, but all of them were pinned like butterflies to the frame of their own morality, and that was that. Kneeling there in the dark, observing her, Martin shrugged. They must try to hold together what was left, and stumble on.

Then Hazel said, "Make love to me."

She was sweaty and feverish, and gave off heat, and when he took her in his arms, seeking to calm her, he found himself caught up in a death struggle. They writhed together, soaking wet. Though he went with her, a part of him stayed behind to watch and listen, like a man uneasy at the edge of the night jungle, to cries of ecstasy which were more like howls, and obscene howls at that; they shook the hut. He clapped his hand upon her mouth. She bit it hard. She gasped, "Oh Jesus, make love to me, screw me, cruel Jesus, damn you Jesus." He reared back in terror and slapped her pale avid face. Hazel lay back on her pillow, her hair crumpled, and gazed at him peacefully for the first time since the death of Billy, and went to sleep as sweetly as a child.

He lay awake for a long time. Asleep, he dreamed that he was peering up into the highest steeple of a great cathedral; through the steeple's translucent skin he could see the night stars of the heavens. A star came down, like a wand of God, and touched the steeple's point; the cathedral dissolved in a burst of ethereal light. All the churches of the world were gathered around this greatest of cathedrals, and they, too, dissolved in showers of light, one by one, as they were touched. But the fragments did not descend to earth; instead they were drawn gently upward, into the starry universe, as if their time on earth had ended—as if God, more rueful than angry, had withdrawn his sanction of man's churches and mankind, saying, No, you have not learned the Way.

With the loss of Heaven, Martin awoke and did not sleep again; he stared at a dull low ceiling of thatch and mud. By morning his eyes were dry and taut, and his every organ ached; lying there on his back, he felt split open, like a dressed animal. A dank fog had settled on him in the night; he lay there helpless in its shroud. The prospect of his journey to the savages filled him with terror, but the journey, with faith or without, had to be made.

Quarrier asked the priest to take Hazel to Madre de Dios; Andy would accompany her, and would put her on a plane and send her home on leave to North Dakota. Hazel offered no resistance to this plan; she had even forgotten that Padre Xantes was a Catholic. She had withdrawn to the asylum of her past, and would have departed with this same serenity for the moon.

Quarrier took her clumsily into his arms and said good-bye to her as to a stranger; she giggled loudly, blushing, and he found himself in tears. "Good-bye, good-bye," called Hazel, to no one in particular; standing there in the early mist, her black shoes square and sensible, she looked like a head nurse on her day off, bound for a nice excursion on the river.

Andy was to wait in Madre de Dios until notified by radio that the Niaruna situation had been resolved; if there was any mission to return to, she would then be flown back to Remate, and Huben would fetch her in the boat.

The only person hostile to these plans was Yoyo. The priest tried to explain to the Indian why he was being left behind, but no one could possibly have made him understand why it was that the white people could commandeer his boat—for though both boat and motor actually belonged to Guzmán, the prestige that went with them on the rivers had adhered to Yoyo, and he regarded them as his own. In his torment he shouted rudely that Padre Xantes did not know how to run the motor, that the priest would surely overturn the boat at the first bend and drown the lot; they would all be eaten by piranhas! Unless he, Yoyo, was there to protect them, the Tiros would foully violate the women! El Comandante would be very angry and would punish *evangélico* and *católico* without distinction!

This address was delivered from the stern of the dugout, from which he refused to budge; then he started up the motor in an attempt at flight, slamming the motor into reverse and churning backward. Quarrier, who had leaped for the boat's liana, was yanked headfirst down the muddy bank into the water, but he held on long enough for Huben and Xantes to rush to his assistance. For one wild ecumenical moment the three holy men, grunting and thrashing in the mud and water, did violent battle with their maddened convert and his outraged machine. Then the clutch slipped and the engine's roar exploded in the jungle morning; the motor belched smoke as Yoyo howled, and the canoe lashed back and forth like a dying dragon. When the motor stalled, they drew the boat ashore. Quarrier seized the raging Indian and hauled him out onto the bank and shook him.

The priest was vexed at having soiled his habit, and Huben was enraged that his wife was laughing. Quarrier too was extremely angry; he was wet and muddy, he had wrenched his knee and was in pain, and worst of all, he had lost his last pair of glasses in the river. This was such a blow that for the moment he did not even wish to think about it; he stood there blinking, trying to regain his breath. Andy was laughing, and although he saw precisely why she laughed, and shared every drop of her despair, he could not laugh himself for fear he might not stop.

He still held Yoyo tightly by the arm. Hatred had drawn the Tiro's small dark face so taut that Quarrier, startled, released him as he might release a snake. Yoyo's hand flicked to his hip; though he did not draw the knife, he did not bother to disguise the gesture. He simply stood there, half turned, body coiled, not even breathing, in his white-man's haircut, his Indian tattoos and the red shirt which, exposing his crucifix, was so large for him that it covered the mission shorts and hung on his bare brown legs like a baby's frock; his yellow eyes were slightly averted, like the eyes of an angry dog expecting to be struck.

Padre Xantes told Yoyo that he was needed to guide Quarrier to the Niaruna, that his was an important mission, that he would be well paid. Yoyo neither moved nor spoke. He did not return the priest's good-bye, or even wince as Padre Xantes, navigating with suspicion and distaste, turned the canoe clumsily about and started downriver.

The skirted forms were soon so indistinct to Quarrier's poor vision that he never knew if anyone returned his wave. This did not matter much, since he himself could not have truly said which of the women he was waving to.

When the boat had gone, he and Huben searched for the glasses in the soft mud along the bank. Leslie poked vaguely at the mud; at one point he reared up in irritation and ordered the Tiro to come and help them. This worsened matters; all three stood stiff until Yoyo broke the triangle, coming slowly down the bank like a man entranced. They hunted together, bent-backed, in the brown slow current of the Espíritu. Finally Yoyo straightened, followed by Huben. Quarrier hunted for a little while longer, his bare feet flinching in his fear of stingrays and electric eels as he moved farther from shore; he only hunted to forestall his dread of sightlessness, and soon he too gave up and climbed out on the bank.

"Well, Yoyo!" He tried to smile. "I'll need you all the more now that I'm blind."

The Tiro gazed at him without expression.

Quarrier changed his clothes and prepared to leave. Huben grew more irritable each moment. He began by questioning the priest's warning; perhaps Guzmán had accepted their assurance that no help was needed. And what made Quarrier think that Aeore's men would not kill him the moment he appeared? Quarrier said nothing. The presence of Yoyo, Huben pointed out, was no guarantee, but the reverse; the Niaruna had already taken Tiro life and would not hesitate to take another, especially if the Tiro was friendly with the whites. For Quarrier to go alone and half blind into Niaruna territory was suicidal; far better to wait and see if Guzmán came, to prepare the boats for flight, to stick together. "We could put up the barbed wire!" Leslie said.

Finally he pointed at Yoyo. "Do you give yourself the right to place this man's life in jeopardy?"

Leslie was afraid to go with Quarrier into the jungle, but he was also afraid of being left alone. Martin understood this and was sympathetic; in Huben's place, with everything to hope for—entirely unsustained, that is, by hopelessness—he too would refuse to go.

Leslie was yanking desperately at the balky rolls of wire, and cut his hands; he seized at every straw of solace, following Quarrier a little way into the forest, then darting back quickly to his wire. "Listen, Martin, you'll be back today now, without fail? Martin? Can you still hear me, Martin?" He was only a few yards away, a thin silhouette in the light of the clearing.

Quarrier turned. "If I'm not back by tomorrow morning, you'd better leave."

"Tomorrow morning! Before dark, you mean!"

"I don't know how far it is," Quarrier called. "It may be a long way."

He started off again. Ahead of him, Yoyo waited. Behind him he heard Leslie call, then call again, his voice much higher. Through the jungle gloom, the lost words searched like spirits of the forest: "Martin?" A pause, a twig, a dry pod falling from the canopy. "God damn you, Martin Quarrier! Why don't you answer me?"

Already Yoyo had picked out the trail, drifting so far ahead that Quarrier kept losing him. The bright red of Yoyo's shirt, spinning in the funebrial shades like a huge butterfly, lured him farther and farther from the light; but for the shirt he would scarcely have known that he had a guide at all, for the Indian's feet and tongue were silent. Several times he had to shout for him; the huge dead weight of leaves submerged his voice.

The penalty of blindness kept increasing; he hurried along, tripping and stumbling, sinking to his knees in murky holes. What was there to stop Yoyo from abandoning him, or worse? And the terror drew tighter each time the Indian reappeared, for he never came from the direction Quarrier expected but would materialize from behind, as if he had followed for some time, listening to the white man shout. Quarrier could not make out his face, but he could imagine the hard mask through which the thin flat Mongol eyes observed him.

It occurred to him that Yoyo meant to kill him. Abruptly he would wave the Tiro ahead, though he never knew just where ahead should be. He had lost all track of time, and all direction, all orientation of any kind with anything he had ever known; he wanted to pray but was no longer confident that God would hear. He had lost all sense of things; in the absence of air and space, of light and sky, he circled aimlessly in the dense core of a huge ball. The feeling that Yoyo meant to kill him grew; he plunged ahead, clambering and falling, pursuing and fleeing the Indian in the same impulse.

The red shirt halted unaccountably, not far ahead. He caught up, gasping with exhaustion, his ears ringing; it seemed to him that he heard voices. The Indian moved ahead, muttering crazily; he seemed on the point of bolting. Soon light appeared, and as they neared the clearing, a loud whooping arose; Quarrier whirled to see three savages who had been escorting them. Two more drifted in on Yoyo's flanks, and now the whole group moved out into the sunlight in a blinding din of dogs and sun and macaws.

Yoyo snapped at him, "Son-of-a-whore, they are going to kill us!"

Naked Indians surrounded them. The air felt charged; he expected to be struck down at any second. He found his voice and cried out, "Moon! I wish to speak with Moon!" But he could not find Moon's painted face among the savages.

24

"Jesu-Moon," Moon answered him at last, in a flat voice. He was incensed by Quarrier's intrusion, by the ugliness of his fright, the blind agonized eyes, the stumbling, the hands outstretched, the muddy rags.

As if goaded, Quarrier plunged forward, his big hands rising up in fists; Tukanu brought him up short by swinging his chonta lance across his shins. Quarrier grunted in pain. "So you've told them you are Jesus!"

"Yee-zuss!" Tukanu exclaimed, and laughed. He seized a lock of the missionary's hair and yanked it out; when Quarrier fell, the other Indians crowded forward.

Moon sat down and gazed at the sprawled missionary. He wondered where Aeore had gone. "No," he said, after a time. "They told *me* that I was Kisu. I didn't know who Kisu was." He explained that Kisu, the bringer of flood, was the most feared of all Niaruna spirits; the benevolent Great Ancestor was named Witu'mai. Quarrier coughed and shook his head; he had never heard of Witu'mai. His big head kept on shaking.

Kisu was actually called Kish'tu; probably it was Yoyo who, to ease his labor as interpreter, had identified Kish'tu with the "Jesu" of Padre Xantes, and come up with the "Kisu" adopted by both sides. When Kish'tu was not treated with respect, he brought the bad floods of certain rainy seasons.

Moon paused, then said almost idly, "Perhaps you understand now why they are resentful of you, why they fear Jesus Christ."

Quarrier kept nodding. His face had gone pale and slack, and his large crude head was bent sideways on his neck like the head of a sunflower on a broken stalk. Moon could not stop; he would have relished telling Quarrier about Kisu all over again in this same remorseless way. The missionary's dogged hope was too raw to endure; it was unbearable. He would flay that unspeakable hope of his, flay the straining pale white hopeful hulk of him—he shivered and ground his teeth. He felt himself in poor control, and recognized the onset of malaria.

"All this time," Moon said, "you have taught them that your Jesu was their Kisu. In other words, you taught them that the white man's God was an angry and evil spirit; you asked them to love their evil spirit." He winced at Quarrier's expression, and turned away. Enough, he thought. Enough, enough. Yet it was all he could do not to vent his frustration on the wretched missionary by knocking him senseless as he sat there. Quarrier looked stunned and stupid, like a man hit on the neck. He was murmuring the news and the warning brought in by the priest; he refrained from pointing out that had Moon stayed away from the mission and from Andy, the epidemic would not have occurred.

Nor did he point out that Moon's presence in the tribe need never have been known; it would have seemed as if the Niaruna had organized and were negotiating for themselves of their own accord, as Moon had planned. But now Guzmán had been given the excuse he needed to make the problem of the Niaruna a political and governmental matter rather than a legal and administrative one. And until the influenza had run its course, the tribe would be in no condition to resist the punitive expedition, which might appear at any time. Moon could undo all his work by persuading the Indians to scatter into the jungle; the

341   *At Play in the Fields of the Lord*

alternative was an open war in which too many Niaruna would die.

Moon sat in silence. He had given drugs to all the people in the village, and thought that most would be spared. But a child whose parents refused the white man's drugs had died the day before, and many others were very sick. Furthermore, the germs had been transmitted to the Yuri Maha through the emissaries who had come to the village since the feast; there was not enough medicine to control an epidemic, even if all the tribes could be persuaded to drop their enmities and suspicions long enough to assemble for treatment. Already the village suspected the Yuri Maha of having poisoned their own allies in the federation.

When Quarrier had delivered his message, he and Moon were silent once again. Then Quarrier cried, "Do you realize what I have taught these people? Not only that Jesus Christ is evil, but that the Christian God is identical with one of their many gods—I don't wonder the poor fellows were confused!" Turning to Yoyo, who was shoved forward at Moon's signal, he asked the Tiro why he had never mentioned Witu'mai.

"Hijo de puta!" the Indian spat. *"Misionero es maricón!"* But seeing Moon's face, he lost his nerve and began to yell that Huben had wanted the name of the great Niaruna god; was that not Kish'tu? How could Yoyo know that he meant Witu'mai, who was beneficent but lived so far off in the sky? Yoyo was naked to the waist because Tukanu had stripped him of his bright red shirt, and Moon ordered the infuriated man placed under guard lest he flee and return again as Guzmán's guide; the Indian was led away, chattering wildly with fear and hatred, and glaring back over his shoulder at the missionary.

"Well," Moon said, "you people made things easier for me. They believed, at least at first, that *I* was Kisu, which is why they did not kill me."

"It's hard to know then," Quarrier said, "in which way I have served them worse." He tried to smile, but he could not.

342

Scratching on the earth with sticks, the two men faced each other. Then Tukanu came and bellowed in Moon's ear, and Moon got slowly to his feet. "Huben's run out on you," Moon said to Quarrier. He walked away without telling the man what he had learned: that Aeore and his men, without consulting him, had gone to the mission to kill Leslie Huben. Had not Huben threatened and insulted them? The Niaruna would not be safe until their enemy was dead.

In the heat and tension of the village, the children seemed to tiptoe; the smallest leaves were still. Aeore was angry that Huben had fled down the Espíritu before he could be killed; this was a bad omen, and he stared malevolently at Moon. The void between them opened further, as if the Indian were standing on the far side of a canyon, beyond reach of Moon's voice.

Moon thought, He will kill Quarrier, and there is nothing I can do to stop him. Boronai, who might have helped, was dying.

Because Boronai was the headman, the owner of the maloca, his death would mean that the whole village would have to be abandoned and a new one erected elsewhere, and this at a season when the plantations were still full of manioc and wild food was scarce. A new planting of manioc could not be made and harvested in less than half a year. The grief in the village was strident and sincere.

Moon did not dare tell Aeore that the white men were on their way; in his present temper, Aeore would fight them. Encouraged by the Ocelot, who was still living in the village, he had been advocating not only an attack on the mission but also on the Tiro villages on the Espíritu, all the way to Remate de Males. Until now Aeore and his men had deferred to Kisu-Mu and Boronai, accepting the theory that the Tiro had guns and would be supported by Green Indians. But his men were less afraid of guns than of committing themselves irrevocably to Aeore, whom they saw as too eager for command, too arrogant, like the Ocelot, his

Yuri Maha clansman. Their doubt had maddened Aeore the more, for he felt he had lost face; he made no secret of his contempt for the clans of Boronai. In recent days his hostility toward Kisu-Mu had grown so overt that Moon now wore his pants continually, to keep his revolver handy in his belt.

In the afternoon Moon paid his last respects to Boronai. Each Indian stood in line to take the headman's hand between both of his own: the men first, then the male children, then the women and girls. They did not exchange words with the dying man, who watched them howl and weep, without expression. Boronai looked no worse than he had for several days; if anything, his fever had receded and his eyes had cleared. But after so many seasons with the tribe, Moon did not question the Indian instinct for the presence of death. Boronai himself had given up the struggle and accepted death, and this quiet resignation of the flesh was instantly apparent to his fellows; from that moment on, the headman was no longer sick but dead, and was so referred to. "He is dead" meant "he is finished, he has given up." By this criterion, Moon reflected, half the people he had known in life could be regarded as defunct.

Quarrier had followed him into the maloca, and his presence there made a bad situation worse. Moon's inability to weep for Pindi had already caused resentment, and this time the Indians studied him to see what he would do. In this closed world, good manners were more crucial than true feelings; those Indians who had visited Boronai, their duty done, stopped howling and weeping the instant they released his hand. But Kisu-Mu's silence was a flagrant discourtesy, first to his woman and now to the dying headman. The Indians watched him as he approached, watched the strange white man who stumbled after him, whispering avid questions; this too was a cause for resentment.

Moon took Boronai's hand as the others had done, and the old man, who only the year before had been a strong Indian of middle age, gazed peacefully into his face. According to Tukanu, the dying man felt that Kisu-Mu had caused his death; yet a spirit was not necessarily an enemy. The mild eyes seemed to know that Kisu-Mu was fond of him, despite the failure to weep and howl. But when Moon, too guilt-ridden to give up Boronai in silence, said to him, "Good-bye, my friend," the headman frowned at this breach of custom and withdrew his hand. To Quarrier, coming next, he refused his hand entirely, and when the missionary, not understanding, groped for it, Boronai muttered angrily and swung his arm away. The onlookers groaned in disapproval, and Quarrier retreated, following Moon into the yard.

When the last infant had been held up and its hand placed on that of Boronai, Aeore painted the older man with fresh streaks of achote and placed on his head a crown of feathers from the harpy eagle, to give dignity to his departure; after this he was left alone in his hammock. Though he seemed alert, he was not offered food or water, nor did he ask for any. The cooking and breast-feeding and the scraping of manioc on the thorn boards went on about him; because the plantations would have to be abandoned, the women had harvested as many tubers as they could, drying the surplus in the sun to make a coarse farina they could take away with them. Dressed in his eagle crown, Boronai observed their preparations, ignored because already dead.

But at Boronai's death the next afternoon, a cry rose as it had for Pindi. The women and children, forbidden to look upon the body, ran into the jungle. As the children's cries rang among the trees, the men came trotting to the maloca in somber files. Moon helped them lay out a reed mat in which Boronai was rolled up with his bows and arrows, his shell strings and his paddle; his canoe was brought and the wrapped body laid in it. Then Aeore chanted a eulogy and a promise of revenge. He invoked the Ancestors and the Great Spirit Witu'mai; he spoke of the gentle soul of Boronai which was the soul of Tukituk, the tanager, and as he did so, some of the others wept without ceremony. Then the canoe was carried to the river. It would drift for many moons toward the East, toward the Ocean River Amazonas, toward the Great Sea of Life. There, in the bright morning where the Sun was born, the canoe would sink, and Boronai's spirit would return into that sky from which, as a star, it had first descended.

The death canoe was slid out from the bank, the head of Boronai high in its stern. But immediately it began to circle, as if struggling to return upstream; it drifted off slowly, broadside. On the first bend it spun a second time, in an eddy, and wedged itself in flood debris on the far bank. A wailing rose anew, for this was a bad sign, but no one was sent to free the canoe and send it on its way. It belonged already to the spirit world and could not be touched.

Aeore drank nipi on the afternoon of the death, saying that he would go to the spirit world to learn the name of the enemy of Boronai. Because he was a jaguar-shaman, a familiar of night cats, Aeore would learn the truth, but Moon was certain that the warrior was intent upon the death of Quarrier, and that nothing his spirit would learn in its night among the jaguars would dissuade him.

The missionary was too near-sighted to read the signs on the faces of the Indians; for a whole day he had badgered Moon for ethnological data on the Niaruna, bemoaning his lack of paper and pencil. His eagerness for information, his stubborn, brave attempt to rearrange the wreckage of his life into some sort of pattern, was exasperating; Moon barely answered this unlucky man who had come at the worst of times to plague him. The man was doomed, had always been doomed, perhaps, and any attempt to intervene might turn the tribe against himself and undo the entire federation.

Aeore had drunk nipi in flamboyant draughts, which evoked sighs of admiration from his tribesmen; seated in an animated circle, they waited for him to vomit, but he did not. The infusion affected him very fast, and by nightfall he lay rigid on his back, near a fire constructed in the center of the plaza. The women and children were forbidden to look at him; his own young warriors tended the fire.

As the moon rose, Aeore's body began to tremble. He shivered and shook, muttering gibberish, and the jaguar necklace twitched upon his chest. "Now his spirit is going," Tukanu said; his eyes were bald with fright. Tukanu had spoken in a whisper, for should Aeore's body be awakened while its spirit was absent, the spirit could not enter it again, and Aeore would sicken and die.

They watched the body through the night. Beyond the black walls of the jungle, down the moonlit river banks, across the high ground and along the swamps where the great anacondas slept, Aeore's spirit hunted in the body of a jaguar.

Though the big cats often circled the village in the night, swelling the jungle with huge hollow coughs, Moon had seen a jaguar only once. It was lying on its side on the flat limb of a low hoary tree found along the rivers, camouflaged so demonically by the deep shade and shifting sun spots that he almost passed beneath it. Because the cat was on its side, the yellow pupil slit burned vertically, a jet of flame; it fixed him in his tracks. In that instant, expecting the jaguar to crouch and leap, he saw the ear twitch and the mad pulse in the throat, the flowering of the black rosettes as the cat breathed, the dead black belly spots, the nervous rippling of the flank, the metronomic thump of the black tail tuft on the rigid wood. And because the jaguar never roared, nor sprang, nor fled, nor even raised its head, but simply watched him, he was shaken for days by the malevolence of this were-jaguar that the Indians so feared.

Now, like the Indians, he awaited in awe and silence the return of the jaguar-shaman. The frogs and the night birds tocked and whistled in the ringing silence, and the bats crisscrossed the clearing, and the scent of the night flowers grew and vanished. *Rawk, rawk; ror-awk:* the rodent Marato, moved by its dim processes, uttered a hollow warning to the world.

The stars turned in the black hole above the clearing, and the Indians sighed. Even Quarrier was infected by the Indians' awe and did not sleep. Though unaware of his own danger, he was as sensitive as the rest to the tremors of the night malaise. "Demons," he told Moon. "There *are* demons. I can *feel* them."

Toward day the body of the shaman twitched again, heaved over and settled. Its tension slackened. In the greenish light the jaguar-shaman stared blankly at the sky. After a time he sat up, slowly and stiffly, his head bent on his chest, arms at his sides, legs and feet pointed straight ahead. The other Indians turned their heads away, out of politeness. In a dull monotone, the jaguar-shaman recounted his travels in the night, how he had stalked and run and climbed great trees and plunged into black rivers, on the trail to the Sea of Life. There he had met with the spirits of the Ancestors. He repeated this, and paused. The others waited.

Slowly Aeore rolled onto his haunches, in a crouch; when he spoke again, his voice was a vibrant singsong. The pupils of his yellowed eyes were still dilated, and his nostrils were flared and flattened, and the sinews of his limbs coiled on the bone.

The Ocelot, grinning, hunched in closer. Moon's mouth went dry. The Niaruna would never doubt what Aeore was about to say, or to restrain in any way this self-appointed judge and executioner, for it was not Aeore who would speak but the spirit world, through the words of their jaguar-shaman. Aeore himself would hear the words as vision and divination, brought from his mouth by nipi. Balanced on his fingertips, head switching back and forth, he spoke his message dazedly, voice mounting, and the tribe repeated his phrases in a chant; his voice did not seem to come from his own mouth, but from the air:

348

"We are the People of the Tuaremi, from the Creek of Agoutis to the rapids of Tai-wi-'an.

"In former days our clans also controlled the Tiro forest. In the Tiro forest, in former days, the clans of our mothers fished and hunted Wutari the tapir, and now Our Time has come again. We will go with all the clans of all the Peoples to the East. We will live again on the Tiro rivers. We will kill the Sloth People, the Tiro, and we will hunt Wutari the tapir.

"The white man is the friend of Tiro, and Tiro is our enemy.

"The white man is emita. He has brought us sickness. He has killed our woman Pindi. He has killed our father Boronai.

"We are the People, and the white man is our enemy.

"The white man now among us is deceitful. He has said to us that Kisu is the only god. He has said to us that Kisu loves the Niaruna. None of this is truth. He has sent poison to the people of our clan, and they have died. He is our enemy.

"We will kill the enemy among us."

Aeore sprang forward and crouched in front of Quarrier. The missionary struggled to his feet, and Aeore rose with him. Quarrier understood that Moon was powerless, and he actually smiled a vague loose smile which, in combination with his sightlessness, made him look as giddy as a baby. Moon turned his head away.

Aeore had been brought a feathered club, and now he set himself to crack the white man's skull. Moon stepped between them. Aeore sprang back, his mouth stretched wide; the Niaruna shrieked and chattered in dismay.

Moon bellowed at them, "Aeore tells you the truth. The white man is the enemy of the People, and all the Peoples to the East. You must drive the white man from your land; this I too have told you. But this man"—he pointed at Quarrier—"is not your enemy. He has come into the forest as your friend. He has brought presents. He has given food. It is true that Boronai has died. But the son of this man has also died. Would he kill his own son? I tell you, he is not your enemy! Your enemy is the white man Guzmán, who is bringing his Green Indians here to kill you!"

The Niaruna awaited Aeore, who clutched the club as if to squeeze it dry. Across a sudden hush of silence, Moon said slowly, "I am Kisu-Mu. I am sent by Kisu. You will obey me."

In the same quiet tone Aeore answered, and he said what Moon had always feared that one day he would say. He said that the People had listened because they thought that the stranger was Kisu-Mu. But Aeore did not believe that this was Kisu-Mu. Now Kisu-Mu must give them sign that he had come from Kisu.

Aeore went down on his knees and lifted his hands, the club still clutched in them. To Quarrier he said, "At the time of the death of Billy, you called to Kisu in this way. We have watched you speak to Kisu-Mu. You do not speak to him in this way. You speak to him as to a man. If Kisu-Mu is a spirit, speak to him now as you spoke on the day of the death of Billy."

Quarrier sank slowly to his knees. He was careful not to face Moon. "Almighty God," he said, "I pray—"

Led by Tukanu, the other Indians got on their knees and prayed to Moon. Quarrier flushed and became silent, then rose suddenly to his feet, shaking his head. "You must not do this," he told the Indians. "You must not pray to this man."

Across the tumult Moon said, "You feel better?" He had taken out his revolver.

Quarrier said, "I appreciate what you tried to do. I'm sorry." He knelt again, then bent his head and closed his eyes. He was very pale, and his voice was high and strained. "I shall pray for us."

"Pray for yourself. If Jesus Christ was as pigheaded as you, I don't know why they didn't kill him sooner."

Aeore, still dazed by nipi, had not chosen his course; he seemed uncertain about attacking Moon. The other Niaruna watched in dread, searching for leadership. Moon thought, If I can just get the jump on him before he makes his move . . . The surest way was to blast him where he stood, in the name of Kisu. He slipped the safety off. "If I have to shoot this man," he said to Quarrier, "I'm going to shoot you too."

The missionary squeezed his eyes shut. "If you can save lives by shooting me," he said, "please do it. While my eyes are closed. They'll kill me anyway." There was a note of martyrdom in the voice, even self-pity, but what seemed to Moon far more disgusting was that Quarrier's voice was resolute, he meant sincerely everything that he had said.

"So get the hell up off your knees," Moon said. "Tell them I am not your precious Jesus. Tell them I am Kisu-Mu, who comes from the Great Spirit of the Rain."

Quarrier stared at him, setting his jaw again. "I can't do that."

"Why, you stinking—*why* can't you, for Christ's sake! It might be true!" Moon kicked him viciously in the side. "Get the hell up, I said!"

At the sight of the kick, Aeore moved forward with the club. Moon lifted the revolver. "Tell him," he said, "or I'll shoot him down to save your neck."

Quarrier pointed at Moon. "Kisu-Mu is not the white man's god," he said, his voice an ugly croak. "Kisu-Mu comes from the Great Spirit of the Rain."

Aeore whooped with rage. He raised his club above Quarrier's head, but this time Tukanu sprang forward. In the second that the maddened Aeore turned to meet Tukanu, Moon seized Quarrier by the collar and yanked him backward, out of the club's reach. Aeore and Tukanu were circling in a kind of dance, chattering so rapidly and angrily that Moon could not understand them. Then Tukanu leaped aside. Pointing at Moon, he shouted, "Kisu-Mu is our friend! Has he not come to the People out of the sky? We have seen it. For many seasons he has lived among us. He has led us against the white man, our enemy, and he will kill the white man who comes here with the Green Indians. Is this not so, Kisu-Mu? Tell the People that this is so."

For a moment Moon was silent; then under the eyes of Quarrier, he said bitterly, "I say to my friend Aeore that this is so. I will kill the white man Guzmán when he comes here."

Aeore threw down his club so violently that it bounded among the tribesmen, scattering them. A moan arose. He stalked away into the maloca, reappearing a moment later with his paddle and bow and arrows, and a net bag of his belongings. He paused in the sunlight, contemplating his people, then started toward the river, trailed by the Ocelot and two of the other Yuri Maha.

Then Tukanu brayed, a long loud sound of ultimate stupidity.

Aeore stopped short. He turned slowly and ceremonially, as in a ritual, and fitted to his bow a fine long arrow with blue and yellow quills. The people near Quarrier moaned and backed away; Quarrier, unable to see what was happening, faced Aeore on his knees.

Aeore stared at Tukanu, then snapped his head and spat. He stared at Moon. Then he raised his bow.

Moon called to him. "My voice is the voice of Kisu. You must not do this."

Still on his knees, Quarrier asked what was happening. Were they going to kill him after all? He did not believe this, and his face was quizzical, almost cheerful.

In the silence of the clearing, a bird called. It was answered by another, then another. Aeore's body trembled. Moon thought he glimpsed, between the savage crisscrossings of color at the eyes, a sign of recognition and regret: If you come from Kisu, very well—then you will punish me.

Death and sunlight, sunlight and death. The shimmering of day: the macaw quills, the bright sun on the forearm sinews, the clean paint on the clean brown of the body, the leaf-shifted morning light, the bird, the river—the very air was of such piercing cleanness that Moon sighed.

Aeore raised his bow again. His fear-softened face, the face of a young boy, became the cold brave terrified face of the last heretic.

"Riri'an." Moon spoke the name quietly, and the Child-Star moaned; his eyes searched the frightened faces of the Indians to learn which had betrayed him. He faltered, lowered his bow, then gave a screech and ran toward his canoe. Behind Quarrier, the three men of the Yuri Maha were snaking for the river. Moon switched the revolver toward the Ocelot, switched it back; he fought down an impulse toward annihilation. He was going to burst. The whole magnificent plan, just to spare this—!

Quarrier reared up off his knees. "What did you—"

Moon brought the revolver around in a chopping backhand arc and smashed the barrel down across the missionary's mouth, sending him sprawling. He aimed the revolver at the blood-smeared head. Quarrier lifted himself slowly, spitting bits of broken teeth. Moon's body was transfixed, all but one finger; the finger tightened. He sighted carefully on a spot of dirt on the missionary's huge forehead. The tears poured down Quarrier's broken face, to the bright red lips, the bleeding mouth; the face filled Moon with horror. He got his breath again, and glanced about him.

Down at the river the men of Yuri Maha drifted free in their canoe, following Aeore. The Ocelot shouted ferociously at Tukanu and waved his bow. Moon called out to Tukanu, "Tell them to stay!"

"No one will stop them," Tukanu said. "The Ocelot says that you are not Kisu-Mu, that you come from the white man."

"Will they come back?"

"They will come back," Tukanu said somberly,

"but they will come back as our enemy." A moment later, apparently forgetting what he had just said, his round face parted in a smile, as if the enmity of Aeore and the Yuri Maha were of no consequence. He was too innocent to conceal emotions; despite the threat to his band, he was chuckling with satisfaction at the prospect of his own leadership. Already he wore upon his chest the green stone cylinder of Boronai.

Moon pointed the revolver at Tukanu, who jumped back in fear. Moon hefted the metal object in his hand—well, so be it. He jammed the gun into his belt as Tukanu watched him.

He will be headman of the tribe, Moon thought, and the tribe is doomed. He cursed Tukanu, cursed every stupid greedy Indian on earth, and at the same time he cursed himself and he cursed Quarrier, and cursed the low thick stupid sky.

At daylight Boronai's canoe still stirred restlessly among the branches. All agreed that the dead man's spirit was unquiet, and they gazed resentfully at Kisu-Mu. Who would revenge Boronai? Could revenge be taken on Kisu-Mu? They did not know. They were unhappy that Aeore's vision under nipi had been disregarded, that the missionary was still walking through their village; if the vision of the shaman was not truth, what faith could they have in anything? Had Kisu-Mu come from Kisu or had he not? They were disoriented and afraid. Some were bold enough to mutter angrily at Kisu-Mu; they had heard what the Ocelot had said.

Tukanu stood on the bank of the river, supervising the departure from the village. New Person was already in the canoe, waving his fat hands at flies. After his birth, his parentage had reverted to Aeore, and Tukanu took no further notice of him; now he was an orphan, tended with indifference by the Ugly One, who had grown lean and cranky. When the Ugly One remembered, she would force her daughter to give the baby suck. The Ugly One said everywhere that this New

354

Person was the get of Kisu-Mu and was an evil omen; it had caused the death of Pindi. All the Indians despised the baby, yet none dared touch it. Moon longed to take the child from the Ugly One, and bounce him and say good-bye to him, but this would further weaken New Person's poor position in the tribe; like Aeore, he would have to fight for a hand-to-mouth existence. New Person peered about him at the world and laughed and bubbled; he had a big voice for a baby and he liked to shout.

The women waited by the river. There was an atmosphere of nervousness and apprehension that expressed itself in general sullenness; few had faith in Tukanu to lead them to a new site, to see that the fields were planted and a good maloca built, to protect them from their enemies, both Indian and white. Tukanu spoke too loudly and gave too many orders; the red shirt bobbed incongruously among brown skins. At one point he cuffed Mutu, who had not moved rapidly enough about his business; this was another bad sign, and the people groaned. Moon had never before seen a child of the Niaruna struck, and when the boy himself stared astonished at Tukanu, the new headman pretended that he was only joking.

Tukanu proclaimed that the People would start eastward, then turn north into a tributary creek above the Monkey Rapids; this was the last high ground near the main river. His people knew that this retreat from the main river was a sign of a dying clan; in the Falling River Time they would have to walk on foot in their dry stream bed, which they considered an ultimate disgrace. Under Aeore, they muttered, the People would have taken Tiro ground and worked it with Tiro slaves. But now they were poor and fugitive, no better than Kori.

In his new role as headman, Tukanu was no longer the feckless Farter. Pompous in his shirt of red, arms folded upon his chest, he addressed Kisu-Mu with ceremony from his canoe. He asked the Spirit of

355   *At Play in the Fields of the Lord*

the Rain to kill the white enemy and drive off the Green Indians; he asked the Great Spirit to go far away once this was done, and leave the Niaruna in peace.

One by one, the canoes drew away in silence. Moon called good-bye, but except from the children, he received no response. Only Tukanu, at the stroke position in the large headman's canoe, lifted his hand off the paddle in a listless wave. Moon sat down on the bank and watched them go. Tukanu skirted wide of the death canoe of Boronai, still stranded among the fallen branches, and then the red shirt was extinguished in the angles of the great green walls, the high dark canyons which led away into another world.

25

In his baggy pants, with the stiff posture and the shy expression of uncertain eyesight, Quarrier awaited Moon. "It's Yoyo," he called across the empty clearing. "Yoyo's gone." Behind him, the Ugly One's old yellow dog, abandoned in the haste of the tribe's departure, appeared and disappeared along the forest edge, like a pariah.

They had forgotten all about the Tiro. He had broken through the rear of the thatched hut, and he would go straight to Guzmán. With Yoyo as guide, Guzmán would have no trouble finding the trail from the Espíritu to the Tuaremi.

A wave of lassitude came over Moon. He grunted aloud and shrugged. "I'll take you to the mission," he told Quarrier. But Quarrier refused to go; he knew it was silly, but he was afraid of Yoyo. He hesitated. "What else?" Moon said, regarding him.

"Well . . . I wanted to dissuade you . . . Are you going to murder Guzmán?"

Moon glanced at him in warning. "Come on," he said, "let's find some supper." They went to an eddy of the river, where Moon speared three small fish; they picked plantains and dug manioc. Toward twilight, gathering firewood, they heard the hum of motors ascending the Espíritu.

They passed the evening peacefully, respecting each other's chagrin. Moon had built a fire inside the main door of the maloca: *This door faces east,* Boronai said, *because the sun's first rays bring strength to us.* When Quarrier repeated his question, Moon answered him quietly, "You heard me promise."

Quarrier said, "Go into the world unarmed."

Quarrier said this naturally and simply, and yet Moon perceived that the missionary had seen into him; he felt his face grow hot with consternation.

"I thought you had given up preaching."

"That's right," Quarrier said, paying no attention to the sarcasm. "I have failed in the Lord's work." When Moon grunted uncomfortably at the phrase, shrugging his shoulders, Quarrier said, "You see . . . a man like me, a cautious man, has his life all figured out according to a pattern, and then the pattern flies apart. You run around for quite a while trying to repair it, until one day you straighten up again with an armful of broken pieces, and you see that the world has gone on without you and you can never catch up with your old life, and you must begin all over again." When Moon made no response, but simply stared into the night, Quarrier said, "I needed badly to talk to someone who didn't refer each problem to the Lord. But maybe we can't talk after all."

"Suit yourself," Moon said. But after a while he said, "How does it feel? Are you afraid?"

"I'm not really afraid of anything that may happen." Quarrier raised his eyebrows, as if surprised by this realization. "I've made such a disaster of my life that I'm not afraid of anything—that is, any change is welcome. Maybe you've never reached that point."

"I've been there, all right. My trouble is, I never left it. I even *like* it." He turned the manioc tubers in the embers.

In the long night silence of the empty village, broken by fits of rain, the voice of the missionary rose and fell. Moon half listened. Quarrier told him of the moment his first doubt came: when Huben announced that Billy's death was surely an expression of the Lord's will, a means of converting the Niaruna. He shook his head. "What arrogance!" he burst out angrily. "And Yoyo! For months I couldn't bear even to think of Yoyo, he was such a reproach to me. For every soul that has been truly saved we have made thousands of Yoyos, thousands of 'rice Christians,' thousands of beggars and hypocrites, with no place and no voice in a strange world which holds them in contempt, with neither hope nor grace! And even the saved—" He stopped, out of breath. "Well, I can't be sure yet. I can only be sure that Martin Quarrier is unqualified to be a servant of the Lord." He looked up, his face laid bare by pain. Moon winced at the sight of the dried blood and broken teeth.

"You'd better give it some more thought," Moon said. He wished to comfort Quarrier, but any comfort in this moment seemed insulting. And Quarrier's defeat made him uneasy, like an argument which, having won, he then had doubts about.

"I'm coming back here, though." Quarrier looked eagerly at Moon. "I'll go back to see to my wife, and get a little stake together, and then I'm going to finish my study of the Niaruna. As Huben says, I've been more of an ethnologist than a missionary right along." His face contorted; he was trying to eat hot manioc without hurting his broken teeth. "That doesn't mean I can't still help them—you know, with medicine and food. But with no strings attached."

Moon laid more fuel across the fire. Near-sighted, leaning forward, Quarrier was searching his face for encouragement; Moon kept his eyes averted. "You better get another pair of glasses while you're at it," he said at last, "or you might wind up with the wrong tribe."

Quarrier smiled in recognition of the joke; out of politeness, he waited a moment before speaking again. But he was so lost in the future he was constructing that he could scarcely contain himself. "If you're still with the Niaruna, perhaps you would let me join you. You could teach me a great deal. What do you think?"

Moon said nothing; he lay down in his hammock. A little later Quarrier said, "It will be very interesting, don't you think so? I mean, to find out whether this tribe is really a lost group of Arawak, as I think it is, or whether it is Tupi-Guarani. Things like that—the sib groupings and everything. Don't you think so?"

Moon rolled over on his back and sighed. "The sib groupings, huh?"

"I don't really know what I'm talking about," Quarrier admitted. Deprived of encouragement, he relapsed into silence once again.

Moon was thinking about how Andy Huben had looked at him the last time they had seen each other, the last time they would ever see each other. But finally he said, "If I don't kill the Comandante, I can't return to the Niaruna. And if I don't go back to the Niaruna, then there's no hope for them."

Quarrier nodded.

"If I *do* kill the Comandante, and don't get myself killed in the process, they'll send the whole damn army in here, and the only Niaruna left for you to study will be Kori." He gazed at Quarrier, who was silent. "As an ethnologist and ex-missionary, Mr. Quarrier, maybe you'd care to suggest a solution to this problem."

Quarrier said, "Come back with me. I'll testify on your behalf. I'll tell the Comandante that you crashed by accident, that the tribe held you prisoner."

Moon shook his head. "This is the jungle, remember? By the time you gave your evidence, I'd be dead." He got to his feet and walked outside. "I can't go back. And besides, I made that promise."

"Yet keeping your promise, as you say yourself, will bring the whole army down upon the Niaruna."

"The Indians are too scattered to wipe out! And I can organize them for guerrilla war!" Moon waved his arms toward the forest. "We have a million square miles of jungle to retreat into!"

"Fighting with the other tribes all the way?" Quarrier sighed. "And at the end, what hope for them?" He paused, then added coldly, "You haven't helped these people as it is."

"So you think I'm beaten."

"Yes, I do. I don't even think you're safe among them any more."

"Misery loves company, eh, Quarrier?"

"You can look at it that way if you like."

"Well, I think I'm beaten, too. But I'm still going to kill Guzmán."

"Because you promised?"

"Because I feel like it."

Moon, running, stopped short in his tracks, caught by the sparkle of light and rain on the golden thatch of his village, by the clear ringing whistles of the birds, by the flower smell floating down from the high canopies, the pale gigantic trees—the painful beauty of the jungle daybreak. He was both hunted animal and hunter.

The invisible plane was circling the mission; if they meant to follow up its raid, the soldiers must be on their way. He stationed himself at the foot of a tree in the downstream jungle; from this point he could cover the whole clearing. He checked the action of the revolver.

Quarrier wandered out across the clearing; Moon called to him, and the missionary came and crouched with him behind the tree. Quarrier said, "What are you going to do?"

"I'll try to make it out through Niaruna territory and down to the rivers in Brazil. The Panoan tribes there are all right, or so I've heard. If I can make it to the Amazon, I'm in the clear." When Quarrier started to speak again, Moon shook him off. "Forget it, man," he said, "it's Guzmán's problem."

The airplane had stopped circling and was headed toward them. Against the sky from which the plane would come, a light breeze stirred the canopy of trees.

361   *At Play in the Fields of the Lord*

Moon licked his lips. "If he comes in low and on a line," he muttered, "into that sun, I'll know this mother has been here before. I'll know it's Wolfie." He shook his head. "The Old Wolf!" he grinned. "Sonofabitch! It's been a long time since I really laughed!" Quarrier looked at him, bewildered, as if Moon were a madman. "When Wolfie's finished," Moon said, "go out and stand in the center of the clearing, where they can see you. If you're with me when the soldiers come, you're liable to get shot." He looked at Quarrier. "That's some mouth I left you with—I'm sorry."

His last words were lost in the roar of the plane, which broke the treetops, broke the sky wide-open; two dark eggs arched forward from its wing racks. Moon threw himself behind the trunk, dragging Quarrier down with him, and clapped his hands across his ears. But the roar of the plane diminished and no explosions followed, only the staggered vibration of the bombs striking the ground. One of the bombs plowed a small crater in the clearing; the other bounded down the bank and spun into the river. When no explosion came, he ran to the first bomb. He was dizzy and feverish, his mouth was dry; at the same time he felt indestructible. He hoisted it in his arms; his idea was to run with it to the river. But as he staggered forth, the plane came in on a second run. He dropped the bomb and fled toward the plane to get below the angle of its guns; behind him, the bare ground jumped and twitched, and the bullets thumped and caromed through the forest. When the plane had passed, he ran back to the trees.

Wolfie roared down on the village twice again. Though the thatch danced on the roofs, the maloca and outlying huts drank up the bullets like great sponges; when the plane flew off toward the west, no visible damage had been done. Nevertheless, Wolfie's aim was good: had there been Indians crouched inside, half might have been wiped out. Moon lay on the ground, no longer laughing. Quarrier had been shouting angrily from the start, "Oh you devils! Oh you murdering devils!"

"Finish your hollering out there, where they can see you," Moon said; he took Quarrier's hand.

Quarrier hesitated. "I don't suppose you'd want a partner, would you?"

Moon pretended that he had not understood. After a pause he said, "You tell Wolfie I sent regards, and tell him to go home. Tell him maybe I'll see him again sometime, up in Barbados."

Quarrier nodded. "Good luck to you, Lewis." He struggled to speak, then turned away. He crossed the clearing, hands slightly in front of him, like a child playing blind man's buff. "Here I am!" he called in Spanish. Moon nodded; how trusting that was—that assumption that someone might care.

"Here I am," the missionary called again. "Don't shoot." With his tatters and great gory head and giant feet, he looked like some sort of mountebank. "Yoo hoo, *mi comandante!*" he called out for Moon's benefit. "It's me!" Turning in a circle, addressing the jungle like an audience, he waved and waddled, making fun of his own presence.

An Indian appeared and disappeared again on the far side of the clearing. At first Moon did not recognize Yoyo, but then the Indian glided out into the open, and the sun fastened on his bright blue shorts and on the crucifix on his breast.

Yoyo glanced back over his shoulder, seeming to listen, then ran forward to meet Quarrier, who revolved, still clowning. Moon never saw the machete until the missionary had fallen; the Indian's arm rose and fell across Quarrier's neck, over and over. By the time Moon got Yoyo in the sights of the revolver it was too late; he held his fire.

Now Yoyo straightened. His breathing was audible across the clearing. He drew a pair of glasses from the pocket of his shorts, and snapping them in half, tossed them on Quarrier's face. Then he turned his head again to listen. A flock of parakeets screeched down the walls of trees, and in their wake the jungle stirred, a murmur, a faint rumble.

In Yoyo's face fear was replacing rage, as if he had just awakened to his surroundings. His head turned slowly, like a cat's; he studied the river bank, the maloca, the huts and the ragged jungle edge. When his eyes met Moon's, he gave a start, and whined with surprise and pain. His body crouched, he glanced again over his shoulder in the direction of the oncoming Guzmán, then back at Moon, repeating this several times, faster and faster; then he scowled horribly and came for Moon, the blade extended.

Moon set himself to kill him. But at the last moment, though he raised the revolver to show Yoyo he was armed, he did not fire.

At the sight of the revolver the Tiro stopped; his face burst with hatred and, at the same time, with a remarkable expression of hurt feelings, as if Moon had misconstrued his actions. Again he whined, in wordless agony. Watching the bright beady eyes, the quick head and teeth, the febrile twitching, Moon was startled by so much hate, and his finger tightened on the trigger.

"Drop the machete," he said.

The weapon fell. It must have come originally from the missions, for it had a cross carved in its haft.

Yoyo seemed to decide that all was lost, that, being an Indian, his word would never be believed by Guzmán, even against that of the outlaw Moon. He glanced once again over his shoulder, then wrenched the chain and crucifix from his neck and hurled them violently to the ground. He ripped off the ragged shorts, threw them down in front of Moon and spat on them. He was trembling so that his skin danced. When Moon only stood there quietly and did not shoot, the Indian whined again in pure frustration. He still believed that Moon would shoot him, and when, a moment later, he sprang sideways and leaped for the cover of the bushes, making away into the forest on all fours, he howled in frenzy from his hiding place. He was still uncertain of his triumph, or whether, in failing to take his life, the white man had not insulted him once again.

Moon glanced about, then ran toward the body. From the forest came a muffled commotion; Guzmán and his men, abandoned by Yoyo, were struggling toward the light.

Quarrier lay sprawled upon the earth as if he had fallen from the sky, and he gazed skyward as he bled to death. The whole side of his neck had been laid open; he was bleeding everywhere. When Moon crossed his line of sight, he spoke.

"I'm dying, aren't I?" He looked shy.

"Yes," Moon said.

Quarrier raised his eyebrows, as if to try them out. When Moon lifted his head, a near smile came to his lips; he actually gave a bubbly cough of laughter. "Martin Quarrier, evangelist," he said, "martyred by savages in the service of the Lord." He looked pleadingly at Moon.

"Yes," Moon said, turning his head away.

"No." The missionary took Moon's wrist in his big hand. "It was Yoyo, wasn't it?" When Moon nodded, Quarrier stared at the sky, unblinking. He coughed again and muttered sadly, "All my life I wanted . . ." His voice trailed off, then said distinctly, "Didn't you?" He tried to speak again, and died with his mouth wide open.

"*Listen,*" Moon called after him; he actually shook him. "Listen to me!" He sat back on his heels in pain and shock. He was smeared with blood.

The green wall stirred, about to burst. Moon ran back across the clearing.

Guzmán called, "Uyuyu!" and then cursed.

A ragged burst of rifle fire: the bullets sang across the clearing, piercing the empty huts. There came a solitary shot, then a loud curse, as if the gun had been discharged by accident; seconds later a squad of Quechuas, twenty or more, pushed and milled into the clearing. Another gun went off.

If Aeore were here with three good men, Moon thought, no Green Indian would ever have reached the Tuaremi.

Huge and pale, Guzmán plowed through his soldiers. He lined them up like a firing squad, and on command they poured successive volleys into the village. The soldiers were nervous, clumping awkwardly in their heavy boots, and talking so loudly that Guzmán could scarcely be heard.

Guzmán came forward cautiously, almost on tiptoe, and overturned Quarrier's body with his boot tip; his soldiers prodded at it with their gun butts. Moon lay in wait while Guzmán burned the village, while Guzmán sent his men into the plantations to hack down the Indian crops, while Guzmán howled for Yoyo. The Comandante appeared nervous about starting back to the Espíritu without a guide, despite the trail that had been made by twenty pairs of heavy boots. *"Oye tú!* Uyuyu!" Yoyo must be crouched near by, but not understanding how things worked, he had made himself a fugitive.

Moon sighted Guzmán's confused, brutal face with the revolver, but already he knew that he would not kill him. He lay back in the jungle gloom, waiting to see if they would bury Quarrier. In the sun's glare, he was seeing spots; he felt dizzy, then cold, in the dark shadows. He was overcome by a sense of unreality: Is this me and who am I and where in hell am I going. Well . . . this was no time for malaria.

They started away without burying the body, and Moon stood up and watched them go. But in a moment a soldier scurried back into the clearing. Squatting, he rifled the old, torn pants. Quarrier's pocketknife turned in his hand, like a bit of fruit in the hand of a marmoset. The sun caught the wet rolling eye in the Quechua's purple face, and Moon blotted out the addled eye with the sight of the revolver; filth could be wiped away so quickly, coldly, without emotion: cleanness through death.

But again he did not fire. He watched the man strip off the missionary's sneakers and tuck them into his bulky green pants, watched him probe the missionary's mouth for gold and silver.

The Quechua stood up again, and started after his companions. But then he stopped, as if awe-struck by the silence. He glanced at the body and started to run; then he stopped and came running back. Without troubling to remove the clip, he used his rifle butt as digging stick, chopping away at the soft ground in a crude paddling motion. As he worked he glanced fearfully after his fellows, who were calling to him. When his small Indian grave was dug, he rolled the large white body into it—or onto it, for the body still remained high above ground. Perplexed, then desperate, the man dug, kicked, scratched, flung dirt at Quarrier, but still the missionary lay there, mountainous.

The soldier whimpered, scratched his groin, then drew the old sneakers from his pants. Kneeling, he returned them carefully to Quarrier's pale feet. He had tied the laces and straightened up again when he caught sight of the solitary man at the edge of the clearing. His mouth made a black hole. He crossed himself, shouted for aid and ran; holding his rifle by the barrel, he dragged it behind him over the ground. As he disappeared into the undergrowth, the rifle's trigger snagged and the weapon fired.

Having no idea where the enemy lay, the soldier's companions commenced firing at random, undeterred by the hoarse shoutings of their Comandante. Bullets flew in all directions. In the pause for reloading, the shattering scream of a man wounded rent the air.

Guzmán's voice boomed from the trees: "*Ay piloto!* You are *aquí?*"

Moon did not answer.

"I es-spik you Ingliss," yelled Comandante Guzmán. "You are prisoner to me!" Abandoning English, he yelled in Spanish, "Tell your savages to lay down their weapons! Tell them we will not harm them, even though they have sorely wounded one of my brave soldiers! But if you do not give yourself up, then we will fall upon them without mercy!"

In the ringing silence, Moon's harsh laugh resounded; it continued as Guzmán bellowed, as his men loosed a tremendous volley at their surroundings. Then came a loud thrashing all along the clearing edge; the soldiers were fanning out.

Still whooping and coughing, Moon scrambled on all fours toward the river. Some soldiers had reached the river bank upstream; they glimpsed him as he skinned down along the bank. He plunged into the water, and the bullets sang over his head; a lucky shot made a thin splash a yard ahead of him. He ducked his head under, fighting his panic, and angled clumsily across the river, holding the revolver clear; the current helped him. He dropped the revolver into Boronai's canoe and swam under it, to the other side; while the soldiers were lining up along the bank in their best firing-squad formation, he hauled it loose. Holding his breath against the corpse's stench, he shoved the canoe toward the middle of the stream, swimming beside it. The dugout, heavy with rain water, was sluggish; bullets smacked into the wood. Already he was drifting clear; the canoe had picked up speed.

"Come back!" El Comandante yelled. "You are surrounded!"

Moon waved his hand, and the soldiers on the bank responded with another burst of fire. In the burned village, from the shroud of smoke, the Ugly One's old dog howled.

26

"Another Christian martyr!

"Since my last epistle to *Mission Fields,* reporting on the work among the Niaruna, the Devil has inflicted a heavy defeat on the forces of God. Pray much for the soul of Martin Quarrier, slain by the savages; pray much for the soul of our young ambassador-in-Jesus, Billy Quarrier, deceased only a short span before his dad. And pray for His childless servant, Hazel Quarrier, in her time of awful sorrow.

"He that loseth his life for my sake shall find it (Matt. 10:39).

"Now, at the same time that we contacted the Niaruna, Satan also got to work, for as you know, Satan never sleeps but always fights the hardest just when it seems that the forces of the Lord are moving ahead to victory. Now Satan sent an emissary to another band of Niaruna, a North American soldier of fortune, a terrible sinner, dope fiend and drunkard. All the time we thought this man had crashed his airplane and died, he was working on the innocent minds of the Indians, going around naked like an Indian, actually encouraging them to remain forever in blackest sin and darkness! And during the absence of the Undersigned in Madre de Dios this outlaw struck the first blow for Satan, sending four of his corrupted Indians among those at the mission. Unfortunately, Mart was too upstanding to suspect anything, but still and all he began to feel that the Niaruna were hostile to him; they were even *afraid* of him. Meanwhile the situation deteriorated. By the time I went in to check on things, our Niaruna were all naked again, which just goes to show you how bad it was!

"Now double disaster struck: along about this time little Billy was taken sick and died. As the Lord giveth, so doth he take away, but we were very upset. Billy was promoted to Glory on the ninth day of last month, in the name of our Lord Jesus Christ. But I saw right off that the Niaruna liked little Billy a whole lot, and, as I said to Mart to comfort him, Maybe little Billy's death is the Lord's way of opening up this Niaruna work, and calling them to the communion of Jesus Christ! Of course Mart was too upset to understand how this could be, and maybe I ought to tell you that he was very nervous and upset right along after that, and so was Hazel—which didn't make the Lord's work any easier for the Undersigned and Andy. Then the black day came when the emissary of Satan actually told us we had to leave or they would kill us!

"Well, a lot of worse things happened which I can't even put down. The Lord led us to send the girls out; and then Mart Quarrier, against the advice of the Undersigned, decided to take Uyuyu and go to the Niaruna village and warn them that their devilish behavior was actually leading to an attack upon them by our local Comandante and the soldiers!

"I was left alone to guard the station. When they didn't appear again by the next day I knew there was trouble, and headed downriver to get help (and by the way, I want to thank all of my friends in Christ for that fine new outboard motor—it's a beaut!). The Comandante was already on his way. Though I pleaded with him to show Christian mercy, Uyuyu, who had escaped, led him back to that village, and they drove away the Indians in a fierce fight, in which one of his own soldiers was killed, and also burned the village, which surely goes to show what happens to people who consort with Satan, just like Sodom and Gomorrah. But anyway, Uyuyu, who went ahead as scout, was taken prisoner or worse, and at the village the Comandante found the body of poor Mart Quarrier, killed savagely by savages.

"In the world ye shall have tribulation: but be of good cheer; I have overcome the world (John 16:33).

"Mart died like a Christian martyr, and we shall certainly miss him here in the Lord's work. But it thrills us to talk to Hazel Quarrier, whose faith is stronger than ever, and who is actually cheerful in the face of all her tragedies. Hazel intends to go back in with us, to continue as her husband would have wanted, although when this will be I wouldn't know. The Comandante says that the outlaw may have survived the attack, and still be at large among the Niaruna. and until he is captured and the Niaruna subdued and civilized, no further mission work will be permitted. So it looks like the Niaruna are to be punished, the good ones as well as the evil.

"Well, that's the story on these savages whom we have come to love in Jesus in spite of the way that they have treated us. The Undersigned certainly hopes there is some better news for the next epistle: one of these days our folks will win these souls and claim the victory which is in our Lord Jesus Christ!

"To Jesus be the glory.

"LES HUBEN"

When he had read out his own name, Huben glanced at his wife. "What do you think of it?" he said defensively. Instead of praising God for his escape, she kept looking at him in a way that made him nervous, as if she were trying to see right through his head. When she did not take the letter, he dropped it in her lap. "It should bring in all kinds of new contributions to the work, the way I look at it."

When Andy got up, the letter fell to the floor. But she had scarcely reached the corridor when Hazel's door opened; the woman lay in wait for her these days like one of the large trap-door spiders that she and Billy had watched so often at the mission. Andy stopped short, out of breath.

"Andy, will you take a cup of tea with me? I get so lonely, you know, without Martin, on these long tropical afternoons—but there, I'm sure you have your own troubles . . ."

She trailed Hazel into her room.

"Oh Andy, you're so *sweet,* dear—"

"Hazel, why don't you go home? There's nothing for you here."

"Carrying the Word of God among the Niaruna —you call *that* nothing? Carrying on the work of that brave man whose widow I am proud to be!" Hazel Quarrier giggled. "Why, I'd call *that* something, Andy dear, yes, I surely, surely would. Each of us must serve our Lord according to our abilities . . ."

Andy thought, Why, she's nothing but a huge crafty child: she's playing a game. Her pity was tainted with revulsion, and during the days since they left the mission, since Hazel became her responsibility, the revulsion had come to dominate. Hazel no longer troubled to keep herself very clean. Her hair looked dead, and on the thin pallor of her face her mustache, heretofore scarcely apparent, had become prominent. Andy had not noticed this new appearance until she glimpsed the creature hid behind it; Hazel's candor, so appealing in the past, had become a front for unctuous wheedling and overblown statements of faith. Even worse, Hazel seemed aware that she was not fooling Andy for a moment; she exploited the loss of her husband and son in compelling Andy to hear out her deceits.

But now she spoke honestly. In a harsh voice, staring at the wall, she said, "Isn't it strange? Martin and I were both such ugly people, and that is why we found each other, yet we never really forgave the ugliness in the other. And do you know why? Because we were both lecherous, and our love was a sin in the eyes of God!" Hazel silenced her with an imperious wave. "Do you know something else? Our families were ugly too, and lecherous—*both* parents, on both sides! And from *way* back!" This was the big, sporty, roadhouse Hazel who had no business in a mission; she laughed so heartily that Andy laughed as well, delighted with her.

And then Hazel said, in a clear quiet voice, "Out of all that lechery and ugliness—generations of it, I mean—how was it possible to bring something so beautiful as my little baby into the world? How was that *possible?*" She gazed at Andy. "Do you know something? The only time in my whole life I didn't hate this big lecherous ugly body of mine was when I remembered that somewhere inside, it must be clean and beautiful, or my beautiful Billy could not have come from it."

In this moment a great peace touched Hazel's face. Andy, undone, was seeking a way to speak, to embrace her and help her. Perhaps the hatred of one's God-given body was the ultimate sin—but Hazel's face shrank back to slyness, and the cute voice of the past days said, "My sin was the sin of pride, of course, and may our Father in Heaven forgive me! He alone made my beautiful little Billy, and caused him to walk this cruel earth so that one glorious day his death might be, as Leslie says, the instrument of the savages' salvation!" With a sweet smile of goodness and infinite mercy, Hazel folded her hands primly in her lap, and bent her head. *"Our Father which art in heaven—"*

"Hazel!"

"Excuse me, honey?" Hazel's tone was lightly reproving.

"I was just going to say . . . you have every right to be proud of Billy—"

"You were very jealous of me," Hazel said, "weren't you, honey? I mean, being barren before God?" When Andy only stared at her, she said, "Of course, you are pretty and I am not. And you were content that Martin lusted after you, I suppose?"

"Hazel, why do you say such things!"

"A little while ago, my dear, you laughed at me when I told you how lecherous Martin was, how ugly. Oh, it's easy enough to *laugh* at my poor Martin, goodness knows!" She humph-ed and sniffed elaborately, to express injury, at the same time biting her lips to restrain her mirth.

"I wasn't laughing *at* anything, I never *thought* about his looks," Andy exclaimed. She stood up, fighting for breath again. "I liked Martin. I admired him as a man. He never once did or said anything suggestive or improper." She longed to say, I admired him most because he had lost his faith and did nothing, even under duress, to weaken mine.

"You deny being aware that he lusted after you?"

"Why do you use that awful expression? Martin liked me, and I am glad he did. We could *talk* together, for goodness' sake!"

"Talk together!" Hazel snorted. Then she smiled

again, with infinite understanding, lowering her voice. "Perhaps you and Leslie have had . . . well, difficulties. I mean, *you* know. You can speak honestly to me—" And she actually shifted herself closer to Andy, chin out, cheek half turned against the blow, adopting a resigned expression which proclaimed the strength to bear all manner of revelation, never mind how terrible or disgusting. Andy was furious that once again she had made herself a party to the woman's games. She said, "I don't like you, Hazel. I just don't like you, not when you're like this."

The big woman cringed grotesquely, bringing her hands up toward her face. "No, of course, how could anyone like me? I'm so upset these days, so strange. Oh, you needn't spare me, I know how strangely I've been acting!"

"You're strange, all right, but not the way you pretend to be." Andy went to the door. "You've found a good excuse for spitting up all that unhappiness of yours, and then afterwards you can say, 'I didn't know what I was doing.'" Hazel cringed again. Andy said, "I'm sorry, Hazel. I wish you would go home. There's not going to *be* any Niaruna work, not for a long time, maybe never. But if you *do* stay here, I'm not going along with your game any more, do you hear me? Do you hear me, Hazel? Maybe Leslie will play along, but I won't."

"Your husband is a good God-fearing man," Hazel accused her. "You don't honor Leslie Huben as you should!"

"Perhaps I don't," Andy said. She went out the door. She had never felt so cold and tough, so deeply angry. She felt cheated.

"What if I tell him?" Hazel shrieked after her, so loudly that her voice carried easily to the adjoining room. "What if I tell Leslie what you said?"

Leslie already knows it, Andy thought. He could never admit it, but he knows it.

"You said you'd have tea with me! You *promised!*"

375   *At Play in the Fields of the Lord*

She went downstairs, with no idea of destination. A fan, the slapping of bare feet, the musings of a hen beneath the courtyard window, a red flower . . . The man Wolfie was in the bar, and when she passed it he came running, glass in hand. But on reaching Andy he seemed to forget what he wanted, and she saw that he had nothing to say. She was shocked by his appearance. He looked like a newspaper picture of some sort of addict.

"I just wanted to say 'Hi,' " he said. "You know? I ain't seen an American in a long, long time."

"Hi," she said.

"You don't look so good," he said, and grinned uneasily. "Your name's Andy, right?"

"That's right."

"I mean, a chick like you don't never drink, I know. But you look like you could *use* a drink."

She gazed at him without expression, watching him withdraw in expectation of the rebuff. But the tart remark which had started automatically to her tongue perished unspoken. Tiredly she said, "Not here." A great inertia had come over her; she could not go back upstairs to those small rooms.

"Oh yeah. Leslie, huh?" He looked at her, astonished. "Well," he said, "well, well, well." Still uncertain of himself, of her intent, he said, "Well, look . . . I mean, can I buy you a drink?"

"Where?" she said, and started walking.

He hastened along at her side, poking his head around in front of her each time he spoke; his fingers rose to her elbow, fell away, came back again and stayed.

"There's only one other place—La Concepción. La Concepción ain't so nice, Andy, only we could sit outside. They got tables outside, see?" He hurried eagerly along beside her.

They went down the mud street, among the hogs and vultures. "Did you see him?" he said to her.

"Who?"

376

"Lewis. Lewis Moon."

"Lewis Moon."

"What I mean is, did you *see* him?"

"Yes," she said. "I saw him."

"How about that?" Wolfie said. "How about that?" Shyly he said, "I don't guess he sent no message, did he? Lewis didn't send no message?"

"No."

"I mean, like, Tell the Old Wolf hello. Somethin like that. He didn't send no message like that, huh?"

Andy stopped and faced him in the street. She wanted to cry, not for Wolfie, but for both of them, for the way of the world. She reached out and touched his arm. "No," she said, "no message. There wasn't time for messages."

Wolfie licked his lips. "I been waitin a long time," he said. "He shoulda sent a message." He looked into her face and sighed. "So," he said gently, "so's how's it goin with you, kid?"

On the way down the street to La Concepción, they held hands. "Tell me about him," she said at the table. She ran her fingers over the cold glass, which she had not touched.

"That's what everybody says t'me: *Tell* me about him. How come they all wanna know about Lewis Moon?" Wolfie laughed tiredly and she smiled. "You know what I finely figured out?" he said. "I figured out that a guy like Moon, everybody wants to *change* him. When they say, Tell me about him, they really mean, Tell me how I can get *at* him, get *with* him. Like, he's too far out there somewhere, we want him back where we can keep an eye on him, make him *care* about somethin. Christ!" he cried out suddenly. "I wish I was a talker. I finely figured this out, see. I could tell you . . ."

"Go ahead. You're doing just fine."

"Well, Moon is kind of like a threat. For most guys this guy is a kind of a threat. He don't seem to care about nothin nobody else cares about, not even his own life hardly; so as long as a guy like that's around, the things you thought were so important, they begin to look kind of stupid."

"And women?"

"That's part of it too. Women can't stand a loner, you know that—they feel like in*sulted*. So long as a guy like this is on the loose, the whole game they been taught to play looks kind of stupid too. But they all think they got the secret—about makin him *care,* I mean. They feel sorry for him, see. They want to mother him. What this guy needs, they yell, is LOVE! So they fall in love with him. But what it *really* is, they want to ball him. I mean . . . you know, excuse me, have *sexual intercourse* with him, because that way they got his number, at least for a few minutes." He looked up at her, out of breath, and laughed. "This is hard work for me. Only I finely figured this thing out."

"I'm sure you're right," Andy said, "as far as you go."

"That ain't very far, huh?" Wolfie shrugged. "Maybe not." He turned away from her. "You goin to drink that drink, or what?" He signaled a woman on the porch and pointed to his glass. Andy picked up hers and drank it off all at once, holding her breath.

"That's not what I mean," she said. She felt a little odd. "I meant, do you think he . . . Lewis Moon . . . I mean, a man like that, do you think he . . . Did he *ever* care?"

Wolfie gazed at her, nodding his head lugubriously. "Don't try it, kid," he said, "don't try it. That Moon'll kill you. That is the hardest sonofabitch I ever seen. Like him and me, we were buddies, for Christ sake. I saved his life more'n one time. And what does he do? He splits without a word, just like *that"*—Wolfie snapped his fingers—"takin the aircraft which half of it is mine. And after all this time, what does he do? Does he send a message? No, he don't."

Wolfie took his new drink off the tray and drank it even before the woman had left the table. She ob-

378

served his distress with sympathy and glared balefully at his companion. Other women had come out onto the porch to look at Andy; they stood there barefoot in gingham dresses, their arms folded on their breasts.

"Rosita," Wolfie muttered, waving the near one off. "Go on, *vamos*. Cut. I mean it. C'mon. All you whores beat it. Don't look at her like that."

"Do they understand English?" Andy laughed; she felt shocked that she was not shocked.

"Only dirty words," Wolfie said. "Just like my Spanish. Some conversation! I done near two years in this stinkin hole and all I can say in polite company is *huevos fritos!*" He shook his head. "So stay away from him. He didn't even send a message."

"Why did you wait here for him all this time?"

"Wait for'm! Who *waited* for'm?" Wolfie glared at her. "Well, whaddya want I should go and do, run *out* on him? How'd I know what happened to him, he coulda come back any day!" He shifted unhappily in his seat, and when he spoke again his voice was quiet. "Well, I'll tell ya. At first, see, I thought it was only he had flipped out on that *ayahuasca,* that he never meant to cut out on me. Lewis cut out on *you,* Wolf?—I says to myself—don't be ree-*dica*lous! Did you or didn't you save his life, many's and many's the time? No, Wolf, I says, you gotta *wait* for him, because Lewis never cut out on you, and you ain't gonna cut out on *Lewis,* I says. Very good. So then I kept rememberin them diamonds he left on my pillow—he had these wild diamonds he picked up somewheres, up on the rivers—and I says, well, listen, man, like maybe Lewis didn't exactly cut *out* on you, man, don't be ree-dicalous, only, well, them diamonds, man, I mean, lay-in *diamonds* on you, man—well, it *looked* like the old payoff for the aircraft, ree-dicalous or *no* ree-dicalous." He raised his head. "And after a while it didn't look so ree-dicalous no more."

"But why didn't you leave when you realized that?"

"How could I *leave?* I tried it only lately. I got

so frantic I tried to give diamonds to Guzmán for my passport and a ticket out, but he only laughed into my face; this Guzmán is so smart he's stupid. He thought all diamonds looked like *diamonds*, see, he thought Moon's diamonds were some nutty kind of *rocks*. Wolf, I says finely, you are castin wild diamonds before swine. So the diamonds wind up one by one"—he waved his hand—"at La Concepción." Wolfie sighed mightily. "Leavin this jungle is like tryin to leave quicksand—you fight like hell, but you don't *go* no place."

"Do you know what he said that night he left here? He said, If there is a jungle there, go *through* it, and come out on the other side."

"Uh-huh. Well, if he thinks Wolfie's goin to plow through I don't know how many million miles of that stuff"—he waved violently toward the jungle across the river—"he better think again, the stupid bastard." Wolfie laughed drunkenly, affectionately, sprawling back a little in his chair. "That's Moon, all right. One night we was down to our last thirty-four pesos, and Lewis says, That thirty-four pesos, Wolf, that's good for seventeen aguardientes each, right? Right, I says. Well, my capacity for tonight is seventeen, he says. And I says, Seventeen of *them* things? In one *night*? I says, Listen, Lewis, like even if we *survive* it is the end of our financial *solvency*. And Lewis says, You want to go somewheres in life, then you got to commit yourself, you got to burn all the bridges behind you, man."

"And how do you feel about him now?"

Wolfie stopped laughing. "I'm gonna tell you somethin. I don't care how this sounds to you, kid, but I admired that maniac, I really did. I don't know why, but I *loved* him. Believe me, I ain't a faggot or nothin, only I really *loved* him, more than I loved even my Ex."

"Your ex-wife?"

"Yeah. While I was sittin around here goin nuts, I wrote Azusa I was lonely for her and Dick the Infint, which this is our kid, and was sick and tired of the road and wanted to come on home. Where was she *livin* at, I asked her. And she wrote me back she was now my Ex and had changed Dick's name to *Richard!*" Wolfie shook his head, incredulous. "Richard, my Ex wrote me, jams all his toys down *toilets;* Richard, writes my Ex, is very hard on *toilets.*" He grunted bitterly. "Richard. I mean, imagine it. But now," he said, "me and Moon ain't friends no more. If Lewis Moon come walkin down this street, I'd kill him."

"I hate him too," she said.

"Do ya?" Wolfie grunted bitterly again. He nodded his head for a little while. "I known all along he wasn't dead; not *him.* I seen guys like that before. I don't mean them reckless guys—them ones don't last. I mean the guys like Moon who *really* don't care— you can't kill *them* guys with a *flame* thrower, for Christ sake!" When Andy said nothing, he said, "How in hell was I to *go* anywhere? No money, no papers, nothin. Maybe if Lewis hadn't split on me like that, he coulda figured somethin out. And Guzmán tellin me every other day if I didn't like, you know, plight my *troth* to this Mercedes, I'd get shipped back across the border and get shot." He sighed. "So I play along with him, like I tell him my intentions are *honorable,* you dig, and he give me drinkin money, waitin for the day. Meanwhile I done what he told me—kept that old car runnin, and maintenance at the hotel—I done every-thin except clean spittoons. Considerin what he give me, he got his money's worth. And now I done the big job for him, and tomorrow I'm goin out on the com-mercial plane, over the Andes. Like, the best years of my *life!* Imagine! And Lewis Moon can screw him-self."

"What was the big job?" Andy said.

Wolfie lifted his eyes. "You mean you really don't know?"

She shook her head.

"Well, Andy, ol' kid, I'm gonna level with you: I hopped in that old Mustang that's out there at the

381   *At Play in the Fields of the Lord*

field, and I bombed and strafed them Indians of yours. The bombs was all duds"—here he shook his head, laughing a shrill, brief laugh—"but the guns worked. The guns worked."

"You couldn't help it," she said after a while. "Oh! When you think of the conscience *he* must have!"

"Don't count on it, baby." He was surprised that she had not left the table.

Wolfie put his hand on hers. He did this without thinking, but once it was there he remembered that she was a missionary's wife, and felt uneasy; he took his hand away. She said in a strange voice, "Are you afraid of me?" and he put his hand back, more uneasy still. Her hand was tight and cold, and his felt numb. He opened her hand to interlock their fingers, and the diamond dropped onto the table. They both looked at it; it gave off faint reflections. With her other hand she put the diamond back into her pocket.

"So you thought maybe you could change him, too," he said, to distract attention from their hands.

"I don't know what I thought," Andy said. "It's been a long time since I let myself think at all."

"That's what keeps you out of sin," he said, and laughed.

"Maybe everybody has to sin once," she said. "I don't even know what a sin is any more."

"I'd be glad to show you," Wolfie said. He laughed again, squeezing her hand. "I'm goin away tomorrow, kid, so you wouldn't have no reminders. What you need is the love of a good Jewish boy." He grinned at her, expecting her to bridle at his teasing, but she only gazed at him. He could not fathom her expression. His heart was pounding, and he removed his hand. "Well, I'm only kiddin," he said. "You already sinned once when you drunk that drink. I mean, a girl like you don't want to fool with nobody like me."

"Would it be a sin for you?" she said.

"Whaddya mean? Look, it ain't the same thing." He stood up, unable to suffer her expression. "For you a sin is different. You'd only be sorry after. Look, kid," he said, when she still gazed at him, "in a town like this, there's no place we can go. We got no place to go."

He was going to ask her if he could walk her home, but he did not want to be with her a moment longer. "I'll see ya, kid," he said. He wanted her badly in the way that he supposed she wanted him: less to make love to than to be warm with. But he was afraid of the look in that open face, and because he was afraid, he repeated angrily, "There's no place we can go."

Jesus, he told himself, these Christer broads are tougher'n any whores alive. She oughta be ashamed of herself—first she's got hot pants for Lewis, and now me! And her a missionary—she oughta be ashamed!

"So long, Andy," he called out, but she did not answer. And he cursed her again for making him feel weak and guilty, just when he had been strong enough not to take advantage of her. He backed away from the table into the darkness of the street. The girl sat there in the yellow light, under the hostile eyes of the women along the porch, her hand on her empty glass. She was still gazing after him, her face sallow and without expression.

"Como puedo decir—no, no, you must not be too—outraged?—about this thing our good Comandante has said to you. Perhaps it is true, perhaps it is not. If it is true, I think he will punish you, for our Comandante is not merciful."

"He already punished me," Wolfie said. "He said that shootin down that missionary is going to cause him a lot of embarrassment, so he's holdin out on me. He's gonna let me get on the plane, but he ain't gonna give me the bread." Too restless to go to bed, he had offered the priest a drink; Padre Xantes, awaiting his supper in the salon, had accepted cheerfully.

"The bread? *Dinero*, yes?" The padre sighed. *"Claro*. No payment for poor Lobo. But permit me to remind you that the Comandante is somewhat emotional about money; if he did not have this reason, he would find another. Besides, he has told me that poor Quarrier was killed by the Niaruna. You see, señor, if you had killed Quarrier with your airplane, or if Señor Moon had killed him, as Guzmán claimed when he came back, the Comandante would not have such a good excuse to attack these Indians. So whether you killed him or not is of no importance; in the official report, the unfortunate evangelist was killed by blood-thirsty savages." The priest drank off his glass in one neat gulp.

"Maybe it's important to me," Wolfie said resentfully. "All I'm sayin is, I never saw no white man, not a sign of one. All I saw was one miserable Indian." He stood up, jamming his hands into his pockets. "I do his dirty work for him, and he screws me."

"So," the padre murmured diplomatically. "You leave us tomorrow, on the way out to the west. And we will not see you back here in the jungle with us soon again, is this correct?"

"This is correct. I ain't *never* comin back!"

Padre Xantes smiled. Though he might have wished another drink, he had detected the long-familiar sounds which signaled the approach of his evening egg, and he was already shifting his attention to his dinner. He extended his hand, and Wolfie got to his feet and took it.

"'I'm surprised you holy people talk to me," Wolfie said suddenly, "after what I done." He swayed there a moment, frowning.

"As a Catholic priest, I must accept men's frailty. And as a European I am too old and tired to expend emotion upon matters I can do nothing about." Xantes smiled again, anxious to bring the conversation to an end.

"Yeah," Wolfie said, "I guess so. Well, so long, Padre. Maybe"—he stood shyly in the doorway—"maybe you'd like to come and see me off?"

"*Encantado*," said Padre Xantes. When one has

been in a place for a long time, he thought sympathetically, and nobody sees one off, the feeling comes that one has never been there. He smiled briefly at the American, then turned his head away and placed his folded hands upon the table. Wolfie swayed in the doorway for a minute more until, finding no way to express himself, he flexed both hands in a sudden spasm of frustration, banged one palm against the wall, and disappeared.

Fausto came in with the soft-boiled egg and toast, and the priest thanked the boy politely. Fausto avoided the padre's gaze, sliding quickly back into the kitchen. Xantes smiled ever so slightly; at his last confession Fausto had finally brought himself to seek forgiveness from the Lord for his several years of remorseless self-abuse.

Very carefully, using a small sharp spoon that he carried with him, Padre Xantes cracked the egg and slid its contents into a small bowl. Using the sharp spoon and a knife, he separated the albumen from the yolk, taking great pains, for the egg was so little cooked that its white was scarcely clouded. During the performance of this operation, he thought vaguely of the day's events. It was sad, of course, but the poor savages would now be persecuted until such time, the Comandante said, as they submitted, or turned the outlaw over to the soldiers, preferably dead. It could have been worse, of course—that is, Guzmán could have been angrier than he had been about Xantes' voyage to the evangelists—but all the same, his own chance of contacting the Niaruna when the Americans were defeated was now gone. This relieved him very much, although he would have liked to test a theory that if one broke up the village structure, changed the shape and juxtaposition of the buildings, the Indians would be totally disoriented, and thus laid open to the first strong faith they were exposed to.

He had coaxed the intact yolk into the spoon, holding his breath at the last moment lest he cut its tender sac; carefully he placed the utensil to one side while he addressed himself with spirit to the albumen, sponging it up with bits of toast and popping it into his mouth.

Smiling, he recalled Guzmán's cheerful mien; Rufino was nothing if not transparent, like a child. Of course, in the great rubber days of a half-century before, not to speak of the long colonial period, the Indians had fared much worse; it was certainly a sign of progress that a present-day prefect such as Guzmán would be held accountable by the government for massacring Indians—unless, of course, the government had sponsored the massacre in the first place. On the other hand, the government need never have become so progressive as to admit Protestant missionaries into a Catholic land; had not the country's Indians belonged to Rome for nearly three hundred years? One trouble with social progress was that it was so impractical.

He would have to write that down, the priest thought. Or better, perhaps: "The flaw of social progress lies in its impracticality." He smiled.

Now Padre Xantes put his knife aside. He cleared his throat, gazing at the soft yolk with intent pleasure. As usual, he began salivating, and he was obliged to swallow several times before daring to pick up the elegant spoon. He wiped his lips with his napkin, then wiped his palms, which had begun to sweat again in the humidity of the evening.

With ceremony, he took up the spoon and lifted it with utmost care into his mouth. First placing the bowl of the spoon upon his tongue, he managed to slide the yolk into his mouth undamaged; holding his breath, he replaced the faithful spoon upon the table. He then sat back gently in his chair and folded his hands upon his stomach. After a moment, satisfied that he was alone in the room and that no invasion was imminent from either street or kitchen, he tested the yolk with a slight, thrilling pressure which, fluttering slightly, it withstood.

Thus Padre Xantes dealt with his brave egg, breathing ever more rapidly in and out until, unable to restrain himself a moment longer, he clamped it savagely twixt tongue and palate, uttering as he did so a tiny squeak of pleasure; the yolk exploded in abandon, mounting deliriously toward his sinuses, then sliding down past the roots of his tongue into his throat. Just at this moment Fausto kicked the door open, banging it hard against the wall.

Fausto cried out, "Does the padre require nothing more?"

And he shook his head. *"No, gracias,"* he answered thickly. "Nothing more."

27

At Two-Bends-in-the-River, he came to the first rapids. The canoe met the rapids broadside, slopping in so much water that when it came again into an open stretch it spun in a slow circle, like a derelict tree. An eddy carried it across a submerged sand bar, and here he found footing and hauled the prow onto the bank, so that the water sloshed into the stern. The malaria was gaining on him, sending advance parties into his brain and body; to warm himself, he tore a large rubbery leaf from a wild fig and with this bailed the canoe, hoisting the water out with both arms. He found hard sap to caulk a split near the canoe's water line; one bullet had lodged itself in the dead body. The matting had unwound, exposing the face with its open eyes in sun-flecked shadow; Boronai retained a dignity which ants and flies and two days' tropic heat had not been able to undo.

Well, he thought, seeing the wound, your bleeding days are over.

When he went ashore, his plan had been to jettison the body, the smell of which was strong on the soft airs. But now the canoe was bailed and caulked, he had taken the dead man's paddle from the mat and was ready to set off, and still the body lay there. He did not want to touch it. He took the canoe by the gunwale to tip it over, then stopped and let it down again.

He was hungry and cold, and felt afraid. When strong and well, with most at stake, he had often risked death as a part of life; how strange it was that the less alive he felt, the more he was afraid to die. Dismayed by his loss of nerve, he took hold of the canoe again and dumped Boronai into the water. He forced himself to meet the flat gaze of the corpse, which revolved once and sank away into the current.

The malaria was draining him of strength; he felt poisoned. The ache in his arms had spread throughout his limbs, and now it seeped into his lungs. He reviled his superstitions, tried to gag, but the bad feeling filled his chest like a huge stone and would not pass.

Below the next rapids, on his left hand, was the creek mouth known as Pariu; up those shadowy streams lay the high ground where Tukanu had led the remnants of his people. This stretch of river, walled with flowering lianas, was sewn in quiet harmonies by the bright arcs of barbets bounding across the bends and eddies and the gold bronze of the open water; small fish dozed in sunny pools under the banks, and a green *jesuchristo* lizard on a low branch caught the sun on its bright eye and signaled him. As he neared, the basilisk dropped from its limb, legs flying, and ran miraculously across the water surface into the under-growth.

He found no peace in the still river; he had the sense of light and death. In the country of the Ocelot he was not safe; he crouched low as an animal in the canoe. He was scarcely below the Pariu when canoes appeared along the bank. It was too late to slip ashore. He forced himself to slide under Boronai's mat and lie there wide-eyed like the body of the dead man.

From the forest edge a moan went up, like wind: *"Wai-Boronai! Wai-Boronai!"* The savages had crowded forward; he could see them as he passed, without raising his head. They were a war party, in macaw-and-monkey headdresses and paint, with white clay drawn like snakes on their brown legs; there were more than twenty warriors, with three canoes like a flotilla in the shadows. Aeore was there and so was the Ocelot, and the Ocelot was wearing Tukanu's red shirt.

With Tukanu one bright river morning he had watched a huge pirarucu in the copper water. *Kisu-Mu? Kin-wee? Kin-wee?*—he tried to blot out that heavy face of brutal innocence. Tukanu was squatting on the sun-warmed sand, his broad feet strong as roots. *Ho, Kisu-Mu?*

Where was New Person? He longed to rear up in the death canoe and threaten them, longed to charge the bank and rip that cheap shirt from the Indian's back and tear it into bits.

Behind him a fresh jabbering arose. Fear and malaria together shook him; he struggled to hold still. The voices faded; he listened for the soft stroke of a paddle. But there was only the whisper of the river, a lone raucous note of some disgruntled bird. Then, as the current turned him in slow circles, he saw behind him, through the branches of the river bend, a kneeling Indian in a black canoe.

He grabbed Boronai's paddle and dug viciously at the water. But he could not hope to outdistance his pursuer, and a moment later he put down the paddle and took out his revolver. The bad feeling filled his chest again, and he shook his head; he gave a great shudder, and the trembling stopped. Screw him, he thought.

Screw it all.

Aeore made no attempt to hide himself; as the river widened and its stretches lengthened, he was constantly in view, in upright silhouette against the western sun. He closed the distance quickly, without haste. Moon yelled at him across the silence to come no closer; the kneeling figure placed his bow in readiness across the thwarts, and then came on again.

One moment Aeore's black silhouette loomed enormous, like the spirit of the Great Ancestor Witu'mai, and in the next it was shadowy and indistinct. Fighting his dizziness, Moon pointed the revolver and blinked to clear his sight. "O Riri'an!" he roared. But he knew that the Indian was steadfast, and did not call out to him again. Leaning back into the stern and steadying both wrists on the gunwale, he braced his gun hand with the other and sighted the weapon on the green stone cylinder that now hung on Aeore's breast. The Indian's outline blurred and broke apart; when it reassembled, it was taking up the bow and arrows. Moon took a deep breath, held it, and squeezed slowly on the trigger.

The crash of gunfire in the wild trees awakened him. Aeore's bow arm had relaxed and the arrow fell into the flood, and Aeore sprawled sideways in the first clumsiness of his life.

The lean canoe, still moving on the impetus of the Indian's final stroke, coasted alongside.

"*Ai Kisu,*" the Indian's voice said vaguely. "*Ai Kisu hai miniti u.*"

The painted boy was shot through the chest, below the heart. Head on the gunwale, eyes staring out across the water, he was breathing steadily, his mouth parted like the mouth of a child about to witness something marvelous. "*Ai Kisu, nepa miniti u. Ai Kisu hai miniti u. Ai Kisu hai u perai'na Riri'an.*"

O Kisu, I did not believe. O Kisu, hear me; I believe. O Kisu, hear the Child-Star calling.

He climbed into Aeore's canoe, letting his own drift alongside. He touched the revolver to Aeore's temple, but could not bring himself to pull the trigger. What was happening? Something of himself was dying; his mind zigzagged like a fly, alighting everywhere and zipping away in the same instant; his ears were ringing, and his heart shriveled with an intense cold.

He stared up at the sky as he pulled the trigger, and the light pierced his own skull in a burst of crystal. He screamed, hurling the revolver from him; it wobbled clumsily through the air and struck a gash in the soft silent current.

He lifted the head of the dead warrior, and taking achote and genipa from the net of fetishes and decorations at Aeore's feet, renewed on the warm face the streaks of red and black. Already a glaze had come to the hungry eyes. He left them unclosed, as Boronai's eyes had been, so that the spirit might guide the canoe on the journey eastward to the sun. He rolled the body and belongings into Aeore's reed mat, pausing each moment to conserve his strength. Then he propped the whole bundle, face up, in the stern of the canoe.

Since he did not know the sacramental phrases, he simply raised his arms toward the sky and summoned the attention of the Great Ancestor. "O Witu'-mai!" Afterward he held his arms raised and his gaze heavenward for a long time, his mind blank and dead.

Boronai's canoe, freed of his weight, had been rescued by the wind from the main current, and now turned peacefully in the side eddies upriver. Too weak to swim or paddle to the bank and drag himself back upstream, he considered dumping Aeore into the torrent and taking the black canoe.

He listened uneasily to the stillness of the river, peered at the encircling green battlements and at the sky. Aeore's face made him more uneasy still; he crept forward and dragged the mat over the face, then fell back again into the bow. They would travel east together.

At twilight the thick tired leaves turned limp and the night creatures stirred. They passed down chasms of dark trees into an underworld.

That first night it rained. The dugout slid past one Yuri Maha village, then another, without incident. In the gray dawn of the next morning, on a roiled river that had widened and grown slow, he saw a derelict craft snared on the bank. He stroked toward shore, but reached the bank well below it. Pulling at branches so violently that his hands bled, he hauled himself far back upstream before he saw that the canoe contained an Indian corpse.

That morning there were several death canoes, trailing and bobbing under the banks. How many others had slipped past unseen during the night; how many had foundered or were still ahead of him, turning slowly in the eddies; how many more, before the influenza ran its course, would drift away from the villages on the Tuaremi . . .

With a wind and rain of evening his fever rose anew. He quaked so that he knew he must disintegrate; the pouring water was his blood. The wind sent the ugly river chop scudding upstream, and on the shore the undergrowth lashed wildly, as if chained to earth; moaning and straining, it reached out at him. He crouched in the stern, shrunk up like a wet spider; behind the mat at the far end of the canoe, the rotting eyes attended him. Enough, enough: he gripped the gunwales until his forearms ached, and watched the rain pour down his fingers.

The canoe descended the mad river in wild turnings, striking the banks in long slow caroms; the mat slipped and the corpse rose a little, half afloat, to watch him. And Boronai—in the deep mud currents far below, Boronai's body accompanied them, bumping soundlessly past sunken trees. Across the wind came the toll of the white bellbird; he thrashed to free the canoe from a dragging bush and fell back again, head spinning.

Then the world flew to pieces in waste and profusion, and did not reassemble.

Heat. The lunatic ringing of cicadas, like rusty gears of an old universe.

Overhead, a creak of wings, and water feeding greedily upon itself beneath the branches. An insect gnawed gently at his temple, seeking access to his brain. The stink of putrefaction—whose? Was God so dead? He laughed. He coughed. The insects reconvened.

The sun killed the tree and pierced its skeleton; on black branches, silhouetted by the sun's dead yellow eye, black fossil birds creaked brittle feathers. The dead birds craned and peered, through a foul mist. "What do you see?" he whispered. "What is it that you *see?*"

He felt beneath the mat for the long arrows and the bow. He raised the dead man's bow, and the arrow shriveled in the sun, and the dead birds craned and peered. The shaft skittered through the branches toward the sun. But the curassows sat oblivious, and he tried again. Each attempt brought the birds closer, craning and peering. At the fifth shot, a bird fell from the tree onto his chest and squatted there, amazed, the arrow quills bright on its burnished breast, the wet point high in the air, catching the sun. The bird bounced, blinking, as he laughed; at the tip of its bill, a drop of blood grew fat.

"It's not you I'm laughing at," he told the being in the bird's round eye. "It's your surprise at what has happened to you."

The white bellbird reappeared, flicking across his vision like a sun spot. Its remorselessness dismayed him, but he could not raise his head. Why not, why not—one might as well as not.

Not what? He had forgotten. He shot idly at the bellbird, and it flew. Well, then . . . He watched his bare foot pushing at the branches, weak and thin. Still twitching, are you? The canoe swung outward and resumed its journey.

The world turned on its endless circle, and the corpse lay downstream, to windward; he could taste it. He coughed weakly and angrily. "God damn you." He spat. "God *damn* you. Enough!" He shook his head; who would have thought that a wild creature so magnificent could have such stink in it? Of the far clear mornings on the Tuaremi, of the first fine days of the great federation, there was nothing left but smell.

He waved at the accumulating sky: We *smell,* right? Can you smell us?

They drifted onward. A vulture, high as a hole in the sky, attended them but did not move. As the sun rolled toward the earth, they passed a canoe caught on

394

a snag, but even as he tried to act they drifted past.

Midafternoon. The vulture flop-flapped down, discreet, onto the dead man's brow. He yelled at it, scaring himself in the almighty silence. The matting had fallen back, baring the corpse. Breathing hard through his mouth, he covered Aeore again, but in the narrow canoe their naked legs embraced. He shook with horror. They were one, a single flesh. All the cold and rot and smell were seeping into him; flies trapped beneath the rotten matting hummed angrily at his belly. Recoiling, he sobbed once, aloud; his breathing rasped his ears like something tearing.

Well, dump him then.

Damned if I will.

Damned if you don't.

The river slowed. From the river reeds, a rude head surfaced. The manatee blinked and puffed like a huge black bald old outraged man. He yelled in fright at the insensible old eyes, then whirled lest Aeore catch him off guard—

He returned Aeore's pitiless gaze.

Don't look the sun straight in the face, Joe Redcloud said, *for the sun will blind you.* And the last old men of the Cheyenne nation grunted and nodded.

He stared straight upward. Kill me or spare me as you like, but either way, expect no thanks for it.

His head split, and he closed his eyes and saw the blood in his own head. How red it was!

Bright red: did they stand over him, imagining him dead? They had caught him then—so much the better. The red shirt had followed like a germ: Uyuyu, Tukanu, the Ocelot, and eastward. His ears rang.

If I knew how, I would ask forgiveness, but of whom? Of Aeore? The Sky? Myself?

Who else?

Are you afraid?

Not of death.

Of what?

Of that enormous sky.

You're going to die.

Well, kill me then, says I.

You're going to die then.

Lewis Meriwether Moon: die soon.

He dozed.

You're going to die then.

Well I said kill me then or else be quiet.

Aeore's face twitched with ants and flies. Aeore whined.

Lo, I am with you always, even unto the end of the world.

STILL HERE, STILL HERE, he howled; he howled at Aeore, but sometimes Aeore was God, sometimes the sun, sometimes himself; and he knew, and remembered afterward, that all of this was true.

So never whine, he said.

He said, Be content with howling.

Night and cold. He was so cold, so cramped, so tired, so weak that he could not get a fire going. Curled tight as a fetus on his naked self, he prayed for the return of the fever that for Christ knew how many nights had kept him warm on his bed of soggy reeds. He shuddered, and reviled his own endurance.

Daybreak.

A country of low forest and savanna.

A strange dugout lay turned turtle on a bend. In silhouette in the eastern light, it looked like a black log. He dared not notice it for fear that his eye betrayed him; he was almost abreast of it when he looked again. Scrambling to his knees, he paddled and splashed ashore and pitched back up along the bank, crashing through the arrow grass, while Aeore's canoe turned once and drifted onward.

The hulk surged mutely in the flood wrack, like a carcass. In his weakness he miscalculated, and fell short when he leaped; he caught hold of a submerged branch before the current took him, and hauled himself whimpering across the hulk and kissed it, panting like a dog.

When his strength returned, he worked the canoe free and guided it down to a break in the bank where he dragged it out and turned it right side up. After resting again, he floated it and got into it and sat in it like a small baby. Then he sailed downstream to the massive pile of flotsam where Aeore's canoe had caught and hung; there he retrieved his paddle and the dead curassow. The last remnants of his pants were gone; he stripped off the belt that had constricted him so faithfully for so long and flung it away after the rest.

Gaunt and naked, leaning on his paddle, he stared at the face in the canoe. Except he willed it so, it was no longer Aeore, and a well of sadness for things irredeemable and gone flowed over him. The Indian nation had grown old; he knelt down like a penitent and wept. He wept for Aeore and the doomed people of the jungle, and he wept for the last old leatherfaces of the Plains. He wept for New Person and Pindi, and he wept for Alvin Moon "Joe Redcloud" and the seventeen thousand volunteers. And he wept for Quarrier, and for himself, who had never wept in twenty years. He wept and wept, and though toward the end he began to smile, he kept on weeping until at last he breathed a tremendous sigh and laughed quietly, without tears.

Aeore said, We are naked and have nothing! Therefore we must decorate ourselves, for if we did not, how are we to be told from animals?

He took up Aeore's achote and on his own chest drew the sun as a child would draw it, rough and bold, with violent rays; he threw his chest out. Then his brain was drowned in blackness, and he fell.

When he opened his eyes, the sky was ringing, and the mist on the east horizon bulged with light; he rose awe-struck to his feet. A wind of dawn had turned the death canoe back to the current; it passed on down the somber flood between high swords of grass. On a wide bend far away where wind and the light of the rising sun had turned the water gold, the canoe of the Child-Star hung a moment in the brilliant mist and then, as the sun appeared, went up in fire.

Hunched on the earth's face as the night came, he contemplated the dead curassow. The thought came: die or eat. He turned the dead thing in his hand, peered at it curiously; how mysteriously it was made! He opened its breast and ate it in small bites, raw.

The dark was crossed by star fire and heat lightning. He stared outward, upward; the Southern Cross and Sagittarius climbed the sky, as if to immolate themselves in the full moon. Silver night-hawks, crisscrossing the pale surface of the river like night swallows, joined the evening hunt; a jaguar coughed from the far bank, downriver. Somewhere a great tree gave way and crashed into the flood with a noise like thunder.

At morning the wind was cold again and brought a brown chop to the river. The river was wide and slow, without tight bends or rapids. The land had flattened, and great tracts of flooded savanna broke the ramparts of the rain forest. In the shelter of the drift wrack, a mud beach had been strained from the brown water. All that day he squatted on this scrap of earth, mouth open: a dead fish beside him on the strand, lone bony trees across the reaches of pale swamp, black circling birds, a gaunt cormorant on the snag of a drowned tree, a dead snake, belly up, in the driven water. There was no sign of man. Under the raining banks, unknown antediluvians gasped and swirled.

He felt bereft, though of what he did not know. He was neither white nor Indian, man nor animal, but some mute, naked strand of protoplasm. He groaned with the ache of his own transience under this sky, as if, breathing too deeply, he might rise on the wind as lightly as a seed, without control or intimation of his fate. He was the nameless beetle probing the pores of his own toe; he twitched in the wind like the dull scale that loosened on the flank of the rotten fish. His was the bald eye of the vulture forming its halo over the mute landscape; far beneath, he saw the solitary man on the humble mud.

On every side there stretched away a vast world without a sun. The savanna was beaten flat by wind and rain, and the sky was so huge that the weight of the whole hemisphere oppressed him. He did not know within a thousand miles where he might be, nor on what river, nor in what country. How close, how far stood the nearest being under this same sky?

A cold sun loomed through the pall and peered at him. He raised both arms to it; the sun withdrew.

He drifted eastward.

The sky turned heavily, battered by wind.

He drifted eastward, eastward, past long sand bars bare of tracks.

He thought, Am I the first man on the earth; am I the last?

On an island shared with swift white birds, he trapped some small fish in a pool; he clutched the live quicksilver things, triumphant. The pool reflected his hunched form against the sky. In a face bare with privation the wide eyes were clear, and behind the face the clouds of heaven rolled majestically across the world.

At noon the sun returned again, resplendent. He entered its sparkle on the water and opened his mouth and drank. The flood was mineral and cold as a prairie river. It coursed his throat, his lungs, the inside of his skin; it bathed his heart. He let the water pour across him, wash in and out of his clean mouth; he rolled in the warm shallows like an otter and washed his skin with sand.

He assembled a fire of dry precious sticks, coaxing a small transparent flame with a makeshift drill; the sun flowed softly in his hands. Clean as the silvered driftwood, strong as wind, he broiled the brilliant fish on sticks, exultant.

The wind was bright. Laid naked to the sun and sky, he felt himself open like a flower. Soon he slept. At dark he built an enormous fire, in celebration of the only man beneath the eye of Heaven.

ABOUT THE AUTHOR

As a naturalist-explorer, PETER MATTHIESSEN has been a member of expeditions to remote regions of all five continents, including the Amazon jungles, the Canadian Northwest Territories, the Sudan, New Guinea and Nepal. A former commercial fisherman and charter-boat captain, he has always been interested in marine biology, and participated as a diver in the worldwide search for the great white shark that culminated in his book *Blue Meridian* and in the film *Blue Water, White Death.* His fiction includes *Race Rock, Partisans, Raditzer, At Play in the Fields of the Lord,* which was nominated for the National Book Award, and his most recent novel, *Far Tortuga,* which was one of the most prominently reviewed novels of 1975.